The House
That Jack Built

GRAHAM MASTERTON

The House
That
Jack Built

Carroll & Graf Publishers, Inc.
New York

First published in the UK in 1996 by William Heinemann

First Carroll & Graf edition 1996

Carroll & Graf Publishers, Inc.
260 Fifth Avenue
New York, NY 10001

Library of Congress Cataloguing-In-Publication data for this
edition are available.

ISBN: 0-7867-0353-9

Manufactured in the United States of America.

For my father, Ian, with love

But every beginning is only a continuation
And the book of fate is always open in the middle.

Polish poem

Mayan priests had a ceremonial calendar which governed
thirteen festivals of twenty days each. The ceremonial calendar
rolled through the year like a wheel, and consequently the
festivals occurred at different days each year but always in
the same sequence. The priests could calculate into the
future or the past exactly what the populace would be doing,
hearing or seeing on any given date. They were dealing
from a stacked deck.

William Burroughs

If time were a pool we could kneel at its edge and gaze at our
reflections and then beyond them to what lay deeper still.
Instead of looking back at time we could look down into it –
just as we could peel back the layers of the palimpsest – and
now and again different features of the past – different sights
and sounds and voices and dreams – would rise to the surface:
rise and subside, and the deep pool would hold them all, so
that nothing was lost and nothing ever went away.

Lucie Duff Gordon

The House
That Jack Built

Tuesday, March 16, 8:07 p.m.

'Can't you try Broadway?' Craig demanded. It was raining so hard that the taxi's windshield wipers couldn't keep up with it, and up ahead of them Eighth Avenue was a jostling carnival of glaring red brake lights.

'Broadway's the same, my friend,' said the driver, placidly. He was swarthy-skinned and narrow-faced, with an odd woven hat that looked like an upside-down flower pot. His medallion revealed that his name was Zaghlul Fuad. 'The whole Theater District's gridlocked solid.' He gave a dry sniff, and added, 'It's raining.'

'It's raining?' said Craig. 'I wouldn't have noticed.'

He checked his watch even though he had last checked it less than a minute ago. He was supposed to have been at Pétrossian by 7:30 at the latest, for Mr Ipi Hakayawa's celebration dinner. Mr Hakayawa was their wealthiest and most prestigious client, and he had invited Craig and his partner Steven to a lavish evening of champagne and caviar – not only to thank them for all of the white-hot legal work that they had put into *Hakayawa vs Nash Electronics*, the most expensive patent-infringement action in legal history, but to brief them on the next stage in his fight against US protectionism, *Hakayawa vs Department of Commerce*.

Craig was sufficiently well versed in Japanese business protocol to know that Mr Hakayawa would make no comment on his lateness; but that privately he would take it as a deep discourtesy. If you pay a man $1.3 million in fees, you expect that man to take account of such a common-

1

place occurrence as a rainstorm.

The traffic crept forward another two car lengths before the brake lights flared up again. Rain drummed viciously on the taxi's roof, and streamed down the steamed-up windows. Craig wiped the window with his sleeve and peered out. Shit. They were only as far as 46th Street – still eleven blocks to go.

'Take a right on 48th,' he snapped.

'I told you, friend, Broadway's the same.'

'Just do it, will you, please? If Broadway's the same, try Sixth.'

'Sixth is the same, Madison's the same.'

'Listen, I don't need some fucking Egyptian to tell me the way around my own city, all right?'

There was a moment's pause. The taxi in front of them crept ahead a little way, but Zaghlul Fuad turned around in the driver's seat and stared at Craig with large, dark liquid eyes. He was unexpectedly handsome.

The taxi behind them blared its horn. Craig flushed, and shrugged, and said, 'I'm sorry, okay? I'm late, that's all. I've had a bad day. I apologise, all right? I didn't mean to lose my temper.'

Zaghlul Fuad continued to stare at him with no expression whatever on his face. Then, without looking around, he switched off the meter and said, 'You had a bad day, my friend? Do you know what happened to me today? My father died today.'

'Listen, I've said I'm sorry. And I'm sorry about your father, too. Now can we just–' Craig nodded towards the taxi in front, which had pulled ahead another three lengths. The taxi behind them was deafening them with a barrage of horn blasts.

'My father was a fucking Egyptian, like me,' said Zaghlul Fuad. He pronounced his words with extreme delicacy. A

2

lisp, almost like a woman. 'He tried his best, the same way I always try my best. Sometimes he was not perfect. Sometimes I, too, am not perfect. Sometimes I fail to take my passengers where they wish to go. I will not take you where you wish to go. Get out of my taxi.'

'What are you talking about? Are you nuts?'

'I said, get out of my taxi.'

'It's raining, for Christ's sake!'

'It's raining? I wouldn't have noticed.'

Craig felt a huge surge of frustration, panic, and almost uncontainable rage. In the US Court of International Trade, he had faced down countless case-hardened lawyers with twice his experience. Smooth, tough, silver-haired men in silver suits with rumbling magisterial voices. But how could he face down a fey Egyptian taxi driver whose ancestry he had just gratuitously insulted, and who had nothing to lose except a few dollars' fare?

'Okay,' he said. 'Let's be conciliatory here. Whatever the fare comes to, I'll double it.'

He took out his crocodile wallet and tugged out a $100 bill. 'Look – I'll give you a hundred. Just get me there, okay? I have an urgent, important meeting with a very important client. I'm late already, and that's a disaster. If I'm late and wet, that's going to be it. I mean, that's going to be–' and he drew his finger across his Adam's apple.

Zaghlul Fuad remained expressionless. 'In Egypt we have a saying that a man who speaks sharp words will always cut his own throat.'

'Oh, do you? Well, in New York we have a saying that a taxi driver is obliged to take his passenger to any destination in the city or else the Taxi & Limousine Commission will take away his medallion.'

Lizard-like, Zaghlul Fuad closed and reopened his hooded eyes as if he wanted to remember Craig's face for-

3

ever. 'Losing my medallion will be a small price to pay for ridding myself of someone who cannot respect his fellow beings. Get out of my taxi.'

'What the hell kind of smartass game is this? Are you crazy? Did they just let you out of Bellevue?'

'Please get out.'

All around them, the salvo of horns was deafening. Craig could hear shouting, too. 'Move your ass you dumb mutha!' 'Get oudda thuh goddamned way!' Craig thought: where the hell are the cops when you really need them?

He took a deep, tight breath. He had already wasted more precious minutes by arguing. There was only one thing for it, and that was to get out and walk. He put away his wallet, and then with shaking hands he wrote down Zaghlul Fuad's medallion number. He was so angry and upset that he could barely hold his pen.

He opened the taxi door, and a sharp fusillade of rain burst in. He jabbed his finger at Zaghlul Fuad and said, 'You're finished. You understand me? I'm going to make sure that you lose your medallion if it takes me the rest of my life. You Egyptian fuck.'

'*Salaam, effendi,*' said Zaghlul Fuad, without the slightest trace of irony.

Craig dodged across 48th Street between the honking, glaring herds of taxis and limousines. He clutched the lapels of his grey Alan Flusser suit close to his neck, but it didn't make much difference. The rain was crashing down in chilling torrents, the gutters were filled to overflowing, and the wreckage of broken umbrellas was strewn everywhere. He was drenched even before he reached the sidewalk, and he stepped right into a pothole and flooded his shoe with ice-cold water.

He picked up a broken umbrella, shook it, and tried to

4

straighten it out, but it was limp and bony and intractable, like a dead pterodactyl, and he swore and threw it away again. He had left his own raincoat and his own umbrella back at the offices of Fisher & Bellman on the 76th floor of 2 World Trade Center. Worse than that, he had left his mobile phone there, too, expecting to collect everything after lunch. But lunch hadn't finished until five to seven, when Khryssa had woken him up with a kiss and said, 'Isn't it time you left?'

The first thunderclap had shaken the windows of Khryssa's apartment, and the little blue teddy bear that he had given her had dropped off the mantelpiece.

All he could do now was jog to Pétrossian and hope that Steven had been keeping Ipi Hakayawa happy and that the maitre-d' could fix him up with a dry suit. He would just have to invent some cock-and-bull story about why he was so unpunctual. He couldn't really tell Ipi Hakayawa that he had spent the whole afternoon in bed with his nineteen-year-old mistress. Maybe he could say that his father had died.

He jogged heavily towards Broadway, his thick brown hair sticking to his scalp like a bathing-cap. He was a big, healthy man, nothing at all like his father (who had actually died more than seven years ago, from lung cancer). He had the kind of square, well-fed face that put people in mind of prosperous farmers or wealthy dynasties of Democratic politicians. There was nothing in the way he looked that suggested an asthma-wracked childhood in a shabby walk-up apartment on Lispenard Street, and a pale, lonely boy in spectacles and a green home-knitted windbreaker, for which he was remorselessly teased.

As he splashed along 48th Street, he may have been soaked, and out of breath, but he still looked affluent, and that was probably why the curly-haired girl came teetering

5

out of the doorway of K-Plus Drugs and snatched at his arm. 'Help me!'

'Hey,' he protested, and tried to pull away, but she screamed, 'Help me! You have to help me!'

He stopped, his shoes squelching. She clung onto his sleeve as if she were drowning, and she practically was. Her face was round and puffy and white, and blood and rainwater were running down her forehead and streaming from her nose. She wore a sodden black-leather blouson and a short black skirt, and she was hobbling on broken shoes. She couldn't have been older than fifteen or sixteen.

'Help me!' she kept screaming, a thin breathy scream. 'They took my friend! They took my friend! Help me!'

'Listen, I'll call a cop,' Craig told her. 'You stay there. Do you hear me? Stay there, and I'll call a cop.'

'You have to help me, they're raping her! Please! You have to help me!'

Craig took hold of her shoulders. 'Quiet, calm down. Who's raping your friend? Where?'

The girl turned around and pointed to K-Plus Drugs. It was only now that Craig saw that the store was closed down and derelict, Bankruptcy Sale stickers criss-crossing the grimy, blacked-out window, along with the faded stickers for Pepto-Bismol and Maalox and Vaseline Intensive Care. The door was ajar, but inside it was impenetrably dark.

Craig let go of the girl and peered without enthusiasm into the doorway. The rain clattered all around him, as loud as a standing ovation. Traffic honked, sirens wailed. The girl looked up at him with blood dripping and beady black eyes like raisins and shivered and muttered, 'Please help me, they're raping her.'

Craig wiped the rain from his face with the back of his hand. 'How many?' he asked her.

'Two, that's all. Please help me.'

6

He looked back towards Eighth Avenue. Then he looked the other way, towards Broadway. The street was blocked with automobiles, with their windows tightly closed. He splashed across to the nearest taxi and rapped on the driver's window, but the driver emphatically shook his head. He stepped through a deep puddle to the car behind, a blue Buick with a balding shirt-sleeved businessman behind the wheel, and tapped on his window, too, but the businessman locked all his doors and wouldn't even turn to him.

He knocked on the Buick's window a second time. 'There's a girl being raped in there! Can you hear me? A girl being raped in there! Call the cops, will you, that's all you have to do!'

The businessman gave a barely-perceptible shake of his head, and edged his car along further.

Craig stood up straight, dripping and desperate. The girl took hold of his arm again, and screamed, 'Please!' at him. 'Please!'

'Listen,' he shouted, over the noise of the traffic and the rain, 'is either of them armed? Do they have guns or a knife or anything like that?'

The girl shook her head. Her face was a sliding mask of glutinous, rain-diluted blood. 'There's just two of them. Please.'

Craig thought: what the hell, I'm already late, I'm already soaked. I can handle two of them, for Christ's sake. How fit are they going to be? I doubt if they jog six miles every morning, and work out three times a week at the Bar Association Athletics Club. And right now, I'm sufficiently pissed off to handle anybody.

He went back to the half-open doorway. He could smell damp, and mould, and urine. He pushed the door wider, and stared into the blackness.

7

'Who's there?' he called out. 'If you can hear me, you'd better get the hell out of there, and fast!'

There was no reply. Only the sound of rain trickling down the walls. Craig's eyes were gradually growing accustomed to the darkness, and he could just distinguish a row of free-standing shelves.

'What's your friend's name?' he asked the girl.

'Susan,' the girl replied, blinking at him, almost as if she didn't expect him to believe her.

'All right, then.' He reached into his pocket and produced a dime. 'You go call for the cops and an ambulance. I'll find your friend for you.'

The girl started to limp towards Eighth Avenue, wiping her face with a handkerchief. Craig stood and watched her for a moment, but he didn't watch her long enough to see her turn her head and smile.

He stepped into the darkened drugstore, his shoes crunching on ground glass and grit. 'Susan?' he called. 'Susan – if you can hear me, Susan, all you have to do is call out, or make a noise. Kick your heels on the floor, whatever.'

He reached the row of shelves and stopped and listened. At first he couldn't hear anything, but then he picked up the faintest tapping. *Trrapp, trrapp, trrapp,* like somebody running their heels from side to side across a bare-boarded floor. His suit dripped onto the floor, a soft, uneven *plip . . . plop . . . plip.* He began to think there was nobody here; that the girl with the blood-covered face had been playing a malicious prank. You never knew in New York City, there were so many wackoes roaming the streets.

'Susan?' he called.

Nearly a whole minute went by, and still no reply. Craig was ready to turn and leave when he heard a muffled

8

mewling sound. It sounded like a cat, but not exactly like a cat. More like a girl with a gag around her mouth.

He blundered into the darkness at the back of the store. 'Susan? Is that you? If you can hear me, kick your heels on the floor! Go ahead, kick!'

He took another step forward and his right foot became entangled with a heap of wire shelves and display-racks. He shook them free, but then he trod on several sheets of glass, and they split underneath his shoes with a sharp, crackling noise.

That was why he didn't hear them when they rushed right up to him and hit him in the stomach.

He had been hit before – in boxing, in racquetball, in athletics – but never like this. He pitched back onto the wire shelving and shattered glass as if he had been knocked down by a speeding taxi. His head hit the wall with a terrible clonking sound and he bit right through his bottom lip. He was so winded that he couldn't breathe, and when he clawed at the floor to try to lift himself up, his left hand was pricked and sliced by razor-sharp fragments of glass.

But somebody seized his lapels and dragged him up onto his feet. Somebody strong and dark; somebody who smelled of rain and cigarettes and alcohol.

There was somebody else, too. Somebody standing very close beside him. Far too close to be friendly.

'What you doin' here, pal?' said the somebody who was standing very close beside him. 'Someone invite you in?'

Craig wheezed and coughed. His stomach felt as if it were blazing. He never knew a punch could hurt so much.

'Looking for Susan,' he managed to choke out.

'Ain't no Susan here, pal. Ain't no muff at all. Just he and me.'

'It's okay, then. I made a mistake. I'm sorry.'

9

'Well, we're glad that you sorry. But sorry ain't enough. Sorry don't pay the man. Sorry don't make nobody feel better 'ceptin' the dude who says it.'

Craig felt appalling. He began to tremble with ice-cold shocks, as if somebody were emptying buckets of cold water over him, one after another. He felt nauseous, but he couldn't bring anything up. His stomach felt as if it wasn't there any more. Why did he feel so cold?

'What do you want?' he managed to ask them, in a bubbly voice.

'Your money, pal. Your credit cards. Your jewellery. Whatever you got.'

He took a deep breath, tried to say something, and then puked up a mouthful of bile and blood and Khryssa's chicken brioche, half-chewed.

'Hey pal, you disgustin'. You sick.'

'Take whatever you want,' he told them.

'Okay, okay. But don't go hurlin' them chunks on me none.'

'Take it, just take it.' He spat food from his mouth, and a string of sour-tasting saliva swung from his chin.

'You one disgustin' dude, you know that? I seen dogs better behaved.'

He waited, quaking, his eyes downcast, his shoulders hunched, while the young man reached into his coat and took out his wallet. Quick, dirty fingers went through his pockets, lifting his pens, his calculator, his loose change.

'You goin' to be glad you did this, pal. Not everybody gets the chance to make a donation to the Aktuz.'

Craig raised his eyes. In the darkness of the derelict drugstore, he could make out very little, only the faint gleam of rainy streetlight on a black cheekbone and a black shoulder; and eyes that glittered like blowflies.

He turned to look at the boy who was standing beside

10

him, and for a split-second this boy moved across the light and Craig caught a glimpse of a tall, cadaverous youth with deep-sunk eyes and a mouth stretched back in a gin-trap disarray of overlapping teeth. What struck him most of all was the youth's hair, which had been gelled up around his head like a gleaming black crown, and the heavy black frock coat that he was wearing. He looked like an extra from a movie about Mozart, except that he wasn't carrying a silver-topped stick or a violin. He was carrying a hammer.

God, thought Craig, no wonder that goddamned blow to my stomach hurt me so much.

'Watch and ring, pal,' the youth told him.

Craig reluctantly took off his Rolex and his wedding-band. He nearly puked for a second time, but he managed to swallow it back. He didn't want to antagonise his attackers any more than they were antagonised already.

The boy in the frock coat came very close beside him. 'We leavin' now. I know what's happenin' inside of you' haid, you thinkin', shit, they makin a fool out of me now, but you wait till I follow those boys and find out where they at and whistle for the man. Well, here's news for you. You ain't followin' us none.'

'I wasn't even going to try,' Craig choked.

'That's what you say.'

'Why the hell should I follow you? I'm soaking wet, I'm sick. All I want to do is go home.'

'That's what you say.'

'For Christ's sake, you've taken all my money. What more do you want?'

'I want a guarantee, pal.'

Before Craig could even ask him what kind of a guarantee he wanted, the other youth seized him ferociously from behind and gripped him tight. Craig tried to wrestle and

11

wriggle free, but the youth in the frock coat slapped his face, left and right, not too hard, but just enough to make his ears sing and his cheeks burst into flame.

Together they slammed him up against the old drugstore counter.

'What are you doing? What the hell are you doing? For Christ's sake let me go!'

But while the first youth kept Craig pressed against the dusty mahogany counter, the youth in the frock coat reached around and unbuckled Craig's belt.

'Get off me! Don't touch me! What are you doing?'

He felt his buttons pulled off, his fly wrenched apart. Then a long-fingered black hand reaching into his shorts.

'Don't touch me! Don't touch me! Don't touch me!'

But the youth in the frock coat roughly scooped his genitals out of his shorts, and laid them on the counter. Craig's penis shrank in fear, and his scrotum tightened so much that the youth could barely take a grip on his testes.

'Listen, I'll give you anything you want,' Craig babbled at him. 'I have a BMW 7-series, you can have that if you want to, it's red, you never drove anything like it. I have much more money, I'm really wealthy, I can arrange to pay you ten thousand dollars each. Twenty thousand, if you like.'

The youth in the frock coat sniffed reflectively. 'Amazin', ain't it, how generous a dude can be when you're holdin his toolbox.'

Craig was sweating and trembling and utterly revolted by the way the youth was slowly kneading his penis and his testes between his long, dry fingers. He was rubbing him and pulling him almost absent-mindedly, but this gave his manipulations a terrible intimacy, as if he were a wife playing with her husband.

'Amazin', how much some dudes would pay for a tool-

12

box. What you would pay, pal?'

'Anything you want. Now just let me go.'

But the other youth said, 'I bid twenty dollars for the right-hand ball.'

'Twenty dollars? Do I hear twenty dollars for the right-hand ball?'

'Let me go!' Craig roared at him, and tried to wrench himself away. But the youth in the frock coat slapped him again, much harder this time, and then he slammed his hammer down on top of the counter, only inches away from Craig's genitals. Craig felt the hard shock of it travel through the counter and bruise his thighs.

'Is that all that anybody goin' to bid?' the youth asked, in mock astonishment. 'Why, twenty dollars, that's *nothin'* for a full-growed fully-functional ball.'

'Thirty,' said Craig. This was the most chilling kind of torture, because he didn't know whether they wanted him to win or lose – or what would happen if he did either. If he won, he was terrified that they would cut off his testicle and give it to him. If he lost – well, God alone knew what they would do. He even began to think about the Bobbitt case, in which a vengeful Laurene Bobbitt had cut off her husband's penis and thrown it out of her car window. He tried to remind himself to look closely where these two tossed his genitals, if they castrated him, so that he could recover them quickly; and he also had to think of places where he could find some ice, so that he could keep them in good condition while he called for an ambulance.

He thought he remembered seeing a bar across the street. A bar would have ice. Then he thought: *what am I thinking? This is a nightmare.*

'Thirty-five,' the other youth bid.

'A hundred,' Craig countered, in a much higher voice than he had meant to.

13

'Hundert-and-twenny five.'

'Two hundred.'

'Five hundert.'

'A million.'

A pause. Then, 'A *million*? Come on, pal, nobody's ball worth a million.'

'Mine is, to me.'

The youth in the frock coat came up very close to him, and said, 'You serious?'

'Sure I'm serious. You let me go, you can have a million dollars, in cash, no questions asked.'

'Well, hey . . . now you talkin'.'

'I mean it. A million, in cash, in used currency, no marked or sequential bills. Delivered anyplace you like, any time you like.'

'I think you serious, pal. I genuinely think you serious.'

'I am serious, for Christ's sake. Just tell me where you want the money, and when. Or else I can give you my phone number, and we can arrange it later.'

'A million,' breathed the youth, and ostentatiously licked his lips. 'What you think about that, bruthah? You think you can bid more than a million?'

'No way, man. I'm out.'

'Okay then. For one million dollars, this valuable ball . . .one of a *fine* pair . . . going – going -'

Craig lifted his eyes in relief. For the first time since the two youths had jumped on him, he clearly heard the sound of the traffic and the storm outside. On the ceiling, he saw the shadowy ripples of rainwater coursing down the drugstore window, and the flickering long-legged images of passers-by.

Then the youth in the frock coat lifted his hammer like an auctioneer's gavel, hesitated for a moment, and smashed it down onto Craig's right testicle. The flesh was

14

flattened, almost as thin as a veal patty, and the hammer-head punched a semi-circular hole right through the skin of his scrotum.

Craig was too shocked even to scream. The youth who was holding him stepped smartly back, both hands whipped up high, so that Craig twisted around and dropped to the floor on his knees, convulsing like an electrocuted ox.

He had never experienced such agony in his life. He felt as if somebody were directing an oxy-acetylene cutting-torch right between his legs. All he could see was wave after wave of dazzling scarlet, and all he could hear was a grinding, churning noise; which was his blood churning in his ears.

He didn't even hear the youth in the frock coat when he leaned very close to his ear and said, 'You must take me for some kind of fool, pal. Once I let you loose, you were still goin' to pay me one million dollars – *one million dollars* – for somethin that was safely tucked up in your shorts? You the fool, pal, not me.'

The other youth whooped and cackled; and then the two of them stepped out of the drugstore doorway and into the rain. They didn't hurry. They didn't have to. They knew that Craig wouldn't be following them, and that they had plenty of time before he called the police.

On the corner of Eighth Avenue, the girl with the curly hair and the puffy white face stepped out of a rubbish-filled doorway, and linked arms with the youth in the frock coat, and the three of them pranced through the storm as if it couldn't touch them, as if nothing could.

Thursday, June 17, 3:11 p.m.

Effie said, 'The car's outside.'

Craig continued to stare out of the window. Below him, East 86th Street was striped with sunlight. He was watching two small schoolchildren trying to cross the street, even though there was scarcely any traffic. A bossy elder sister and a little boy, just like him and his sister Rosie used to be, except that these children were obviously wealthy, from the Sutton Place School. Every time the street was clear, the elder sister insisted that they wait at the kerb. Whenever an automobile was approaching, she ventured out, and then they had to scuttle back to the kerb again.

Craig wondered if they would ever make it; or whether they would still be here in twenty years' time, trying to cross the street, while their mother grew old and their supper turned to dust.

Effie came up to him and laid a hand on his shoulder. Very carefully, because he was still hypersensitive to sudden touches. He still jolted violently during the night, dreaming about that hammer. He still sat up sweating and gasping and trying to say something which nobody could have articulated.

If only I hadn't said it. If I could cut out my tongue.

'Listen, I don't need some fucking Egyptian to tell me the way around my own city, right?'

Effie said, 'Come on, Craig, it's time to go. I want to get to Cold Spring by eight.'

He turned, and awkwardly held her wrist, and nodded. 'Okay, whatever. I was watching those kids, that's all.'

16

Effie nearly blurted out, 'You can have kids. You can have kids like any other man.' But she had learned not to raise the subject of potency. It still led to red storms of uncontrollable rage, and endless screaming matches, and then terrible quaking aftershocks of deep remorse, which were worse, in a way, than the arguments. It had been three months now since Craig had been attacked, and she was tired of his tears.

He had always been so steel-sprung, so positive. Sometimes *too* positive. But *too* positive was infinitely preferable to this complete collapse. It was like trying to drag around a shuffling, forgetful parent.

Effie's best friend Shura Janowska had lost her right breast to cancer; and yet Shura was brave and funny and never believed that she was any less of a woman. Why did Craig seem to think that he wasn't a man any longer?

Craig picked up his walking-cane and limped after Effie to the door. Jones the porter was waiting outside, ready to lock up for them. Craig took a look around the quiet, high-ceilinged apartment. The afternoon sun filled it with buttery light. His huge success at international corporate law had enabled him to furnish it with colonial antiques, gilded mirrors, and elaborate cream-and-yellow curtains. Over the fireplace hung an abstract painting by Max Weber – over three-quarters-of-a-million-dollars' worth of vibrant blues and singing crimsons. The whole four-bed-roomed apartment looked as if it had been furnished for a spread in *Architectural Digest*, but Craig took no joy in it any longer. He had a premonition that he would never see it again, and he wasn't at all sure that he would be happier if he didn't.

On one of the sofas, an embroidery cushion was propped, with the handstitched inscription, 'I Fought The Law & The Law Lost'.

17

The door closed behind them. 'How long are you planning to stay upstate, Mrs Bellman?' asked Jones. He was a black man, uniformed, smooth, very smooth. Even when he was carrying their suitcases he walked with a supernatural glide.

Effie glanced around to make sure that Craig was following. 'We're just going to play it by ear. We're visiting my sister in Albany, and then we may spend some time up at Glens Falls.'

'Planning on fishing, Mr Bellman?' asked Jones. 'They say you can't beat Oscawana Lake trout.'

Craig said, 'Fishing? No. Well, I don't know – I might. It depends if we get that far. Going upstate isn't exactly my idea of time profitably spent.'

Effie linked arms with him, and smiled, although her smile was strained. 'Any time spent getting your head straight has got to be profitably spent.'

Craig twisted his arm away. 'I see. Now my head's not straight. Tell me some part of my anatomy which is.'

Jones looked embarrassed, and remained silent with his gloved hands clasped in front of him as they descended in the elevator to the lobby. He and Effie watched each other in the elevator's mirrored walls, but neither of them gave anything away. Jones was the perfect porter. It wasn't his place to express opinions about any of The Sutton's residents, even when that resident had turned so suddenly irascible.

Effie thought she looked pale. She was a small, dark brunette, with an oval face that one of her two previous lovers had always compared to paintings by Bernini – slightly medieval, with a thin, straight nose and very full lips, like angel's bows, and eyes the colour of Stradivarius violins, hazel, amber and the thinnest of honeys, one transparent layer of varnish painted on another, until they shone.

18

She wore a plain linen suit in periwinkle blue, which was smart, but a little too city-smart for a drive to the country. She had chosen it because it made her feel calm and controlled, and today she needed calm and control in spades. It also made her feel comfortable. She always believed that she was too large-breasted for her height, but the way this suit was cut made her feel slim. She could date her feelings about her figure right back to the day that Craig had said to her, 'You know something? You remind me of Elizabeth Taylor.' And Effie had never been able to tell him that she hated Elizabeth Taylor, or at least the way that Elizabeth Taylor looked.

Control, that was what she needed. Calm, and control.

Only the purplish circles under her eyes betrayed how stressed Craig's accident had made her.

He insisted on calling it an 'accident', instead of a mugging, and Effie could understand why. It was far too disturbing for him to think that, every year of his life, his destiny had been taking him step by step to the darkened entrance of K-Plus Drugs. How could he have been born and raised with all that love and dedication for no other purpose than to walk into that doorway and come face-to-face with that terrible youth with the hammer and the black frock coat? His parents hadn't sent him to law school for *that*, had they? Surely he hadn't argued and struggled and battled his way to the top of his profession to have his manhood pulverised by some freak in a derelict building.

He refused to believe that it was meant to be, because if it was meant to be, God must have marked his card. Surely God couldn't be that sick. Why had God allowed him to be so successful, if only to show him how vulnerable he was? That was why he called it an accident. Accidents are nothing more than bad luck – the cards don't come up, the dice go cold. Destiny is something else altogether. Destiny is

19

something terrifying that's waiting for you round the next corner, except that you don't know it.

Jones said, as he stowed their bags into the trunk of Effie's scarlet BMW, 'You take good care now, Mrs Bellman. You know what my granma used to do, before she took a trip anyplace?' He flicked his right shoulder with his hand. 'That's to brush off the devil, so he don't ride along with you, whispering no evil nonsense in you' ear.'

'Evil nonsense?' said Craig, raising one eyebrow.

'You never know, Mr Bellman. The devil's full of tricks, and he's got breath like chimney smoke. Choke you before you know it.'

'Thanks for the tip,' Craig told him. He climbed into the car and slammed the door.

'And thank *you* for the tip,' said Jones, under his breath, as the Bellmans drove away.

They drove north on the Henry Hudson Parkway, playing *Madam Butterfly* on the CD. Effie had been brought up in a house filled with opera, and in the seven years they had been married she had gradually converted Craig to a liking for Verdi and Puccini, although he wouldn't listen to Wagner. 'Warbling tubs of lard in tinplate Wonderbras,' was how he described *The Ring*.

'I really don't need this,' said Craig, as they crossed the Harlem River into the Bronx. Directly in front of them, a huge grimy truck was toiling along, its rear doors decorated with a grinning Joker. Lucky Times, Inc. But no indication of what Lucky Times, Inc., might be selling.

Effie said, 'You need to take some time away from work, darling, that's all. You had a bad experience, you must give yourself time to recover, to think it all through.'

'Think it all through? I've been thinking it all through ever since it happened, every hour on the hour. For

Christ's sake, Effie, it's been almost impossible to think about anything else.'

'Craig, it's *over*. It's really over. There's no point in torturing yourself. You were fantastically brave.'

'Fantastically stupid, more like. Why didn't I just tell that girl to take a hike?'

'Because you're you; and because you care about people.'

'I didn't go into that drugstore because I cared about people. I went into that drugstore because I was pissed with the weather, and I was pissed with goddamned taxi drivers who don't know where the hell they're going, and I was pissed with Hakayawa for making me feel like a clumsy hamfisted Occidental who couldn't even arrive for a goddamned dinner on time.'

They passed a sheer wall of tawny-grey concrete, and then they were out in the sunlight again. Butterfly was singing *Un bel vedremo*. Effie said, 'You know what Dr Samstag told you. You have to think about yourself differently. You have to revise your whole view of yourself. What happened in that drugstore, that made you question your manhood, your sense of being in charge, everything. They could have killed you. They could have done anything to you, and there wasn't a damned thing that you could have done about it.'

'Don't you think I know that?' Craig barked at her. 'Don't you think I fucking know that?'

'Yes,' she said, restraining her anger. 'I do think you know that, yes. That's why you should have the sense to see what a few days' break is going to do for you. Maybe you can get rid of some of that anger. Maybe you can learn that there are some things in life which are way beyond your control; things that you can't do anything about, no matter how much of a wheeler-dealer lawyer you are.'

Craig said nothing, but looked out of the window at the dreary warehouses and half-derelict projects of the Bronx. In the orange summer sunlight, it looked like a landscape from Morocco. Next to them, a black family were driving in a sagging bronze Mercury, father and mother and fat daughter and dreadlocked kids, and Craig was struck by their obvious happiness, the way they were smiling and laughing. If that old wreck had been *his* only car, he would have thought about fixing a hose to the tailpipe and killing himself. God, to be satisfied. Just to be satisfied once – with his career or his wife or his friends or his life, or anything.

Unconsciously, he brushed his right shoulder.

Friday, June 18, 7:54 a.m.

Effie opened her eyes and looked up at the ceiling. The sun was dancing across it like a row of dancing-dollies. Beside her, Craig was bundled up in the comforter with only his hair sprigging out of the top of it, his breathing harsh and aggressive. Effie listened and all she could hear was swans honking, and the tap-tap-tap of the curtains against the window catch.

Not for the first time, she wondered how her life had come to this. No child, when she had always wanted a child. No time to paint, when she had always wanted time to paint. No time to do anything, except work all day at Verulian Galleries on Third Avenue, and then rush home to change for dinner so that she could decoratively attach herself to Craig's arm while he entertained his clients. It was always the same. Lutece on Tuesday, Le Bernardin on Wednesday, La Cote Basque on Thursday and La Reserve on Friday.

22

Evening after evening of nodding and smiling at the wives of Japanese and Korean businessmen. Evening after evening of brittle, meaningless conversation. Effie knew that it was her duty; and she couldn't pretend that she didn't like the wealth that it had brought them. But she hadn't married Craig for this. She had married Craig because he was tall and shy and self-deprecating, and he had always made her laugh.

She thought about those early days together, on Lafayette Street, and she could remember every detail of the window sill over the sink, with the pickle jar filled with cornflowers, and the wild-haired worn-out pot scourers, and Marmaduke the cat sleeping with his paws tucked up, and she could have cried, except that she didn't cry, because she was Effie, and as her mother had once told her 'Effies don't cry.'

'Ohaya gozaimas, ogenki des ka?' she recited. That was Japanese for 'Good morning, how are you?'

'Hajimemashte,' she answered herself. 'Pleased to meet you.'

She sat up. The room was hushed and richly furnished in reds and yellows, summer colours, with a rocking-chair next to the fireplace, and a huge oak armoire. An oil painting of a retarded-looking shepherdess hung on the opposite wall.

Craig was still breathing as if he were deeply involved in some complicated dream, so she kissed his shoulder and climbed out of bed. She walked naked to the window and looked down onto Main Street, with its freshly painted turn-of-the-century houses, and its neatly planted maples. In the distance, down at the bottom of the slope, she could see the river glittering, and an early windsurfer setting up his rig.

She let the net curtain fall back. She turned around, and

23

she could see herself in the cheval mirror on the other side of the room, a pale curved back; a dark cascade of hair, the colour of blackberries, in that moment when the morning light first catches them. She felt the carpet beneath her bare feet. She always felt so calm and beautiful when she returned to Cold Spring, so much at home. She believed that people have an affinity for certain places, even if they weren't born there. Craig, she was sure, was a city dweller. He needed carbon monoxide and the perfumed, airless atmosphere of international-class restaurants.

She knew that he would have to go back. He would fret, otherwise – start drumming his fingers at mealtimes and checking his watch every five or ten minutes and start making phone calls back to the office. But maybe she could persuade him to stay long enough to get his confidence back, especially his sexual confidence. She needed him to make love to her, just once, to show that he hadn't been emasculated. She needed to feel his single remaining testicle, and to reassure him that was all she wanted.

He still kept his towel wrapped around him when he came out of the shower. He still wouldn't let her look at him and touch him.

She went to the mirror and stood in front of it looking at herself. She tried not to blink. Movie actresses were trained not to blink. Her breasts were pale with veins like the tracery of tree-roots. Five small moles formed a cluster on her left shoulder. I am a real person, she thought, watching her chest rise and fall as she breathed.

She heard Craig stir. He grunted, like a dog grunts when it scents an animal that it doesn't particularly want to catch, like a skunk. He opened his eyes and blinked at her.

Naked, she came and sat on the edge of the bed, and kissed his forehead, and ruffled his hair with her fingers. 'It's a beautiful day,' she told him. 'It's a beautiful day and

24

every minute of it belongs to us.'

'What time is it?' he asked her.

'Eight-oh-two.'

'Jesus, eight-oh-two. Listen, why don't you take a shower? I have to call Steven. He's due in court this morning with Filipino Oil.'

'Craig, you don't have to call Steven. Steven is perfectly capable of taking care of Filipino Oil by himself.'

Craig sat up. 'Filipino Oil is a very complex case. It's *my* case.'

'For sure, sweetheart. But Steven knows just as much about it as you do. You said so yourself. So why don't you let him get on with it, without poking your nose in?' She patted the tip of his nose with the tip of her finger, smiling. She knew she was pretty; she knew she looked good. If only Craig would just forget about K-Plus Drugs and that damned hammer, that damned hammer which had beaten them apart.

'Craig,' she said, and looked him straight in the eye. 'Craig, I love you.'

He covered his mouth with his hand.

'Craig, I love you, and I think it's time you tried to forget what happened and think about me.'

Still he said nothing. She stroked the fine pattern of hairs on the back of his hand, and said, very softly, 'You have to let this go, Craig. Nobody could have done more. It didn't make you a coward. It didn't make you a fool. It didn't even take away your masculinity. We can still have children. You heard what the doctor said. Nothing's changed, nothing at all. Especially the way I love you.'

Slowly, she traced her fingertip down his wrist, down to his elbow, and up to his shoulder. He wasn't looking at her directly, his eyes were fixed for no apparent reason on the electric socket next to the satinwood bureau. He looked

25

infinitely sad, as if he had suffered the greatest disappointment of his life. She ran her fingertip down from his shoulder, and touched his left nipple, so that it knurled slightly. She tugged the few dark hairs around it, and then her fingertip continued its journey down his side, tracing the outline of each lean gym-trained muscle, until it reached his naked hip.

Now he looked at her. 'No, Effie. This isn't going to work.'

She didn't answer. Instead, she slipped her hand beneath the comforter, and took hold of his fat, soft penis. She could feel his single testicle touching her knuckles, and nothing had changed, not really. She felt breathless, she wanted to feel it, she wanted to squeeze it, she wanted to reassure him that he still excited her, that he was still a man.

'For Christ's sake!' he snapped at her, twisting himself away from her. 'Don't you understand English?'

Effie reached out for him again, but he pushed her off. She sat up straight, feeling embarrassed and frustrated and angry, too.

'Craig . . . you have to try sometime.'

'So you keep telling me. So Dr Samstag keeps telling me.'

'I love you, Craig. You can't keep pushing me away.'

He said nothing, but she had never seen him look at her with such resentment before. His bitterness was so strong that she could almost taste it, like a mouthful of pennies with a squeeze of lime.

He climbed out of bed, keeping his back to her, and picked up the oversized terry robe that was hanging over the back of the chair. She watched him wrap himself up in it, but she made no attempt to cover herself.

'I need some more time, that's all,' Craig told her.

26

'Dr Samstag said the longer you put it off, the more difficult it was going to get.'

'Dr Samstag wasn't hit in the balls with a goddamned hammer.'

'Craig – you have to make an effort to recover. You can't go on feeling sorry for yourself for ever. You're still virile, you're still a man. I still love you just as much as I always did. But I can't help you unless you try to start helping yourself.'

He thought about that, but he didn't reply. Instead, he said, 'What do you want to do today?'

'I don't know. Anything you like. Maybe we could go to the Boscobel Restoration and look at the furniture.'

'You'd better get yourself dressed, then.'

She stood up and faced him. She wanted to say something angry, but she knew that it would only make matters worse. What was worse than feeling frustrated was not knowing whether he still loved her or not. She couldn't live without love, and without approval, and she was beginning to feel that she might have to go somewhere else to get them.

She could have shaken him. She could have dug her nails into his shoulders and scratched him until he bled. But all she did was open the bureau drawer and stare at her clothes as if she had never seen them before.

Friday, June 18, 11:47 a.m.

They spent a quiet morning strolling through the grounds of the Boscobel Restoration, a Federalist mansion set in apple orchards and rose gardens, with sparkling views of the Hudson River and the Hudson Highlands beyond.

27

'We should have brought a picnic,' said Craig, quite unexpectedly, shading his eyes against the midday sun.

Effie linked arms with him, and this time he made no attempt to pull himself away. 'A picnic? After all that breakfast? *Three* helpings of pancakes, wasn't it?'

'Have to keep my strength up, if I'm going to be a man again.'

'You're a man now.'

'So you keep telling me.'

They walked around the mustard-coloured house, and then ambled back through the orchard towards their car. Effie said, 'If you're really hungry, there used to be an inn not far from here, just the other side of the Bear Mountain Bridge. Do you want to try to find it?'

They drove down the winding road beneath the noisily-rustling trees. Effie said, 'My father used to take us to this inn almost every Saturday, for lunch. The Red Oaks Inn. He always had a Bloody Mary, and let me suck the celery stick. My mother said he was going to turn me into an alcoholic. He said he was trying to turn me into a vegetarian.'

They drove around three curving S-bends, and then suddenly Effie said, 'Stop! Stop! I think that's it, off to the left!'

Craig backed up the BMW around the curve, its transmission whinnying. A small downsloping side-road disappeared darkly between the oaks, so angled and overgrown that they probably would have missed it if Effie hadn't known what she was looking for. A faded wooden finger-post was engraved with two barely-legible names, Red Oaks, and underneath, Valhalla.

'Valhalla?' asked Craig, as he turned the BMW around. 'What's Valhalla?'

'Somebody's house, I don't know whose. I looked it up

in my encyclopedia, when I was a kid, Valhalla. It comes from one of those Norse legends, you know, like Odin and stuff. It's the hall of dead heroes. My father always used to say that it was a warning that he should never eat at the Red Oaks Inn, ever again, or else he'd wind up joining them.'

'Well, he was pretty imposing, wasn't he?'

'Imposing? You don't have to be PC about him, just because he's dead. He was F–A–T, fat.'

They turned down the side-road, and immediately found themselves plunged into a cool, hushed world of low branches and dense bushes. Occasionally they glimpsed bright sunlit clearings through the undergrowth, but for the most part the road was shadowy and damp, and smelled strongly of decaying leaves.

'You sure this is the right turnoff?' asked Craig, as briars squeaked and lashed against the BMW's bodywork.

'It must be. It said Red Oaks, didn't it? And Valhalla.'

'Right. The hall of dead heroes.'

The road began to rise up the side of the hill, growing steeper and steeper with every turn. The bitumen had crumbled on both sides, and it was running with herring-bone eddies of springwater. On one side, they could see nothing but treetops. On the other, they were treated to a dank cross-section of the earth's interior, with twisted roots and layers of leaf mould and pale, pungent-smelling fungi.

'Doesn't look like anybody's driven up here for years,' said Craig. 'Maybe we should turn around and find some-place else.'

'Well, we can't turn around here,' said Effie. 'We may just as well go on to the inn.'

They crept round one hairpin after another, but at last the trees began to thin out and the road was dappled with sunlight. A faded board by the roadside said Red Oaks

Inn, 200 yards. Open Hearths & TV.

The inn looked much smaller than Effie remembered it, and it wasn't just closed, it was half tumbled down. It was set in a clearing on the left-hand side of the road, over-shadowed by giant oak trees, an empty clapboard building with a sagging verandah and a skeletal roof. Most of the windows had been broken, and the gutters were filled with landslides of weather-bleached shingles.

Craig turned the car into the parking-lot, and tugged on the handbrake. 'Looks like lunch is off,' he said. 'Where shall we go to now?'

Effie climbed out of the car and walked up to the inn's front steps. Nineteen years ago, climbing these steps with her father, she never would have believed that she would ever come back here, to find the inn looking like this. She stepped up to the front doors, and peered inside. The doors had once had panels of decorative stained glass, through which she could peer while she was waiting for her parents to finish paying the bill or powdering their noses or whatever it was that parents did to drag each minute beyond the bounds of endurance. She used to imagine that each pane of coloured glass gave her a secret view of a world which was never normally visible: a red world, a green world, and a sickly amber world.

Once – through the red glass – she had seen a man in a homburg hat walking across the parking-lot. When she had looked through the clear glass, he had vanished.

She heard the car door slam behind her as Craig came up to join her. The front doors were chained and pad-locked, but she could clearly see through to the dining-room, with its view of the stream that ran down the rocks at the back, although the stream was clogged with grass now and there was no furniture in the room except for a single tilted-over chair.

'Memories, hmh?' said Craig, looking up at the dilapidated roof.

She nodded. 'Dad took me here on my eighteenth birthday.'

Craig unexpectedly laid his hand on her shoulder, and gave it a squeeze. Effie turned and looked at him, but his head was turned.

'I like it here,' he said, almost as if he couldn't believe it himself.

'I'm pleased. I always did. There were two lovely people who used to run it, Mr and Mrs Berryman. They loved cooking and they loved making people feel contented and happy. Mrs Berryman used to let me go into the kitchen and make pastry-people.'

They went back down the steps. In the distance, they could see the blueish peaks of the Hudson Highlands, and the darker cloud-cloaked outline of Storm King Mountain. They could have been alone in the world, here by this deserted and broken-down inn, explorers of a long-lost civilisation. Whippoorwills called sadly from hill to hill.

'Did you ever go up as far as Valhalla?' asked Craig.

She shook her head. 'We came up here to eat, we ate, we went home. Dad was always promising to go for a walk in the woods, but he never did. He was always too full.'

'I'd like to see what Valhalla is.'

'It's just somebody's house.'

'All the same, I'd like to see it.'

Effie said, 'Okay.' She didn't mind what they did, so long as Craig remained as affable as this. He hadn't been so relaxed since the day before his 'accident', and she was beginning to think that this enforced vacation was really going to work.

This morning, he had dressed in a camel-coloured linen suit, with a sky-blue shirt, a city dweller's ultimate concession to the countryside. But now he stripped off his coat and rolled up his sleeves and twisted open two more shirt buttons. 'I shouldn't have worn these goddamned loafers,' he said. 'I'll see if I can pick up some Timberlands when we get back to Cold Spring.'

'You? In Timberlands?'

He grinned, and patted her on the back. 'I'm on vacation, I'm allowed.'

Up above the Red Oaks Inn, the gradient was so steep that Craig had to shift down into 2. But after a few minutes of laboured climbing, the road began to level out, and described a gradual left-hand loop to follow the upper contours of the hill, between slopes of tawny dried-out grass and nodding, undernourished wildflowers.

They were so high up now that the wind began to fluff and whistle through the open windows. As they reached the crest of the hill, a thick barrier of hunched old oaks came into view, like an army of ogres rising to their feet. Although they were all mature, these oaks, most of them were so exposed to the weather that they had grown stunted and deformed, and several had been dramatically split apart by lightning strikes. But they formed a natural barrier from one side of the hill to the other, so that Effie could only imagine what lay beyond them. When she was a child, she had thought it was quite romantic for somebody to name their house Valhalla, but now when she was here, now she was actually standing in front of its gates, it seemed unsettling and perverse.

The house might just as well have been named Purgatory; or Mictlampa, which was the Mexican land of the dead, where skeletons danced. Her parents' housemaid Juanita had told her all about Mictlampa, when she was little, and the memory of those stories still made her shiver.

'This is *so* spooky,' she said.

But Craig kept on driving with a look on his face that was almost one of dawning recognition. 'It's fantastic. I love it.'

The road surface deteriorated into broken asphalt and shingle, with weeds and grass growing through it, but Craig continued to follow it at the same speed as it curved around the trees, even though it looked as if it came to a dead end. Past the last stand of oaks, however, a pair of tall wrought-iron gates came into view, sagging between two tall stone pillars. Craig drew the BMW right up to the gates, and stopped.

'This must be it,' he said. 'Valhalla.'

In places, the wrought-iron was rusted through, and the pillars were pockmarked and spotted with lichen. But all the same, the gates were gaunt and deeply impressive, as whoever had raised them had obviously intended them to be.

Beyond here, these gates said, *you are trespassing on land that belongs to me.*

Craig climbed out of the car and looked around. The summer wind whipped the grass around his ankles. Effie climbed out, too, her denim dress flapping.

'What a place to have a house,' she said. 'Can you imagine trying to get up here in the winter?'

Craig limped up to the gates and shook them. The left-hand gate had rusted completely off its hinges, and the bottom rail was buried in the shingle, but it would probably be possible to swing open the right-hand one. Beyond the gates, the road curved off to the right and down the other side of the hill, and so it was impossible to see anything but more trees.

'I feel like . . .' Craig suddenly began, and then stopped, and looked around some more.

'*What* do you feel like?' Effie prompted him.

'I don't know. It's really strange. I feel like I was meant to come here.'

She thought of his 'accident', and his repeated denials that destiny had guided him to the darkened doorway of K-Plus Drugs. Yet here he was, trying to suggest that destiny had brought him here.

'You're feeling relaxed, that's all,' she told him. 'Your mind's off-guard. It's kind of like *déjà vu*.'

'No, no,' he said, shaking his head. 'It's not like *déjà vu* at all. I don't have any feeling that I've been here before. I can't explain it. I just feel that I was *meant* to come.'

Effie took hold of the gate, and tried shaking it, too, but it didn't even rattle. 'You may have been meant to come, but you sure weren't meant to go inside.'

Craig paced up and down for a few moments. 'We could try pulling them open with the towrope.'

'Craig – are you kidding me? This is somebody else's property. We could be sued. Besides, I don't want you ruining my car. Supposing you strained the engine? Supposing one of the gates fell onto the back of it?'

'Okay, okay. Just an idea.'

Effie stood watching him for a while. He seemed extraordinarily agitated, yet pleased, too, because he kept chivvying the palms of his hands together, the way he always did when he was excited or inspired.

'What is it?' She took hold of his arm, and his face was radiant. 'Tell me what it is.'

He grasped her shoulders, and then he hugged her close, really hugged her, for the first time since he had left home on the morning of March 16. Effie was so surprised and touched that she suddenly felt as if she had burrs in her throat, and her eyes filled up with tears. It had been so long since he had spoken with any affection at all, let

34

alone showed it, that she was overwhelmed.

'I was *meant* to come here,' he repeated. 'I don't know how, or why. But it's like hearing music, almost.'

'Music?' Effie was moved, but completely baffled.

He released her from the hug, but he still kept hold of her hands.

'I can't explain it. I just can't explain it. But do you know what it's like, when you're passing somebody's house, on a summer afternoon, and they've opened all the windows, and you can hear music playing? Dance music, do you know what I mean? Dance music – tango, foxtrot, that kind of thing. And you think to yourself, I wonder what memories this is conjuring up, for the person who's listening to it. Is it happy, or is it sad? Maybe they danced to this music with somebody who's dead. Maybe they never had anybody to dance with.'

'*Craig*,' said Effie, half-pleased and half-concerned. He had delighted her, with this sudden burst of affection, but he had alarmed her, too. She had never heard him talking this way before, even when they were first married.

'It's all right,' he said. 'Everything's fine. Everything's going to be fine.'

After a while, they climbed back into the car, and he started the engine. He turned around in his seat to back the BMW along the road. Effie took a last look at the rusting gates. They reminded her of Edward Gorey's drawings; the sort of sinister Gothic gates that might have been familiar to The Dwindling Party or the Gashlycrumb Tinies ('A is for Amy who fell down the stairs').

'We must be able to find out whose property this is,' said Craig. 'One of those realtors in Cold Spring should know.'

'What does it matter whose property it is?'

'I want to see it, that's why it matters.'

'I expect it's all run down, just like the Red Oaks Inn.'

35

'I want to see it, is that such a bad thing?'

'No, no, of course not,' said Effie. She didn't want to upset him now that he was being so effervescent. If it took a visit to some derelict old house to lift him out of his trauma, then terrific.

They had almost backed up to the point where Craig could turn the car around when she saw something moving, beyond the gates, where the oaks were darkest. It could have been nothing at all, a stray flicker of sunlight through the leaves. But she was sure that it was a figure; a very slim pale figure dressed in white or cream, watching them go.

She didn't know why, but the sight of this figure alarmed her out of all proportion. She opened her mouth to say something to Craig, but then the figure was gone, or dissolved, or vanished. She suddenly thought of the man in the homburg hat she had seen through the red stained glass segment of the window at the inn.

Red world, green world, and sickly amber world. Perhaps there was another world, too. A world glimpsed through closed gates and half-closed doors. A world where dance music was always heard through other people's open windows. She looked at Craig and he looked back at her, and she wondered if she had actually understood what he meant.

Saturday, June 19, 3:23 a.m.

She opened her eyes. Somebody was standing at the end of the bed, watching her. A bulky, shadowy shape, its eyes glistening in the darkness. She was clutched with such fright that she couldn't breathe, couldn't speak. She tried

36

to whisper, '*Craig*' and reach out for him, but her voice wouldn't work and her hand wouldn't do anything but grip the sheet.

'Sweetheart?' said the shape, all of a sudden. 'Are you awake?'

She let out an exhalation of relief that was practically a scream. 'God, you scared me! God, you almost gave me a heart attack!'

He came around the end of the bed and sat down close to her. He was wearing his white cotton pyjama pants, but that was all. He gently held her wrists and kissed her on the forehead. 'I'm sorry. I couldn't sleep.'

'I thought you were a ghost or something.'

'A ghost, weighing 200 pounds?' He kissed her again.

'Do you want a Nytol?' she asked him.

He shook his head. 'I don't feel like sleeping. I feel like I've just woken up.'

'What do you want to do, then? Play Scrabble?'

'I know this sounds crazy, but I thought I might drive back to Valhalla.'

'Well, I don't mind. But I thought you were going to talk to a realtor first.'

'I can't talk to a realtor at three-thirty in the morning.'

Effie propped herself up on one elbow. The sheet slid down, and her breasts were bare. 'You want to drive back there *now*?'

'I don't know. I have the urge to, that's all. I never felt this way before. It's like, if I go there, I'm going to find the answer to all of my problems.'

'Oh, Craig, that's impossible. We can't. I don't mind going back with you in the morning, when it's light. But not now.'

He sat up straight. For a moment she was afraid that she might have lost him again; that he was going to lose his temper. But then he nodded, and nodded again, and said, 'You're right. We'll talk to the realtor first, then we'll go back.'

He climbed back into bed. She thought for a split second that he might make love to her, but then he turned his back like he always did, and by the time the clock in the hallway below struck four he was deeply asleep.

Saturday, June 19, 10:19 a.m.

'Mr Van Buren can see you now,' announced the secretary with the fiery hair and the firetruck-coloured lips and the huge circular spectacles. She waggled her way along the corridor in front of them, her bright green dress swinging from side to side.

Walter Van Buren turned out to be an amiable old coot in a beige seersucker coat and brown Staprest pants and a necktie that proclaimed him to be a friend of the Hudson Valley Philharmonic. He had a soft, beige, jowly face, and the palest eyes that Effie had ever seen, eyes that were strained to the colour of weak tea.

On his beige hessian-covered walls hung photographs of his children and grandchildren, and framed awards from the Hudson Valley Realty Association and the Cold Spring Elks. Out of his window there was a view of a parking-lot, where a 10-year-old full-sized Buick baked in the morning sun; and a children's playground, where a lone mother sat reading, while her scarlet-suited child went around and around on the merry-go-round.

'Understand you're interested in Valhalla,' said Walter Van Buren, indicating with a wave of his hand that they should sit. They sat. 'Valhalla's stayed empty since 1956.

There's been some restoration work, but the only reason it's still standing is that it hasn't fallen down and nobody's gotten around to knocking it down.'

'I'd still like to see it,' Craig put in. His hands were resting calmly in his lap.

Walter Van Buren shrugged. 'You can see it, I guess. But if you're looking for large, high-class Hudson Valley property, then I can show you scores of homes you're going to like better, and which are much better value. One of them came onto the market just last week . . . here, look, Oscawana, a very fine property with seven bedrooms and four bathrooms and two half-bathrooms, not to mention a pool and a squash court and a view of Lake Oscawana. Here, take a look.'

He nudged a brochure across his desk but Craig didn't touch it; didn't even drop his eyes to look at it.

Walter Van Buren eased himself back in his chair and blinked with those colourless eyes and said, 'Valhalla . . . I have to be frank with you . . . Valhalla is more what I'd call your serious developer's buy. The house was something special, once upon a time. But it would take hundreds of thousands just to make it liveable. Millions, maybe. We had an approach from Trump but when their surveyors took a look over it . . . well.'

'I thought realtors were supposed to sell realty,' Craig riposted. 'You know, stretch the truth a little. Make their property sound tempting, even when it's nothing but a crock.'

'Oh, no, don't get me wrong,' Walter Van Buren retorted, holding up his hand. 'Valhalla has one of the finest locations in the Hudson Valley Highlands. Unparalleled views. Privacy, seclusion. It's a house in a million.'

'But it's badly run down?' asked Effie, trying to stop

Craig from badgering Walter Van Buren so intently, and to see some sense.

'I can't tell you a lie, Mrs Bellman.'

'How badly?' Craig wanted to know.

Walter Van Buren took a worn green manila folder out of his in-tray and opened it up. He passed over an architectural side-elevation of Valhalla, and a blurry black-and-white aerial photograph. The house was designed in the neo-Gothic style, with tall chimneys and leaded windows, and it was huge.

'My God,' said Effie, and laughed.

'Let me put it this way,' said Walter Van Buren. 'This is a house you'd really have to have a passion for.'

Craig picked up the photograph and stared at it for a long, long time. 'It's incredible. It really is.'

'Well, it belongs to another time,' Walter Van Buren explained, watching him keenly. 'It belongs to the Rockefeller days, the FDR days, the Vanderbilt days. A very big house for a very big man.'

'Do you know what needs doing to it, roughly?' asked Craig.

'As I say, Mr Bellman, I can't tell you a lie. The whole roof needs fixing, most of the windows need replacement, and like most of these older properties, it'll probably need rewiring, and replumbing, too.'

'But it could be restored?'

'By somebody who really had the passion for it, yes.'

'Craig,' said Effie, 'I hope you're not seriously thinking what I think you're thinking. We need a house like this like a hole in the head.'

'Oh, come on, sweetheart, I'd still like to take a look at it,' Craig told her. 'Who owns it now?'

'Well, what does it say here?' said Mr Van Buren. 'A realty trust fund managed by Fulloni & Jahn, up at Albany.

40

That's unless they've sold it or transferred it without letting us know. We haven't had any enquiries about Valhalla for well over a year.'

'Maybe I should talk to these Fulloni & Jahn people.'

'You could, for sure, if you really wanted to. I could give you their number. But I'm just trying to be realistic here, Mr Bellman. Valhalla could seriously damage your financial health; and I wouldn't want that; because you'd never forgive me for it. Every time you drove past this office or saw me in the street, you'd say, "That's Walter Van Buren, who sold me that goddamned house, and ruined me." ' He gave a little dry laugh that was more like a dog barking.

'Mr Van Buren,' said Craig, 'I don't think you understand. I haven't even seen Valhalla from the outside; never laid eyes on it. But the moment we drove up that mountain and stopped outside of those gates – well, I don't know. I felt like I was there for a reason. I felt like I was *meant* to be there.'

Walter Van Buren glanced edgily at Effie and cleared his throat. 'And, uh, what do you think, Mrs Bellman?'

'I think–' said Effie, and Craig lifted his head. 'I think that–' Craig focused his eyes on her. 'I think that, really, yes, maybe we could take a look, at least. If that's okay with you.'

Walter Van Buren drummed his fingers on the green folder. Then he said, 'Okay . . . if that's what you folks want to do, then do it, by all means. As you so rightly say, Mr Bellman, I'm here to sell realty, not to discourage you.'

He stood up, and crouched in the corner of his office, where a small grey safe sat, and started to turn the combination lock. 'When would you care to view?'

'Today?' Craig suggested. 'How about right now? We don't have any plans.'

Effie said, '*Craig* – don't forget we have a one-thirty

41

lunch reservation at the Vintage Cafe –' but he waved her into silence and said. 'That's okay, that's okay. We'll make it easily.'

Walter Van Buren produced a brown envelope containing keys. 'Here you are, then. But if you want to view today, I'm afraid that you'll have to view it alone. I have six or seven other clients calling today. We have a very desirable house just outside of Rhinebeck . . . you may like to look at it yourselves. It's a stunner. Five bedrooms, three Carrara marble bathrooms, and a view that's only second-best to the view from Heaven itself.'

'That's quite a pitch, Mr Van Buren, but all we want to look at is Valhalla.'

'Let me tell you something, Mr Bellman . . . and I'm going to be serious now. When you see Valhalla, you should either want to own it with all of your heart, or else you should turn your back on it and forget it. It's very much more than most people can manage, and I don't just mean financially. Valhalla is the kind of house that people fall in love with, and then it breaks them, breaks their spirit, bit by bit.'

'I'm not the breakable type, Mr Van Buren,' said Craig, although Effie could hear that his voice was filled with rain and hammers and mocking mushroom-haired boys in swirling frock coats.

'Well, let's hope so,' Walter Van Buren replied. 'But Valhalla was built in 1929, by Jack Belias, the textile millionaire; and when he died in 1937 or thereabouts it stayed empty until World War Two, when the Army rented it as overflow accommodation for West Point Military Academy. The trouble was, five officer cadets committed suicide while they were staying there. I might as well tell you before anybody else does that a story started going around that Valhalla was haunted.'

'Haunted?' asked Effie. 'Haunted by what?'

'I don't know, and quite frankly I don't believe it. But you know what people are. I've been selling property up and down the Hudson River Valley for thirty-eight years, and I haven't come across a haunted house yet. My opinion is that those boys were frightened of going to war, that's all, and who can blame them?'

'What happened to the house after that?' asked Effie.

'As far as I remember it stayed empty for a while. Then it was leased to a woman called Turlington who wanted to turn it into a riding school for the sons and daughters of well-heeled Manhattanites. She didn't do too badly to begin with, but then she took out a party of young riders during an electric storm. One of her wealthiest charges was struck by lightning, and killed, and of course that was the end of her – financially, because she was sued for millions, and psychologically, because the boy was killed right in front of her.'

'Oh, my God,' said Effie. 'Talk about jinxed . . .'

Walter Van Buren shrugged. 'It depends if you believe in jinxes or not. My feeling is that large, expensive properties attract folks who like to take risks – folks who are larger than life, if you know what I mean. Those kind of people live their lives right on the very brink. If you live your life right on the very brink, you're always in danger of losing your balance and dropping clean over.'

'Who was the last owner?' asked Effie.

Walter Van Buren leafed through his file. 'Technically – before Fulloni & Jahn took over – Valhalla was owned by the Fishkill Hotel Corporation. They were planning on turning it into a resort hotel, with a golf course and you name it. Fishkill spent over three-quarters of a million dollars on restoring the old ballroom and some of the bedrooms, but then they went bust. Most people who come up

43

the Hudson Valley for a weekend break want cutesy bed-and-breakfast places like Pig Hill Inn and the Beekman Arms. They're not too interested in ritzy, expensive golf resorts. Nobody's shown any serious interest since.'

'You're right,' said Effie. 'We're staying at Pig Hill. The only reason we came up here was to be comfortable and cosy and quiet. By the way,' she added, 'do you remember Mr and Mrs Berryman, who used to run the Red Oaks Inn? I was wondering whatever –'

But she was interrupted by Craig, who had picked up the brown envelope, and torn it open, so that the keys dropped noisily on Walter Van Buren's desk.

'Look at these. The keys to the hall of dead heroes,' he proclaimed.

Walter Van Buren gave him a look of faded perplexity, so Craig added, 'Valhalla, that's what it means. That's what my wife told me, anyway. The hall of dead heroes; from the old Norse mythology.'

'Hall of dead plaster, more like,' Walter Van Buren responded, dryly.

Effie picked up the keys one after another and turned them over in her fingers. For some reason she didn't like them. One key was green with verdigris, and unusually large, like the key to a monastery. A second was small and rusted, and looked as if it would fit only the tiniest of cupboards. The third was oily and almost new. 'That opens the padlock on the gates,' Walter Van Buren explained. 'The large key opens the front door.'

'And the small one?'

'I don't know. I never found out. All I ask you to do is lock up after you leave.'

'Sure we will,' said Effie.

But Craig said, with a sly smile, 'Supposing we decide to buy the place?'

Walter Van Buren let out another of his sharp, barking laughs. 'If you decide to buy the place, Mr Bellman, just remember one thing. It's your own decision, I'm not trying to influence you. So don't blame me.'

Saturday, June 19, 12:03 p.m.

As they drove back over Bear Mountain Bridge the wind was getting up. There was a sense of hurrying everywhere. The clouds were running over the dark skyline of the Hudson Highlands like a pack of pale grey dogs. Grit storms leaped up from the side of the highway, and helter-skeltered across the road.

Below the bridge, the river was almost black, and anxiously chopping.

'Feels like a storm's rising,' said Craig. 'Hope it's really humungous. I love storms.'

'Oh, thanks. We're having our first vacation for three years and you want it to storm?'

'It'll freshen things up. Besides I'm in the mood for it.'

'What kind of mood is that?' asked Effie. 'Apocalyptic?'

'*Excited*, for Christ's sake. Why can't I just be excited? Is there some federal statute against it?'

'I'm sorry. It's just that I never saw you act this way before.'

'You never saw me act *excited* before?'

'Of course I have. I've seen you act excited about a court case that really came together. I've seen you act excited about a new car. But I never thought I'd ever see you act excited over some derelict building that even Donald Trump doesn't want.'

'Donald Trump can make errors of judgement, just like

anybody else.'

Effie went *phph!* And gave a tight, exasperated shake of her head. To the north-west the sky was rapidly darkening, and they saw the first twitches of lightning. She hadn't been keen on visiting Valhalla to begin with, but now she seriously didn't want to go. If this was how Craig felt about it without even seeing it, what was he going to be like when he could actually walk around it? She was enjoying his new excitement, but at the same time she hoped to God that Valhalla would turn out to be so badly dilapidated that no amount of excitement could ever repair it.

She thought of the steel engraving in her encyclopedia of the Norse warriors, hoary and bearded and blind-eyed, their armour dented and pierced with spears, marching back to Valhalla as the sun went down.

Craig became aware of her silence. He glanced at her once, twice, and then laid his hand on top of hers. 'We're only taking a *look*,' he cajoled her. 'I have a law business to run, I couldn't simply afford the time for a house like this.'

'Or the money.'

'Effie, when you really want something, "afford" doesn't come into it.'

'Oh, come on, Craig, be serious. You heard what Walter Van Buren said. Valhalla has thirteen bedrooms, nine bathrooms, four reception rooms including a ballroom. A place like that would cost us millioins, and we don't have millions.'

'It's only money,' said Craig, without even looking at her.

He knew the way now, and didn't miss the dark, cavelike turning that was signposted Red Oaks Inn and Valhalla. They sped beneath the overhanging branches, and the bushes snapped and tinkled and pinged on the car. Effie could smell ozone in the air, that strange fresh restlessness

46

before a heavy storm. But it wasn't only the storm that was restless. Craig was driving as if he couldn't wait another second to get to Valhalla, as if the keys were beginning to glow warmer and warmer in his pocket.

Trying to distract him, Effie said, 'This man Jack Belias, who built Valhalla. Did you ever hear of him?'

They were rising up out of the woods now, and they were squealing around the first of the hairpin bends.

'Jack Belias? Sure. He was quite famous in the '30s . . . or notorious, depends on which way you look at it. We had to study some of his business dealings in law school. He could twist the law so far that it looked like a pretzel. He made all his money with this non-crease fabric, I can't remember what it was called. He made a fortune before nylon was invented. He put something like ten million dollars into the Empire State Building when John Jacob Raskob was running short of finance. It was because of him that the Empire State went up so quickly. Belias bet Raskob fifty thousand dollars that he couldn't erect it in three hundred ninety-nine days.'

'But it took four hundred.'

'That's right. And that's another reason why Jack Belias was so rich. He gambled a lot, and he usually won.'

Effie said, 'I'm just wondering what kind of man would want to build a house way up here.'

'A man who wanted his privacy, I guess.'

'There's a difference between privacy and total isolation.'

'So what's wrong with total isolation? Maybe he wanted some time to think. Maybe he wanted some time to find out who he was, without other people trying to tell him all the time.'

Effie glanced at him in genuine surprise. He had said that with extraordinary vehemence, as if *he* were the man

47

who was deprived of privacy; as if he took the whole idea of Valhalla personally, its creation, its neglect, and the tragedies that had happened here. His impatience to see it was almost visible, like the warping of a plate-glass window just before it shatters. He had never driven so fast, or so erratically, and Effie was shaken from side to side as he swerved around bend after bend, and jounced into pot-holes and stretches of loose shale.

'Craig, for goodness' sake! We're not in any kind of a hurry. Come on, I know I complained, but we're not booked for lunch till one-thirty.'

Craig didn't say anything, but slid the BMW around the next bend with its tyres squittering. Effie's stomach went weightless for a split second, and the car snaked, and she was sure that he had almost lost control.

'For Christ's sake will you slow down? This is my car and I don't want to die in it!'

They drove through rippling surface water in a high cloud of spray. 'What's the matter?' Craig laughed at her. 'Don't you trust me, or what?'

'Of course I trust you, but–'

They sped past the Red Oaks Inn. Just as Craig was slowing down to take the curve, Effie saw somebody sitting on the front verandah. A man, with his arm lifted, and his mouth open, as if he were trying to call out to them.

Instantly, she gripped Craig's knee and said, 'Stop, Craig! *Stop!* There's somebody waving!'

He swerved into the parking-lot and slithered to a stop.

'For Christ's sake, what was that all about?' he demanded.

'He's waving at us, look!'

'So what? He's only some kid!'

Effie opened the car door. 'He waved, all right? I want to see what he wants.'

48

'He *waved*? For Christ's sake, people wave at anything. People wave at trains. It doesn't mean they want them to stop!'

Effie turned to him furiously. 'If you really want to know, I don't care why he's waving. But I wanted to slow you down. You never drove like that before.'

Craig puffed out his cheeks in resignation. 'All right. I'm sorry. But what's the use in having a fast car if you never go fast?'

'What's the use in having a fast car if you're lying in the cemetery?'

They were still arguing when they climbed out of the car. They slammed their doors much more forcefully than they needed to, and they kept an angry distance as they walked up to the inn. As they approached, they were watched with obvious trepidation by a skinny bespectacled youth with very long chestnut hair who was sitting on the front verandah with both heavily-booted feet raised on the rail. He wore a yellow-and-black checkered work-shirt, and a sleeveless vest of thick gingery tweed. In spite of his outdoorsy clothes, his face was the colour of semolina. He had large brown eyes that were magnified by his spectacles, and a large sharp nose that was simply large, no magnification necessary.

Parked on the opposite side of the inn was a dusty '69 Dodge Charger which presumably belonged to him. Most of it was black, but its hood was off-white and its driver's door was metallic green.

'Hi, there!' called Craig, with forced, over-loud friendliness, as they climbed the steps up to the verandah. The young man watched them without saying anything, without taking his boots off the rail. He had righted one of the inn's occasional tables, and Effie was immediately fascinated by the picnic lunch which he had meticulously

49

spread out on it, on an opened-out copy of *National Enquirer*. Two or three slices of pumpernickel, an orange, a small half-empty jar of blueberry jelly, a carton of Philadelphia Cream Cheese, four Saltines, a tomato and a dill pickle.

'You waved,' said Effie, brightly.

The young man slowly blinked at her, and then blinked equally slowly at Craig.

'Did you want something?' asked Effie. 'Or were you just . . . waving?'

'Oh, sorry, I wanted something. You're Mr and Mrs Bellman, right? I was trying to catch your attention.' His voice was surprisingly deep for his pasty, juvenile appearance, and he had a very distinctive Massachusetts accent. Effie would have guessed that he came from Boston's North Shore originally, Salem or Marblehead.

Craig put on his martyred talking-to-retards tone. 'You were trying to catch our attention?'

'That's right.'

'Well, you caught it. You caught our attention. Here we are, all attentive. Now what?'

'Do you live around here?' Effie asked him. 'The reason I ask is, I used to come to the Red Oaks Inn when I was a girl, I mean my parents brought me here, and I was just wondering if you happened to know what happened to the owners.'

'Oh,' said the young man. 'The owners.'

'Effie, sweetheart,' Craig put in. 'This young man has attracted our attention, or so he says. Do you think we can ask him why?'

Effie persisted. 'Mr and Mrs Berryman, do you remember them? She was kind of plumpish with white hair and he was tall and very skinny with eyeglasses. I asked at our bed-and-breakfast and down at the Country Goose but nobody could clearly recall.'

'I guess people wouldn't,' the young man nodded. 'People, like, forget things here, when they don't particularly want to remember them.'

'Do *you* know what happened to them?' Effie coaxed him.

'Jesus,' said Craig. 'We're driving past, he waves, and we still don't know why. All of a sudden, it's old folks week, and we're talking long-lost inn owners.'

The young man said, 'I don't know the whole story.'

There was a long, taut pause. Lightning crackled in the near distance, with a sound like tearing calico, and then the hills echoed with a muffled drum-roll of thunder. Craig said, 'What was it?'

The young man blinked and looked around. 'Thunder I guess.'

'I know it's thunder. What I meant was, what happened to Mr and Mrs Berryman?'

'Oh, them. Well, this was six or seven years ago. Business got worse and worse, and in the end they went bankrupt. Then Mrs Berryman died in a fire. I don't know what happened to Mr Berryman. Right after the fire he left, and nobody ever heard from him again. Some people say that he went to Minnesota, but I don't know.'

'Oh, I feel so sorry for them,' said Effie. 'They were always such happy people.'

The young man lifted his feet off the rail. 'My mom always says that happiness is finite. That's what makes it happiness. If it lasted too long, we'd all grow to hate it. Like, if we had prime rib for every meal, or orgasms went on for a week.'

'Your mom sounds like quite a philosopher,' said Craig.

'My mom? Forget it. My mom could use a head transplant.'

51

Effie laughed. 'That's not a very complimentary thing to say about her.'

'Hey . . . she's the first to admit it. If you ever talked to her, you'd think she just arrived from Mars about an hour ago. If you're staying in Cold Spring, you probably met her already. She runs the Hungry Moon Natural Nourishment Store on Main Street. Health foods, crystal balls, occult stuff. You know how she got here? My grandparents brought her to Woodstock in '69 and like left her behind. Forgot her. Can you imagine it? Just forgetting your kid like that, like some umbrella?'

Effie said, in disbelief, 'The woman who runs the Hungry Moon is your *mother*?'

'Sure. That's right. Have you met her? You don't mind if I eat my lunch?'

'No, no. Go ahead. But your mom is so young-looking!'

The young man laboriously spread one slice of his pumpernickel with Philly cheese. 'She's young-looking because she's young. She was only twelve when my grandparents left her at Woodstock. I guess she must have been tough, though, because she lived with this busload of hippies for three or four years afterwards. Actually my grandparents did come back looking for her after a couple of months, but by that time she didn't want to go.'

'When did she have you?'

'Well, she was sixteen years old when she got pregnant, that's all. But I guess she was lucky. Mr and Mrs Berryman gave her a live-in job right here at the Red Oaks Inn. She saved up just about everything she earned, and then she opened the Hungry Moon. That's it; the story of my dubious ancestry.'

'Your mom's name is Pepper something, is that right?' asked Effie. 'I've talked to her once or twice.'

'That's right, Pepper Moriarty. My name's Norman.

52

Actually on my birth certificate it says No Man because mom wanted to name me after my father, and she wasn't exactly sure who my father was. Sometimes she says I was born by virgin birth. She was lying in this field one night with her dress pulled up around her waist, and this shooting-star came streaking down from the sky and, like, penetrated her. She said she saw a terrific flash of white light, and that was it: she was knocked up with me.'

He frowned beneath his dangling hair, and spread blueberry jelly on one of his Saltines. 'I'm very open-minded, and all, but I don't actually think that's very likely.'

'Whatever, it's still a nice story,' Effie smiled. 'Is that one of your mom's diets you're eating?'

Norman frowned at his jelly-smeared Saltine. 'Actually it's my own diet. It's very balanced, and you can actually *see* that it's balanced. Black is the opposite of white, so I eat black bread with white cheese on it. Blue is the opposite of yellow so I eat yellow Saltines with blueberry jelly. Red is the opposite of green, and so on. I went to art school,' he added, with obvious regret. 'I guess I should have gone to dietician school instead.'

Craig was impatiently jingling the keys to Valhalla in his pocket. 'It's been great talking to you, Norman, but we have to make tracks. We're getting a little pushed for time here.'

'You never saw Valhalla before?' asked Norman.

Craig was visibly irritated. His eyes always went foxy and small when he was irritated. 'How do you know we're going to Valhalla?'

'You couldn't be going anyplace else. After the Red Oaks Inn, Valhalla is all that's left on this mountain, apart from the view. Besides, I was supposed to meet you here. That's why I waved. Mr Van Buren called me, see, and asked me to tag along. As an adviser, kind of, and a guide. I didn't realise you were going to be so quick. I went to Pig Hill and they said you wouldn't be back until after lunch, so I guessed you were going to go eat first.'

'Craig's very impatient to see Valhalla,' said Effie. Impatient? God, he was jingling those keys like a jittery warden at Sing Sing.

'Why don't you finish your – uh – lunch?' Craig suggested. 'Then you can catch up with us.'

'Oh, I guess I shouldn't,' said Norman. 'Mr Van Buren said I should keep you company the whole time, because some of the building is like pretty unsafe. Besides, he said you'd probably want to know what it would cost to put it all back together, and that's where I come in. Restoring local houses, that's one of the things I do. Admitted, I never restored a house as big as Valhalla, but I'm very good on floors and ceilings. I can render. I can tile. I've put in three spiral staircases, two timber, one cast-iron. And a whole limed-oak kitchen, too.'

'We're just viewing,' Effie explained. 'We don't need a builder.'

Norman crammed the rest of his Saltine into his mouth, and wrapped up everything else in his *National Enquirer*. 'Sure, I know you are. But Mr Van Buren said that it wouldn't hurt.'

'All right, then,' Craig agreed, still foxy-eyed. 'It won't hurt. Now, shall we go?'

He stalked back to the BMW just as an ear-splitting clap of thunder exploded right over their heads. There was a moment's pause, and then fat, warm spots of rain began to fall. Norman took Effie's elbow and said, 'Better hurry. The good old firmament's just about to open.'

Craig climbed into the car and slammed the door. Norman was just about to open the passenger door for Effie when she held his arm and said, 'What did Mr Van

54

Buren tell you, Norman? I mean, we're *viewing*, that's all.'

Norman shrugged. 'Mr Van Buren said that anybody who wants to look at a house like Valhalla usually wants to buy a house like Valhalla, and who is he to stand in their way. You know what houses are like. They're the same as crack cocaine. Either you don't even think about it, or else you'll kill for it.'

'And what do you think?'

'I don't know. Whatever makes you happy.'

'Look at us. Do you think Valhalla could make us happy?'

Norman raked his hair back from his forehead with both hands, and shrugged. 'For a while, I guess. But there you go. It's just like my mom says. Happiness has to come to an end sooner or later, otherwise it isn't happiness.'

Saturday, June 19, 12:36 p.m.

Norman followed them up the track, only two or three feet behind their rear bumper. His silencer was holed, and his engine burbled so loudly that Craig and Effie could hardly hear themselves think, let alone talk.

'You look annoyed,' Effie shouted.

'I would have preferred it if we could have looked around the house on our own.'

'Norman seems okay. A little eccentric.'

'A little eccentric? A guy who thinks that a balanced diet means eating food in complementary colours?'

Effie laughed. Although she was perplexed by Craig's extraordinary itch to look at Valhalla, she was pleased and relieved by the way in which he seemed to be relaxing. Maybe that was what he needed – a diversion, something else to think about apart from Japanese businessmen and anti-trust suits and nightmarish 'accidents' with hammers.

'Do you know something. I forgot how spectacular the Highlands can be,' said Craig. 'Especially in this weather. Look at that lightning, down in those valleys. Spectacular.'

'You wouldn't like to live here, though, would you? You're a city boy. You always said that lightning striking the Empire State was spectacular.'

'Well, you know what they say. Home is where the heart is.'

Effie shrugged. She was irritated, in a way, that Walter Van Buren had sent Norman to meet them, because Norman would give Craig all kinds of ideas about restoration and what it would cost. Walter Van Buren might have appeared soft and colourless and laid-back, but it was obvious that he hadn't been selling million-dollar properties up and down the Hudson River Valley for thirty-eight years without learning quite a lot about the psychology of realty, and which houses virtually sold themselves, and to whom, and why. But maybe it was a good thing, in a way, because it would give Craig something to take his mind off his 'accident'.

They would never be able to afford Valhalla, not by any stretch of the bank balance, even if its previous owners had kept it in habitable condition; and she didn't think for a moment that Craig would seriously want to make an offer for it. But if it occupied his attention for a week or two, if it helped to restore his masculinity and his sense of pride, then she was happy to go along with it.

She didn't understand why Valhalla interested him so much. He didn't understand it himself, not yet. He had never imagined in his whole life that he would want to live in the Hudson Valley Highlands; and he had warned plenty of his own clients against overstretching themselves

56

when it came to buying property. Too many of them had lost their houses in the late '80s. His best friend Josh Marias had lost a beautiful waterfront property in East Hampton, along with his equally beautiful wife.

Maybe the wild and isolated setting appealed to him; and the name Valhalla, hall of dead heroes; and something else – something as strong as hunger or thirst or sexual desire. It was the feeling that you had to be a man to live here, king of the mountain. Rich, successful, and smouldering with self-esteem. You wouldn't have to go out looking for the world. The world would come looking for you.

Craig, annoyed as he was that they hadn't been able to view Valhalla alone, wasn't altogether displeased that Norman was here. Norman could show Effie that Valhalla was not just a dream but a practical possibility. Norman could tell her in dollars and cents.

If Norman could work out a bare-bones budget which Effie could accept, then later he could add some of those luxury items which the grand mansions of the Hudson Valley deserve. Gilded taps, marble floors. A library pungent with oak shelving and leather-bound books. Swags and curtains and carpets as hushed as sin. A billiard-room.

The rain lashed against their windscreen harder and faster, just as the line of dark, deformed oak trees rose into view. Craig drove right up to the gates and then slewed to a stop. He forced his way out of the car door against a wind that was gusting up to 50 m.p.h. and shouted at Effie, 'Let's hope this is the right goddamned key!'

He went up to the gates and lifted the heavy rusted padlock. The wind sounded hollow and threatening, like somebody blowing across the neck of an empty jar. Rain spattered his cheeks and measled his shirt. Lightning danced across the horizon as he twisted the key into the padlock's opening; and he thought, apocalyptic? Yes, I'm

57

going to be apocalyptic. I'm opening up the gates to a whole new life. Thunder bellowed right over his head, just as Norman came running through the rain to help him.

'That's probably pretty stiff!' Norman shouted. 'It hasn't been opened in years!'

'I can do it,' Craig told him. 'I didn't do gung-fu wrist-exercises for nothing.'

'Okay, great. But if gung-fu doesn't work, I have a couple of cans of easing oil in the car.'

'I can do it, okay?'

'Okay, sure. But let's get hustling, right?' Norman's trousers were snapping in the wind and he was obviously trying hard not to be panicky. 'It's not such a dazzling idea, you know, standing about on top of a mountain in a full-scale electric storm, holding a pair of iron gates. Well, actually, it could be a *very* dazzling idea.'

The padlock was stiff, and gritty with rust, but slowly it yielded. The levers clicked open one by one, and then Craig was able to drag out the rusted hasp.

'Hey, how about that?' said Norman. 'Eat your heart out, Sylvester Stallone.'

Together, inch by scraping inch, Craig and Norman forced open the right-hand gate, and fastened it back with a corroded old hook buried in the grass.

'I guess you know Valhalla pretty well!' shouted Craig against the wind as they did so.

Norman's glasses were steamed-up and speckled with rain, and his hair was flying everywhere. 'Me and my friends used to play here, when we were kids. Ran around everywhere: sitting rooms, ballroom, kitchen, halfway up the stairs. No further, though. Didn't dare, because of the ghosts.'

'Ghosts! You and that Walter Van Buren guy, you're as crazy as each other!'

Norman shouted, 'Who knows? I don't believe in ghosts. I did then, though, when I was eight years old. Didn't you?'

'Let's get moving,' Craig told him.

'You're the supremo, supremo.'

'That's right. I'm the supremo. And, listen, no more crap about ghosts. I don't want you upsetting my wife.'

They drove through the gates of Valhalla and into the shadowy avenue of oak trees. The day was already dark, but the trees blotted out so much light that Craig had to switch on his headlamps to see where he was going. Behind him, Norman switched on his headlamps, too, and Craig had to flick his rearview mirror into its night-driving position to prevent himself from being blinded.

'Jesus, he's all brains, this young pal of ours,' he told Effie sarcastically, his eyes wincing against the bright reflected light.

'What do you expect? He's a kid. Give him a break.'

'What? He must be twenty-two, twenty-three, easy.'

'That's still a kid.'

'What kind of a kid runs his own house-restoring business?'

'An enterprising kid, I'd say. And I happen to like him, stupid diet and all.'

'Maybe you're right.' Then he gripped her hand and unexpectedly kissed it. 'I love you, do you know that? I don't know how you've managed to put up with me, but I do. And, yes, I like Norman, too. He could use a haircut, but I like him.'

As the BMW jounced between the oaks, Craig deliberately slowed. Now that he was here, he wanted to savour his first view of Valhalla, he wanted to tantalise himself. He knew it was ridiculous, of course. But he felt Valhalla drawing him closer and closer; and what was strangest of all, he *wanted* to be there, he *needed* to be there. He felt a magnetism as strong as gravity.

At the same time, he felt the first needlings of a sharp and inexplicable sense of regret. *I should have been here long before now – I would have been, if my life had turned out different. This is where I belong. Why did I never find this place before?*

'Do you know what?' he asked Effie. 'Did you ever feel that your whole destiny was waiting for you, just around the corner?'

She looked at him – his broad-jawed, handsome face, his thick Kennedy-style hair. He was smiling in a way that she hadn't seen him smile for months, since long before his mugging, and she suddenly felt that she had managed to set him free. He looked like Craig Bellman again, the tall, humorous law student who had pushed in beside her at the Corner Bistro on Jane Street, and asked her if she liked Mallarmé.

'What's Mallarmé? A drink?'

'He's a French writer. He wrote, "Oh, mirror! How many times, for hours on end, saddened by dreams and searching for my memories, have I seen myself in you as a distant ghost!" '

She had stared at him in astonishment. 'And?'

'And, I don't know. You just looked like the kind of girl who would find that really impressive.'

Maybe he had reminded her too much of her father. He had always liked to take charge of everything. The only difference between Craig and her father was that her father had grown gentler and more understanding with every new responsibility, a warm and loving patriarch; whereas Craig had grown harder and more obsessive and had eventually lost the courtesy that it always takes to compromise.

Now that they were here, at Valhalla, she began to

60

recognise him again. It was unexpected, and frankly it was wonderful. It gave her the same warm, confused feeling that she had experienced that night at the Corner Bistro. Who is this man? How can he talk like this?

'*Que de fois et pendant les heures, désolée des songes et cherchant mes souvenirs, je m'apparus en toi comme une ombre lointaine.*'

'What?' he said.

'Don't you remember? Mallarmé.'

For one split second he looked cross. Then he seemed to realise what she was talking about, and smiled.

'*Une ombre lointaine,*' she repeated, and rested her head against his shoulder. 'A distant ghost.'

Lightning cracked and cracked again, and the whole world turned electric white. Thunder bellowed so loudly that Effie felt as if the sky was literally collapsing on top of her, and she covered her head with her hands.

'It's okay, sweetheart,' Craig told her, cupping his hand reassuringly around the back of her head. 'Come on, sweetheart. There's nothing to be scared of.'

They jostled along the coarsely-shingled driveway through the trees. On either side of them, the oaks were champing and churning in the wind, like panicked horses. Quite suddenly, however, they drove out onto an open crest; and below them they saw a wide, wide field of long, rain-beaten grass – a field that had once been a croquet lawn, or a tennis court, or several tennis courts. Overlooking the field was a stone terrace, like a low medieval rampart, black with moss, with a derelict fountain and overturned urns.

Beyond the terrace was the house itself, Valhalla. It was raining so hard now that Craig had to switch the wipers full on; but even through the cascading rain and the madly-flapping wiper blades, they could both see what a

61

breathtaking building it was.

'Will you look at that,' said Craig, stopping the car for a moment.

The house was huge, three storeys high, built of dark brownish-red brick, with stone-framed windows. It had originally been constructed in the form of a giant cross, like a cathedral, but later additions of outbuildings and stables had changed it into an L-shape. It was unashamedly Gothic, in the style popular after World War One, especially among successful speculators and war profiteers. This was a house that had been built to give its owner dignity, and status, and a feeling of old inherited wealth.

The sky behind the house was as dark as a poisoned pond, but Valhalla's rooftops shone, and its windows glittered, almost as if it were occupied. Its chimneys were so tall that they trailed in the clouds, and they could have been smoking. It was only when the lightning crackled that Craig and Effie could see that the windows were blacked out and broken, and that the roofing had collapsed in places, exposing the rafters to the rain. As they drove closer, the extent of Valhalla's dereliction became increasingly apparent.

'My God, it's a disaster,' said Effie. Immediately, she wished she hadn't. But then immediately after that, she was glad she had. She couldn't go on treading on eggshells for ever. She wanted Craig to recover from his 'accident', but part of that recovery was getting back to normal, allowing herself to speak her mind. He had been so angry lately, so impossibly angry, that she had fallen into the habit of biting her tongue; and she didn't want to do that any more.

But Craig said, 'You're right. Just look at the state of that roof.'

He continued to drive slowly through the rain down the

winding driveway that curved around the right-hand side of the lawns. Effie could see hardly anything except streaking rainwater and gloomy shadows, and the dazzling reflection of Norman's headlamps in her rearview mirror. But then the driveway rose in a gradual gradient until it reached a wide brick-paved circle in front of Valhalla's main entrance. In the centre of the circle stood the sinister, headless statue of a naked woman, her back encrusted with lichen, like a diseased cloak. In one hand she carried a broken dagger. In the other she was holding up something that looked like a sackful of dead puppies, although it was too burdened with dripping moss for Effie to see it very clearly.

Norman pulled up behind them, climbed out of his car and came scuttling towards them through the rain. He knocked on the window. 'Do you have an umbrella?' he shouted, over the thunder.

'Two,' Effie reassured him.

'Good. You're going to need them. There's a couple of places the roof has come down.'

Effie took hold of Craig's hand. 'Craig . . . really, do you think there's any point in doing this? It must have been a beautiful house once, but look at it now. We couldn't even afford to repair the roof.'

'You said yourself that we were only looking, okay?'

She didn't know what to say. He had that old, warm look in his eyes. He kissed her forehead, and then kissed her cheek, right beside her nose, and then he kissed her on the lips.

'There's no harm in looking, is there?'

She kissed him back. He must have shaved very closely this morning, because his cheek was unusually smooth, like well-polished leather.

Norman's hair was beginning to drip, his nose wrinkled

63

against the rain. 'Are you coming, like, or what? I mean, I don't mind standing here for the rest of my life catching pneumonia, but I was kind of concerned for you guys. People can get a cramp if they stay in cars too long.'

'Come on,' said Craig, and opened the car door. And Effie thought, with a smile of resignation: I won't be able to stop him, not just yet. Today, he's all excited. Tomorrow, or the day after, he'll have seen how bad it is, and worked out the costings to put it right. Two or three million just to make it weatherproof again, and even half-habitable; another three to four million to furnish it and carpet it and make it look like home.

Craig hobbled around to the back of the car, took the umbrellas out of the boot and opened them up. Even so, Effie screamed as they hurried through the rain. 'God, it's cold!' They climbed the semi-circular brick steps which led up to the portico, and found themselves facing Valhalla's double front doors – weathered, dull, with scarcely any paint left on them. In the centre of each door was a heavy, corroded knob. On the right-hand side hung a bell-pull, cast in bronze in the shape of a snarling wolf.

'Do you think we ought to ring, just to warn the ghosts that we're here?' joked Craig.

Norman didn't seem to think that was particularly funny. 'You see this bell-pull? It's supposed to be Coyote, the Native American demon. If you pull it and you're not welcome, or you've come to the house with evil in your heart, it'll, like, bite your hand off.'

'Where'd you learn that hogwash?' asked Craig. He took out the key that Walter Van Buren had given him, and fitted it into the door.

'Excuse me, that's not hogwash. My mom told me. She's an expert on all that kind of stuff. She said it's something to do with the doorway facing east.'

64

'Your mom's been here?' asked Effie. Craig was having trouble with the lock.

'Oh, sure, we used to bring picnics up here, pretend we were rich. It's pretty nice when it's sunny.'

At last Craig managed to turn the key in the lock. He pushed the door and it swung open in complete silence. 'Come on, then,' he said. 'Let's see just how much of a disaster this is. Or maybe it isn't.'

They stepped through the doorway into a huge oak-panelled hall, with a pale marble floor. There were two wide oak staircases, one on either side of the hall, both leading up to a galleried landing. On the newel posts of each staircase stood bronze statuettes of naked women, each holding up a torch. The glass flames from each torch were broken, and one of the women was headless, like the statue outside.

Effie looked up. There were high leaded windows on either side, through which she could see the lightning still flickering. Dozens and dozens of panes of glass had been broken, and the marble floor was crunchy with grit and splinters.

There was a strong, strange smell in the house, too. Not dry rot or wet rot, which she would have expected, but a pungent smell like some kind of liniment – camphor and menthol and aniseed. It reminded her of changing-rooms and clinics and the hospital where her father had died. She suddenly thought of her mother, standing at the very end of a long, brightly-lit corridor, her face devastated by what had happened, like a smashed jelly-jar.

Norman had brought a powerful flashlight with him, and he switched it on. The beam darted up to the landing, then back down again, then pointed at the floor. 'This hall area is pretty sound. The floor's good, just needs cleaning up. There's a marble restoring company in Albany,

65

Schuhmacher's, they'll probably do it for you for less than four thousand.'

'Four *thousand*?' Effie repeated. 'Just for cleaning the floor?'

'It's terrific marble, imported from Belgium. Beautifully brecciated. That means kind of a broken pattern. You don't see marble laid like this, not these days. It's not purbeck, it's proper genuine marble. It would be worth the money, like, just to see it, the way it was.'

'Four thousand isn't bad, for a floor like this,' said Craig, with his back turned. His voice echoed so much that it sounded as if he were hiding under the right-hand staircase and speaking from there; and that his twin was speaking from the gallery.

The flashlight beam jumped up to the windows. 'The floor may be reasonable, but the windows will cost you. These are all handmade, full lead glass. Some of them are overscaled, like these. Some of them are underscaled.'

Craig turned around. For a second, he looked foxy-eyed again, but then he said, 'What does that exactly mean, overscaled and underscaled?'

'Oh . . . it means that some of them are bigger than they traditionally ought to be, right? and some of them are smaller. It's kind of an architectural trick, you know, to make them look more varied. Whatever, none of them are standard, so you're looking at two or three hundred thousand dollars' worth of specialist glazing; and that's if we can find somebody cheap, who'll do it for the glory.'

Craig nodded, but said nothing. It seemed to Effie that his nod was echoed; albeit silently; as if the house understood that here was somebody who found it exciting. She had seen women at cocktail parties unconsciously imitating Craig's affirmative nods, *oh, yes, Craig, yes, Craig, yes,* and that was usually when she ostentatiously linked arms

66

with him, in case there was any mistake about the fact that he was happily married.

The flashlight darted up to the galleried landing, and illuminated a coat of arms, carved out of mahogany. 'See that?' said Norman. 'That was put up by the guy who built Valhalla, Jack Belias. There's a bobbin in one quarter . . . that's to represent his textile business. Then dice in the opposite quarter, because he was crazy for gambling. Then a dragon, because the name Belias was supposed to be something to do with dragons, like. Then a skull.'

'What was the skull for?' asked Effie.

'I don't know. Life and death, maybe. Jack Belias was known for taking ridiculous risks. I guess he was so rich, he thought what the hell. He flew airplanes, drove race-cars and powerboats and all that kind of stuff. He used to have a revolver on his sideboard, that's what they say, with one bullet in it and every day before breakfast he used to spin the cylinder, stick the muzzle in his mouth and pull the trigger.'

'That motto underneath . . . do you know what that means?' asked Craig.

'*Non omnis moriar*? Who knows?'

Effie said, 'That means something like, "Not all of us shall die". No, no, wait a minute, it's first person singular. It means, "I shall never completely die".'

'Pretty creepy for a haunted house,' said Norman, and shone the flashlight under his chin so that his face looked like a glowing, disembodied death mask.

'I thought I told you no ghost talk,' Craig reminded him, sharply. 'My wife doesn't like it.'

'I don't mind,' said Effie. 'I like a good ghost story. Just don't ask me to spend the night here, that's all.'

Thunder rumbled indigestively, but the storm was obviously moving away south-eastwards.

'Come take a look at the ballroom,' Norman suggested. 'Fishkill really did a job on it. It's a pity they ran out of money.'

He led them beneath the broken windows where the rain sprayed in, and along the panelled corridor that took them along the southern side of the house. Their feet crunched on shattered glass and grit. Through the over-scaled and underscaled windows, Effie could see the terrace outside, and the rain steadily sifting across the lawns. Most of the terrace was humped with lumps of black, half-liquefied moss, and impossibly tall thistles grew up between the bricks. She felt as if she were walking through Sleeping Beauty's castle, neglected for a hundred years. She could almost believe that there were people still sleeping in the bedrooms upstairs. She couldn't explain it, but there was certainly a feeling that Valhalla hadn't been deserted. While the roofing collapsed and the rooks made nests in the chimney stacks; while rainwater poured through the ceilings and windows cracked in the summer heat, the house hadn't died, but simply closed its eyes and slumbered.

She reached out and took hold of Craig's hand, and he clasped it warmly.

'Can't you just see us living here?' he asked her. 'Talk about style. We'd have to dress for dinner every single evening.'

'Dress for dinner? We'd have to dress to go to the bathroom.'

He laughed, and kissed her. 'I forgot you. I forgot how funny you were.'

She kissed him back, and what started out as a small peck on the lips became a sudden, urgent embrace. It was only broken up by Norman turning around with his flashlight.

'Oh, excuse me. Didn't mean to break anything up or nothing.'

'That's okay,' Effie told him. 'Realty over one hundred thousand square feet always has that effect on me.'

But Craig held her hand in both of his hands; pressed it like a lily in a bible; and his eyes were bright.

'Then shall I awake to the original fervour, upright and alone in an ancient flood of light, lilies! and one of you for innocence.'

'Mallarmé,' Effie breathed.

'You remembered.'

'Remembered? I never forgot.'

They followed Norman along the corridor until they reached a wide pair of double oak doors, with an arched Gothic-style architrave. 'My mom says the ballroom is definitely haunted. In fact it's one of the most haunted loci in the whole house, except for one bedroom upstairs, which is so seriously haunted that she won't even go within fifty feet of it.'

'I thought you were supposed to be encouraging us to think about buying,' said Effie, squeezing Craig's hand tighter. 'Not scaring us half to death.'

Norman shook his long wet hair. 'Hey, don't worry about me. I don't care if you want to buy it or not, except that it could give me some work if you did. I'm here to give you the guided tour, for which Mr Van Buren will slip me a ten-spot. And a few ballpark costings, if you want them. That's all. Anyhow, you'd be amazed how many people love the idea of a house with ghosts in it. They even pay extra.'

He opened the double doors. 'Besides,' he added, 'you shouldn't pay too much attention to what my mom has to say on the subject of the supernatural. My mom thinks that just about every building in the Hudson River Valley is possessed by spirits. Even the Cold Spring supermarket. She says that, at night, the shopping carts roll up and down the aisles on their own. Nobody pushing them.'

'That's even spookier than a haunted ballroom.'

But it wasn't. Because when Norman opened both doors, and they saw the ballroom for themselves, they saw a silent, dusty room that must have been peopled by the kind of memories that, for most of us, are only fairy stories, and dreams, and half-forgotten snatches from black-and-white movies.

It was over a hundred feet square, with a high pillared gallery all the way around it. Its ceiling rose right up to the roof of the house, and was pierced by an elegant oval skylight. None of the glass in the skylight was broken, but it was clogged with fallen leaves and obscured with livid green lichen. From the centre of it, a long chain hung down. Presumably it had once carried a large chandelier, but now it ended in nothing but a huge hook and four electric wires bound with insulating-tape.

Effie walked through the diagonal beam of the flashlight across the floor. She was entranced. The room was dusty, but it had been immaculately restored, with gilded acanthus leaves on the pale stucco pillars, and elegant bronze wall-lights in the shape of women's hands holding up blazing glass torches. The window frames and the panelling had been stripped and polished, although the polish had a breathed-over look from damp and neglect. The floor had been completely relaid and still looked highly-burnished even beneath a two-year coating of dust.

'See this floor?' said Norman, darting the flashlight right and left. 'Canadian maple . . . best possible dancing floor you could find. It actually springs when you step on it.'

Craig kept turning around and around, looking up at the pillars and the gallery and the decorated ceiling. 'Isn't

70

it amazing?' he breathed. 'You can almost imagine the music. You can almost see people dancing.'

'This room doesn't need anything more than a clean-up,' Norman remarked. He peered at a small scabrous patch on one of the walls, and then prodded it with his finger. 'There's some damp coming through, but you could soon fix that.'

Craig took Effie in his arms and danced three or four steps of a waltz with her. Outside, the skies were beginning to clear, and the first wash of sunlight lit the ballroom windows, and formed patterns on the floor. Craig said, 'Mr and Mrs Craig T. Bellman request the pleasure of your company at a grand summer ball. Dress: amazing, if you please. Supper at ten, breakfast at four, carriages at six.'

'You're mad,' laughed Effie.

'Mad? Me? I'll buy the house Monday and have the invitations printed by the end of next week.'

'Let me show you the kitchens,' said Norman, switching off his flashlight. 'The kitchens aren't haunted.'

Two more rooms led off the ballroom: a huge morning-room with french windows overlooking the gardens; and a derelict room that might once have been a library. The ceiling had partially collapsed, and the plaster on the walls was bulging with damp, like leprosy sores. The flooring was covered with damp grey sheets, and it must have been water-damaged, and warped, because it rattled under their feet as they walked across it, as if they were wearing clogs.

They reached another wide staircase. Effie went halfway up it to have a look. It led up to a large, high-ceilinged landing, with clerestory windows all around it. When it was built it must have been airy and bright, but most of the windows were obscured with grime, and water had penetrated one side of the landing, creating a hunched figure out of fungus and diseased plaster. It even seemed to have one dripping eye, this figure – glaring at Effie from underneath a heavy elephant-man forehead of bulging moss.

'The water's got in pretty bad all around this side of the house,' Norman remarked. 'There's a whole area of flat roofing that's been leaking since the house was built. These days, it's just got worse, that's all, and most of the north-facing bedrooms need new ceilings and new floors.'

'How much?' asked Effie, holding Craig's arm.

'One point seven-five, give or take. That's if you want it to look something like the way it did when it was first constructed.'

'You mean one and three quarters of a million dollars?'

'Give or take.'

'I don't think I need to see the kitchens.'

'Come on, they're like really interesting. They have all the original equipment, in amazing condition. An Elkay sink, a Westinghouse icebox.'

'Norman,' Effie interrupted him, 'I'm sure the kitchens are very interesting, but if it's going to cost one and three quarters of a million dollars just to stop the rain from coming in, we'll just have to say thank you but no thank you.'

'Come on, sweetheart,' Craig cajoled her. 'There's no harm in looking.'

'Well, I don't *want* to look. If we're rich enough to buy a house like this, we're rich enough to have servants. You don't think this Jack Belias ever visited the kitchens, do you?'

'It's pretty historical,' said Norman. 'An original 1929 kitchen, in showroom condition.'

'You mean an antique kitchen that's going to cost half-a-million dollars to renovate?'

Norman chewed on his hair. 'I guess that's one way of putting it. But I know a guy in Newburgh who puts in

72

brilliant imported kitchens at fantastically low prices. You like Neff? He can do Neff for practically nothing.'

He took hold of Craig's elbow, and led him across the hallway to the kitchens. Effie thought: oh well, I guess it's historical, I guess I ought to be interested, and she was just about to follow them when she thought she heard something.

She stopped, and listened, looking up towards the landing where the dripping moss-creature stood. Norman was still talking to Craig, explaining how Elkay's 1929-model Butler's Pantry sinks came in copper, nickel, white metal, crodon plate or monel metal, and how–

They pushed their way through the squeaking kitchen door, and it swung closed behind them. Effie stayed where she was, straining her ears.

The wind was still moaning through the broken windows; and thunder still crumpled in the distance. But she was sure that she could hear a woman sobbing.

She hesitated, then she took two or three steps up the staircase, and listened again.

She was sure she could hear it. The low, agonised cries of a woman who was really desperate, really in pain. It was very far away, in one of the upper bedrooms, but there was no mistaking it.

She turned around and called, 'Craig!'

There was no answer, so she went to the kitchen door and pushed it open. The cream-decorated kitchen was deserted, although the door to the cellar was ajar. Presumably Norman had taken Craig down below to see Valhalla's boilers.

'Craig!' she called, but there was still no reply.

She waited for a moment, then she went back to the hallway. She listened and listened and she could still hear it, that terrible agonised sobbing.

She started to climb the stairs.

Saturday, June 19, 1:11 p.m.

She held onto the banister rail as she climbed, because some of the stairs were darkly rotted where water had been pouring down the wall. Three-quarters of the way up, one of the stairs lurched downward an inch, and Effie heard nails pulling out of old, pulpy wood. She hesitated for a moment, holding her breath, not sure if she ought to continue.

But then she heard that anguished sobbing again; and it seemed much nearer. Whoever it was, she couldn't leave her. She sounded so much in pain.

Effie reached the top of the stairs. The landing was covered with a thin, rucked-up carpet. It had once been yellow, and patterned with flowers, but now it was water-stained and faded to the colour of old skin. On the opposite side of the landing, the grey-green figure of leprous plaster watched her with its single rheumy eye. She stared back at it, defying it to move, and of course it didn't; but there was still something horribly animate about it, as if it were brooding with deep resentment about its own hideous face, like the Elephant Man.

Two corridors led away from this landing: one to her left, to the bedrooms over the kitchens – the other to her right. But directly beside her, another staircase led up to Valhalla's third storey.

She paused, and listened, and it seemed as if this was where the sobbing was coming from: somewhere in the half-collapsed roof.

She heard a door banging downstairs, and she turned

74

back and called out, 'Craig?' hoping that he had finished his tour of the cellars. But it was only the library door, banging in the wind that blew in through the broken windows.

The sobbing had become almost a mewling now, an endless self-pitying litany of indistinguishable words. Although she held her breath so that she could hear better, Effie still couldn't make out what the woman was crying about. She went to the foot of the second staircase, and held onto the decorative newel post. Halfway up the staircase there was a stained glass window, glazed in very pale ambers and yellows and faded pinks. It depicted a woman in a nun's habit, her eyes closed, standing in a field of lilies. Behind her, in the middle distance, stood a man dressed in black, with his back turned. Even further away, on the horizon, stood a castle with black pennants flying from it.

It was the strangest window that Effie had ever seen, and even though she wanted to find the weeping woman as quickly as she could, she stopped on the first stair to look at it, one hand clasping the banister, one foot raised. At the foot of the window, a stained-glass banner was unfurled, with the words *Gut ist der Schlaf, der Tod ist besser.* She didn't know any German, but she guessed that *Schlaf* was something to do with sleep, since the nun appeared to be sleeping. But why standing up, in a field? And who was the man with his back turned? It reminded Effie of a scene from a tarot card, mystic and pseudo-medieval, magical rather than historical.

For a moment, while she looked at the window, it seemed to Effie that the sobbing had stopped. But then she heard the woman cry out, a thin high-pitched cry, and then start to weep and beg as if somebody were hurting her and wouldn't let her go.

She went quickly and quietly up to the top of the second

75

flight of stairs. As she passed it by, the stained-glass window threw the pattern of the nun's closed eyes across her cheek, and then the black banners momentarily flew across her forehead.

At the top, she found herself at the crossroads of three corridors: one directly in front of her that was shadowy and thick with dust-bunnies, leading across to the north side of the house; a second that led to the western wing, which looked as if it had once been the staff quarters, because there were so many small bedroom doors; and a long corridor which led back to the east, to the front of the house.

This corridor was partly in shadow and partly sunny, because the roof had collapsed in several places, and clogged it with fallen rafters and ceiling plaster and heaps of tiles. She could see the crippled oaks that guarded Valhalla's gate, and beyond them, to the highlands, where heavy charcoal-coloured clouds still hung, and lightning flickered spitefully at the treetops.

Because so much of it was open to the sky, the corridor was still dripping from the storm, and wet tarpaper flapped in the breeze like the last feeble convulsions of a wounded crow. There was a strong smell, too: a smell that Effie didn't like at all. It wasn't just damp and decay, it was death, too, and when she started to climb over the first heap of broken tiles, she found out what it was. Her foot crunched through splintered clay, and rotten laths, and into a rancid underworld of feathers and straw and tattered fabric. The stench of this material was appalling, but it was only when Effie was able to extricate her foot that she realised what it was. A huge, thick layer of squirrels' nesting, as springy and fibrous as a mattress. It was thick with the bodies of squirrels' young: some skeletal, some partly mummified, some that were liquefied horrors of

76

hair and claws and glutinous yellowish-grey slime.

Effie felt her stomach contract, and she gagged. She dragged out her foot – then skipped, half-hopped along the corridor. Her heart was palpitating as if she had a huge moth trapped inside one of her ventricles, desperate to get out.

She stood still to steady herself, her hand pressed against her forehead. God, she had once heard a handyman warning her father not to allow squirrels to nest in his rafters, but until now she had never known why.

She took six or seven deep breaths to steady herself. The corridor was silent now. The sobbing seemed to have stopped. Effie crunched over another heap of broken tiles, keeping one hand against the wall to steady herself. Then she stopped, and listened, and very far away she could hear the sound of traffic on Route 9.

For a moment, she wondered whether she had been imagining the sobbing. Maybe it had been nothing more than the sound of the wind, blowing through the roof. After all, who could be here, and why would they be weeping so desperately?

She was plucking up her courage to step back over the crushed tiles and the squirrels' nest when she heard the sobbing yet again: and, this time, it sounded very much closer.

She called out, 'Hallo? Hallo? Can you hear me? Where are you? Which room are you in? I'm coming to help you!'

There was no reply, but the sobbing went on. Effie walked a few steps further along the corridor and opened the first door that she came to. It was swollen with damp, and she had to push it with her shoulder. It juddered on its hinges, and then stuck fast. Inside was an empty, unfurnished bedroom, with a pale blue carpet that still showed the rusted imprints of bed castors and the rectangular

77

impressions of a nightstand and a large chest-of-drawers. The carpet was blotched with a large brownish stain close to where the bed must have stood: a stain in the shape of a goat's head, with asymmetric horns.

There was a small rusted fireplace. Its grate was filled with damp ashes and some unpleasant-looking rags, some of them singed.

Out of the dusty, grease-smeared windows, Effie could see the sloping roof of the house, and a cluster of tall earthenware chimney pots, and the treeline in the distance.

The room gave her a feeling which she didn't like at all. It wasn't the coldness, or the damp, although the room was very draughty and the rain had soaked down behind the wallpaper and left it peeling and colourless and foxed with brown spots. It was a feeling of terrible *closeness*, a feeling of unsolicited and unwanted intimacy, as if somebody very unpleasant were following her around, staying so near to her that she could almost feel their breath on her cheek.

She stepped back towards the door, her movements stiff, trying to suppress her alarm. She had never believed that houses could be haunted, but the atmosphere in this empty bedroom was deeply unsettling. It was even worse than being followed, it was like being *touched*, like having to submit to prurient caresses from somebody she couldn't bear.

She opened and closed her mouth, trying to speak, but she had lost the breath for it.

Then she jolted in fright, because suddenly she heard the sobbing again, and it sounded more agonised than ever. She was sure that she could make out a miserable plea of, 'Don't – please don't – please don't.' But it could have been the wind, distorting the weeping into words, or it could have been her own imagination.

The worst thing was, though, that it seemed to be coming from *here*, from right inside this bedroom with nobody in it.

She heard a noise on the staircase. 'Craig!' she managed to call out. 'Craig, can you hear me? I'm up here, on the top floor!'

There was no reply. She hesitated, her fist clenched, her heart palpitating more furiously than ever. She had never felt so ridiculous in her life; but then she had never felt so frightened, either – at least of something, or somebody, not even there. There was no such thing as ghosts. She simply didn't believe in them. People died and when they were dead they were gone for ever. The sobbing was more muted now, and when she listened to it more intently she realised that it could be the wind, it *must* be the wind. It had freshened up in the wake of the storm, and it was probably sobbing down the clogged-up fireplace.

All the same, she still felt deeply unnerved. The bedroom with the pale blue carpet and the smeary windows disturbed her more than any room that she had ever been in before. It felt like a sickroom, a room which its occupant would never leave alive; a room in which there was nothing to do but watch the long days go by, the shadows on the chimney stacks; rain, fog, winter sunshine. It was a room of unbearable pain and utter desperation.

Effie started to go back to find Craig, to bring him up here. Craig could show her for sure that she was imagining things. But after only two or three steps, she stopped. *Don't. Don't call him up here, whatever you do.*

She frowned. Why did she think that? What was wrong with calling him up here?

Just don't.

She turned back and stared at the half-open door. All

she could see was the fireplace and the mark on the carpet where the chest-of-drawers had once stood.

Am I thinking for myself or is somebody else thinking for me?

Don't call him up here.

Why? Because he won't believe me? Because he'll make fun of me?

Because you'll regret it.

Effie cautiously made her way back along the corridor. She felt like turning around, just to make sure that she wasn't being followed, but she kept telling herself, it's empty, the bedroom's empty, there's nobody in it, just the wind.

She climbed over the tiles and the broken rafters, and she was almost back at the staircase when a man in a dark suit appeared from the corridor that led off to her right, crossed the landing, and started to hurry downstairs.

Effie called, 'Pardon me!' and ran to the head of the stairs.

The man paused at the turn in the stairs and looked up at her. The stained-glass window gave his face a sallow look, as if he were Italian or Greek. His glossy hair was brushed straight back from his forehead. His eyes were very dark and deepset, and oddly *blurry*. In fact, Effie found it quite difficult to focus on his face at all, as if she were shortsighted.

'Pardon me, sir, do you think you could help me?' she said. 'You see, I thought I heard a sound like a woman crying in one of the bedrooms here, and–'

The man stared at her for one moment longer, and then continued down the stairs at the same brisk pace. She heard him cross the second-storey landing and carry on down to the first floor below.

Effie was stupefied. Hadn't he heard her? He must have

80

heard her. Why hadn't he said anything, or even acknowledged her?

Slowly, she descended the stairs. As she did so, she heard Craig and Norman noisily climbing up from the first floor, talking about heating-pumps.

'Effie!' said Craig. 'We were wondering where you'd wandered off to!'

'You have to be pretty careful in a property like this,' Norman cautioned her, tossing the hair from out of his eyes. 'Some of the flooring joists are rotten, especially where the rain's been coming in. You could drop right through from the attic to the cellar. There's been some termite infestation, too. One or two of these beams look like solid oak, like, but you could punch a hole in them with your finger.'

Effie said, 'Who was that man?'

'Who was what man, sweetheart?'

'That man who just came down the stairs.'

Craig looked baffled. 'We haven't seen anybody coming down the stairs, have we, Norman?'

'You must have done! He must have passed you on the way! A man in a dark suit.'

Craig shook his head. 'We haven't seen anybody. Really.'

'Maybe it was just a trick of the light,' Norman suggested, trying to be helpful. 'These stained-glass windows, you know, they throw all kinds of weird shadows and all.'

'He wasn't a trick of the light. He was as solid as you are.'

'Maybe he went off down one of these corridors.'

'He didn't. I'm sure he didn't. I heard him go right down to the first floor. I heard his footsteps!'

'Then he must have walked right through us.'

'What did I tell you?' grinned Norman. 'The place is haunted.'

Craig put his arm around Effie's waist and gave her a

81

squeeze. 'Come on . . . it was probably some bum who's been squatting here. You remember the old Regency Hotel on Lexington Avenue? They found winos and derelicts in practically every room when they demolished that. It had more people in it when it was closed than when it was open.'

'Craig . . .' Effie protested, 'this wasn't a derelict. He had a smart suit, and his hair was brushed, and – well, he just didn't look like a derelict. Besides, derelict or not, where did he go?'

Norman said, 'Don't worry, if there is anybody squatting here, our less-than-friendly local police chief can soon clear them out.'

'You shouldn't have come up here anyhow,' Craig told her.

She was right on the tip of telling him about the sobbing that she had heard, when she felt a deep wave of resistance run through her. It wasn't as strong as a proper electric shock; but it gave her a cold crawling sensation all the way across her shoulders, and an odd feeling of nausea, as if she had stepped off a carousel.

Don't let him come up here. You'll regret it.

'Did you see any of the bedrooms?' asked Craig.

She said, 'Most of the roof has come down. They're not really worth looking at.'

'I can use my imagination.'

'They're full of tiles and rubbish like that. You really shouldn't bother.'

'But Effie – if we're going to buy this place –'

'What do you mean, if we're going to buy this place? There's no question of us buying this place! It would ruin us!'

'I could sell my share of the partnership.'

Effie stared at him. 'I don't believe what I'm hearing.

82

You've worked yourself half to death for that partnership. Now you're going to sell it, for a rotten overblown dump like this?'

'I think Mr Van Buren prefers, like, "imposing character dwelling, with considerable scope for improvement",' Norman put in.

'It's a rotten overblown dump and that's all there is to it. And if you even *think* about buying it, I'll – I'll –'

Craig was smiling. She couldn't believe how warmly he was smiling. He took her in his arms, right then and there on the staircase, and he kissed her forehead and he kissed her hair, and he said to her, very softly, so that Norman couldn't hear him, 'What if it made me happy? What if it made me really, really happy?'

Effie looked up at him. There was something in his eyes which she couldn't understand at all. It was *triumph*, almost. A look of inspiration; a lighted-up look. She hadn't seen such obvious strength in him since his accident, and she had never seen such warmth.

'Just a quick look at the bedrooms,' he said, and this time she didn't resist him.

He stood for a long time in front of the stained-glass window.

'I like it,' he nodded. 'I really like it.'

'Do you know what it means – *Gut ist der Schlaf, der Tod ist besser*?' asked Norman.

'Something about sleep being good?'

'That's right. Sleep is good, but death is better. Goethe, or Heine. One of those.'

'Is this some kind of allegory, this window?' asked Effie.

'Who knows? Don't sleep standing up. Don't face the wrong way when you're having your portrait painted. Could be anything.'

They climbed up the last flight to the bedrooms. Effie was beginning to feel even more nauseated, and the palms of her hands prickled with nervousness. Supposing the sobbing started up again? Logically, she wanted Craig to hear it. Maybe it would help to put him off the idea of buying Valhalla, or dampen his enthusiasm, at the very least. On the other hand, she desperately *didn't* want him to hear it. She couldn't think of any logical explanation for feeling so anxious. In spite of what she had heard, and in spite of what she had seen, she really couldn't bring herself to believe in ghosts. But she did believe in *atmospheres*: and she did believe in ill fortune. If she spilled salt, she always threw a pinch over her left shoulder; she never walked under ladders; and she never looked at the new moon through glass.

Her mother always said that the house in Briarcliff Manor where she lived with her sister Rhoda was 'a happy place', as if there could be 'unhappy places' too.

'Roof's pretty bad here,' Norman commented, as they crunched along the corridor. 'But, you know, it's fixable, like I said, for a price.'

Craig climbed awkwardly over the tiles and the rafters and the squirrels' nest. He looked out over the distant hills and then he looked back again and now he appeared disconsolate.

'It's worse than I thought it was going to be.'

Norman said, 'One point seven-five should cover it, though. Like, give or take fifty, depending what you find.'

'The question is – is it worth it?' asked Effie. Craig was standing right next to the half-open door of the bedroom, the bedroom where the sobbing had been coming from, and she felt an inexplicable twinge of panic. *Don't let him in, you'll regret it. Don't let him in.*

Norman gave her a quick, disapproving glance. Behind

84

his hair and his glasses, it was difficult to tell what point he was trying to make. Maybe he was frowning like that because he wanted the job of restoring Valhalla to its former magnificence, with all the profit he could make from timbering and tiling and pest-control. On the other hand, maybe he wasn't so mercenary after all. Maybe he could sense that there was a bad atmosphere here; unhappy memories and bad luck; and rooms from which his mother, the psychic sensitive, stayed well away.

Craig looked further down the corridor; and he was just about to climb back over the slates when he said, 'What about this bedroom here? Is this pretty typical?'

'This is one of the guest bedrooms, yes,' said Norman. He sounded nervous, as if he would rather be anywhere else but here. 'Take a look inside, if you want to. This is one of the bedrooms that–'

'Yes?'

'Well, this is one of the bedrooms.'

Craig pushed the door wider, and stepped inside. He paced to the window, and looked out. Then he paced around the carpet. He ended up right in the centre of the stain that looked like a goat's head.

'Well?' asked Effie.

He was standing with his back to her. All the same, she could see that he was thinking; that he was *listening*, almost – either to what the house was telling him, or his inner heart. Or maybe both.

He lowered his head. His fists were clenched and he was quivering.

'Craig?' she said. 'Is everything all right?'

He turned around. His eyes were wide and his face was bright. 'This is it,' he told her, in a voice that was high-pitched with exhilaration. 'This is absolutely it.'

'You want to buy it,' said Effie, thinking, *Oh God, I knew that he would.*

He nodded, again and again. 'We have to buy it. It's all here, everything. I can't describe it. It's like all of my life fits into place.'

He stepped out of the room and took hold of her arms. 'This house is like a map, do you understand what I mean?'

'A map? No, I'm sorry.'

'Norman, do you understand what I mean? It's like the house was built as a model of my life. The entrance-hall, the ballroom, the library . . . Valhalla is me.'

'Well, Mr Bellman,' said Norman. 'I don't know what to say.'

'Say you'll restore it, that's all.'

Norman looked at Effie, and again she had the strongest feeling that he was trying to tell her something, but she couldn't understand what it was.

Then he said, without taking his eyes off her, 'Sure, I'll restore it, if that's what you want. I'd love to. But it could need more than restoration, couldn't it, don't you think?'

Craig ignored him, and started to walk further down the corridor. 'Let's go see the master bedroom, shall we? That's what I really want to see.'

Effie stayed behind. She looked into the bedroom with the stained blue carpet and the rag-cluttered fireplace and she knew that there was something badly wrong here. The sobbing – well, she could have imagined the sobbing. The man on the stairs, he could have been a derelict. But it was the thick and terrible atmosphere that frightened her the most. Throughout Valhalla, the very air that she inhaled seemed to be denser, and pungent with antiseptic, as if somebody had committed the most hideous of all imaginable acts, and had been scrubbing and scrubbing in a futile attempt to expunge it.

Valhalla was filled from attic to cellars with the unbearable tension of unforgiven sin.

Effie was about to follow Craig and Norman when she glimpsed a quick dark shadow crossing the landing behind her. Without a word, she scrambled back over the heaps of broken tiles, until she reached the head of the stairs. The same man was standing halfway down, staring up at her. His face was unfocused, his eyes were black as smudges of ink.

'Who are you?' she said. She was so frightened that her lips could scarcely form the words.

He leaned his head forward, as if he were trying to focus on her. He looked bewildered but hostile at the same time.

'Who are you?' she repeated.

The man hesitated for a moment longer. Then he shook his head, and continued to hurry downstairs.

Saturday, June 19, 9:36 p.m.

'Mother? It's Effie.'

'Effie, how are you, darling? How's your vacation? More to the point, how's Craig?'

'Well, Craig's much better.'

'Why do I have the feeling that you're not ecstatic that Craig's much better?'

'He's better because he wants to buy a house.'

'A *house*? Where?'

'Here,' said Effie. 'You remember the Red Oaks Inn . . . there was a house beyond it called Valhalla.'

'Valhalla? Yes, I remember. But didn't they tear it down? That's what I heard.'

'Actually it's still standing. It's in terrible shape. Part of the roof has caved in. There's dry rot and wet rot and every other kind of rot. It needs reroofing, replumbing, rewiring, you name it.'

'And Craig wants to *buy* it?'

'He's so excited about it, you wouldn't believe! We went to look it over this morning, and he hasn't stopped talking about it!'

'You don't really want to live way up here in the valley, do you, darling? What about Craig's law business?'

'He wants to give it up.'

'Give it up! And do what?'

'I don't know. I can't understand him at all. He says we'll manage.'

'Your father always used to say that. No disrespect meant, but look at me now, living with your Aunt Rhoda. I'm not quite a charity case, but the next best to it. You tell Craig to think again.'

'I'm trying, mother, but he's so determined. Not only that, he's so enthusiastic, he's so *excited*. It's got him right out of his depression, in just one day.'

'Effie . . . you have to think of the future. You're going to want children soon.'

'Well, that's if our love life ever gets back to normal.'

'He still won't –?'

'No. But he *has* been much more affectionate.'

'Oh, darling. I wish there were something I could do to help.'

'There's nothing, mother. It's just this house. I can't understand why he wants it so much. I mean, it's huge, thirteen bedrooms – *thirteen* bedrooms! Not to mention four huge reception rooms and a library and a ballroom. What are we going to do with a ballroom?'

'My God,' said Effie's mother.

'I know,' said Effie. 'But he loves it, and he wants it, and it's changed him so much. What on earth am I supposed to do?'

'Well . . . if you want my advice, you'll humour him. Just for the time being. He's still in recovery, remember. As soon as he finds out what this house is really going to cost him, I think you'll find that his enthusiasm starts to wane.'

'I hope you're right,' said Effie. 'But there's something else, too.'

'Effie . . . what? You don't sound happy at all.'

'It's hard to explain. It sounds so stupid.'

'For goodness' sake tell me. Your father was always saying "this sounds so stupid", and that was when he wanted to tell me the most important things ever. Like he'd lost his job; or fallen in love with his secretary.'

'You never told me he'd fallen in love with his secretary.'

'Of course not. You were only seven; and nothing came of it.'

'Mother –'

'Tell me what you were going to tell me, *please*.'

Effie took a deep breath. 'We were in the house – Valhalla – and Craig was downstairs in the cellar, looking at the boilers – and – I thought I heard a woman crying. I mean really crying, as if she were hurt. I went upstairs to look for her, but I couldn't find her. I got frightened, so I went back downstairs, and half-way down the stairs I saw a man. He was smart, he was dressed all in black, or maybe dark blue. His hair was combed back. I asked him why this woman was crying, but he didn't seem to hear me. He disappeared downstairs, and even though Craig was coming upstairs, Craig didn't see him; or at least he said he didn't. The man just vanished, like a ghost.'

'Effie . . . you're ridiculous. There are no such things as ghosts.'

'Then who *was* he, mother, and how did he manage to run downstairs without Craig bumping into him? And what was more, I saw him again, only a few minutes later, in exactly the same place.'

'You need a rest. You need Craig. If you want my opinion. When you're sexually frustrated . . . well, that causes all kinds of problems. You remember Mrs Teeman? After her husband died, she kept imagining there were men in her bed. She said she even saw the sheets all humped up; and heard breathing.'

'I saw this man with my own eyes. He was there. He was real.'

'Did he speak to you?'

'No.'

'You spoke to him, but he didn't speak to you?'

'That's right.'

'What did he look like? Tell me.'

'I don't know. Pale. Shocked. He looked like he'd seen a ghost.'

Sunday, June 20, 1:34 a.m.

She dreamed that she was being buried, and that heavy clods of earth were dropping onto her coffin. She felt a rising sense of panic, because she knew that she was still alive. But they kept dropping earth on top of her, and the weight felt heavier and heavier, and in the end she knew that she was going to be pressed to death, like the Salem witches.

She started to gasp, and struggle, and then she woke up and opened her eyes. Her nightgown was pulled up around her waist, and Craig was on top of her, naked. His

90

hot breath blasted against her cheek, and she could feel his hairy thighs forcing their way between hers. She reached up and put her arms around him, and felt his back muscles, which were tensed-up and hard as pebbles. He had kicked away the duvet because the night was so warm, but all the same he was slippery with sweat.

'Effie . . .' he breathed, so close to her ear that it sounded like thunder. He grasped her breast, and tugged at her nipple. He kissed her forehead, he kissed her eyes, he kissed her lips. He took her chin between his teeth and he bit her neck, teenage love-bites that really hurt, but which suddenly excited her, so much that she wanted him to bite her and bite her and make an indelible mark.

He took her nipple between his teeth and bit that, too, and she dug her fingers into his hair and pulled at his roots.

She was frightened and excited at the same time. Even when they had first slept together, he had never made love to her as violently as this. His whole body was totally tense: his stomach muscles bunched hard and his thighs corded.

He bit her nipples again and again, nipping them and stretching them until she gasped for him to stop.

With his right hand, he pinned her upraised arm against the pillow. With his left hand, he reached down between her legs and opened her vulva. She was very wet: she could feel it. He pressed the head of his penis between her parted vaginal lips, and it felt huge and taut and silky-skinned, the size and texture of a large plum. There was a moment when everything stood still. Time, the world, and all the stars that anybody could ever count. Then he slowly plunged himself inside her, as deep as he could, and she closed her eyes and threw back her head on the pillow and all she could feel was his erection, right inside her. Every ridge of it, every swollen vein.

She reached down and opened herself even wider, so that he touched the neck of her womb with every thrust, and made her jolt. With her right hand, she grasped his scrotum, with its single heavy testicle.

To her, this one testicle seemed enormously potent, because he was just as capable of impregnating her with one ball as he was with two. But when she took hold of it, he jerked reactively, and drew himself out, and stayed out, and she thought she might have made a terrible mistake.

'Craig,' she whispered. 'Craig, I want you.'

Still he hesitated, his juicy cockhead touching her lips, touching, and tantalising.

'Craig,' she repeated. 'Please, Craig, it doesn't make any difference. Don't you understand that? It doesn't make any difference. I want you.'

She thought for one teetering moment that her marriage was over for ever. If he couldn't do it now, then he could never do it. But then, without a word, he thrust, and thrust again, and soon his penis was flying in and out of her, and both of them were clutching and gasping and greasy with sweat.

She felt such pleasure that she laughed out loud. But Craig made love to her with urgency and deadly seriousness, almost as if he wanted to punish her. He thrust and he thrust, grunting harshly with every thrust.

'Oh Craig I want you,' she panted. 'Oh Craig I need you so much.' The antique wooden bed went *squonk – squonk – squonk* with every thrust and she was sure that everybody else in the inn could hear them, but she didn't care. In fact, she wanted them to hear, because now she had passion back in her life, passion and fire and greedy, ferocious sex.

She reached her orgasm long before he did. It wasn't violent, although his thrusting was violent. It poured all over her, warm and dark and slow, like oil pouring over a polished floor, one of those subtle ever-expanding climaxes that seemed to reach all the way to the furthest and darkest horizon. Craig kept on gasping and pushing and she was sure that he hadn't realised that she had climaxed.

'Bitch,' he gasped, and the sweat dropped from his forehead onto her face. 'Dirty, disobedient bitch.'

She grasped the tensely-knotted muscles of his thrusting buttocks, trying to restrain him. He was ramming himself into her so hard that he was beginning to hurt her. His single testicle swung against her again and again.

'Bitch!' he repeated. 'Filthy conniving bitch!'

'Craig!' she said. She was frightened now, yet she was still excited. In a strange way, her fear aroused her even more. He was thrusting himself in and out of her so forcefully that she was pushed up the bed with every thrust, until her head was pressed against the carved wooden panel. She thought the whole bed was going to be shaken apart, disassembling right underneath her.

There was a second of tightly-compressed silence. Craig stayed stock still, holding his breath, every sinew tight as a twisted-up cord. Then Effie felt his penis pulsing inside her – pulse, pulse and pulse again – and he let out a cry that was closer to pain and frustration than deep release.

He dropped onto the pillow next to her, his chest heaving, his body glistening in the darkness. He was too breathless to speak. She curled herself in close to him, sliding her hand down his chest and over his stomach and grasping his juicy, softening penis. She kissed his shoulder again and again, like a supplicant kissing a holy effigy. 'You were wonderful,' she whispered. She kept squeezing him and squeezing him. 'You were absolutely wonderful.'

At last he managed to catch his breath. 'It's all so clear,' he panted. 'I never saw everything so clearly before.'

She kissed his shoulder, again and again. 'I love you,'

she told him.

'You know what I said about Valhalla being like a map. I understand it now. There's a room for every part of my personality. A room for my pride, a room for my ambition, a room for my anger. A room for my sense of humour. Everything.'

'Craig . . .' said Effie. 'Valhalla's only a house, and a derelict house, too.'

'No, no. It's much more than that. It's me. That house is me. It's just as if somebody analysed my whole personality and then turned their analysis into a building.'

'I still don't understand.'

'I was drawn there. You saw how much I was drawn there. And when I went inside, I felt as if I knew it. I felt as if I'd lived there all of my life. I can't describe it. But I felt as if I belonged there. I felt as if I was home.'

She let go of his penis, and wrapped herself up in the sheet, pressing her arms protectively down by her sides. 'Then you're not going to change your mind about making an offer for it?'

He propped himself up on one elbow, and kissed her on the forehead. 'Hey . . . I'm not going to be stupid about this. I'm going to have the house surveyed first. We don't want to pay over the odds for it.'

'But I don't like Valhalla. In fact I hate it. And the very last thing I want to do is spend the rest of my life and the rest of my money trying to restore it. Valhalla may be you but it sure as hell isn't *me*.'

'Come on, Norman's going to help us. He knows a guy upstate who can supply us with roof-timbering at cost.'

'I thought you said you weren't going to rush into this.'

'I know. But the minute I walked into the door, I felt so *alive*. I thought about all of those corporate law suits and all of those Japanese board meetings and I thought, no . . .

this is where I want to be. Here, in Valhalla.'

Effie didn't know what to say. For herself, she didn't mind the idea of giving up her job at Verulian art galleries and moving upstate. She certainly wouldn't miss any of those effortful business dinners ... 'I hear that Kyoto is very beautiful at this time of year. Do you grow bonsai trees?'

She would be nearer to her mother; and maybe she and Craig could even start talking about a family.

She didn't like Valhalla at all. But she had managed to convince herself that her mother was right, and that there were no such things as ghosts, or ghostly sobbing; and that the atmosphere which had disturbed her so much was nothing more than damp, and neglect, and her own feeling of disaffection.

More importantly, Valhalla had filled Craig with so much energy and so much enthusiasm; and tonight he had made love to her – not weakly or reluctantly, but with all the carnal fierceness of a man possessed.

'All right,' she said, at length. 'We'll have a survey.'

Craig didn't answer, but kissed her on the lips. Then he dragged off the sheet which she had wound around herself, and straddled her, and when she reached down she discovered that his erection was just as hard as it had been before.

He pushed himself right into her. He was so hard when he arched himself back, he almost lifted her hips off the bed. 'Bitch,' he whispered, and this time she felt degraded more than stimulated.

'Craig,' she said, touching his lips with her fingertips. 'Craig, darling, don't call me that.'

'Bitch,' he repeated, and she could actually feel him smiling.

Thursday, June 24, 11:11 a.m.

Morton Walker parked his beige Buick station wagon next to the statue of the headless woman holding up the sackful of dead puppies. He eased himself out of the driver's seat, and stood beside the open door for a while, methodically mopping his forehead and the back of his neck with his handkerchief.

It was a hot, oppressive morning, and the landscape around Valhalla looked as if it were covered with a thin coat of amber varnish. Valhalla itself seemed unnaturally large and out-of-scale, as if the heat had magnified it.

Morton had visited Valhalla just once before, for a Dutch hotel group called Kuypers, but he had recommended that they look elsewhere if they wanted to open a health resort and golf complex. In his opinion, it would have cost over $51 million to bring Valhalla up to luxury hotel standards, with very little guarantee that Kuypers would ever recoup their investment. The terrain wasn't suitable for the Gary Player championship golf course that Kuypers had envisaged, the weather up here was notoriously unpredictable, and the simple fact was that Valhalla was far too isolated, especially for weekenders. Jack Belias had built it on this awkward and inhospitable hilltop for the specific purpose of shutting himself away from the world around him.

Still, a private buyer was a different matter. A private buyer wouldn't have to concern himself with all the health and safety regulations that a resort complex would have been obliged to meet, such as fire doors and emergency

96

exits and entrances widened for wheelchairs; and a private buyer could take as long to restore the house as he felt like. Years, if necessary – and it probably would take years. Why the hell anybody should want to buy a decaying mausoleum like Valhalla, Morton couldn't understand. As far as he was concerned, it was fit for nothing but demolition. He was a Federalist man himself: he hated Gothic.

He reached across to the passenger seat and picked up his cassette-recorder, his flashlight and his notepad. His assistant Brewster Ridge was supposed to have been here to meet him; but it didn't surprise him that he wasn't. Brewster had probably been too carried away by the Snoop Doggy Dogg CD whomping on his car stereo to have noticed the Red Oaks–Valhalla turnoff. Morton and Brewster didn't get along particularly well, although Brewster had genuine respect for Morton's experience in detecting the kind of flaws in construction that slipshod builders would do their best to disguise, like hiding subsidence cracks with folded-up slices of bread and flexible filler, and nailing clean sheets of expanded polystyrene over walls that were running with damp. Morton for his part was grudgingly impressed by Brewster's college qualifications in the work of residential architects. He definitely knew his Irving Gill from his Barry Byrne.

Morton slammed his station wagon door and trudged towards the house. He was big and balding, with a face that had the pale lumpy texture of a root vegetable. He blinked a lot and wore rimless spectacles with clip-on sunglasses, which he lifted up whenever he went indoors, so that he looked like a croupier. His shirt was already stained with sweat and his beige cotton trousers were impossibly creased. They were held up with withered, once-jazzy suspenders, in scarlet and green. They were the last Christmas present that his wife Audrey had given him, before she took seventy-six paracetamol tablets and died of liver failure. He had never known why. She hadn't even given him the consolation of a suicide note.

He took out the keys to Valhalla and sneezed twice. Hay fever. Or maybe he was allergic to huge, half-collapsed buildings. As he turned the key in the door, he thought he heard Brewster's car coming, but when he turned around there was nobody there: only the mossy, overgrown terraces, wavering in the mid-morning heat. Only the shrunken oaks; and the overgrown tennis courts; and crickets chirruping from the cracks in the bricks.

He stepped inside and closed the door behind him. He looked around him, right and left, with a feeling of profound misgiving. Even in the hallway, he could sense the extent of Valhalla's collapse. It was like ground beef, when you knew that it had turned. It didn't smell too bad, but nothing would ever persuade you to eat it.

'Well . . . the general structure of the entrance hall seems reasonably sound,' he told his cassette-recorder. 'All of the glazing will require repair or replacement, but the ultimate cost will depend on how closely you wish to reproduce the original windows. The glass is bubbled and slightly yellow-tinted. It was made by hand, and fitted by hand, too. I couldn't give an exact estimate on replacing the windows, not without finding out if anybody today is still capable of doing glazing work like this. Obviously we're talking six figures; and this is just the entrance hall.'

He walked across to the left-hand staircase and bent over to examine its treads and its risers. 'Left-hand staircase is original . . . it's been repaired, here and there, and probably quite recently by the Fishkill Corporation. It's unusual in that it's been constructed without the use of nails, and with only a minimal number of pegs. In fact it's virtually self-supporting. Very interesting. Good thing it's

98

in reasonable condition: a modern carpenter just couldn't do it. None that I know of, anyhow.'

So Morton wandered from silent room to silent room, his voice occasionally echoing from the marble floors and the dulled oak panelling and the high, flaking ceilings.

Slanted bars of sunshine lined the corridors, and Morton walked through them in swirls of golden dust. He had the strangest feeling that he was intruding – a feeling which he only had when the house that he was surveying was occupied. He stopped, and listened, but all he could hear was the miniaturised sound of distant traffic, and the cawing of a raven in the oak trees.

He was satisfied that the ballroom would need little more than cleaning up; but once he had walked into the library he began to see the scale of Valhalla's decay.

'Dry rot, wet rot, extensive termite infestation. . . . some of the floor joists are on the point of collapse, and all of the panelling has to be replaced.'

He left the library and paused for a moment at the foot of the secondary staircase, looking up to the landing. From here, through the balustrade, he could just see the hunched figure of plaster and moss that had unsettled Effie so much. He stared at it for longer than he meant to; almost as if he were expecting it to move. It stared directly back at him with its soulless, dripping eye.

He shook his head, and said, 'Jesus H. Christ, Morton, what's the matter with you?' Then he carried on through to the kitchens.

The kitchens were chilly and shadowy and cavernous, and fitted with all the latest equipment for 1929. Along one wall there was a cream-coloured enamel range which was large enough to cook for a decent-sized hotel, and along the opposite wall were glass-fronted cupboards capable of storing hundreds of plates. The floor was quarry-tiled, and seemed solid enough, but many of the tiles were cracked, and there was no doubt that the entire kitchen area would have to be gutted and brought up-to-date.

The kitchen window looked out onto a surrealistically-overgrown vegetable garden, where knobbly sprouts had grown to the size of small trees, and asparagus waved tall and feathery in the summer breeze. There were huge rhubarb leaves and giant thistle-like artichokes and everything was tangled with creepers and tendrils as if the vegetables were deliberately strangling each other in their struggle to survive.

At the far end of the kitchen, on the left, Morton saw a cream-painted door. He checked it on the faded blueprint plan that Walter Van Buren had given him. This led down to the cellars. He turned the key in the door and peered inside. A flight of wooden steps led directly into total darkness. He took out his flashlight and pointed it one way, and then the other, but the darkness was so intense that the pencil-thin beam scarcely seemed to illuminate anything at all, except the wooden handrail, and a dangling light-socket, and a bundle of greasy-looking rags that were hanging from a hook on the ceiling.

He was just about to go down into the cellar when he was sure that he heard footsteps. It sounded like somebody running quickly downstairs: a man, wearing light-soled shoes. He hesitated, one hand clasping the doorframe, one hand pointing his flashlight into the darkness. He listened, but Valhalla had fallen silent again.

'Brewster?' he called. 'Brewster, is that you?'

Silence. Dust fell ceaselessly down, in every room, as if Valhalla were quietly demolishing itself, a process that might take centuries. *Look on my works, O ye mighty, and despair.*

'Brewster, if that's you I'm in the kitchen . . . just going down to check out the cellar.'

Still no reply. He must have been hearing things. He ventured cautiously down the cellar steps, making sure that he held on tight to the handrail. He had heard of too many surveyors falling ass-over-apex down the steps of unfamiliar basements, and he had trodden through too many termite-infested treads to trust the appearance of even the most solid-looking staircase.

He reached the cellar floor. Like the kitchen, the cellar was quarry-tiled throughout, and stretched all the way from one end of Valhalla to the other. The floor was slippery with wet, and Morton could hear dripping from several directions, although the vaulted arches that held up the ceiling made it difficult for him to see where the water was coming from. He shone his flashlight towards the front of the house, and he could see that it was drier there, although apparent dryness didn't mean that the foundations weren't rotten. He took out his penknife and scraped at one of the walls, just to make sure that the limestone wasn't dissolving. There was no future in restoring Valhalla if it was in danger of complete collapse.

Whistling between his teeth, he walked between the first two vaulted arches until he found the oil-fired boilers. They were dulled and rusted, but he could still see traces of red enamel, and the words Capitol Red Top embossed on them. Good boilers, in 1929. If they were restored, they could probably do the job of heating Valhalla, even today.

He explored a little further. He heard rats scurrying and scratching in the furthest recesses of the cellars. They weren't used to intrusion. They must have proliferated in this lightless subterranean kingdom for so long now that they thought it was theirs. Well, Morton knew a man at Albany Exterminators who could show them different, but that was another expensive item to add to the estimate.

Some of the pipework to the radiators had been half dismantled: maybe it had sprung a leak and somebody had tried to cap it off. A single vertical pipe, five feet high, stood in the centre of one of the alcoves and led to nothing at all. Morton shone his flashlight at the ceiling immediately above it and saw that it was black with wet rot and speckled with mould. God almighty, this house was going to take a fortune to put to rights, even if the Bellmans cut corners.

He was still looking around when he heard footsteps crossing the ceiling above his head. They sounded the same as the footsteps he had heard before: lightly-shod, in slippers or pumps, but a man's footsteps, no doubt about it. They seemed to cross the room above diagonally, and he guessed that it was probably the library, where he had noticed before that the floor was seriously rotted.

'Brewster!' he shouted out. 'I'm down here, Brewster, checking out the boilers!'

He waited for Brewster to come down the steps, but Brewster didn't appear. Nobody appeared. He thought about exploring further, but when he shone his flashlight directly ahead, he saw a tawny-grey rush of rats at the very end of the cellars, and he decided against it. He could make a full inspection if and when the exterminators had done what they had to do. He took a last perfunctory look around the alcoves on either side, and then started to walk back.

'The integrity of some of the load-bearing limestone piers looks suspect . . . we'll have to carry out some analysis. They could be reinforced with concrete pilings, but without detailed structural analysis it's going to be hard to tell how extensive that reinforcement would have to be. Again, we're talking six figures. Low six figures, but six figures all the same.'

He climbed the steps back to the kitchen, closed the door and locked it. Outside, in the kitchen garden, the giant rhubarb leaves still glittered with the morning dew, and cobwebs glittered, too. He crossed the kitchen and opened the door to the hallway.

As he did so, he glimpsed a shadow on the wall at the top of the staircase, and he heard the *chiff—chiff—chiff* of shoe soles on the stairs.

'Brewster?' he called. 'Brewster, is that you?'

He started to climb the stairs after him, pulling himself up with the banister rail. 'If you're not Brewster, then you'd better come on down here, mister, because this is private property and you're trespassing!'

He reached the top of the stairs, and looked up to the next flight. Halfway up, the nun stood in the lily field with her eyes closed. Morton paused for a moment to catch his breath, then continued to climb up. But when he reached the third-storey landing, there was nobody in sight. Not down the left-hand corridor, not down the corridor right in front of him, not down the corridor that led off to his right, the corridor with the half-collapsed ceiling.

Morton listened keenly. The wind was very light, but the day was hot, so that Valhalla creaked and complained with the normal expansion of metal and wood. He couldn't get over the feeling that he wasn't supposed to be here at all, that he was intruding. When he spoke into his cassette-recorder, he spoke in a very quiet voice indeed, in case he was overheard (though by whom? or by what?).

'Third storey, south corridor, headed east. Serious roof collapses for the first hundred feet; and water penetration, too, going right through the building, floor after floor.'

He climbed with difficulty over the heaps of broken tiles and splintered rafters and squirrels' nest. 'Again . . . seri-

103

ous rodent infestation in the loft spaces . . . in fact the whole of this house is a goddamned menagerie. We're talking five-and-a-half thousand for extermination minimum.'

He pushed against the door of the first bedroom that he came to. It was stiff, but two or three good shoves managed to get it open. It was carpeted in pale, faded blue, and there was a dark rust-coloured stain in the centre of the floor. Morton paced across the room to the window. He looked at the view of Valhalla's chimneys, and the trees beyond. Then he turned back to look at the floor stain. It looked to Morton like a devil, or a goat, or the shadow that his grandmother used to cast on the wall when she was telling him stories all those years ago, when he was a boy. She used to fold her headscarf into peaks, so that she looked as if she had horns. Grimm's fairy tales, she used to tell him, crowded to the rafters with child-eating ogres and hunchbacked hobgoblins.

Something lurched. Just an old joist. Somewhere, a door closed. Even the softest of draughts never closed a door that quietly.

Morton looked around, his breath wheezing asthmatically. Empty houses had never alarmed him before, but this one did. He was sure that he could hear people breathing, just behind his back. He was sure that he was not alone, and that somebody was standing very close to him, watching every move that he made.

This room in particular felt stifling and claustrophobic, and he was beginning to realise that it *stank*, too, of kerosene and cheap women's perfume and cockroach powder and something worse, he didn't know what it was. He hadn't noticed it before, but maybe the wind had dropped. Yet how could it smell so strongly if nobody had occupied Valhalla for so many years? Somebody must have been squatting here recently, or the stench would have

104

faded long ago. Maybe somebody was squatting here now.

He turned back to the bedroom door. He had opened it flat against the wall, so that anybody could have hidden behind it. He hesitated, then slammed it shut, shouting out loud as he did so. But of course there was nobody there. Only a brownish cruciform mark on the wallpaper where an effigy of Christ had hung.

'Goddamn it,' said Morton. He reopened the door and looked out into the corridor. All he could see was heaps of tiles, and a flapping black wing of abandoned tarpaper. Through the collapsed roof, the sun was burning off the morning mist, and everything was blurry and gilded. The landscape was so dazzling that, for a moment, he was temporarily blinded.

'Okay, I know there's somebody here!' he shouted, very emphatically. 'There's somebody here! I know you're here! There's no use hiding!'

He waited, sweating; and then he thought he heard somebody say something abusive, right in his ear, quietly. It sounded like '. . . cretin', with an unintelligible swear-word. He turned, furious, but there was nobody there. It was only when he turned back the other way that he saw a man in a dark suit walking away from him, at the very far end of the corridor, a man who appeared to be brushing his sleeves and buttoning his gloves.

'You!' he called out. 'You, sir! What the hell do you think you're doing here? This is private property!'

The man stopped at the very end of the corridor, and peered back at Morton with obvious bewilderment. Then, still buttoning his right-hand glove, he turned the corner and disappeared.

Morton hadn't taken any exercise in years. But he was determined to catch this trespasser. He shouted, 'Hoi!' and 'Hoi!' and 'You just wait up there, pal!' and he started to

105

run along the corridor in lumbering pursuit.

For a few seconds, he was running like an athlete, his head held high, his lungs expanded, his fists punching. He ran through all the golden triangles of sunlight that fell across the corridor.

'You're trespassing!' he bellowed. And then his left foot went right through the floorboards, in a thick, woody explosion of dry-rot dust and stick-thin lathes and rendering.

He thought it was impossible, to drop clear through a floor, and that was why he didn't shout out. But he burst out of the ceiling into the music-room below, lacerating his arms and tearing his face and ripping his shirt into plastery rags, and then he dropped another twenty feet. He felt that he was flying, with nothing to grab on to, but then he hit the floor, with a thudding impact that broke his collar bone and knocked the wind out of him. Immediately, the music-room floor collapsed, too, in a powdery shower of timber-dust and plaster, and Morton dropped again, another twenty feet. He saw a window fall past him. He saw shelves and walls. Then he plunged concussed like a diver through the wet rot that had turned the library floor into sodden flakes of yielding wood, and into the cellar.

The vertical, capped-off heating pipe was waiting for him. He dropped directly onto it, and it tore through his upper left thigh muscle and into his pelvis, penetrating his large intestines, piercing his liver, and puncturing his right lung, missing his heart by less than a quarter of an inch.

He roared in agony, and a fine spray of blood blasted out of his mouth. He was transfixed, helplessly kicking and waving his arms. His feet were three or four inches clear of the cellar floor, so that all he could do was to pedal, and the more he pedalled the deeper the heating pipe sank

106

into his body.

'Oh God help –' he tried to shout out.

'Then, '*Oh God help me!*'

The pain of being impaled by a cold metal pipe was more than he could bear. He could feel it running right up inside him, right through his bowels and into his stomach. He could feel it in his lung, which blathered and wheezed like a wet balloon. But when he struggled, the pipe inched up further, until it was touching the inside of his ribcage, the pain was even greater, and he forced himself to stay still.

He felt agonised, half-concussed, but he couldn't believe that he was still alive. He didn't know whether he wanted to live or die. God knows what damage the pipe had done to his insides. Blood was trickling down it, and spreading across the tiled floor. If he couldn't get himself free, he would probably bleed to death in a matter of minutes, and then what he wanted would be academic.

Where the hell was Brewster? If Brewster were here, he could help to lift him off. But then the pain was so cold and intense that he didn't know whether he wanted to be lifted off. He couldn't bear the thought of the pipe sliding out of him.

Oh Christ, he thought, what did I do to deserve this? Maybe this is my punishment for what happened to Audrey. Maybe she took her life because of me, because I ignored her, because I took her so much for granted, and this is what I have to suffer in return.

He closed his eyes but all he could see was scarlet. He was trying to remain still, but his weight was gradually pushing him further and further down. He could feel the top of the pipe pressing against his upper ribs now, and that was a very special kind of pain that made him suck in his breath and start to whimper.

It seemed as if hours went by. He faded in and out of consciousness, but the pain never went away. He dreamed that he was sitting at home, talking to Audrey, asking her what she was doing. Audrey had nearly completed a jigsaw which was spread out on a tea tray on her lap. Her face was very pale, the colour of uncooked pastry. The light which came through the sitting-room window was scarlet, and lit up her hair. The jigsaw was very strange. It showed people walking around a garden with their eyes closed. They looked as if they were asleep. Audrey said, 'Life is just like a book. Don't you understand?'

'Which book?' he asked her (or thought he asked her).

'Any book. Life is like any book. That's why I took all those pills.'

'I still don't know what you mean.'

'You will, Morton. You will.'

He opened his eyes and he hoped he was dead, but he wasn't. He was still alive, still transfixed, still in appalling agony. He took a deep, gurgling breath, and then he screamed, and screamed again, and he could hear his scream echoing around the house. Where the hell was Brewster? Why was Brewster always late?

He tried to calm himself down. He had only succeeded in hurting himself even more; and making himself feel more helpless and frustrated.

He tried to think about anything else except pain. Like, what were the odds against his falling through three floors, and finishing up pierced by this pipe? I mean, what were the *odds*? A million-to-one. A *billion*-to-one. Yet here he was, so accurately impaled that he could only believe that God had done it on purpose.

He wondered if he tilted himself sideways, the pipe would bend sideways, too. If it fell over horizontally, then he could crawl off it. But when he leaned to the left, only half an inch, the pipe touched his heart and he went into such an agonising spasm that he bit right through his lower lip and clenched his fists until his fingernails punctured the palms of his hands.

It took him over a minute to recover. When he did so, he was still trembling and sweating, and now he was convinced that he was going to die. He whispered 'Our Father. . .', or tried to, but somehow he got it all mixed up with the 23rd Psalm. 'Give us this day our daily bread . . . for thy rod and staff, they comfort me . . .'

He heard a scurrying noise. Then another.

'Forgive us our trespasses . . . as we forgive them who trespass against us . . . and spreads a table in the sight of mine enemy . . .'

It was hard for him to see. He was deeply shocked and half delirious, and apart from the pale reflected sunlight that penetrated the alcove from the hole in the ceiling through which he had fallen, the cellar was utterly dark.

But he heard another scratching, scurrying noise, and then a rustling sound, as if somebody were dragging sacks across the floor; and he didn't need to glimpse much more than a wriggling rug of brownish-grey fur to know what was happening. The rats in the cellar had gathered around him. He could smell them. He could see their beady jet black eyes glittering in the shadows. They were lapping up the blood that had trickled down the pipe, and one or two of them were already venturing up to the pipe itself and following the blood to its source.

Morton bellowed in panic and disgust. The rats flinched, as if he had hit them with a stick, and some of them scurried away. But they soon came back again, sniffing and chittering and crawling all over each other in their eagerness to lick up his blood.

One of them managed to scramble up the heating pipe

and bite into Morton's left foot. He was hurting so much already that he scarcely felt it; but even when he swung his foot backward and forward, the rat clung on, pirouetting heavily with every swing.

Another rat jumped up and bit at his ankle, and then another dug its teeth into his heel. He kept on swinging his feet, and every swing was torture, but the rats refused to let go, and soon he was doing nothing more than heaving great festoons of rats from one side of the pipe to the other, like a man wading through thick grey seaweed.

It hurt so much that he couldn't understand why he didn't die. Maybe he *was* dead, and this was Purgatory, where he would have to swing impaled on a pole, eaten alive by rats, until somebody prayed for his soul, and he was saved. He tried to think of somebody who might pray for his soul, but the only person he could imagine doing it was Audrey, and she was dead already.

'Life is like a book,' she told him.

'Yes, Audrey, but *which* book?'

'Any book. Don't you understand?'

Any book? What did she mean? Maybe she was trying to say that when you were born, it was like opening a book, and you lived your life from page to page, and when you died the book was snapped shut. But he still didn't get it.

A huge rat jumped up and dug its teeth into his chest. Another scrambled onto his shoulder. An even heavier rat clawed its way up his back, its claws digging into his skin, and perched itself on top of his head, like a terrible parody of a trapper's hat.

Morton twisted his head around and around but the rat dug its claws into his scalp and he couldn't dislodge it. Then another rat bit into his upper lip, and another bit into his cheek, and then he was wearing a living, swaying mask of greasy sewage-smeared fur.

He tried to shout out, but a narrow-nosed rat bit into his tongue, and then thrust its head into his mouth. He tasted sick and sewage and blood.

A *book*, she said, and at last he understood.

Thursday, June 24, 1:04 p.m.

Brewster Ridge slewed his TransAm to a halt outside Valhalla, grabbed his briefcase, and ran up the steps to the front door. Morton was going to kill him. He knew that Morton was going to kill him. He had promised himself that he would never give Morton the chance to criticise him for anything any more: not for lateness, nor over-optimistic surveys, nor wrongly identifying termites or parasites or wood-boring beetles. Morton had already complained about him to Leonard Braun, their senior executive surveyor, and Leonard had given him the same sort of look that he had given Ray Philips, Brewster's fellow junior, a week before Ray Philips had found himself out of residential surveying and into utensil control (in other words, clearing tables at St Andrew's Café).

Brewster found the front doors of Valhalla unlocked, and that was one relief. At least he wouldn't have to ring the doorbell and wait for Morton to answer. Apart from that, he didn't particularly like the look of Valhalla's bell-pull: a snarling bronze beast that almost dared you to put your hand on it.

He stepped into the entrance hall. He had worked for Braun Bannerman for less than a year, and he had never visited Valhalla before, although he had heard about it. It was featured prominently in Carole Rifkind's book on American residential architecture, and there was a view of

111

its south elevation on Mr Braun's office wall, next to his framed diploma and a photograph of his late Doberman with its tongue hanging out.

Mr Braun had said that he ought to assist Morton in his survey 'because they don't build houses like Valhalla any more, just like they don't breed men like Jack Belias any more'.

Brewster didn't know what that meant, not exactly, anyhow. Brewster was 27 years old and black and extremely lanky. He looked like Eddie Murphy if Eddie Murphy had suddenly grown serious and ten inches taller. He could have been a brilliant basketball player except that he had always hated basketball. He was Poughkeepsie born and bred, and remembered Poughkeepsie in the days when it was safe to walk around at night. His father worked for the railroad, and was devoted to the railroad, and in many ways his father's appreciation of physics and mechanics and fine old-fashioned engineering had influenced his choice of career.

He walked into the entrance hall and looked around. Valhalla had looked enormous, as he sped towards it down the drive, but this was something else. His father's whole house could have fitted into this hall, with plenty of room to spare. He crossed the marble floor and his footsteps echoed. He turned around. This was really something else. Huge, grand, and falling down. It put him in mind of *Citizen Kane*.

'Morton, are you there?' he called; and his voice echoed, and changed, until it sounded as if he had called out something else altogether.

Brewster wasn't surprised that there was no reply. He knew how quickly Morton worked, marching from room to room with his cassette-recorder, prodding the walls with his ballpen, chipping off woodwork with his penknife, jumping up and down on suspect floors. He was probably halfway finished already, up in some attic, testing the copper on the roof.

He was also probably showing his annoyance that Brewster was so late. This time, however, Brewster had an excuse that was almost legitimate. His wife Gala had called him from the clinic to say that she was pregnant, after two years of trying.

'Morton, it's Newt! I'm sorry I'm late!'

Still there was no reply. Brewster walked along the corridor and opened the doors to the ballroom. He stepped inside, and stopped for a moment, looking around him in amazement. He had seen some enormous private residences, up along the Hudson River Valley, but Valhalla was something else. This house hadn't been built simply for comfort. This house had been built as an overwhelming declaration of its owner's wealth and self-importance. From the coat of arms in the hallway to the stratospheric ceiling in the ballroom, every feature of it was designed to make the visitor feel intimidated, and to enhance the stature of the man who had constructed it.

Brewster didn't like it at all. He never liked houses that were deliberately unwelcoming; and Valhalla was positively bullying.

'Morton?' He called. 'Morton, listen, I'm real sorry to be so late! Just give me a clue where you are!'

He went through to the library. On the left-hand side of the room, just below the window, the floor had completely collapsed, and there was a gaping hole in the parquet that was big enough to drop a sofa through. He looked up, and saw that the ceiling had collapsed, too, almost as if that imaginary sofa had fallen right through to the cellar from the floor above. He could just imagine the expression on Morton's face when he saw *that*. Morton thought that the

113

art of building sound domestic residences had been lost before the turn of the century.

He found himself at the foot of the secondary staircase. 'Morton!' he shouted, and his voice echoed, 'Morton, it's Brewster . . . I didn't mean to be late but Gala's having a baby!'

He stopped and listened, but even this news didn't provoke a reply. There was only one thing he could do, and that was to start his own survey and hope that he ran across Morton while he was doing it. He hunkered down on the library floor and clicked open his briefcase. He took out a large legal-sized notebook, a flashlight and a tape measure.

He was still rummaging through his papers looking for a copy of Valhalla's blueprints when he heard a thick gurgling noise, apparently coming from the large, ragged hole in the library floor. It sounded like a cistern emptying, or a sink that was suddenly unblocked. Brewster stood up and cautiously approached the edge of the hole, testing the strength of the floorboards with every step. He had seen houses in which entire floors had collapsed as soon as they were trodden on, and he didn't fancy the idea of a short cut down to the cellar.

He heard another gurgle. This time, it didn't sound like a cistern or a sink or anything else mechanical. It sounded like a large animal, struggling for breath. Brewster hesitated. The floor creaked ominously underneath him. He took one step nearer the edge of the hole, then another, and this time the wood crumbled wetly, and he almost fell through.

As he tilted forward, however, he glimpsed something down in the cellar. Something grey, and hunched, like an old motheaten fur coat hanging over a dressmaker's dummy. Except that it couldn't have been a coat, because

114

it shifted and wriggled as if it were alive. Rats. Jesus. A whole heap of nothing but rats, nearly six feet high.

Except that it couldn't have been nothing but rats, because two or three of them lost their footing, and dropped down into the darkness, revealing for one single hideous instant the face of an agonised man, scarlet with blood, both eye-sockets empty, and his mouth crammed with a huge brown rat, its hind claws scrabbling at his chin as it tried to force itself further and further down his throat.

Thursday, June 24, 5:54 p.m.

They returned from a day trip to the Vanderbilt Mansion to find Walter Van Buren waiting for them in the garden of Pig Hill Inn, accompanied by a tall and serious young black man.

Mr Van Buren was sitting in the shade of a large oak, sipping iced tea.

'They told me you'd be back around six,' he said, standing up and shaking their hands. 'This is Mr Brewster Ridge, he's one of the surveyors from Braun Bannerman.'

'Well?' asked Craig, impatiently.

'I regret we have some bad news,' said Mr Van Buren.

'How bad? Don't tell me the foundations are rotten.'

'It's not the house, Mr Bellman. Well, not directly. There was an incident earlier today, when Mr Ridge and his colleague Mr Walker were conducting their survey. Mr Walker fell through the floor, I'm afraid, and was killed. Of course the police were informed but it was clearly a tragic accident.'

'I'm very sorry to hear that,' said Craig. He took hold of

115

Effie's hand. 'Please accept our condolences.'

'Thank you,' Walter Van Buren nodded. 'Morton Walker was a very close friend of mine, and a first-class surveyor, too. We're going to miss him.' He paused, and took a minuscule sip of tea. Then he said, 'The reason I'm here is to ask you if you still wish to continue with your plans to purchase.'

Craig frowned. 'Why shouldn't I?'

'I just thought that under the circumstances, you ought to be given the opportunity to back out. Some people are not especially happy to buy a house where a tragedy like this has taken place.'

'I doubt if there's an old house anywhere that hasn't seen its share of tragedy,' Craig replied. 'I'm very sorry to hear about your friend, but that doesn't change my mind about wanting to buy.' He turned to Brewster. 'He fell through the floor? Which floor?'

Brewster swallowed. 'As a matter of fact, he fell through three. From the third-storey corridor to the music room, from the music room to the library, from the library through to the cellar.'

'Jesus,' said Craig. 'How much damage did he do?'

'He dropped onto a disused heating pipe. He was impaled. He must have suffered a great deal of pain.'

'Yes,' said Craig, doing nothing to disguise his impatience. 'But how much damage did he do?'

'Excuse me? You mean, to the house?'

Craig turned to Walter Van Buren and said, 'Are you sure you commissioned the right surveyors?'

'Braun Bannerman are excellent surveyors,' snapped Walter Van Buren, 'and Mr Ridge here is one of their best.'

'It's all right, Walt,' said Brewster. 'I can understand Mr Bellman's concern.' He glanced at Effie, and she could tell that he was making a considerable effort to keep his tem-

116

per. In recent years, she had seen that look on the faces of Craig's business associates many times. Maybe she had just grown accustomed to his boorishness, taught herself to ignore it. Maybe he had always been that way, and that was an integral part of what made him so attractive. Maybe she had a thing for brutes. Craig had been making love to her every night this week, and often in the morning, too, with a ferocity that she found frightening, breathtaking, but flattering, too. He swore at her; he told her that she was a whore. But he made love to her as if he wanted to drive her through the mattress and into the floor.

Brewster opened his briefcase and took out a blueprint. 'Mr Walker fell through the floor here, and here, and here. There's an area of dry rot extending along fifty or sixty feet of the flooring of the upstairs corridor, and at this point the rotten timber was unable to carry his weight. Unfortunately the dry rot had spread through the vertical timbers to a thirty-foot area of the floor below, and he dropped right through that, too. The library floor as you've probably seen for yourself suffers severe wet rot.'

'So how much is it going to cost to repair all of this falling-through?' asked Craig.

'If you were thinking of buying this property, Mr Bellman, you would have had to replace all of these areas of flooring in any case, and maybe much more besides.'

'You can cut out the rot, though, can't you?'

'It depends how extensively it's spread, sir. You have a form of dry rot known as *Merulius lacrymans*, or weeping fungus. It's been caused by water penetrating from the roof. It starts off as white threadlike growth on the surface of the wood, but then it penetrates the tissues and destroys them. Later it forms this thick reddish growth which is a reproductive structure, a fruit body, which produces spores, like a reddish-brown powder . . . and this powder

117

can be carried all around the house by insects or birds or rats or even air currents. First of all you have to deal urgently with all of your leaks and water penetration. Then you have to think about removing all diseased timber, and treating the whole of the rest of the property with fungicide.'

Craig was staring down at his shoes, his head bowed. For a moment, Effie thought that he was going to give in, that he was going to say forget it, a house riddled with dry rot and wet rot, a house with broken windows and only half a roof and a pervasive atmosphere of doom and decay. Not to mention the fact that one of their surveyors had been killed in it, only just today.

But he looked up after a while and said, 'Okay . . . give me the most pessimistic scenario you can, and then put a price on it.'

Walter Van Buren finished his iced tea. 'You have the passion, don't you, Mr Bellman?' he said, and his voice was almost regretful. 'That house has hypnotised you, just the way I was afraid it would.'

'Passion?' Craig replied. 'It's not a question of passion, Mr Van Buren. It's a question of finding out who you really are. You said it yourself: Valhalla is a very big house for a very big man. You think that's arrogant? Let me tell you this: most men go through life without understanding even a fiftieth part of what they can really do. They think small, they do small things, they live in small houses. They're *small*, Mr Van Buren; even though they could be big. That's why I want Valhalla so much. Valhalla isn't just a house. It isn't just a place to live. It's *me*.'

Effie watched him as he spoke. He surprised her, yes. He embarrassed her, too. But he talked with such determination that she found herself laying her hand on top of his sleeve, in a gesture of affection and affirmation. She felt his

118

warmth; she smelled his skin. She loved him. He was like a different man.

Brewster said, 'You want me to finish the survey?'

Craig nodded. 'So long as you don't start swan-diving through the floors.'

'I'm not amused by that, Mr Bellman. Mr Walker was a close colleague and a friend of mine.'

'Then why don't you make sure that you do his memory proud?'

Brewster stared at him, his chin uptilted, his eyes wide. 'I will, Mr Bellman. I will.'

Saturday, June 26, 6:24 p.m.

'We ought to spend the night there,' said Craig.

Effie put down her book. She was sitting up in bed, with four plump pillows banked up behind her, drinking sparkling wine. Outside the afternoon was still sunny, and the sky was as blue as dinner plates. The quilt was drawn up demurely under Effie's arms, but beneath it she was naked. As soon as they had returned to the inn from their lunch at La Parmigiana in Rhinebeck, Craig had insisted on making love to her. She was still looking flushed, and she was wet between the thighs.

'We ought to spend the night *where?*' she asked him.

'Valhalla. Just to see what it's like.'

She stared at him. 'Valhalla? It's a ruin! I'm not going to spend the night in a ruin!'

'We could take an inflatable bed, and borrow a quilt.'

'I don't want to take an inflatable bed and borrow a quilt. I want to stay here. I want a good bath and breakfast in bed.'

Craig sat down on the end of the bed. He was dressed in nothing but his thick towelling bathrobe, loosely tied up. 'Come on, Effie, it'll be great. It's about time we had an adventure.'

'I *love* adventures. But sleeping in some draughty, dilapidated old building is not my idea of an adventure. That's my idea of Purgatory.'

He looked at her steadily for so long that she averted her eyes in sheer embarrassment. She didn't know what to make of him. She didn't know why he kept swearing at her when they were making love. She couldn't even begin to understand what it was about Valhalla that attracted him so strongly. But she was afraid of breaking the spell. She didn't know where their relationship was going. She had lost all sense of certainty. But she didn't want to go back to the miserable, argumentative days after Craig's 'accident', and she certainly didn't mind if she never had to say again, '*Ohaya gozaimas, ogenki des ka?*'

She would have preferred the droll young man who had once said to her, 'Oh, mirror! how many times, for hours on end, saddened by dreams and searching for my memories, have I seen myself in you as a distant ghost!'

'No,' she said. Then, 'absolutely one grillion per cent no.'

He turned away and lifted his hand as if he were fending off the evil eye. 'It's all right, don't worry about it. It was only a suggestion. I just thought that if we could spend the night there – well –'

He poured himself a Scotch. She could see his face in the oval, gilt-framed mirror over the drinks table. His expression was unreadable. Usually she could tell what kind of a mood he was in, even when his back was turned, but even his back told her nothing.

'If we could spend the night there *what?*' she asked him,

after almost an entire minute had gone by.

'It doesn't matter. Forget it.'

'If we could spend the night there *what*??' she demanded, even more stridently.

'I said forget it, okay? You don't want to do it, we won't do it.'

'Craig, I didn't say I didn't want to do it, I said it wasn't my idea of an adventure, that's all.'

'What you said was, no. You said one grillion per cent no, that's what you said. So forget it.'

'God, you're obstinate!'

'And you never stop bitching.'

'Is that the only word you know? Bitch? What happened to your vocabulary all of a sudden? Come to think of it, what happened to you? You're in love with some crummy old tumbledown house, you can't make love without calling me names. A man was killed and you showed about as much compassion as Adolf Hitler.'

Craig slammed his glass on top of the drinks table and turned around and his eyes were wolf-like with anger. 'I could have been killed in that pharmacy! As it was, I was nearly turned into a eunuch! Now I've found Valhalla and Valhalla means something to me. Don't ask me why. It doesn't matter why. I don't even fucking know why. But it's everything. It's me. It's what I am.'

'Oh, please. Spare me the consciousness-raising.'

He approached the bed. He was dark and he was threatening and he was quaking with rage and she was genuinely frightened that he was going to hit her. 'You talk to me about consciousness-raising? You talk to *me* about consciousness-raising? You spend your life in some dumb art gallery filled with incomprehensible squat painted by a gang of overpaid pretentious jackasses who don't know one end of a paintbrush from another? Yes? And you talk to *me* –'

121

Quite unexpectedly, she started to laugh. It was probably fear. But on the other hand, it could have been amusement, too, because he had articulated exactly what it was about Verulian galleries that she found so numbing. The art *was* all incomprehensible squat. Craig was absolutely right. Canvas after canvas of incomprehensible squat, painted by jackasses who couldn't paint for jackasses who couldn't see; and the more incomprehensible they were and the squattier they were, the more expensive they were. Their costliest artist, Paul Firman, was such a bad draughtsman that he couldn't have drawn breath.

She laughed because she was upset, and because she was frightened. But she also laughed because he had said something completely true. After years of building up his law partnership, after years of pleading to erratic, egocentric judges and juries who couldn't tell the difference between a balance sheet and a grocery list, after years of bargaining and compromising, Craig was actually speaking the truth and saying what he wanted, what he *really* wanted, regardless of the risks.

He said, 'What? What are you laughing at? What?' but all she could do was laugh even harder and shake her head.

He started to laugh, too, and dropped onto the bed next to her, and took her in his arms.

'Listen,' he said. 'I'm sorry. I shouldn't call you a bitch. I shouldn't *ever* call you a bitch.'

She wiped her eyes with the pillowslip. 'Maybe I deserve it. Maybe I am a bitch. You seem to be finding yourself and all I can do is complain.'

He kissed her. He kept his eyes open. He stared at her from very close up. 'I'm sorry. What I said earlier, about staying the night at Valhalla, just forget it.'

She kissed him back, more greedily. 'Maybe I am a bitch.

122

Maybe we should spend the night. Maybe we could spend the whole night making love. Think of it! In that draughty, mouldy, drippy old building!'

He stared at her and his face was so near that she couldn't focus on it properly. 'You'd really do that?'

'Sure . . . if that's what you want.'

'No, you're just trying to humour me, aren't you?'

'Did I ever humour you before, ever?'

Craig sat up. 'I don't know. Sure you did. You and that – Gaby.'

Effie said, 'Gaby? Who's Gaby?'

He pressed his forehead between fingers and thumb, as if he had a headache. 'I don't know why I said that. I don't know anybody called Gaby.'

'You definitely said Gaby.'

He climbed off the bed, went across to the drinks table, and picked up his drink. 'I don't know. I don't know why I said that. I don't know anybody called Gaby.'

While Craig bathed, Effie finished her drink and read some more of her book. She had found it in the Cold Spring Library yesterday morning: *Only The Rich – Jack Belias and the Greek Syndicate*. It was the history of the greatest gamblers of the 1920s – Nico Zographos and Gordon Selfridge of Selfridge's department store and Andre Citroën the car manufacturer, among many others, men who won millions of francs in a single night, and lost them, too. But mostly it was the story of Jack Belias. While other heavy gamblers played because they were addicted to it – 'like morphine', said Zographos – Jack Belias played because he wanted to ruin and humiliate those he played with.

He was phenomenally lucky at baccarat, and one afternoon at the Deauville casino he brought Zographos, who was one of the most skilful card players in Europe, right to the brink of bankruptcy. Only the turn of one card saved Zographos from ruin – the nine of diamonds. Afterwards, Jack Belias sent him a lapel pin with nine diamonds in it, a mocking souvenir to remind him how close he had been to poverty.

But again and again, Jack Belias stripped his fellow players of their fortunes, and what they couldn't pay in money he took in kind. At one point, Gordon Selfridge had to borrow £155,000 from his own company to pay his gambling debts to Jack Belias; and a few days before Andre Citroën died, already impoverished by the failure of his latest automobile, Jack Belias stripped him of £64,000 in eight successive coups of £8,000 each, and took less than ten minutes to do it.

There was a black-and-white photograph of Jack Belias in the centre of the book. It showed a tall, unsmiling man in a large black hat and a long black overcoat, standing alone on a sandswept boardwalk. He had a strong, squarish face and dark-circled eyes. He looked vaguely Turkish. He was leaning on a cane as if he were impatient to be off.

The caption read: *Jack Belias in Deauville in 1934. The only known photograph in existence.*

'What's that you're reading?' asked Craig, coming back into the bedroom, towelling himself.

Effie showed him the jacket. 'It's all about Jack Belias. I found it in the library while you were down at Mr Van Buren's office.'

Craig sat on the bed beside her. 'Walter Van Buren told me he was quite a gambler.'

'He was. He made his first million dollars out of textiles, but he just about trebled it by gambling. He used to bet on anything and everything, and he almost always won. That was how he made the money to build Valhalla. The only

124

trouble was, nobody liked him very much.'

Craig peered at the photograph. 'Hmm. He doesn't *look* very likeable, does he? It's strange, though. He seems familiar. I almost get the feeling that I've met him somewhere.'

'I don't think you could have done. He died in 1937, and it says here that this is the only known photograph of him.'

'That's pretty strange, don't you think?'

'What's strange?'

'You'd think that a man like Jack Belias would have had his photograph taken thousands of times. He ran one of the country's biggest textile companies, after all. Don't tell me he was never interviewed by *Fortune* or *Business Week*, along with a picture. Don't tell me he never made presentations to staff, and had his photograph taken there.'

'Maybe this caption is wrong. Maybe they haven't expressed it very well, and this is the only known photograph of him in Deauville.'

Craig stood up, letting the towel fall from his waist. He walked over to the bureau and took out his underwear, and made a deliberate show of dressing himself in full view.

'What else does it say?' he asked Effie. 'Does it mention Valhalla?'

She licked her thumb and turned to the index. 'Yes . . . here we are. Page 209. "In 1929 blah-blah-blah Jack Belias had won over £300,000 at Deauville, Cannes, Monte Carlo and the Cercle Hausmann in Paris . . . he used all of this money to build a huge Gothic mansion overlooking the Hudson River Valley. He named it Valhalla after the hall of dead heroes in Norse legend, because he claimed that the money which had built it had cost the suicides of eleven bankrupted men." '

Craig, tugging on his jeans, said, 'Not exactly Mr Nice Guy, was he?'

' "In 1931 Jack Belias was briefly married to the French actress Jeannette Duclos, but after three months she died in mysterious circumstances." '

'What mysterious circumstances?'

'It doesn't say. It just goes on to mention that Jack Belias was involved in a scandal in 1937 involving the wife of the British financier Douglas Broughton, and that about a year later he disappeared. His car was found abandoned by Bear Mountain Bridge and it was presumed that he had taken his own life by drowning in the Hudson.'

'That doesn't tell us very much, does it?'

'This is mainly about his gambling career. But I guess there must be other books about him.'

Craig buttoned up his blue check shirt and then pulled on a navy-blue sweater. His hair stuck up at the back like a little boy's.

'I thought we were eating at Le Pavillon tonight,' said Effie. 'You're not going dressed like that, are you?'

'I thought we'd agreed to stay the night at Valhalla. We can buy pizza on the way.'

'You're really serious, aren't you?'

'Of course I'm serious. We're going to live there. We're going to be spending most of our money on it. In fact we're probably going to be spending *all* of our money on it. I want to find out what it's like.'

Effie closed the book and threw back the quilt. Craig took hold of her and held her close, and kissed her forehead and her hair. He tried to touch her breast but she covered herself with her hands. 'What, are you, shy?' he teased her.

He sat in one of the velvet-upholstered chairs and watched her while she dressed. She didn't really like it, the

126

way he looked at her while she stepped into her white lace panties and fastened up her bra, but she didn't say anything because she felt that she would annoy him if she did. Besides, it was a compliment, wasn't it, if your husband still wanted to watch you after all this time together? She buttoned up her Calvin Klein jeans and pulled on her cream Paul Levy skinny-rib poloneck. She brushed her hair, and static made it fly up fine and shining in the marmalade-coloured sunlight.

She turned around and half-expected Craig to pay her a compliment, but he simply smiled and grunted as if he were thinking of a private joke. All the same, she went across the room and kissed him, and he kissed her back, very measured, very thoughtful, like a man tasting wine.

'Where are we going to find an inflatable mattress?' she asked him.

'I'll ask Norman. He looks like the kind of guy who'd know where to find an inflatable mattress. He looks like the kind of guy who'd know where to find an inflatable *anything*.'

'Do you have his number?'

'Of course. He lives with his mom, over the Hungry Moon.'

He leafed through the local phone directory. 'Norman went back to Valhalla yesterday with a couple of friends from the building trade. He's going to give me a price on the roof. Once we fix the roof, the rest is going to be easy. Cutting out the dry rot, fixing the floors, plastering the ceilings. Easy. So long as we don't get impatient, so long as we're systematic.'

'You're really going to sell out of Fisher & Bellman?'

'Can you really see me going back? "Y'r honour, my clients have been trading in *ngapi* for five generations. Medical records show that nobody in the United States has fallen ill or died as a consequence of consuming *ngapi* for over forty-seven years. Why now has the Food and Drug Administration suddenly taken steps to ban its distribution? After all, it's only semi-rotted shrimp paste." '

'But what are you going to *do*?' asked Effie.

He kissed her again. 'I'm going to start taking risks. I'm going to gamble. I'm going to put my life on the line, every single day. In fact, I'm going to *live*, like I never lived before. By the time I'm through, Valhalla is going to be too small for me.'

'You don't seriously mean gamble? Not roulette, or poker, or whatever?'

'Maybe . . . but there are much bigger games than that.'

'Such as?'

He looked at her and his eyes were dark. In fact they were just like Jack Belias' eyes, as he stood on the board-walk in Deauville, with a flag waving in the distance, and a little girl running out-of-focus just behind him. That little girl would be an old lady today, if she were still alive; but what of the beach at Deauville, and the flag, and what of Jack Belias? His Lincoln Zephyr coupe parked by Bear Mountain Bridge, its lights gradually dimming and its driver-door left open?

Effie said, 'Valhalla will cost us a fortune. We couldn't run it on . . . luck . . . or whatever it is you're thinking of doing.'

'Listen, I was lucky that night in K-Plus Drugs. They could have killed me. But they didn't. They sent me here, to recover. They sent me to Valhalla, didn't they? The hall of fallen heroes. And I've discovered myself; and that's all I care about.'

'What about me? Do you care about me?'

'Do koi care about water?'

She kissed his freshly-washed hair. 'Koi? Those Japanese

128

fish? I guess they do.'

Although later she thought: no, they probably don't. Any more than birds care about the air. Koi take water for granted the same way that birds take the sky for granted; and the same way that Craig took her for granted. He needed her. He couldn't live and breathe without her. But being needed wasn't the same as being loved.

Craig dialled the Hungry Moon. Effie was close enough to hear the rich, breathy voice that answered. 'Hungry Moon . . . Natural Nourishment.'

Craig glanced up at Effie and grinned. Then he said, 'You must be Norman's mother.'

'This is the Hungry Moon. Who is this?'

'I'm sorry. This is Craig Bellman. Norman may have mentioned me. My wife and I have been thinking of buying Valhalla.'

'I see. Yes. Norman did mention that somebody was interested in it.' The voice was just as breathy, but suspicious.

'Is Norman home? The reason is, I wanted to borrow an inflatable bed, or a camp bed, or a futon, or something like that.'

'You want to borrow a what?'

'An inflatable bed. Or maybe a camp bed. Or even sleeping-bags. My wife and I are planning on spending a night there . . . you know, just to get the feel of it. . . .. we were wondering if –'

'*You were planning on spending a night at Valhalla?*' The harshness in Pepper Moriarty's voice made Effie's scalp prickle like the effervescence from a freshly-opened bottle of tonic water.

'Sure,' said Craig, nonchalant male, winking at Effie.

'You were planning on spending a night at Valhalla, after everything that happened?'

'Ms Moriarty, I don't know what you mean by "everything that happened", and I don't think that I want to know. Norman told me that you had some views about Valhalla having a non-conventional ambience, but I don't think that it's anything to get excited about.'

'Non-conventional ambience? Are you a lawyer?'

'Yes, as it happens.'

'Let me tell you this, then, Mr Lawyer. I've been to Valhalla, and I know what's wrong with Valhalla, and "non-conventional ambience" isn't it. Valhalla has seriously bad psychic vibrations. Valhalla is not the place for you to spend the night; or for anybody to spend the night.'

Craig put on his flat, patient, attorney-speak voice. 'Mrs Moriarty, I know what you think about Valhalla. Norman told us. But personally I'm afraid that I'm not a great believer in what you call psychic vibrations. And I really would take it as a favour if you kept your views to yourself, in case we have trouble hiring builders, or staff, or anybody else who might be deterred by the idea of working in a haunted house. I presume that's what we're talking about, isn't it? A haunted house?'

Pepper Moriarty said tightly, 'I'll go find Norman. Don't hang up. Or do, if you can't afford it.'

'I can afford Valhalla, Mrs Moriarty.'

'Then you can afford to stay on the line, can't you? And it's Ms.'

Saturday, June 26, 10:28 p.m.

Norman was waiting for them when they arrived at Valhalla. He was slouched in the passenger seat of his Dodge Charger wearing a red check overshirt and a black

130

T-shirt with a picture of Kurt Cobain on it, and he was eating a hamburger stuffed with kumquats. 'Brown, orange, they're complementary colours.'

'You could have had cheese. That's orange,' said Effie, wrinkling up her nose.

'I don't know. It's all to do with karma too. You can't eat the flesh of a domestic animal along with the curdled milk of another domestic animal. You have to have something completely inanimate, and remote. Something that came from a long way away and can't answer back.'

'Well, that probably makes sense,' said Craig, slapping him on the back. 'I never heard of a kumquat that answered back. But come to that, I never heard of a hamburger that answered back.'

'I guess you never went to McDonalds.'

He carefully folded up his paper napkin and tucked it into his glovebox. Then he climbed out of the car and stretched and shook himself like a dog. 'The day I've had. Me and two other guys, we're restoring a Dutch barn over at Nelsonville, and we, like, replaced the pentice and we hung new doors, all in one afternoon. Seventeen-hundred seventy-five that barn was built, the year before Independence. They knew how to build a barn in those days. That barn's going to be standing in another two hundred years, I'll bet you.'

'How much?' asked Craig.

'How much what?'

'How much do you bet me?'

Norman frowned at him from out of his hair. 'What does it matter? Even if you win, you won't be around to collect it.'

'You want to bet on that, too?'

Norman opened the Charger's boot and took out a large bundled-up futon, tied with sisal string. 'Hope this is okay.

It's all I could find. It used to belong to some old hippie but mom washed it since then.'

'Looks fine to me,' said Effie. She could smell herbs on it, and flowers. Obviously Pepper Moriarty had kept it in the storeroom at the Hungry Moon. Norman carried it up the steps for them, past the statue of the headless woman, to the front door.

The sky was dark blue and glossy as lapis lazuli, and it glittered from one horizon to the other with millions of stars. That was one of the things that Effie missed, living in the city. They gave the night such depth, and such a feeling of timelessness. She loved the idea that she was seeing the stars as they used to be, thousands of years ago. She loved the idea that somewhere far away in space, if they had telescopes that were powerful enough, people could look towards Earth and see her as she was when she was a little girl, skipping up the steps of the Red Oaks Inn, hand-in-hand with her father. They would still be able to see her hundreds of years in the future, when she was long dead and lying next to her parents in Cold Spring cemetery.

If someone in the furthest reaches of the galaxy can still see you, dancing and laughing, how can you ever die?

'What are you looking at?' Craig asked her.

'The stars. Look, the Dragon, *Draco* – and there's Ursa Minor, the Little Bear.'

He grasped her elbow and led her to the house. 'You always were a romantic, weren't you?'

But all that Effie could think about was that Valhalla's black bulk completely blotted out a whole section of the sky. She could feel its coldness and its vinegary dampness; and as Craig turned the key in the lock, she could feel its unwelcoming atmosphere, too. The wolfish bell-pull glared at her through the shadows, and she remembered what Norman had told them about it: that it would bite off your hand if you rang it when you weren't welcome. She could almost believe it.

Norman tossed back his hair and followed them into the gloomy hallway. 'My mom wasn't too pleased with what you said about psychic vibrations.'

'Oh, no?' said Craig, with a conspicuous lack of interest.

'She said that people who can't sense psychic vibrations are suffering from mental gangrene. Like, a piece of their consciousness has gone dead, and has started to rot, and gives off this very offensive odour.'

Craig turned and stared at him. Norman shuffled from one foot to the other, an odd little skip of embarrassment.

'Your mom said that?'

Norman looked uneasy. 'She has a way of saying what she thinks, like right out front.'

'Maybe she should keep her thoughts to herself.'

'Come on, man, she's my mom. She's entitled to have her opinions. Besides, she may be right.'

'And she's lent us a futon that was slept in by Wavy Gravy?'

Norman shrugged, and gave a slopy smile. 'I guess that's an opinion in itself.'

'Craig, for goodness' sake,' Effie interrupted. 'Where are we going to sleep? I didn't realise this place was going to look so creepy at night.'

Craig walked to the centre of the hallway and looked around. The starlight fell through the broken windows like chilled milk. He stood in the middle of the marble floor, tall and dark and unsmiling. Effie could sense that he was trying to pick up the feeling that Valhalla had given him before: the feeling that he belonged here, that the house wasn't just meant to be his, it *was* him.

'This place is going to be amazing,' said Craig, his voice echoing from everywhere. 'Can you imagine it?

133

Chandeliers, polished marble floors, music.'

'Isolation,' put in Effie.

'What are you talking about, isolation? We'll have house parties every weekend!'

'Oh, yes? And how are we going to pay for them?'

'We'll have a few card games. Win a little here, win a little there. That should cover it.'

Effie couldn't believe what she was hearing. ' "We'll have a few card games"? Are you kidding me, or what? You're going to invite your friends up here for house parties, and then you're going to fleece them at poker?'

'People love to gamble. Especially people with lots of money. We'll be famous; we'll be rich; and we won't have to answer to anyone.'

'What the hell are you talking about? I can't even understand what you're talking about! Take me back to Pig Hill, I really don't like it here.'

He stepped towards her. The soles of his shoes squeaked on the fine grit that covered the marble floor. He laid his hands on her shoulders and stared directly into her eyes.

'Effie . . . for my sake, try to like it. This is where I belong. This is the house that I always wanted. This is the house that I always *needed*.'

'I just don't like it. Besides, it's unsafe. Look what happened to that poor surveyor.'

'Oh, Effie,' he said, and she could feel the warm breath on his face, and for some reason his closeness disturbed her. 'You're just feeling tired, that's all. We'll stay well clear of the library, and all of that side that has dry rot. We don't we go upstairs to the bedroom and make ourselves cosy.' He reached into his pocket and took out a pack of playing cards. 'See, look what I brought. We can even get some practice in.'

'I don't *believe* you sometimes,' said Effie. She didn't

134

know whether to feel angry or exasperated or whether to laugh and admit defeat. But he stroked her forehead, touched her hair, and kissed her, and that made her feel good enough to look up at him and smile and say, with exaggerated reluctance, 'O-*kayy*. Maybe it could be fun.'

'Listen,' said Norman, 'if it makes you guys feel any better, like, I'll stay, too. I've always wanted to spend the night in a haunted house.'

Craig looked up. 'Norman – no matter what your mother says, Valhalla isn't haunted. Damp, I'll give you. Derelict, yes. But not haunted.'

'Whatever you say, supremo. But I'd still like to stay. It'll give me some time to look around, make you up some estimates. That roof is going to take some serious fixing.'

'I don't know,' said Craig. 'This was going to be a private party. Just Mrs Bellman and me.'

'Hey . . . I won't get in your face. I'll have to do some measuring and some tapping and some running up and down stairs, but that's the only way you'll know that I'm here. Mr Discreet strikes again.'

Craig said to Effie, 'What do you think?'

'I don't think we have very much to fear from a kid in a Kurt Cobain T-shirt, do you?'

'I'm not sure. I'm not sure about anybody who worships the dead.'

Norman said, 'Come on . . . serious for a moment. Houses are different by night. During the day they show you all of their good side, do you know what I mean? By night they give up their secrets. All their creaks and groans and bad little memories. I always do a night inspection, when I'm planning to work on a house. You like catch the house unawares. It doesn't expect anybody to be looking at it, and you can be surprised at what you find . . . like a floor that didn't creak at all, during the day. Or a damp

135

patch that you couldn't see by daylight.'

Effie gave Craig a direct kiss on his mouth. His lips were unexpectedly cold, as if he had been pressing them against a winter window. 'Norman can stay,' she told him.

'All right, then. Norman can stay. But careful where you walk, Norman, okay? I don't want *you* kebabbed, the way that surveyor was.'

'Do you mind not saying kebabbed?' asked Norman. His eyes were very large and swimmy behind his spectacles. 'Morton was a friend of ours. You know, my mom and me.'

Craig cleared his throat, said 'Sorry', although he didn't sound it.

They climbed the left-hand staircase. The risers creaked, and they could hear the pegs straining, but the stairs on the whole were very firm. Norman's flashlight played swordfights between their legs, and cast humped and jumping shadows on the walls.

'It's a good thing it's summer,' Norman remarked, shining his flashlight down to the hallway below them. 'This place would be freezing, else.'

'I think it's cold enough now,' said Effie. She could feel a terrible deadness in the house; a sense of memories that had gradually sunk to the floor, and gathered in crevices; and words that had turned into powdery ash. They reached the landing that overlooked the hallway, and Craig opened the double doors, which swung back silently, to reveal a gloomy red-carpeted anteroom, with a single tilted-over chair in it. At one time, there must have been sofas to sit on and mirrors on the walls. The screw holes for the mirrors were still visible. Norman flicked his light around, from floor to ceiling, and then diagonally across the walls, and said, 'This part of the house is pretty good. You're looking at decorating costs here – paint, paper, carpeting, that's all. You could leave it till last.'

136

There were two doors on the opposite wall of the ante-room: a single door on the right which led to the corridor that ran the length of Valhalla's second storey, and a pair of solid oak double doors, stained and marked but still in near perfect condition. Effie approached them, and touched them with her fingertips. They were elaborately hand-carved with roses and briars and lilies; and the faces of scores of hooded women with their eyes closed, all with their eyes closed. Above the women's heads were curly carved clouds, like a Dürer etching, and ravens flying.

'This is so strange,' she whispered. But she found it alluring, in a way. It had the same allegorical quality as the stained-glass window on the other side of the house: a riddle, but an explanation too, if only you knew what it was trying to explain. 'They're not dead, these women, because they're standing up . . . But why are their eyes closed?'

'And look at this,' said Craig, coming up behind her. 'There's a man with his back turned, just the same as the window . . . and a tower, with flags. And look at this writing, on the flags.'

Cut into each of the banners, in exact serif script, were the words *Samvi, Sansavi, Semangelaf.*

Norman peered closely at the doors, lifting his spectacles so that he could see them in more detail. 'They're really wild, these doors. You couldn't reproduce them today. Where would you get the craftsmen? I mean look at those *faces*, man, you could almost believe that they're living and breathing. You could almost believe that they're going to open their eyes, and scream at you.'

'Don't,' Effie admonished him. 'I'm edgy enough as it is. If I thought for one moment that they were *really* going to open their eyes –'

Craig rapped one of the women's faces on the bridge of

137

the nose, hard, with his knuckle. 'Happy?' he asked Norman, half jocular and half aggressive. 'What did I say to you before? No more haunted house stuff.'

Effie was tempted to mention the sobbing that she had heard in the blue-carpeted bedroom. She even started to say, 'You may not *think* it's haunted, but –'

But she thought she heard somebody catch their breath – a woman – and her tongue curled up in mid-sentence and she stopped herself. She looked around, both frightened and excited. Yet neither Craig nor Norman appeared to have heard anything, and they both carried on as if nothing had happened. Craig took hold of her arm, and said, 'It's spooky, I'll give you that. But spooky isn't real. Spooky is all in the mind.'

'I'm pleased *you're* so confident,' said Norman.

Craig twisted both handles of the double doors, and opened them up. They stepped into the master bedroom, a huge room with floor-length windows overlooking the gardens (although they were inky black now, because it was night). Above their heads there was a domed ceiling with small clerestory windows pierced in it, and faded murals of flying angles with immense feathery wings and coral-snakes like venomous zigzag bangles, and diving cormorants and yellow macaws.

Norman flicked his flashlight from one side of the dome to the other, and Effie saw fruit trees and flowering vines, and a forest thick with pale cream lilies. A nude man stood with his back turned. A woman in a black nun's habit stood with her eyes closed.

'My mom thinks it's supposed to be the Garden of Eden,' Norman remarked.

Craig paced around, looking up at it. Time and grime had mottled the flesh colours and rotted the apples on the Tree of Knowledge. In fact, on closer inspection, it wasn't

138

just time and grime that gave it such an air of decay. There were thistles growing up between the lilies, the waterways were clogged with weed, and many of the trees were infected with parasitic fungus. If this was the Garden of Eden, it was the Garden of Eden after the Fall.

'It wouldn't take much to clean this up.' Craig asked Norman, 'Do you happen to know who painted it?'

'It was a local artist, Ruden McCane. He used to paint covers for *Collier's* and *Woman's Home Companion*. He was pretty famous. But Jack Belias could have afforded anybody. He could have afforded, like, Norman Rockwell. Or Maxfield Parrish. Or even Magritte, I guess.'

'I like it,' said Craig, nodding with enthusiasm. 'I really like it.' Then, 'How about this picnic? I'm starved. You going to join us, Norman?'

'Sure thing.'

Craig tossed him the car keys, quite hard. 'In that case you can bring up the hamper, and the lamps, too.' Norman held up the key ring with one finger, and Effie thought for a moment that he was going to refuse. But he gave Craig an exaggerated grin and said, ' "Please"?' and off he went.

When he came back they unrolled their futon in the centre of the floor, shook it to plump it up, and then positioned four pressure lamps, one at each corner. Craig spread out the large plaid blanket from the car, as well as a waterproof groundsheet, while Effie opened up the picnic hamper that Pig Hill Inn had prepared for them, complete with plates and glasses and silver cutlery and red-check napkins. The hamper was packed with cold roast chicken, stuffed tomato salad, fresh colonial bread dotted with fragments of pecans and candied peel. Craig opened a bottle of Lanson champagne which had been kept chilled in a plastic wrapper.

139

'This is the life, hunh?' said Norman, sitting cross-legged and throwing his hair back over his shoulders. 'You wait till you get this place, like, all fixed up. You won't know yourselves.' The pressure lamps cast his shadow huge and wavering on the wall behind him, like the shadow of a witch or a hooded nun.

'So you really think you can do something with this place, then.'

'Sure. I've got the feel, that's the great thing. Got to tell you, though, I'm not really an expert. I studied a year at art school, in New York, but I could never draw too good and I quit. I mean I drew better than Picasso, but who couldn't. So I studied architecture for three years. I thought I was going to be Frank Lloyd Wright the second, but I didn't have the brain. I couldn't get it together with all those stress factors and all that load-bearing stuff.' He rolled his eyes. 'All that calculatin'. And concrete left me cold. But I did have a real good feel for old buildings, and taking care of them, and respecting what the men who first built them had been trying to achieve. So I started helping some of the local builders, real craftsmen that were friends of my mom, guys with beards, like, who knew about gambreled roofs and shingle-sheathing and rusticated brick-work.'

He took a glass of champagne. 'I guess I'm more of an entrepreneur, if you know what I mean. I'm good at, like, getting people together. But restoring this place, that's my dream. When we came here for picnics, my mom and me, I used to look at this house and think, you know, what was it like when it was new, and perfect, and there was shiny copper on the roof, and flags flying.'

Craig sat down beside him. His face looked oddly distorted in the upward light from the pressure lamp, large nose, puffy eyes. 'Let me tell you something, Norman . . .

Valhalla's going to look like that again.'

'Oh, hey,' Norman interrupted. 'I forgot to tell you. I found a window guy. A glazier, in Kingston. He's an old guy who used to do churches and stuff like that. I showed him the blueprints, and he's sure he can restore your windows. He can still make window-glass by the crown method, that's where they spin it around into a big circular sheet, like, and then cut it up . . . but you always end up with what they call a bullion, you know, that knobby bit in the centre. But of course they didn't have bullions here at Valhalla . . . the place was too quality. In the old days,you could tell that somebody didn't have too much money because they used the bullions as well as the plain part.'

Craig slapped him on the shoulder. 'Don't worry . . . we'll get it all back together. And that's great, about the window guy.'

Sunday, June 27, 1:58 a.m.

They had finished their third bottle of champagne and Effie was growing drowsy. She would have given a hundred dollars to be back in her bed at the Pig Hill Inn, but Craig and Norman were both still talkative and hyped-up. They played cards for over two hours, with a seriousness that was completely out of proportion to the fact that they were staking only nickels and dimes; and while they played they devised grandiose plans to replace all the carved oak panelling, and restore the floors with patterned parquet. They discussed the gardens, and the tennis courts, and who they could find to restore the landscaping.

At last, however, Norman ran out of loose change, and

they exhausted the subject of restoring Valhalla, and fell silent, and finished what was left of their champagne. Effie felt that Craig and Norman had begun to develop a strange bond between them. They disliked each other in almost every way that she could think of, and were completely indifferent to each other's values; but their enthusiasm for restoring Valhalla was so great that they had reached a complex kind of compromise.

Norman's digital watch beeped the hour. 'Don't you think it's time we tried to get some sleep?' asked Effie.

'I want to do some prowling around first,' said Norman. 'I want to do some *listening*. It's amazing what you can tell about a house just by listening.'

Craig looked around. 'I'm not ready to go to sleep yet. This place has such a *feel* to it.'

'How about a horror story?' Norman suggested. 'We always used to tell each other horror stories, when we were like camping out.'

'I don't know any horror stories,' Craig told him. 'I guess you could say that international commercial law is pretty horrific, but I don't think that *US Treasury vs Hong Kong Securities* would make the hair on the back of your neck stand up.'

'Oh, come on,' said Effie snuggling the blanket around her shoulders. 'I feel creepy enough already. And cold. And tired.' She didn't say frightened, although she was. She didn't like the way that their huge shadows kept dancing and dipping on the bedroom walls. And she couldn't help listening for footsteps of a man running downstairs, or the anguished, remote sobbing that had come from the blue-carpeted room on Valhalla's third storey.

Norman drained his champagne in three swallows, wiped his mouth, and said, 'Okay . . . I'll wander around for a while, then I'll grab some zees myself. Oh – don't

142

worry. I brought my own sleeping bag. I have to put up the roof on my car anyway, in case it rains.'

'It won't rain,' said Craig, flatly.

'The forecast said that it might.'

'It won't. Believe me, it won't.'

'It might, and if it does, I don't want my car filled up with water, okay?'

Craig reached into his pocket, took out his slim Gucci billfold, and slapped a $50 bill onto the futon. 'Fifty bucks says that it won't.'

Norman stared at it, and then said, 'Okay, man, you're on. But I don't have fifty dollars on me right now.'

'I'll trust you. So long as you leave the roof of your car down.'

'Hey, supposing I win, and it does rain?'

'Then you can spend your fifty drying it out.'

Effie said, 'Craig . . . you never made bets like that in your life!'

She was not only astonished: she was upset. She detested gambling. Her parents had always worked hard for their money, and so had she, and that was why she felt protective about it – unlike her Uncle Bernard, who had lost automobiles and jewellery and savings accounts at Saratoga Race Track. One evening, he had lost his house at the poker table while his family unsuspectingly slept in it. The next morning, Effie's cousins had all turned up on their doorstep, three of them, dazed, bewildered and homeless, carrying blankets. Only the kindness of Uncle Jack's creditor had made it possible for them to keep a roof over their heads.

Norman stood up, a little unsteadily. 'You know something? I never drank champagne before. But I think I could get used to it. If my restoration business works out good. I'm just going to take a look around. I want to catch

143

this sucker by surprise, know what I mean? Houses move, when you're asleep. I could tell you a story about a house that was never the same, from one long day to the next. Houses *move*, man. They're living: they're animate. Can't you feel this place breathing? I've seen doors change position; I've seen beams rearranged. One of the guys I use for carpentry, old Henry Sneider, he swears a whole Dutch barn rebuilt itself once, in like two or three days. He was supposed to be knocking it down, but every morning he came back and it was halfway built back up again . . . with nothing to show who did it. No footprints, no wood-shavings, nothing. You can still see it standing today, over at Salisbury Mills. I could tell you more, man. There's a house in Manitou where the windows turn red. I mean solid red, like blood.'

'Come on, buddy,' Craig told him, standing up, and resting his hand on Norman's shoulders. 'I think it's time to call it a night, don't you?'

'Guess so . . . yes, sure. See you tomorrow. Bright and early, I guess!' He teetered slightly to the right, and then teetered back to the left. 'Jeez . . . this champagne. You could drink this stuff all night, couldn't you?'

'I could,' said Craig, with unexpected coldness, as Norman walked diagonally to the doors. 'I don't think *you* could, though, little man.'

Effie reached across and tugged at the leg of Craig's jeans. He didn't flinch or resist, but on the other hand he didn't look any too pleased, either. 'Are you sure he's going to be safe?' she asked him quietly. Her voice sounded flat and muffled, as if she had a cardboard box over her head. The interior acoustics in Valhalla were very unpredictable. One minute your words could be carried all around the house. The next, you couldn't hear anything but that slow magnificent creaking, and the showering-down of dead

144

plaster, and your own expensive watch frantically ticking your life away.

'Oh, he'll be safe,' Craig told her. He waited for a while, till Norman had said 'goodnight, folks' for the fifth time and had weaved his way out of the double bedroom doors. Then he got up and walked lithely and silently across the underfelt, to close the doors firmly and lock them. 'There. Just in case he takes a wrong turning, during the night. This is our adventure, after all.'

He walked back across the room, stripping off his sweater as he did so, and tugging out his thick brown leather belt with a loud, unpleasant snap.

'Craig, I'm tired. And I really don't like this house very much.'

He lay down next to her, and kissed her. The pressure lamps hissed at every point of the compass. 'You'll grow to like it, I promise you. I know it's damp, at the moment. I know it's cold. But you wait till it's finished. This is going to be your palace, princess. Princess Effie, of Valhalla, how does that sound?'

Effie stared at the crumpled futon inches in front of her face, with a sprig of verbena still clinging to it. She had read about verbena: it was supposed to have the power to turn the sun blue.

She could hear Craig tugging off his socks. Then he was naked, and close up behind her. She felt his erection bobbing against her jeans. 'Princess,' he whispered, close to her ear, but he wouldn't have done, if he had known how much she hated anybody to call her 'princess'. It made her feel like a prom queen at a rundown inner-city high school, or a daddy's girl (which she was, and always would be, but not in that way).

He reached around and tried to unbuckle her belt, but she twisted and resisted and pushed him away. 'Come on,

Craig . . . I just want to get some sleep.'

'Heyy, sweetness . . . that's not what you said before. You've been begging me for it for months.'

'That was before. And that wasn't here.'

'What's the matter with here?' His voice was hard. She knew that there was going to be trouble, whatever she said.

'It's old. It's falling down. It's uncomfortable. That's the matter with it.'

He pulled her quite roughly onto her back, and climbed astride her. He looked down at her and he was very handsome, in that broad-faced Kennedy kind of way, with questioning eyes and thin lips which were almost smiling but not quite. He took hold of her hand and forced her to hold his erection. It was hot, hotter than her own body temperature, and her fingertip touched a snail's trail, just at the tip. She really didn't feel like this at all. The lamps made his eyes look uneven, as if one were set higher than the other, and there was something absurd and threatening in what he was doing to her. She didn't want to hold his cock. She didn't want to be lying on this herby-smelling futon. She wanted to be snuggled up in bed, in the longest safest nightgown she could think of, with her toes curled up, and be left alone.

Sunday, June 27, 3:07 a.m.

Craig was snoring.

He lay on his back with his arms and his legs spread out as if he had dropped from the top of a high building. Every now and then he twitched and muttered, and Effie knew he was dreaming.

Once he said, 'Gaby, you're a bitch.' Then, 'Gaby' again.

Effie couldn't sleep at all. She had dropped off for a few minutes after Craig had finished having sex with her, but she had been woken up by a violent and terrifying nightmare in which she was throwing herself through a window. She had crouched under her blanket, gasping for breath, convinced that she had actually heard the glass breaking, and convinced that she had miscarried. She reached down between her legs, expecting to find blood, but of course it wasn't blood at all.

Since then, she had been lying close to Craig, watching him sleep, and wondering if her life would ever be the same again.

She wondered, too, why she had imagined that she had miscarried. She had never been pregnant; although she had always wanted to have children, when Craig became established as a top-flight lawyer. Perhaps her unconscious had been trying to tell her that her chance of becoming a mother was dwindling by the day. Perhaps her unconscious had been trying to tell her that she had no chance at all.

'Gaby, if I catch you –' Craig murmured, and then boisterously turned over onto his side, dragging most of the covers with him.

Effie waited for a while, until he started snoring again, and then sat up. She felt exhausted and hung-over and her left hip ached. She would have done anything for a hot cup of lemon tea, but all that Craig had brought was a bottle of Perrier water. She shuffled across the floor, unscrewed it, and drank it straight from the neck.

It was then that she thought she heard the sobbing again. It was so faint that it could have been anything: a shutter swinging, an owl calling. Even the crackling of bubbles from the open Perrier bottle made it harder for her to make out what it was. She stood up, and listened

147

again. It was still impossible to distinguish what it was.

She tiptoed in her socks to the door which led out to the corridor, turned the handle and eased it open.

It was dark, because the moon had yet to rise, but Effie could see that the corridor ran the whole length of the second storey to the landing where the hunched plaster-creature stood. Most of its windows were broken, but the tattered remnants of net curtains still silently billowed at every one, like a procession of ghostly brides.

She listened again, and this time she was quite sure. It was a woman sobbing – not high-pitched, not keening, but the terrible deep lung-wrenching cry of utter desolation.

Effie waited and waited. She was growing cold and her neck was stiff, but she couldn't make up her mind if she should go upstairs again or not. After all, there had been nobody in the blue-carpeted bedroom the last time she had ventured into it. If Valhalla were haunted, maybe this disembodied sobbing was as far as it went.

She looked back at Craig but he was still sleeping as if he had been struck on the head. She hesitated a little longer, and then she crept out of the room and closed the door behind her. Her heart was beating quickly but she was determined not to be frightened. Not too frightened, anyway. If the sobbing was only that, and nothing more, then she had nothing to worry about. But if there were somebody there, a real woman who needed real help, then she would never forgive herself for having ignored her.

She passed room after room: a sewing-room, in which she glimpsed an empty embroidery frame; a room with a closed door and a recent sign saying Danger Keep Out, which was the music-room; and then two doors which led to the upper gallery of the ballroom. The sobbing grew louder, and even more anguished, and Effie thought: this time, I'm going to find you. This time, I'm going to help

148

you. Whatever's wrong, whatever's happened, I'm going to stop you from sobbing. Because this woman sobbed in the way that all women sob, whether they do it outwardly or whether they keep it silently locked up inside themselves. They sob because they realise, one day, that they were born on a planet of men, and that short of death or spinsterhood they can never escape.

Effie's Aunt Rachel used to say, 'Even the slaves could run away, but where can women go?' Effie had never understood what she meant until Craig had started working in international law; and she had become his acquiescent geisha, just like the wives of all the other lawyers and vice-presidents and managing directors. *Good evening, I am the wife of Craig Bellman. Who are you?*

Suddenly she found herself out on the second-storey landing where the plaster-creature lived. She stopped. The sobbing was so distinct now that she could almost hear what the woman was saying. The moon had just appeared over the horizon, and the stained-glass window gleamed like a giant spiderweb. *Gut ist der Schlaf, der Tod ist besser.* Perhaps she could understand that, too.

She was just about to climb the stairs when something made her look jumpily around. At first she couldn't think what it was, but then she realised, and the realisation made her feel as if centipedes were crawling down her back, inside her sweater. The plaster-creature was gone. Where it had stood, the wall was scabby and stained, and the laths were exposed, like the ribs of a half-collapsed mummy. But it had completely disappeared – that lumpy, dripping thing with its hideous Elephant Man head and its one glutinous eye.

Effie stood at the bottom of the stairs with one hand on the rough, flaking banister rail and she felt faint with fright. *If the plaster-creature wasn't here, where was it?* She had a horrifying vision of it shuffling painfully through the darkened corridors of Valhalla, hunched and distorted, trying to find where she was. It may even have climbed up the stairs ahead of her, and be waiting at the top.

'This is crazy,' she said, out loud. 'You're imagining things. You're just working yourself up into a panic.'

She took half a dozen deep breaths. Then she said, 'I can't believe I said that out loud! I must be going out of my mind!'

Cautiously, she raised her eyes. The moon had risen even higher now, and the hooded woman in the stained-glass window had taken on a cold, beatified shine. The banners on the distant battlements seemed to be slowly furling and unfurling, and the lilies quivered as if somebody had just walked through them. *Sleep is good, but death is better,* the window whispered, and for the very first time in her life Effie felt mortally afraid.

But it was too late for her to turn back. The sobbing still echoed down the staircase, and she knew that she was going to have to find where it was coming from, and face it, whatever it was. She took a huge, steadying breath, and lifted her right foot onto the staircase. It felt as if she had been sitting on it for too long, and it had turned numb.

Help me, the woman begged her, between her sobs. *Please, if you can hear me, help me.*

Oh God, thought Effie, as she climbed the stairs. Her legs felt too weak to carry her, and her will was draining away from her with every step. Yet she knew she had to go on. If she didn't discover who was sobbing, she would never be able to live here, and if she couldn't live in Valhalla, then she couldn't live with Craig any longer, because the house, to him had become such an overwhelming obsession.

She passed the window and carried on upward. On the

150

third-storey landing she hesitated fora few moments, to calm herself down. Then she walked along the moonlit corridor towards the blue-carpeted bedroom, looking as spectral herself as any ghost.

Since Morton Walker's fall through the floor, most of the broken tiles and squirrels' debris had been cleared away, or swept to one side, and a tarpaulin had been rigged up over the open roof. Further along the corridor, where Morton had actually dropped through to the music-room, two criss-cross planks barred the way, and the hole itself had been covered with a sheet of heavy-duty ply.

Effie reached the bedroom. The door was half open, and she could hear the woman sobbing quite distinctly. She wasn't imagining it or dreaming it; and it wasn't the wind blowing down the chimney, because there was scarcely any wind tonight.

Please, please, please, if you can help me –

She grasped the door handle. She didn't know whether she had the courage to open it. She waited and waited, and all the time the woman sobbed and sobbed as if she could never stop.

She pushed it open.

For one instant, she thought she saw a woman dressed in white, standing by the window. But then Craig said, 'Effie? Eff, what the hell are you doing?'

Effie turned around, her whole nervous system tingling with shock. Craig was standing at the head of the stairs, wearing nothing but his jeans and his shoes, with his flash-light in his hand. She turned back to the bedroom, but the flashlight had dazzled her, and when she looked again, the woman (if it had been a woman) had disappeared.

Craig came up to her and put his arm around her shoulders. 'You shouldn't wander around up here, it's dangerous.'

151

'I thought – I thought I heard something.'

'I woke up and there you weren't. You had me worried.'

'I'm sorry. I didn't want to disturb you.'

'Come on, let's go back and see if we can catch some more sleep.'

'Craig –'

'What's the matter, sweetheart?'

'I think there's somebody here, apart from us.'

'Well, sure there is. Norman.'

'I mean apart from Norman, too. I think there are people living here.'

He ushered her gently out of the bedroom and closed the door behind him. 'I don't see how that could be.'

'But I keep hearing things, seeing things.' She swallowed, and she felt as guilty as if she were breaking somebody's confidence. 'I heard a woman crying, I'm sure of it.'

He paused at the top of the stairs. 'You can't hear it now, can you?'

'No,' she admitted.

'Old houses always make weird noises. Come on, you've drunk too much champagne, that's your trouble.'

She wrapped herself up in the blanket and fell asleep almost at once. It was like falling down a black, echoing well. She dreamed that she was walking into the blue-carpeted bedroom and a woman dressed in white was standing by the window. The woman was silent. She didn't turn around. She didn't speak. Effie found that she was gliding across the floor towards the woman, even though she wasn't moving her legs, even though she didn't want to.

She was terrified of what the woman's face might look like. She had a feeling that it might be diseased, or disfigured, or even a flesh-bare skull. She kept gliding nearer and nearer and she wanted to put out her arms to stop

152

herself but she couldn't.

And then the woman turned around and she had the misshapen face of the plaster-creature, with one glistening eye, and an awful scabby maw encrusted with white mineral salts.

She woke up, thrashing and gasping. She sat up and found her wristwatch. She had slept only twenty minutes. The moon was still shining, and the bedroom was silent. Even Craig had stopped snoring. In fact, when she reached out for him, he wasn't there at all.

'Craig?' she called. 'Craig, are you there?'

She got up and walked across to the bathroom. He had probably gone for a pee. 'Craig?' she called, in a stage whisper, although she didn't know why, in a huge empty house like this. 'Craig, are you in there?'

She opened the bathroom door but the bathroom was empty, and dark. The moon gleamed on sea-green tiles, and a bath with a rust-coloured stain down one side. She saw a pale, blurred face on the other side of the room, and for a split-second it gave her a jolt of fright, until she realised that it was her own face, in the dusty mirror over the washbasin. *Une ombre lointaine.*

She was returning to the futon when she thought she heard a scream, somewhere in the house. She listened and listened but it wasn't repeated and she wasn't sure that she had heard it at all. Owls? she thought. She hoped that Norman hadn't fallen and hurt himself. And where was Craig?

She knelt down and lit one of the pressure lamps. She was clipping the top back on it when the door from the corridor opened and Craig came back into the room. He looked sweaty and agitated, although he was grinning.

'Thought you were sleeping,' he said, sitting on the futon to ease off his shoes.

'I was.'

'Do you want to turn that lamp off again? Maybe we can get some well-earned sleep.'

'Where did you go?'

He lay down, and turned his back to her, and said nothing.

'Craig . . . I asked you a question. Where did you go?'

'What's this, the third degree? I just went for a leak, okay?'

'The bathroom's right here.'

'Sure, but there's no water-supply, is there?'

'Oh . . . no, I forgot about that.'

He turned back and stared at her. He didn't look himself at all. There was something *gross* about him, something coarse. She couldn't exactly say what it was, but she didn't like it at all.

'So, are you going to kill that lamp, or what?'

'Oh, sure. Sorry.'

She lay back and stared up at the ceiling. After a while she said, 'I thought I heard somebody screaming. Did you hear that?'

He snorted and jostled as if he were annoyed at being disturbed. 'Nobody screamed, honey. You've got the jittery ab-dabs, that's all. Now will you please try to sleep?'

'Sorry.'

But she found it impossible to sleep. She lay on her back; she lay on her side. She turned over and lay on the other side. She kept thinking about the woman dressed in white, standing by the bedroom window. Had she really seen a woman, or was it an optical illusion, an oddly-shaped assembly of wallpaper and moonlight? She remembered stepping out of the Red Oaks Inn once, when she was nine, and seeing a dark, enormous man leaning against the side of her father's car. She had walked

154

along the verandah, staring at the man in horror, and as her viewpoint had changed, the man's arm had magically turned itself into a shadow beneath the side-mirror, and his head and shoulders had revealed themselves to be nothing more than reflections in the windshield of sky and clouds and a nearby oak tree.

Craig was sleeping deeply now, groaning and snorting like a man trying to swim a quarter of a mile underwater. She kept trying to push him away, but he kept turning over until he was leaning against her, and his face was only inches from hers.

'*Impossible*,' he said, in his sleep. The moon began to appear around the other side of the house. '*Yussuchabitch.*'

'Craig,' Effie protested, but she couldn't wake him.

'*No such – jusslike – Gaby –*'

She was almost on the very edge of the futon now, with her right elbow against the thick, prickly underfelt. She reached down to turn him over bodily, and it was then she felt his flaccid penis against the back of her hand. It was cold and wet, but not with urine. It was actually slippery, as if he had ejaculated in his sleep. She knew that could happen, especially if a man hadn't had sex for a long time, but his thigh wasn't wet and neither was the futon.

She lifted her fingers up to her nose and sniffed them, and the salty, bleachy smell told her at once that it was semen. Yet she detected another smell, too. An aromatic smell, more like a woman's sexual fluids than a man's.

She lay on her back while the moon rotated around Valhalla and her brain leapt and juggled in the shadows. Had he simply climaxed in his sleep? Or had he left the bedroom to masturbate somewhere? Why should he do that? If he wanted sex, she was there, right next to him, and she wouldn't have denied him if he had really wanted it desperately.

155

But the other possibility that kept haunting her was that she was right, and that they weren't alone in the house. The other possibility was that Craig had crept out of the bedroom to find another woman, and to make love to her. But who could such a woman be? Not the woman dressed in white, surely – even if there really *was* a woman dressed in white.

Why would she sob? Why would she scream? What was she doing in the house, and why would she make love to a total stranger in the middle of the night? That was if Craig *was* a total stranger.

Could this woman be 'Gaby'?

Effie's thoughts went around and around in a carousel of prancing bewilderment and fleeting doubts. She was tempted to go back upstairs, to search Valhalla room by room. But it was well past four o'clock now, and she was aching and tired, and she didn't know whether she wanted any of her questions actually resolved. If there was a real woman here, a real 'Gaby', Effie didn't want to face her, not here, and not now. And if the woman was nothing more than a white-dressed figure in the moonlight, or a trick of the light, or a sobbing voice that nobody could exorcise, she didn't want to face her, either.

Especially if she turned around, as she had in Effie's dream, and showed her the half-melted face of the plaster-creature.

In the morning, prowling barefooted around the house, she found Norman in the middle of the ballroom, wound up tight in an old pink blanket. He was still holding his architects' tape-measure in the palm of his hand. His eyes were closed and his mouth was wide open, and he sounded as if he were singing a song.

Monday, June 28, 3:33 p.m.

The Hungry Moon was half way down Main Street on the left-hand side, a small storefront in between Hautboy Antiques and The Goose & Gander Kitchenware Store. Its frontage was painted olive green and gold, and its shiny windows were filled with gilded moons and mounted crystals and patchwork cushions filled with pot-pourri, as well as occult books and mirrors and tarot cards.

Effie came down the sunny, brick-paved street, enjoying the cool wind that blew off the river and the shade of the maples that lined the sidewalk. She stopped and peered up at the sign which hung outside the Hungry Moon. She had never really looked at it closely before. It was a copper casting of a crescent moon, with nose and eyes and a wide-open mouth, but what Effie hadn't realised was that the mouth was crammed with a cat, a violin, a cow's legs, a frightened-looking dog, a plate and a spoon. The moon from the nursery-rhyme 'hey-diddle-diddle' had greedily swallowed everything else. It was folksy, picturesque, but curiously disturbing, too, as if some warm and folksy friend had suddenly turned out to be a dangerous psychopath.

The door was open and Effie stepped inside. The store was small, with bare polished boards, but the shelves were stacked with every imaginable herb and spice and occult device. Black tin witches hung from the ceiling, and revolved slowly in the summer breeze. There were old-style broomsticks and crystal balls, witch-dolls and glazed mandrake-fruits, and heaps of books and pamphlets on

157

everything from wholesome eating to flying spells. The fragrance was overpowering, cloves and orange peel and jasmine, and some hauntingly rotten-sweet odour like waterwort.

There was nobody behind the red-painted wooden counter, so Effie rang the little bell that stood beside the baroque brass cash register. Nobody appeared so she rang it again, and eventually a young woman came through a screen of beads, carrying a stack of books.

'You'll have to forgive me,' she said. 'My son usually helps me out, but he's preoccupied with other things right now. Right at the beginning of the season, of course.'

Norman's face was rarely visible behind his curtains of hair, but what Effie had seen of it didn't much resemble his mother's. Norman was thin-faced and large-nosed. Pepper Moriarty had broad features with strong bone-structure and a small, straight nose. Her ash-blonde hair was tied in an indigo-dyed bandana, and she wore huge dangly hoop earrings. Her eyes were strange. The irises were very pale grey, so that when the light caught them they looked almost silver. She had a wide smile with more than her fair share of extremely white teeth.

She put down the books and came around the counter. Woodstock had obviously left an indelible impression on her. She was very big-breasted but she wore a thin butter-muslin blouse without a bra, although she had an Afghan waistcoat on top of it embroidered with tufts of red-and-black wool and beads and stars and tiny sparkling mirrors. Her stonewashed denim jeans were skintight at the top, but widened into raggedy flares. She wore high-heeled tan-leather boots, but even in these she wasn't more than 5ft 5ins tall.

'Your son's been working with me and my husband,' said Effie. 'I'm Effie Bellman. We're the people who are thinking of buying Valhalla.'

'Oh,' Pepper Moriarty replied. 'You're the one with that less-than-polite lawyer for a husband.'

Effie felt herself blushing. 'I'm sorry about that. It's just that Craig's been through quite a difficult time. He was – well, he had an accident. We came to Cold Spring to give him some time to get over it. You know, get a little rest.'

'I wouldn't have thought that buying Valhalla was very restful. That place is a ruin.'

'My husband's set on it,' said Effie, trying hard to smile. 'He's really obsessed with doing it up.'

'Well, best of luck, that's all I can say,' said Pepper. 'I wouldn't live in Valhalla if you gave it to me. In fact, I wouldn't live in Valhalla if you gave it to me and paid me a thousand bucks a night to stay in it.'

Effie hesitated, and then she said, 'That's the reason I came to see you.'

'Oh, yes?' Pepper started to take small coloured-glass bottles off the shelf next to the counter, dust them, and put them back. She paused, and focused those almost-silver eyes on Effie, and said, 'You stayed the night there, didn't you? You really went ahead and did it.'

'That's right. We did.'

'How sensitive are you?' Pepper asked her.

'Cat-hairs make me sneeze; and some of the summer grasses. Why?'

'I wasn't talking about hay fever, I was talking about psychic vibrations.'

'Well . . . if it *was* a psychic vibration, I heard a woman upstairs in one of the bedrooms.'

'What was she doing?'

'She was crying. She went on and on, and kept saying "help me." '

'So what did you do?'

159

'I tried to find her, of course.'

Pepper puffed out her cheeks. 'Phew! You're crazier than I thought!'

'I just had to know if she was real or not. I mean, if Craig and I are actually going to live in Valhalla –'

'Did you find her?' asked Pepper, sharply.

'I'm not sure. I found the room where the crying was coming from – and I thought I might have just glimpsed somebody, only for an instant. But – I don't know. I'm not sure what I saw.'

'Did your husband hear it, too?'

Effie shook her head. 'If he did, he didn't say.'

'But you told him that *you* could hear it?'

Effie kept on shaking her head. 'Something stopped me. I don't know what it was. I felt that I shouldn't, that's all.'

'That's very interesting,' said Pepper. 'One of the tests of a true psychic vibration is that it's very selective ... it doesn't make itself known to every Tom, Dick or Harry.'

Effie said, carefully, 'I had the feeling that the woman specifically didn't want Craig to know that she was there.'

'*Very* interesting,' Pepper nodded. 'And is that all you've heard, just this one woman crying?'

'It's all I've *heard*. Well, apart from something that could have been a scream, but I think that was only an owl. I did *see* somebody, though. A man, in a dark suit. He was going downstairs and I called out to him, but he looked at me as if he couldn't even see me.'

'You're sure he wasn't a squatter, or a trespasser? Or something worse? A realtor, maybe?'

'I don't think so. He was much too elegant. I called out, but he looked right through me, as if I wasn't even there.'

'Well . . .' said Pepper, hanging up an arrangement of dried thorns and weeds and mandrake roots, 'I've been to Valhalla, too, as Norman probably told you. I never heard

160

anything and I never saw anything, but that place has absolutely the worst psychic atmosphere I ever encountered. Especially the ballroom, and some of the upstairs corridors. I sensed such *dread* there. I sensed such *malevolence*.'

'But what is it?' Effie wanted to know. 'Is it haunted, is that it?'

Pepper pursed her lips. 'By haunted you mean ghosts.'

'I guess so.'

'You don't really believe in ghosts, surely?'

'I don't know. I didn't till last night.'

'But now you're not so sure? Well, let me put your mind at rest. There are absolutely and irrefutably no such things. There are psychic vibrations, yes. There are very strong psychic vibrations; good and evil; and at some locations those psychic vibrations can make themselves felt so strongly that people can hear and see and even smell them. It can happen in houses, in hotels, or right out on the street. We call them a psychic nexus. There's a woman who lives over on Fair Street whose daughter died when she was just eight years old, and that little girl loved lilac. Every year, on her birthday, you can smell lilac flowers in the room where the little girl died. I've smelled them myself. That's not a ghost, though – that's a psychic vibration, and what you've been hearing and seeing, they're psychic vibrations, too.'

'Are they dangerous?'

Pepper made a see-sawing gesture with her hand, as if to say 'kind of'. 'They're not dangerous in themselves, no. But any psychic nexus is dangerous; just like any physical nexus is dangerous. Like, most of the time you can walk around on the Earth's surface and you're perfectly safe, right? But if you stand too close to a place where the surface is broken, like a volcano or a geyser or something like that, then you're taking a risk. It's the same with the psy-

161

chic world, do you follow me? Most of the time, it's safe, but it has its ruptures, it has its fissures and its weaknesses where the psychic equivalent of molten lava or steam-heated water are liable to burst through.'

'And that's what's happened at Valhalla?' asked Effie, although she didn't fully understand what Pepper was talking about. 'A kind of . . . bursting through?'

'In a manner of speaking, yes. That's what I think, any-way.' She picked a small green bottle off the shelf. 'Do you see this stuff? Oil of Foxgloves. You get it by boiling down foxglove flowers. It's poison . . . witches used to use it in the seventeenth century to kill off babies born deformed. But it also contains digitalis, which doctors are still prescribing today to help cardiac patients.'

'I'm not sure that I –'

Pepper looked at her patiently. 'What I'm trying to tell you is that psychics and healers like me aren't fakes. We're not snake-oil sellers. What I'm trying to tell you is that I know what I'm talking about, okay? You heard a woman crying up at Valhalla and you want to know what you can possibly do about it. And my answer to you is: you can't do anything about it. She lives there, just the same as you're planning to live there, and I'm afraid that you and your less-than-polite lawyer of a husband are going to have to grow used to the idea.'

'If she's not a ghost, I don't see how she can live there.'

Pepper dusted and replaced another bottle. 'You see this? Flying ointment – eleoselenium, aconitum, frondes populeas, and soot. It's supposed to contain the fat of young children, too, but that doesn't meet federal require-ments these days. Women used to rub it on themselves, hoping they would fly. Of course they never physically flew, but it used to penetrate any cuts or lice-bites they might have had, and get into their bloodstream, and at

162

least two of the ingredients are strong hallucinogens. They may not have actually left the ground, but they sure *thought* that they were flying.'

Effie said, 'Mrs Moriarty . . . I don't want to be a nuisance, but I have to know what's happening at Valhalla, if I'm going to live there.'

'It's Ms, not Mrs, and anyhow please call me Pepper.'

'I'm sorry. But I'm genuinely frightened.'

'Listen,' said Pepper, in a businesslike way. 'Everybody thinks that haunted houses are full of the souls of dead people, wandering around looking for revenge or lost opportunities or where the hell they left their glasses because they can't see to read *The Heavenly Herald*. But when you're dead, you're dead. You don't come back in any shape or form. I hate to tell people that, but I've been dabbling since Woodstock. I've tripped and I've tranced and I've ouija'd, I've done it all, and I'm *very* sensitive. But the dead are dead, believe me.'

'So this sobbing woman . . . she's real?'

Pepper briefly closed her eyes in assent. 'Yes. She's real.'

Effie's mouth felt dry. She thought of Craig, waiting until she was asleep, and then sneaking off to meet – who? and how? And why did the woman sob like that?

'If she's real,' she said, 'how come I can hear her but I can't see her?'

'I thought you said you did see her.'

'I'm not sure. It was only for a second.'

Pepper put the last bottle back on the shelf, and then she laid her hand on Effie's shoulder. 'Come into the back. I'll brew us some tea. A friend of mine went to see his guru in Poona and sent me some wonderful Nilgiri. I also have some great cream cakes. They make them at the Riverview Bakery and I can't resist them. You'll put on five pounds just by looking at them.'

163

Effie hesitated. 'You *do* have time, don't you?' asked Pepper.

'Well, sure, but this whole situation has left me really confused. I don't know why Craig's so set on buying Valhalla, and I don't know what you mean about this woman living there. I feel like I'm totally missing out on something somewhere.'

Pepper led the way into a small back room with a hob and a kettle and more shelves crammed with herbs – betony, houndstongue, mugwort and spikenard – all the ingredients of the magic pantry, in blue ceramic jars with gilt lettering. One of the jars was marked 'Moriarty.'

'I didn't know there was a herb called moriarty,' said Effie.

'There isn't. That's blood root. It's the root of deception, so you always have to store it with a false name.'

While the kettle boiled, Pepper led Effie into the garden at the rear of the store. They had to step over a monstrous grey cat sleeping in the open doorway. The garden was overgrown with wild flowers and it didn't look as if the grass had been cut all year. A cast-iron table and chairs stood beneath a gnarled old apple tree. Pepper spread a faded flower-patterned cloth over the table, and invited Effie to sit down.

'What about the store?' asked Effie.

'I hardly ever have stuff stolen,' said Pepper. 'The kind of people who come to the Hungry Moon leave their money on the counter if they can't find me. If somebody did steal something – well, it would probably be the worse for them. Every item in the store has been touched by centaury plants, and if a thief smells centaury he goes into mad delusions of terror.'

'I'll make sure I don't take anything without paying for it, then,' said Effie. 'I think I'm having mad delusions of

164

terror already.'

'It's the vibrations,' Pepper told her, emphatically. 'Whatever happened in that house when Jack Belias was living there, it's still happening.'

Effie frowned. 'I read somewhere that if some really powerful emotional event occurs in a house, the walls can sort of absorb it, like a photograph.'

Pepper shook her head. 'That's hooey. Walls are walls. You can't store an emotional event in a brick any more than you can store your voice in a jam jar.'

'But these psychic vibrations . . . what can you do to get rid of them?'

'What do you do when your tap leaks?'

'Call for the plumber, I guess.'

'So what do you do when your psychic vibrations are acting up? And don't say call for a vibrator.'

For the first time since she had entered Valhalla yesterday evening, Effie laughed. She liked Pepper. She was one of the first matter-of-fact people that she had met since Craig had taken up international law, and she hadn't realised how much she missed the company of women who laughed, women who spoke their own minds, women who didn't give a shit for anything.

The kettle whistled. Pepper stood up and said, 'Don't go away. When you need help with psychic vibrations, you need a psychic, and that's me.'

Monday, June 28, 6:28 p.m.

Pepper closed up the Hungry Moon at six o'clock and they went across to the Old Post Inn for cocktails. The evening was warm and the sky was glazed in pale violet. Main

165

Street was still busy with tourists and lights and slowly-creeping automobiles.

They sat at a small corner table and Pepper ordered two Fish House punches: dark rum, cognac and peach brandy, with lime juice and plenty of sugar.

'I drink this on purpose,' she said, lifting her glass, her eyes shining silver in the light from the tablelamp. 'The Fish House in Schuylkill was the first men's club in America, and this was their special tipple. Another bastion falls.'

'This is going to knock me out,' said Effie, sniffing her drink as if it were hemlock.

'That's the general idea,' Pepper replied, and clinked glasses with her. 'Here's to psychic harmony: and you; and that poor sobbing woman, whoever she is.'

They drank for a while without talking. During the afternoon, they had grown to like each other more and more, in spite of the radical differences in their backgrounds and their politics and their points of view. Effie found that Pepper was convincing, direct and immensely liberating. She believed that everybody had a spirit life. She believed in souls. She believed, too, that the natural world was teeming with energy that anybody could harness, and use to their own benefit, if only they weren't so cynical. But she didn't subscribe to the conventional ideas of spiritualism or faith-healing. 'If I was a ghost, and some old biddy asked me, "Is anybody there?" I'd tell her to stick her crystal ball where she didn't need Ray-Bans.'

But she still hadn't explained who or what the sobbing woman could be: at least, not in any way that Effie could understand it.

'I'll tell you the truth, Effie,' she said, leaning back in her chair, and crossing one booted foot over her knee. 'And the truth is that I don't honestly know. There are no ghosts,

166

okay? But I don't really understand this crying, and I don't understand this man you said you saw.'

Effie had half-finished her punch and she was already feeling more than a little unreal.

Pepper said, 'Why don't I come up to Valhalla and give it another look? I'll bring some hazel twigs and some salt and we'll see what's what. Hazel twigs for sensing the psychic vibrations: it's just like water-divining. Salt for keeping off evil.'

Effie looked down at her drink. She liked Pepper, but she really doubted that she could give her any serious help, especially with divining-rods and magic remedies. All the same, what else could she do? Call the police, and have them search Valhalla for squatters? Search it herself? Or simply pretend that she couldn't hear anything at all – that the woman's sobbing was imaginary, the first delusions of an early menopause?

Pepper said, 'How about the day after tomorrow? That's if you can square it with Big Chief Craig.'

'Craig's going back to the city tomorrow morning. He has some business to settle up. He said he'll be gone for only two or three days at the most.'

'Then maybe we can exorcise your sobbing woman and your dark-haired man before he gets back.'

'Well. . . . I don't know. Craig's very possessive when it comes to Valhalla. He says it's not just a house, it's like *him*. It's like a map of his whole personality.'

'He really feels that way?' Pepper frowned.

'It's changed him, completely. After his accident he was very withdrawn, he had no confidence at all. He was mugged, if you want to know the truth, and very badly hurt, and it kind of disintegrated his ego. There were times when he could hardly feed himself. But as soon as he saw Valhalla, he changed. He started talking about giving

167

up his law partnership. He started talking about rebuilding the roof, and gutting the kitchens, and laying out the grounds. It was just as if somebody gave him a shot of something.'

'So how do you feel about it?' asked Pepper.

'Buying Valhalla? Not totally committed. I guess I could learn to get used to it. But I'm not totally committed, the way that Craig is. I'm not obsessed.'

'Tell the truth,' said Pepper. She didn't blink once. She didn't raise her voice. Effie knew that she had found her out.

'All right,' Effie quivered. 'At first I didn't like Valhalla. Now I hate it. It frightens me, because it's going to eat up all our savings and all of our investments, and nobody will ever want to buy it from us because people don't buy thirteen-bedroom mansions on the Hudson any more, do they? Except for Craig.'

Pepper gave her a slow, soft handclap. 'So don't buy it,' she said.

'It's what he wants. He's so determined.'

'It's your life, too.'

'Yes, exactly. It's my life, too, and I want Craig in my life. I want him the way he used to be, before he became a hotshot lawyer, and started treating me like a geisha. I want him the way he used to be, before he was mugged. Valhalla's given him some of that back. I hate Valhalla, I really, really hate it, and it scares me to death. But I'm not going to lose my husband to some sobbing woman, and I'm not going to lose him to a house.'

She paused, and then she added, breathlessly, 'No matter how grand or special that house may be.'

Pepper lifted her glass, and said, 'Here's dry rot in your eye.'

168

Tuesday, June 29, 3:39 p.m.

The doorbell rang again and again and in the end Steven turned over and said, 'Khryssa – can't you answer it?'

'It's nothing,' Khryssa murmured, and snuggled down even further into the sheets. 'Just somebody forgot their keys, and wants the front door open.'

But the doorbell kept on ringing, and in the end Steven climbed out of bed and went to the intercom. 'What?' he demanded, standing naked and pot-bellied in the criss-cross sunlight.

Khryssa said, 'Don't be so aggressive, Steven. It doesn't suit you.' Her long brunette hair flowed over the pillow like a lazy sea-swell filled with weed. She was very tall and long-limbed and oddly pretty, with a snub nose and full lips and slightly-squinting eyes. She was wearing a three-stranded pearl necklace and a gold watch and a gold chain bracelet from Tiffany's.

Beside the bed stood a half-empty bottle of tequila and two glasses. It was Mezcal tequila, with the saguara worm in it. Steven had already eaten the worm, although it had-n't appreciably improved his performance. Since return-ing to Khryssa's loft, they had spent two hours wrestling and sweating and Khryssa still hadn't climaxed once. Mind you, she suspected that Steven hadn't, either. Most of his grunting and 'oh-Godding' had been 60 per cent alcohol and 40 per cent simulated.

Steven said, 'Who?' and then he covered the intercom receiver with his hand. 'Khryssa . . . it's Craig, for Christ's sake.'

169

She turned over and propped herself up on one elbow. 'Craig? Craig who?'

'Craig Bellman for Christ's sake, who do you think?'

'I don't believe you! Craig went to Cold Spring, to convalesce.'

'I know he did,' said Steven, his round face looking boiled and red. 'But he's here now, and he wants me to let him in.'

'Tell him I'm not here. Tell him you're my cousin, and you're taking care of my apartment while I'm away.'

Miserably, Steven hesitated, and then he said, 'She's not here. That's right. I'm her cous –'

He took the receiver away from his ear and stared at it as if it had personally affronted him.

'Well?' said Khryssa.

'He hung up. That's all.'

'That's okay, then, isn't it?'

'You don't think he recognised my voice?'

'He went away, didn't he?'

'Sure, but we've been partners for how long? Jesus, that was a shock!'

Khryssa said, 'Stop worrying and come back to bed. He doesn't own me. I haven't seen him since he was mugged. He called, sure, but calling isn't the same as making love, is it? Come on, Steven, get back into bed. The sheets are getting cold and your tequila's getting warm.'

Steven paced uneasily up and down, the sunlight shining in his wild, sparse hair; his penis bobbing. 'I don't know, Khryssa . . . maybe I ought to leave.'

'You promised me the whole afternoon. You promised to take me to Lola's.'

'I don't know . . . this whole thing seems to have got out of hand.'

Khryssa sat up, and tossed back her hair. 'Well, if you're

170

going, Steven, go! At least Craig always knew what he wanted!'

Steven came back and sat on the edge of the bed. He took Khryssa's hand between both of his hands, and patted it, and kept on patting it. His upper lip was decorated with tiny little glass beads of perspiration.

'Maybe this isn't working out, I don't know.'

'You feel guilty?'

'I feel like I'm trespassing, if you want to know the truth. Craig and me, we go back to law school.'

'Not forgetting your wife, of course.'

'Margo? Jesus. Who could forget Margo?'

'You could, if you put your mind to it. You could forget Craig, too. I have.'

Steven looked disconsolate. 'I just don't think that I'm cut out for this kind of thing. I have to think of the kids, too.'

' "Both of whom look like Margo? And both of whom are goddamned intolerable brats"? Excuse my quoting you.'

Steven managed to look directly into her eyes; a disappointed 34-year-old lawyer with thinning hair and a Rolls-Royce and a summer house at East Quogue. He owned a minor Andrew Wyeth, a watercolour of piercing-blue pieberries in a pail, and when he looked at it he didn't even understand what he was looking at; just as he didn't understand Khryssa, or the half-melted marmalade light that filled her loft, with all its Mexican tapestries and hangings and its strange salt-glaze pottery. He understood only that he had succeeded in life way beyond his wildest expectations, and yet he had totally failed. Khryssa had asked him, 'What is a Rolls-Royce *for*?' and he hadn't been able to answer her.

'I'll, unh, see you next week maybe,' he told Khryssa. 'You don't mind taking a raincheck on Lola's, do you? I mean I *like* Lola's, but you have to be feeling *exuberant* for Lola's.'

'What about Mortimer's?' she suggested. She leaned forward so that her small bare breast touched his arm. 'Mortimer's is quiet, and I can wear that black dress you bought me.'

He kissed her. 'Khryssa . . . I'm really sorry. I've kind of lost the mood.'

She stared at him for one intense moment. Then she flounced back onto her pillow and said, 'Screw you, Steven. At least Craig had the balls to take me places.'

Steven stood up, his cheeks flaring. 'Pity he doesn't have the balls now, hunh?'

And it was then that they heard a hard, insistent knock at the door.

They looked at each other in alarm. 'Are you expecting someone?' Steven hissed.

'Of course not. It's Craig.'

Steven ducked down and found his blue-striped boxer shorts. 'Jesus, Khryssa, this is insane.'

The knock was repeated: louder, more insistent.

'Give me time to dress, give me time to dress. For Christ's sake, Khryssa!'

'Khryssa!' called Craig, through the reinforced steel door. 'Khryssa, it's Craig! I know you're in there! You left your bike in the hall!'

'Oh, shit,' said Steven, scrabbling into his trousers. He lost his balance and fell over sideways onto the bed. Khryssa angrily pushed him off, and he ended up sitting on the floor.

'Khryssa, are you going to open this door, or what?'

Steven's head appeared over the end of the bed. His finger was pressed to his lips. 'Say nothing, for Christ's sake, say nothing!'

They waited and waited. A minute went by. There was no more knocking. They waited even longer – three minutes, four. Khryssa looked at Steven and Steven looked at Khryssa, and Steven whispered, 'He's gone. I'll bet my ass.'

'You don't know Craig,' said Khryssa, nervously.

'What do you mean, I don't know Craig? He and me, we graduated together. We were brothers. He was the bright one and I was the dogged one. Craig did the fancy summings-up. I did the spadework. That was what made us so goddamned good. We had balance. We had yin and yang or whatever.'

He prodded his finger towards the door. 'He's out of here, believe me. He never had the staying power. Sparkling one minute and bored the next. No patience, that was always Craig's problem. Why do you think he got attacked? All he had to do was sit in the goddamned cab for ten minutes more, and make some excuse to old Hakayawa about his wife getting pregnant or something like that, and who would have cared? But not Craig, oh no! He had to run through the night and rescue a damsel in distress who didn't even exist, and end up with crushed *cojones*.'

Khryssa sat up in bed, piling her hair up in her hands, bare-breasted. She was 19¾ years of age and she looked like every man's dream. 'Do you know something, Steven,' she told him. 'That was what made Craig a man.'

Steven stood up. 'Fine, okay, fine. As I said, I'm trespassing. I'll go.'

But at that moment the lock clicked, very quietly. Then it clicked again, and again, and Khryssa remembered with rising panic that she had given Craig a key. He had returned it, by mail, after his 'accident,' with a confused letter about 'manhood' and 'betrayal'. But, of course, he

173

would have had a duplicate cut. He may not have been as dogged as Steven, but he had always been deeply methodical. The two of them stared frozen as the last lock-lever clicked, and the door swung open.

'Craig,' said Steven, 'this isn't what it looks like.'

Craig stepped into the loft and closed the door quietly behind him. He was wearing a dark, discreet suit and a charcoal-grey poloneck. He looked like Craig – and yet, in a peculiar way, he looked like somebody else, too, somebody they didn't know. He seemed shorter and stockier and coarser, and he walked with a strange slow-motion glide that reminded them of ballroom dancers, *Begin The Beguine*.

But his voice was unmistakably Craig's voice when he said, 'What *does* it look like, Steven? You tell me.'

'Hey – I had a heavy lunch with Chon International. I needed a couple of hours' rest before I went back to work.'

Craig came close up to him, and even though he appeared shorter than he had before, he was still a good three inches taller than Steven. 'Breathe on me,' he demanded.

'What? What are you talking about?'

'You heard. Breathe on me.'

'For Christ's sake, Craig, nothing happened here, believe me. I drank too much, I ate too much, I needed a rest . . . I remembered that Khryssa lived here in the neighbourhood.'

Craig half turned away, as if he were no longer interested. But then his right arm swung around so fast and hard that Steven didn't even see it coming, and he slapped Steven across the face so hard that he fell back onto the bed as if he had been struck by lightning.

'*Craig!*' screamed Khryssa, but Craig fixed her with such a nail-eyed look that she grabbed the blanket and pulled it

174

up around her and stared at him and said nothing else at all.

Craig stood over Steven and said, 'I trusted you.'

Steven struggled to sit up. 'For Christ's sake, you can trust me. Nothing happened.'

'You lied. You perjured yourself. You never ate Korean.'

'Who says I ate Korean?'

'Tell me one executive from Chon International who doesn't? Your breath should smell of *kim chee*. But what does it smell of? Tequila, my friend, that's all. Tequila, and Khryssa, and lies.'

Steven half-fell off the bed, but managed to get up on his feet. 'You listen to me, Craig. You were hurt, you were badly hurt, and everybody at Fisher & Bellman was sorry about that. I miss you. I need you. You're my partner, and I love your work. What did I say to you? Watching you reel in those juries is better than watching *A River Runs Through It*. But you've been gone, Craig . . . and life carries on. You can't expect Fisher & Bellman to wait for you, in suspended animation, any more than you can expect Khryssa to wait for you, in suspended animation. She's a young girl. She's got a life; and life goes on.'

Craig listened to all of this, and then said, 'You finished?' He turned to Khryssa, and his voice was oily with menace. Dark, but swirled with captivating rainbows.

'You didn't do this on purpose, did you, sweetheart? This was all a mistake.'

Khryssa nodded yes.

'You knew I was coming back to you, didn't you? I wrote you how much I cared for you.'

Yes, yes, you did.

'I was injured; you knew that. But you didn't doubt me, did you? Or did you? You knew that when I was well again, you knew that I'd come back.'

175

No nod. No nothing. Only a terrified stare.

Steven said, 'Come on, Craig, for Christ's sake. You're scaring the girl. You're scaring *me*.'

'Good,' said Craig. He turned around, and walked through to the kitchen area, and pulled open the cutlery drawer.

'What the hell are you doing?' Steven shouted at him.

'What the hell do you think I'm doing? You bet your ass that I wasn't there. I heard you. Well, you made a bet and you lost it. I *was* there. And now I want your ass.'

'Oh, come on, what is this? *The Merchant of Venice?*'

Craig reappeared and he was carrying upright in his right hand the largest-sized Sabatier carving knife. French tempered steel, a bright triangular shard of razor-sharp metal that could cut open a fillet steak like opening an envelope.

Steven backed away, his hands slowly rising to protect himself. 'Fuck, Craig. You don't know what you're doing.'

'I don't? I always thought I did. I always heard you praise my intellect; my acumen; the way I could cut right through to the heart of a problem, just like that. How about I cut through to the heart of this little problem, Steven?'

He raised the knife and Steven stumbled backwards but Khryssa screamed, '*No!*'

Craig immediately lowered the knife, and touched his forehead with his fingertips, as if he had a headache, or had just woken up from a daydream. Steven stayed where he was, tense, biting his lips, his eyes darting at Khryssa now and again. Khryssa cautiously began to move across the bed towards the telephone.

'The trouble is, you can't trust anybody these days,' Craig said, and his voice seemed quite different. 'You can't trust your girlfriend to wait for you. You can't trust your business partner to keep his hands off your girlfriend. You can't trust your wife to support you. You can't trust your friends. You can't even trust your enemies.'

'Put down the knife, Craig,' Steven said, trying to be soothing.

Craig looked up. 'Time was, people gave you their word, and you could rely on it. Not any more, though. Not any more.'

'Put down the knife, Craig,' Steven repeated.

Tuesday, June 29, 7:28 p.m.

Zaghlul Fuad drove up the ramp of the 51st Street garage and out through a cloud of steam into the street, turning right towards Lexington. He had hardly driven thirty feet before he was hailed from the front of Loew's New York Hotel by a tall, well-built man in a dark double-breasted suit and a poloneck. He pulled over to the kerb and the man climbed in.

'Think I'm okay for Pétrossian?' he asked.

'Pétrossian, what's that?' asked Zaghlul, drawing away from the kerb and stopping at the traffic signals.

'Don't you remember? It's a restaurant.'

'Okay, so it's a restaurant. Where's it at?'

'182 West 58th, close to Seventh Avenue. You don't remember that either?'

'Why should I remember? I never went there before.'

The man sat back. 'No, you didn't, you're right. You never went there. You're absolutely right.'

Zaghlul was about to turn around in his seat to see who the man was, but at that moment the signals changed and the car behind him was blaring its horn.

'At least it's not raining,' the man remarked.

'Raining?' Zaghlul laughed, shaking his head. 'It hasn't rained in two weeks. Not likely to, neither.'

'That's good. Maybe I can get there safely this time.'

Zaghlul spun the wheel flat-handed and the taxi swerved around a lumbering tractor-trailer and bounced across Park Avenue while the signals were changing. 'What are you talking about, safely?' he said. 'I always get everywhere safely.'

'You're quite an optimist, Zaghlul.'

Zaghlul frowned into his rear-view mirror, trying to see what his passenger looked like, but all he could see in the back seat was darkness, and the shape of a head.

'Have I picked you up before?' he asked the shape of a head.

'Sure, Zaghlul, you've picked me up before.'

'You remember names that much?'

'No-o-o, not particularly. Not genuine people. Not friends. But I do remember people who screw me: or put me down; or try to take advantage.'

'But you remember my name?'

The passenger leaned forward so that Zaghlul could smell alcohol and bittermints on his breath. 'I always remember a good name. Zaghlul Fuad, that's quite a name. How's your father, Zaghlul?'

'My father died.'

'Oh, that's right,' Craig whispered. 'I remember now. Your father died. Your father, who was not perfect, the same as you.'

They reached a red signal on Madison, and Zaghlul braked the taxi hard and turned around. 'Do I know you?' he demanded. His flower-pot hat was tilted at an angle. 'Who are you to say my father was anything at all?'

The man's face was craggy and handsome, but unnaturally handsome, like a dead Kennedy. 'You said it, Zaghlul. You were the one who said that your father wasn't perfect. He tried his best, like most of us do. But you – you never tried your best, did you, Zaghlul? You never tried to be helpful, when people needed you. You were always so goddamned right and everybody else was so goddamned wrong; and apologising didn't help, even when you were right, because you never accepted apologies, did you? You never understood stress. You never understood need. You never thought that you and this fucking cab could make all the difference between success and failure, between life and death, between a man being a man and a man being a eunuch. You never thought that, did you?'

'Hey, you wait a minute –' Zaghlul began, but the signals changed and the man said, 'Better get moving, Zaghlul. And better look the way you're going, don't you think?'

Zaghlul's fender collided with a trash-container at the side of the street, and he swerved and almost hit a stretch limo that was wallowing down the street right next to them, gleaming mysteriously with opera-lights and black-tinted windows.

'Shit!' he said. Then, 'Sorry; I apologise.'

The man shifted forward in his seat. 'Too late for apologies now, Zaghlul. The damage is done.'

Zaghlul pulled over to the kerb, and stopped. 'Listen, friend, I don't know what I ever did to you to make you feel this way, but whatever it is, it's all in the past, okay, and I just want you to exit my taxi.'

The man paused for a moment, his head tilted to one side, giving Zaghlul a slanted and provocative smile. 'This is a habit of yours, isn't it? You don't like one of your fares, you pull over and throw him out. Or her, too. I guess you throw out women as well, don't you, any woman you don't like, regardless of where you leave them?'

Zaghlul opened his door. 'I'm telling you, friend, either you get out of this taxi or I'm calling a cop.'

The man grunted in amusement. 'Oh . . . they'll come running soon enough. Once they know that you're dead.'

Zaghlul said, 'Please, friend, why don't we forget it, okay? Just get out, and you can have the ride for free. Let bygones be bygones – sweep them under the rug.'

'Forget it? How can I forget it? Don't you know what you did to me?'

Zaghlul said, 'I'm sorry. I don't know who you are. I don't have any idea what you want. I don't know you and I don't want to know you. Whatever you do, whoever you screw, that's your business. So let's call it quits on the fare, and shake hands, and forget it.'

The man thought for a while. Then he said, 'Okay . . . let's forget it. You don't remember one rainy night in March – March sixteenth, if we're going to be precise – when you told me to get out of your taxi because you didn't like the way I talked to you?'

Zaghlul shook his head. 'I don't remember that. I take thousands of fares, friend. I can't remember one from another.'

'You should remember me.'

'I don't think so. But if I upset you, I apologise.'

'You *will* remember me,' the man smiled; and with that he reached over the seat, yanked Zaghlul's head back, and drew his hand in front of Zaghlul's face like a cellist drawing his bow. The gesture was so effortless and elegant that Zaghlul himself didn't realise what had happened until blood cascaded wet and hot down the front of his Hawaiian shirt. He clutched his throat, and all he could feel was pumping arteries and sliced-open skin, like another mouth.

'You will remember the night you threw me out of your

180

cab when it was storming with rain; and I was mugged; and I was hurt; and I was hurt worse than you will ever be, Zaghlul. You fucking know-nothing, pock-faced Egyptian.'

Zaghlul couldn't speak; he couldn't breathe; he couldn't think. As Craig climbed out of the taxi and quietly closed the door, he dropped sideways onto the seat, and his flowerpot hat fell off, and blood ran in thin glutinous rivers onto the taxi's rubber mats. He had thought when he started out that the evening was sunny, when he first set out, but it seemed to be darkening all the time. Soon it was so dark that he thought that it must be time to go home.

He was sure that he could hear his father talking. In fact, he was talking louder and louder, so loud that Zaghlul could scarcely bear it.

'Zaghlul, didn't I tell you not to be so arrogant? You were always so arrogant! And now where are you?'

A woman tapped on Zaghlul's window and asked him if he could take her to Columbus Circle. Then she backed away.

He heard traffic; and hundreds of feet, pounding the sidewalks.

Tuesday, June 29, 11:11 p.m.

They called him many different names. Some of the younger kids called him The Prince. His close friends called him Up, because he was always wired. His mother called him Samuel, which was his given name. His father called him Useless, because he was, but not to the Aktuz, the gang who dominated the theatre district, preying on theatregoers and tourists and anybody else who happened along.

This evening he was preening his black mushroom-shaped coiffure in one of the dressing-rooms at the Lyceum, watched admiringly by his curly-haired girlfriend Scuzz (real name Susan) and his closest friend and body-guard Tyce (named for Mike Tyson, with whom he shared the same collar size.) Up was a frequent visitor backstage, both on- and off-Broadway, because he knew all the door-men and the security guards, and they humoured him because he gave them very little trouble, apart from strut-ting around like a vain and self-opinionated actor-man-ager, and because he was capable of giving them a great deal of very serious trouble if they didn't. Vandalised hoardings, ransacked dressing-rooms, and intimidated staff.

'Where we goin' tonight sweetheart?' Scuzz asked him.

'Au Bar,' said Up. 'Then maybe on to The China Club. Depend on my mood.'

'You're puttin' me on.'

'Sure, I'm puttin' you on. We goin' to Tony Roma for some ribs.'

Tyce said, 'Lookin' good tonight, man. You ought to audition.'

Up swivelled this way and that way, turning up the col-lar of his coat and pouting at himself. 'I don't need no audition. One day they goin' to be lookin' for a new Othello, and they goin' to come beggin' on they hands and knees. "Be sure of it; give me the oracular proof." '

Tyce applauded. 'You got it, man. You could hold that stage any time you want.'

'I told you. They'll come beggin' on they hands and knees.'

He took out a cigarette and Tyce instantly reached out to light it. At that moment, however, there was a sharp knock at the dressing-room door.

182

'What you want?' Tyce demanded. 'Private party goin' on here.'

'Looking for somebody name of Up.'

'What for?' asked Tyce. He glanced at Up, and then reached into his black leather coat and took out a switchblade knife.

'Special delivery.'

Tyce said, 'Special delivery of what?'

'Don't ask me. I only deliver.'

Up stepped cautiously towards the door. The Aktuz had recently suffered some vicious run-ins with a neighbouring gang of Puerto Ricans, the Red Scorpions, who hung around the Port Authority Bus Terminal snatching purses and luggage. Two Aktuz had been stabbed last week, one seriously, and it was well known that the Red Scorpions had put a price on Up. Any Scorpion who brought back Up's scalp back to the lair would be rewarded with all the crack he could carry.

'That ain't no greaseball,' Tyce whispered.

'So what? They could have paid a ghost.'

Up drew back his long black coat and lifted out the hammer that hung in a loop from the lining.

'Okay you can come in now. But take it slow.'

Tyce opened the door with his left hand, holding up the switchblade in his right. There was a moment's pause, and then a tall white man stepped in, with one arm held behind his back. He didn't look like the kind of man who delivered packages for a living. He was dressed in a dark expensive suit and a charcoal-grey cotton poloneck.

'Are you Up?' he asked, still keeping his arm behind his back.

'Maybe I is and maybe I ain't. Who want to know?'

'I do. I've been looking for you. You're a difficult man to find.'

'What you holdin' in back of yourself, man.'

'I told you. Special delivery.'

The tension in the dressing-room was quickly rising. Scuzz moved back towards the corner, and her chair made a teeth-edging squeak on the floor. Tyce sprang his knife and the double-edged blade winked and sparkled in the intense light from the dressing-room mirror.

'You better lay that special delivery down on the floor,' said Up.

The man shook his head. 'I'm sorry, I can't do that. I have to lay this on you personally.'

Up rhythmically slapped his hammer-head in the palm of his hand. 'You tired of being conscious, man? I said to lay it on the floor.'

Tyce gave a toothy, exaggerated grin. 'You ever see what a hammer like that can do to a person?'

The man turned and stared at him seriously. 'Yes, I have, as a matter of fact. But I never saw what a hammer like *this* could do to a person.'

Without warning, he twisted his arm out from behind his back, and before Tyce could raise his hand to defend himself, he had whirled a long-handled sledgehammer round in the air, and knocked Tyce straight in the face with it.

Tyce's nose burst apart, and his upper jawbone broke in half with an audible crack. He fell backward, toppled over his chair, and collapsed in the corner, one leg twitching, his eyes rolled up into his head.

Up crouched down, and swung his hammer in a vicious criss-cross pattern, almost as if he were sword-fighting.

'You want me, man. You better say you prayers.'

The man remained completely expressionless. He lifted the sledgehammer and brought it down so hard on Up's right wrist that his hammer flew across the room. Up

184

screamed out in pain, and staggered back towards the dressing-table. The man swung the sledgehammer again, and hit him on the shoulder, a blow that broke his collar-bone. Up lifted his hand, trying to protect himself, but the man hit him in the chest – once, twice, three times, and each time they could hear his ribs cracking.

Up fell back against the mirror. The man hit him on the forehead. The mirror smashed into hundreds of brightly-lit fragments, and the front of Up's skull caved in.

The man beat him and beat him, again and again, destroying both him and the mirror. He went on beating him long after he was dead – long after his bombastic pompadour had been reduced to a mash of blood and hair and bone-fragments and jellyish brain. One eye looked accusingly out of his squashed face, but apart from that it was almost impossible to tell that he was human.

Scuzz cowered in the corner and her face was as white as the wall.

'Don't hurt me,' she begged him.

The man stood over her, hefting the sledgehammer in both hands. 'You don't remember me, do you?' he asked her.

Mutely, she shook her head.

'You don't remember the K-Plus Drugstore on 48th Street, one rainy night in March?'

She looked completely baffled.

' "Help me, help me," ' he mimicked. ' "My friend's being raped." '

Still she couldn't remember. Too much dope, he thought to himself. Too few brain cells. She had no more intelligence than a housebound mongrel.

He turned away.

'I won't tell no one,' Scuzz whimpered. 'I swear to God I won't tell no one.'

185

'You promise?' he asked her, with his back to her.
'I swear to God.'

Wednesday, June 30, 11:29 a.m.

When Effie came downstairs, Pepper was already waiting for her in the hotel entrance hall, flicking through a copy of *Architectural Digest*. She was wearing a maroon kaftan and black broad-brimmed hat with maroon ostrich feathers in it. And a huge ungainly woven bag lay on the floor beside her like a slumbering dog.

Effie said, 'I'm sorry, Pepper. I'm not sure that I can go. Craig just called. His partner was found dead this morning. Somebody stabbed him.'

'Oh, you're kidding! That's just awful. Do they know how it happened?'

'The police didn't tell him very much, only that he was found in some girl's apartment. The girl was murdered, too.'

'God, that's terrible. You don't feel like you're safe anywhere any more.'

'Craig's calling me back later to tell me what he's doing.'

'Let's take a raincheck,' said Pepper, laying a hand on her arm. 'Really. You won't feel like doing any psychic stuff today.'

'No, I do,' said Effie; and she did. She was beginning to feel that her life was being swept away, like a paper boat in a storm drain. Valhalla, Gaby, and now this. She needed to do something positive to bring her destiny back under control. 'It's just that Craig said that he might want me back in the city.'

Pepper looked at her watch. 'If you really want to go, we

186

won't take very long; no more than an hour. Why don't you leave a message at the desk?'

'Well, I guess,' said Effie. She thought for a moment. She knew that Craig was distressed. She was distressed, herself, even though she hadn't liked Steven from the moment that Craig had first introduced him. He may have been a balding, boring, out-and-out chauvinist; but he was a human being; and somebody had once been sufficiently in love to conceive him, and give birth to him, and bring him up. However unappealing anybody had been, it was always tragic when they died too young.

But she thought of her future; and Valhalla; and she said, 'Okay,' and went to the desk and rang the bell.

'Was he a close friend of yours, Craig's partner?' Pepper asked her, leaning against the desk.

Effie crossed her fingers. 'He and Craig were like *this*. Inseparable. Craig had known him since law school. I know I shouldn't speak ill of the dead, but I never liked him very much. He was always so pushy. I don't think that Craig would have been so aggressive if it hadn't have been for Steven. Apart from that, he was always making eyes at me, following me into the kitchen at parties. One of those guys who can never keep their hands to themselves.'

'I know the kind. I used to call them octopi until I found out how intelligent octopi are. They say that octopi could write poetry except that their ink keeps running.' She paused, and then she said. 'Joke. Except that it's almost true.'

Wendy O'Brien the innkeeper came out and Effie asked her to take any messages from Craig.

'Are you all right, Mrs Bellman?' Wendy O'Brien frowned at her. 'You're looking a little pale, if you'll forgive me for saying so.'

'I'm fine,' Effie assured her. Pepper took hold of her

187

hand, and squeezed it; and Effie suddenly realised that she had made a very close friend.

They drove through the trees and up past Red Oaks Inn. The sky was filled with huge, creamy cumulus clouds, as if the whole of Georgia's cotton crop had been lifted up and carried north-east by the wind, on its way to Labrador, or who knew where. Effie said, 'Norman told us you used to work for the Berrymans.'

Pepper smiled. 'Oh, yes. They were great, the Berrymans. I think they probably came from another planet, because I never met Earth people so nice. They had that unearthly quality about them, don't you think, like people in the *The Twilight Zone* or *This Island Earth* or one of those old fifties science-fiction movies.'

'We probably saw each other, back then,' said Effie. 'My father used to take me here for brunch, as a special treat.'

She smiled at the memory. 'I used to look through the stained-glass window, do you remember that? They had a stained-glass window in the front door. I used to look through it, and I could see people walking about, people who weren't really there.'

'*What?*' said Pepper.

They were driving through water, in a sizzle of spray.

'I saw people in the window, in the coloured glass.'

'Which colour, in particular?'

'The red. It was always the red. But why? They weren't real, were they?'

'The *red*, for God's sake,' said Pepper.

'What's wrong with that? It was only imagination. There was nobody there. I used to open the door and look out of it, and there was never anybody there.'

Pepper said, 'You weren't to know it, but red is the only colour of the spectrum through which you can perceive

188

parallel reality.'

'What does that mean?'

'Well, let's put it this way. Some people think that time is like a continuous line . . . and we're all moving along it like driving down some long highway that goes off towards the horizon like an endless ribbon. But other people think it loops in a circle, which means that one day, we're going to be doing the same thing all over again. Eternal recurrence, that's what Nietszche called it. Poor old Nietzsche, so misunderstood. So *misinterpreted,* but aren't we all? And then some people think that time is like a loop, a Moebius strip; and other people think that it goes fast or slow.

'But time isn't like that at all. Time isn't linear; and it isn't sequential. Everything that ever happened is simultaneous. You were born today. You graduated today. You met your husband today. You grew old today. You died. Everything happens at once. It's only the way you perceive it that makes it seem like one thing happens after another.'

'I don't understand you at all,' said Effie. 'I know what happened yesterday; but yesterday's gone, I've lived through it, and now it's gone. How can it still be there?'

'It's there because it's there. That's all. Didn't it *feel* real, when you lived through it?'

'Of course it did.'

'It felt real because it *is* real. Life is just like a book, that's what you don't understand. That's what nobody understands. Life is like a book because it's all there, all in one piece. The beginning, the middle and the end, and you can pick it up at any time, wherever you want. You can read the end of *Gone With The Wind* . . . "After all, tomorrow is another day" . . . and then you can go right back to the beginning . . . "Scarlett O'Hara was not beautiful" . . . or anyplace else you like, the dead man's head bumping down the stairs and Melanie covering her ears, Atlanta burning . . . Atlanta *before* it was burnt . . . it all happens *now*. Like, there isn't any "yesterday". Why should there be? It wasn't "yesterday" when you were living it, was it? Just like we're driving up this road now. Are we driving "yesterday"? We'll think we were, tomorrow. But "yesterday" we were driving up here "tomorrow." '

'I think I lost you about three sentences ago,' laughed Effie.

'No, you didn't. Because you looked through the red glass and you saw people who weren't really there. The point was, they *were* there. Or they *had* been there, at one time. If you look through red glass, you can see things that were; and things that are going to be.'

'You mean, when I saw that man crossing the parking-lot –'

'Outside the Red Oaks Inn, when you were a child? Yes . . . that was somebody from the past, or maybe the future.'

Effie shook her head. 'I don't believe it. I *can't* believe it.'

Pepper laid a hand on her sleeve. 'It doesn't matter, so long as you know about it.'

They drove on towards the gates of Valhalla. 'Maybe this is a bad idea,' said Effie. She was beginning to feel deeply disturbed; not only by what had happened, but by Pepper's interpretation of it. If she understood Pepper correctly, she was saying that your entire life happened simultaneously, that, and that all you did was move forward from one sequence to the next, like reading a book. But if the past still existed, did that mean you could also move *back*?

Pepper said, 'You'd be surprised how many good things happen as the result of bad ideas.'

Valhalla lay under the shadow of a large cloud, which made it look unnaturally dark and forbidding. Ravens wheeled around its chimney stacks.

'Norman used to love coming here, when he was a boy. I never liked the house itself, but I love the location, don't you? It's so wild and so weird. Did you ever read *Tanglewood Tales*? "The border between the seen and the unseen." It makes me shiver!'

They drove up to the headless statue and climbed out of the car. Pepper dragged her big woven bag out of the boot and hefted it up the steps. Effie sorted through Craig's key ring until she found the right key, and opened up the front doors.

As they stepped into the hallway, a pigeon suddenly burst from its perch on the balcony and fluttered furiously around the ceiling. They both jumped in fright.

Although they could see bright blue sky through the broken windows, the hallway was shadowy and cold. Pepper put down her bag and opened it up, rummaging through books and bottles and rattles and tins and extraordinary hanks of hair and vegetable-dyed rags. At last she produced a dried-up hazel twig, a slender fork in the shape of a wide Y; a greenish copper salt-shaker; and an amber glass jar.

'Essence of lilies,' she explained. 'I thought I'd bring some along.'

'What's that supposed to do?' asked Effie.

'The lily is the flower of the moon. It brings madness, the same way the moon brings madness. Essence of lily is very good for quietening places where psychic vibrations have gotten out of hand. It disrupts the nexus, turns the vibrations in on themselves, stands logic on its head.'

She twisted her wrists around and took hold of each branch of her hazel twig.

'Where did you *learn* all of this?' asked Effie, with a smile.

Pepper slowly swung the hazel from left to right, and

back again. 'My parents left me, after Woodstock. I talked to shamans and witches and all kinds of people. Some of them were crazy. Some of them were *very* crazy. But between them, they taught me so many things. How to make candles in the shape of human hands, the Hand of Glory, so that I could find treasure. How to throw horseshoes over my shoulder, to stop the Devil from following me. They taught me all about vegetables and herbs and the magic pantry. It doesn't work, most of it. But some of it really does; and when it does, it's incredible. It blows your socks off.'

She paused, feeling the twig. Then she said, 'There's a twitch here, but nothing too much. Let's move on.'

'A twitch?'

'It's like somebody trembling . . . here, feel it. It's like somebody trying to pull your hands away.'

Effie touched the twig, and it was quivering. Electric, erectile, like the tail of a dog on heat.

'It's incredible,' she said. 'How does it work?'

'Hazel picks up psychic disturbance the same way that iron attracts lightning. But it doesn't work for everybody. You have to be very passive. You have to think *inward* rather than *outward,* if you understand what I mean. You have to encourage the vibrations to enter your head, welcome them in, and not many people can do that.'

She walked across the hallway until she reached the door, pausing every now and then to make sure that she was following the strongest of the psychic currents. 'You remember *Ghost Busters*? They would never have found any psychic phenomena. They were far too aggressive. You can't hunt down a memory, or a feeling of regret, or a moment of terror. They're too elusive, too faint. They exist right on the very edge of yesterday, or in the very first suggestion of tomorrow.'

192

Effie thought that Pepper was beginning to sound very much too Aquarian, but she didn't say so. She could see the hazel frantically quivering, and nobody could have made it do that simply by shaking it. Every now and then, it twitched upward, quite violently, as if somebody had flicked it, and when it did so, Pepper let out a little gasp of effort. 'It's strong here . . . I never felt anything so strong before.'

'What do you think it is?'

'Right here, in this corridor, it's movement, it's almost certainly human movement. I get the feeling of lots of very excited people, rushing along the corridor towards the ballroom. They're rushing along here all the time, a stream of them. They're excited. Frightened too. I get this feeling of delicious dread, like they're all hurrying to see something really terrible.'

The hazel twitched upward again and again, and each time it twitched up further. Soon it was rearing up so high that Effie couldn't understand how it didn't snap.

Pepper began to walk faster. 'There's so much panic,' she said. Her face was drained of colour and her eyes were wide. 'There's so much *fear*! They don't want to see it, but they don't want to miss it, either!'

By the time they reached the ballroom, they were practically running. The doors were closed, and they stopped in front of them. Effie had the irrational feeling that beyond there was nothing but a vacuum, and that if they opened them up, they would be sucked into absolute emptiness. Her feeling of terror was so strong that she could hear her heart beating like somebody wildly beating a cushion with a stick.

'Oh my God,' said Pepper. 'I can hardly hold it.'

The hazel had bent back so far that it was pointing at the runic medallion that hung around her neck. Effie took

193

hold of her arm and she could feel the effort that Pepper was having to make just to keep the twig from flying out of her hands. All the same, it didn't crack, didn't even splinter.

'What is it?' she asked, aghast. 'Why is it bending itself back like that?'

'I can't – it won't – it *refuses*!'

'What do you mean it refuses? *Pepper!* It's only a twig, and you're holding it!'

Pepper stared at her with those glittering silver eyes, swallowing hard. 'I mean that *I* won't go any further. Not in there. I can't.'

She hesitated for one more moment, and then she flung the twig away from her, across the corridor, as if she had suddenly seen an earwig crawling up it. It fell beneath one of the windows, and gradually unbent itself.

'Pepper,' said Effie, 'what is it? What's wrong?'

'I don't know,' she trembled. She was shaking, and she kept anxiously rubbing her arm. 'Whatever it is, I can't face it. It's far too strong . . . it's so much stronger than it ever was before. Maybe it's me, maybe it's you. I don't know. But if you could feel what I felt –'

Effie glanced at the twig. 'Maybe I should try.'

'No, don't. You probably wouldn't feel anything, but you never know. You may be more sensitive than you think.'

'But what was it?'

'It was like a *darkness* . . . a kind of *emptiness*. I can't describe it. I just felt that something totally grotesque was going on.'

Effie bit her lip. She didn't know what to think about any of this. There was obviously something wrong here at Valhalla, but was it really 'psychic vibration'? She enjoyed Pepper's mysticism, her magic pantry and her lexicon of spells, but could Pepper really give her a rational explana-

194

tion of what was happening, so that they could exorcise it, or whatever they had to do? She was beginning to feel that the answers to her problems would be found in the real world, rather than the world of spirits and dreams and hedge-magic.

'You don't want to try again?' she asked Pepper.

Pepper shook her head. 'I'm sorry, Effie. I didn't want to let you down. But –' she looked towards the closed ballroom doors and her eyes said it all. 'There's *dread* in there, Effie. You don't have any idea.'

Effie shook her head. 'You haven't let me down, I promise. I'll just have to talk to Craig about it, and see what he thinks.'

'You're going to tell Craig?'

'What else can I do?'

'But that feeling you had, that you *shouldn't* tell him about it. I wouldn't ignore that feeling, if I were you.'

'I have to do *something*. I can't think of living here, the way it is, no matter what's wrong with it.'

'Effie . . . a woman from another time was appealing to you. . . . begging you not to tell him. Don't you think that you ought to respect that appeal, at least for now? At least until you find out *why* she doesn't want you to tell him.'

Effie said, 'I'm very confused. I really am.'

Pepper looked quickly at the ballroom doors. 'We ought to go.'

But Effie stayed where she was, thinking. There had to be some rational explanation for all of this – for the sobbing woman and the man on the stairs. *Gut ist der Schlaf . . . der Tod ist besser.*

'You really can't do any more?' she asked Pepper.

Pepper said, 'I'm sorry.' She clasped her hand against her forehead as if she had a headache. 'It makes me feel as if I'm just about to die.'

'I just want to know what it *is*? You say there's dread in here, but what does that mean? *Dread?*'

'Effie, leave it.'

But Effie, in frustration, pushed the doors wide open. She wasn't sucked into oblivion. There was no vacuum, no darkness. Only the stately gloom of the ballroom, with the clogged-up light from the glass dome high above it, and the pillars and the balcony.

And then – in the blink of an eye – she was right in the centre of the floor, and the lights suddenly brightened, and she was dancing. She couldn't think how she had got there, or why she was dancing. She couldn't hear music at first, but then she could. It was Strauss, and she hated Strauss, but she couldn't stop dancing. She went around and around the floor, and all she could see was a circling blur of pillars and lights and blurry faces.

Because there were *people* here, the ballroom was crowded with people.

She was so startled that she couldn't catch her breath. She felt as if she had suddenly stepped into the ocean, out of her depth. She twisted her head around, trying to see where Pepper was, but all she could see were pale, unfocused faces. She tried to stop herself from dancing, but strong male arms enclosed themselves around her and swept her away, and she turned back in amazement to see that she was dancing with a tall man in white tie and tails. She could feel the grasp of his warm, white-gloved hands. She could feel his pristine shirt-front. He danced with power and rhythm, and there was nothing she could do but follow him wherever he led.

She tried to focus on his face, but even though they were dancing they were dancing so close, all she could see were dark smudgy eyes and a wide grinning mouth. It was like trying to look at him through a pane of glass smeared with

196

Vaseline.

'Stop,' she tried to say, as he circled the floor for a second time. Her voice sounded flat and plugged-up, and she wasn't certain that she had managed to speak at all.

But the man didn't stop and he didn't reply, either. He kept on dancing to that damned Strauss and everybody watched them as they spun and swayed.

Effie thought that she could hear the people making a dull, baying sound, but it hardly sounded like people at all. They could have been pigs and donkeys dressed up in tails and evening-gowns. She was reminded of some nightmarish nursery-rhyme world, in which animals wore clothes and hats and disdainfully squinted at their human inferiors through monocles, even though they were still just as bestial and dangerous underneath.

'*Stop, you're hurting me!*' Effie pleaded. But the man continued to sweep her around, with that same irresistible rhythm, and that stretched, almost lunatic grin. What was worse, he *was* hurting her. He was crushing her fingers together with his right hand, while his left hand seemed to dig into her back. And as her perception heightened, she became conscious of something else, too. A sharp, agonising pricking in the soles of her feet. She tried to break her stride and to pull herself free, but she couldn't – not only because she wasn't strong enough, but because she was just as much caught up in the waltz as he was. She felt as if she were dancing on sharpened kitchen knives, and every step made her calf muscles spasm because she knew that it was going to hurt so much. Yet, madly, she carried on dancing, even when she thought she felt blood on her ankles.

The man said, in a deep, indistinct voice, '*I bet them that you would waltz for me.*'

Effie said, 'What? What did you say?'

'*I bet them that you would waltz for me, barefoot, on broken glass.*'

197

'What do you mean? Who are you? What do you mean?'

'I said that you would do anything for me . . . and one of them said, I bet she wouldn't dance for you, barefoot, on broken glass. But here you are, my darling. Here you are!'

'What?' screamed Effie. But the man didn't repeat himself. He swept her round again, and laughed; and the people in the ballroom laughed, too, that hideous sub-human baying. The man turned to the people in the ballroom and lifted his hand in triumph – and in that one instant when he was acknowledging the applause of his admirers, and the waltz momentarily paused, Effie at last managed to twist herself out of the man's embrace, and stop. When she stopped, the music died away, too, disintegrating into discordant squeaks and scrapes and spasmodic drumbeats. The lights dimmed all around the room, until they gave off nothing but a sickly, intermittent flicker. The man stood in shadow, his arms by his sides. She couldn't see his face but she could tell by the way that his shoulders were hunched and his fists were clenched that he was angry with her. Not just angry. Quaking with rage.

For the first time, she looked down at the floor. It was littered with broken champagne glasses, slices and shards and shattered stems. Then she looked down at her feet. At first she thought that she was wearing scarlet socks, but then she realised that her feet were bare, and that the broken glass had cut thin bloody curves into her heels and her soles, and that the top of one of her big toes had been almost completely sliced off, like the top of a boiled egg. She felt chilled with shock. She stood where she was, shaking, and she didn't know what to do.

The man approached her. It was too dark for her to see his face, and besides she didn't want to. *'I bet that you would happily waltz for me,* The Blue Danube, *barefoot, on broken glass. Look how many glasses I've broken for you, and all of them the finest French crystal.'*

He reached out with the finger and thumb of his left hand as if he were going to tilt her chin up, so that she would *have* to look at him. But as he did so, Effie bit into his finger, hard, and she heard him bellow in pain and devastating fury.

She twisted herself away, and at the same time she felt an extraordinary wrench, like somebody pushing her too quickly through a revolving door. She stumbled, and lifted up her hands to save herself in case she fell, but then she realised that she was still outside the ballroom, in daylight. Pepper was only two or three feet away, bending over to retrieve her hazel twig.

'I –' she started; but she couldn't find the words. She stared into the ballroom with a mixture of fear and astonishment. For one split second, she could understand why people went mad.

'What's the matter?' Pepper asked her. She held her hazel wrapped in a yellow Nepalese scarf, so that she would be insulated from any psychic vibrations.

'I thought that I was – *dancing*,' Effie breathed.

'You were standing right there,' said Pepper, perplexed.

'No, no, I was right inside the ballroom and it was full of people in evening dress and I was dancing.'

Pepper came up to her and looked her straight in the face, her silver eyes darting from side to side like restless fish, looking for clues, looking for reality. 'You mean it, don't you?' she said. 'You're telling the truth.'

Effie's self-possession began to dissolve, and her eyes were suddenly crowded with tears. 'I just opened the doors, and there I was, right in the centre of the ballroom, dancing with this tall dark man. The whole room was filled with people, I swear it. I could hear them. I could see them. And they were playing *The Blue Danube*.'

Pepper took hold of her hands. 'Did you see any faces? Did you see who any of these people were?'

Effie, her mouth crumpled in misery, shook her head. 'I thought they looked like animals, dressed up. They made a noise like animals. It was horrible.'

'My God, you're sensitive all right,' said Pepper. 'You're so damned sensitive you don't even need a hazel twig.'

'But it was horrible. It was so horrible. I felt a pain in my feet and I looked down and I didn't have any shoes on, and I'd been dancing on broken glass. And there was so much blood. And the man said – the man said –'

'Hey, come on, honey,' said Pepper, wiping her eyes for her. 'This wasn't real. None of this was real.'

Effie swallowed. 'He said that he'd made a bet that I would dance for him, dance for him happily, on broken glass.'

Pepper said nothing for a moment, then held her close, shushing her and patting her on the back. After a while, though, Effie pulled away. 'What was it?' she asked. 'How could anything like that happen?'

'I told you. It's a psychic vibration. I felt it, but you actually saw it. You were actually part of it. You must be acutely sensitive, Effie; and whatever vibrations there are in this house, they must be very powerful. I never knew such power.' She leaned cautiously into the open ballroom door, and sniffed. 'Christ, you can even smell it, can't you? That smell like scent, and thunderstorms, all mixed together.'

'What are we going to do? I can't possibly live here if that kind of thing keeps happening to me. I'd go out of my mind.'

'The first thing we can do is go find ourselves a stiff drink,' Pepper suggested. 'After that, I'd better start thinking about a full psychic cleansing – floor by floor, room by room. That's going to be difficult, and it could be very

200

dangerous too.'

'Is that like an exorcism?'

'Unh-hunh. An exorcism is supposed to send demons back to hell, or unquiet spirits off to join their relatives in heaven. But exorcisms don't work because you can't exorcise something that doesn't exist in the first place. Did you ever see a demon? Do you *know* anybody who ever saw a demon?

'No, a psychic cleansing is totally different because the psychic vibrations come from people who lived *right here*. You can't send them back anywhere, to heaven or to hell, mainly because there's no such place and also because they belong here, they didn't just live here "yesterday", they live here now, and they're going to be living here tomorrow . . . the same way you will, too.

'The Bible was right about one thing. People are immortal. They're always being born, they're always growing up, they're always growing old. Time isn't, like, an endless ribbon. It's a series of locations. It's walking from place to place, from street to street.'

'But if these people belong here, how can we get rid of them?'

Pepper rubbed her eyebrow with the heel of her hand. She was looking tired. 'We don't get rid of them. We just find a way to keep them in their place. Anyway, let's get out of here.'

Effie took one last nervous look into the ballroom, then she started to follow Pepper along the corridor. At once felt sharp, slicing pains in her feet; and she stopped, in horror.

'*Pepper!*' she called. '*Pepper! My feet!*'

She was still wearing her white rope-soled deck-shoes. But the canvas was heavily soaked in dark red blood, and there were spatters of blood on her ankles. She felt ragingly hot, and then cold, and her head felt swimmy. She

201

leaned against the panelling for support, but she was sure that she was going to faint. Pepper came jangling up to her in her beads and her bells and held onto her before she could fall.

'My feet,' she whimpered. 'Oh God, Pepper, my feet.' She kept thinking about her big toe, and how the top of it had been sliced almost completely off.

Pepper said, 'Sit down. Sit right here. I'll go to the car and call for help. Don't try to take your shoes off, whatever you do.'

Effie awkwardly but carefully sat herself down on the floor. 'I'm okay,' she told Pepper. 'I'm okay.'

But when Pepper ran off to call for the paramedics, tears started to roll down her cheeks, and then she sobbed, with clenched fists, until she felt that she was going to break in half. All she could think about was the pain in her feet, and that terrible frightening waltz, and Craig swearing '*Bitch!*' at her every time they made love, and his hideous incomprehensible obsession with Valhalla.

Her feet bled inside her shoes, she could feel the wetness welling between her toes. She tilted her head back against the wall and sobbed and sobbed, until at last she stopped, from sheer exhaustion.

It was only when she heard Pepper running back that she realised what she had sounded like, when she was sobbing. She sounded like the woman in the blue-carpeted bedroom, exactly. The same desperation; the same inconsolable sadness. She bit the edge of her hand to stop herself. She was hurt, and she was shocked, but she wasn't going to allow herself to go right over the edge. She wasn't going to be part of whatever was happening, here in Valhalla, this psychic vibration, this haunting.

Pepper hunkered down beside her. 'I called for an ambulance. They won't take too long. They said to keep your shoes on, just for now.'

Effie tried to smile. 'I'm okay. Really, I'm quite okay.'

'I think I made a slight error,' Pepper admitted. 'This *is* real, isn't it, this psychic vibration? It's actually intruding on us physically.' She held Effie's hand and squeezed it. 'You ought to stay away from Valhalla, Effie. Stay well away. I always thought this house had a bad feeling about it . . . but, Jesus.'

'Don't worry,' Effie told her. 'I've made up my mind. Craig can buy Valhalla if he wants to, but not with any of my money; and he needn't expect me to live here.'

'Are you serious?' Pepper asked her.

Effie didn't reply, but rested her head back against the wall, and sat there quietly conserving her newly-discovered strength until she heard the whooping of an ambulance siren echoing across the derelict tennis courts.

Wednesday, June 30, 10:18 p.m.

He burst into the room as if demons were after him. 'Effie! Jesus Christ! What happened?'

She was lying on her bed at the Pig Hill Inn reading a slew of glossy magazines which Wendy O'Brien had brought up for her: *Vanity Fair* and *Architectural Digest* and *Vogue*. On the nightstand, there was a half-finished mug of hot chocolate and home-made cookies. Effie had washed her hair and her head was wrapped in a towel turban. Her feet, in their bandages, looked the same. She was very white: waxy-candle white, but she looked – and felt – very composed.

'I told you,' she said, trying to smile. 'I cut my feet on some broken glass.'

203

He sat down on the edge of the bed. He was gripping a bunch of yellow roses as if they were a weapon. 'What broken glass? *Here*, at the inn? We could sue them!'

'I went to Valhalla with Pepper Moriarty. There was broken glass in the ballroom.'

'I don't understand. You went to Valhalla with Pepper Moriarty? For why?'

'She's a sensitive, Craig. I wanted to find out what was going on there. I wanted to exorcise it, if I could. Cleanse it. There's something badly wrong with Valhalla, Craig, something really abnormal, believe me.'

'Taking some crackpot like her around it, trying to play exorcists? Come on, Effie. Be serious. These are the 1990s, not the 1790s.'

'Well . . . I'm not so sure about that. I'm not sure *what* these are,' said Effie; and managed to look at Craig strongly and steadily. There was a long, oblique pause between them. She knew now that they were no longer partners but combatants.

'So how did you cut your feet?' he asked her. 'Weren't you wearing shoes?'

'Of course I was . . . in the 1990s.'

'What does that mean?'

'I think it means that I cut them some other time, when I wasn't wearing shoes.'

'Some other time? When? I don't understand.'

'Why are you so impatient with me? Why do you keep trying to suggest that I'm talking nonsense? I cut my feet when I was dancing barefoot in the ballroom, with a man in evening dress. The ballroom was crowded with people; the orchestra was playing *The Blue Danube*.'

Craig smacked his forehead with the flat of his hand. 'Effie – I don't know what this Pepper Moriarty's been telling you, but I've had it up to here. Steven was

204

murdered. They cut his throat and made him look like a Happy Face. I'm in shock. I'm in grief. I'm mourning here, can you understand that? And you cut your feet because you weren't sensible enough to wear shoes and you blame it on some fantasy. Some goddamned psychic crap.'

'I'm really sorry about Steven. But that doesn't alter what happened. I'm asking you to believe me, Craig. I really need you to believe me.'

He suddenly smiled, shrugged, changed his expression. 'Listen . . . hey, I didn't mean to come on aggressive. I'm still kind of shaken by Steven, that's all.'

She reached out and held his hand. 'Me too. It doesn't matter how he died; and it doesn't matter that I didn't particularly like him. I still didn't want to see him dead.' She rotated his wedding-band around his finger. 'I just want you to do something for me.'

'Oh, yes?'

'I want you to visit Valhalla with Pepper Moriarty, so that she can show you what it's really like. I want you to experience those psychic vibrations for yourself.'

'With a view to what?'

She pressed his hand tight. 'With a view to not buying it, Craig. I don't want that house, and I don't want you to buy that house.'

'I paid the deposit already. We've agreed a price.'

She was shocked. 'What? When?'

'I called Walter Van Buren from the office. He said that Fulloni & Jahn were prepared to accept two-point-five. I said two or nothing; and they agreed. I mean, what could I do? I called you to discuss it but you weren't here. They're drawing the papers up now.'

'You've agreed to buy Valhalla and you've paid the deposit and you haven't even discussed it with me?' Effie felt as if she had

been abruptly immersed in a tub of chilled water.

Craig gave her a boyish pout. 'I had to. Fulloni & Jahn said that, for that price, they had to have an immediate decision. What else could I do?'

'You could have said *no*,' said Effie, in a high voice, and now she was really quaking.

'I couldn't say no.'

'*Why not?*' she screamed at him. '*I hate the place! I don't want it! I'm scared of it, and I hate it, and I won't even set one foot in it, ever again!*'

She paused for breath, her eyes filled with tears. Spots of blood were beginning to show through the bandages on her feet. 'You've agreed to pay two million dollars for it? Two million dollars is more than everything we own, everything we've ever saved, everything.'

'We can manage,' he said. 'You know we can manage. When the partnership's sold –'

'Who to? Steven can't buy you out – he's dead. How can you sell a law firm that doesn't have any lawyers?'

'We can manage,' he repeated, doggedly. He was staring at the model on the cover of *Vogue* as if he could happily kill her. 'I can make plenty of money here and there . . . you'll see.'

Effie looked at him for a long time and didn't know whether she hated him or whether she felt sorry for him. She cursed those hoodlums who had hit him with a hammer; but it was too late for that; and later than she even knew. 'Let me tell you something, Craig,' she said, 'what's ours is half mine, and you can't touch my half of anything without my permission. Call Walter Van Buren first thing tomorrow, and tell him you made a mistake.'

'Norman's ordered the roof tiles already, and five thousand dollars' worth of joists.'

'*Well tell him to fucking un-order them!*' Effie screeched.

206

Craig recoiled from her, but only slightly. Then he smiled. For Effie, that was the most frightening thing that he could have done, because it meant that no matter how much she protested, he was absolutely convinced that he was going to have his own way.

That night, when she was still sleeping, drugged with paracetamol, he dragged up her nightdress, spread her thighs, and pushed himself into her. He woke her up when he started thrusting; but she lay back with her eyes closed, floppy and unresponsive, because she didn't want him to think that she needed him, or that she liked him. She was conscious of every grunt; and when he finally ejaculated she could feel his semen running out of her. But she still feigned sleep. She nearly *was* asleep: she kept sliding in and out of dreams and unconsciousness and wakefulness and pain. But she didn't want to give him the satisfaction of knowing what she felt; or that he had actually excited her.

She turned over onto her side and listened to him snore. It was strange, but she was sure that he had smelled different. Nothing to do with deodorant, or aftershave. A different body-smell. Slightly oilier, somehow; and a different feel, too. Smoother – and again, oilier.

There was something else, too. She was sure that she had felt *two* testicles swinging against her when he had been thrusting himself into her. He couldn't have sneakily undergone a prosthetic operation in the two days that he had been back in the city; he wouldn't have healed yet; and he would have told her, wouldn't he? She had probably made a mistake. Too shocked, too exhausted, far too sedated. She tried to sleep but she kept thinking of dancing on broken champagne glasses, and the man with the blurry face, and in the end there was nothing she could do but huddle herself close while the sun rose behind the floral curtains and the birds started to twitter; her feet throbbing and her mind aching; and the unwanted semen of the husband she could no longer understand dripping coldly down her thigh.

Thursday, July 8, 11:49 a.m.

She opened the door and it was Pepper and Norman. Pepper was wearing a Cossack-style blouse in yellow and orange, and carrying a huge bunch of bright yellow chrysanthemums. Norman was looking pale and his jeans and his denim jacket were covered with plaster. 'I've been loading up gypsum boards,' he explained, brushing his shoulders and his sleeves until he almost disappeared in clouds of dust.

'Hey – come on in,' said Effie. For the past week she had been staying with her mother and her Aunt Rhoda at her Aunt Rhoda's small, white-painted house in Carmel. It overlooked a steeply-sloping country road, and it was almost unnaturally peaceful. At night Effie could smell the woods, and see shooting stars. There wasn't room for her to stay for very long. There were only two bedrooms, and most of the house was crowded with furniture – everything that her mother had brought with her when her father died – nests of tables, clocks, armchairs, knick-knacks, whatnots and statuettes. But Effie had found it an ideal place to recover from her experience at Valhalla, not only the lacerations to her feet, but the shock and disorientation to her soul.

'My pickup's suffering from tired blood,' said Pepper. 'But I persuaded Norman to drive me over here. I'm beginning to wish I hadn't. He drives like Ben Hur on Prozac.'

Effie, still hobbling a little in her mother's carpet slippers, led them into the living-room. Her mother was sitting reading by the window, a tortoiseshell cat in her lap. She looked distinctly like Effie: small boned, slightly Italianate, with grey hair pinned back with a mother-of-pearl buckle. As soon as her cat saw Pepper, it jumped off her lap and came trotting across the carpet, climbing on its hind legs up against Pepper's leg. Pepper scratched and tickled it under the chin, and it followed her so closely that it almost tripped her up.

'You sure have a way with cats,' smiled Effie's mother. 'That one usually runs away when strangers call by.'

'She can smell the witchery on me,' said Pepper.

'More like that fish you were cleaning,' put in Norman.

Effie's mother said, 'You run that herb shop, don't you, down in Cold Spring? I bought one of your spells once, to stop me feeling faint.'

'Yes,' smiled Pepper. 'Peony root, peony seed, nutmeg and fine sugar. Did it work for you?'

'The wonderful thing was that it did.'

Norman said to Effie, as if he'd just remembered an errand he was supposed to have run, 'We're all ready to start stripping the roof. Just thought you'd like to know.'

'I know. Craig called me yesterday.'

'Soon as the sale goes through,' Norman added. 'I gotta tell you, I can't wait to get my hands on that place.'

'Well, don't count on it,' said Effie.

Norman said, 'Like – I know that Valhalla gives you the creeps. I know you don't like the atmosphere and all. But you have to admit that it's some house, hmh? And when we've finished, it won't be creepy any more. I mean, it's some house.'

209

'Yes, Norman. It's some house.'

Norman abruptly left them for a while. He said he was going to visit the J. Register Hardware Store on the outskirts of Carmel, because it was the only store in the Hudson River Valley to sell old-fashioned steel barn door hangers and braced barn-door track. Effie's mother made tea.

Pepper said to Effie, 'I wouldn't have come over to bother you but I think I know what's happening.' She reached into her bag and produced a dog-eared book. 'I was talking to one of my friends about what happened when you cut your feet, and he came up with this. *Coincident Lives.*' She passed it to Effie, and said, 'Page 108. There – there's a marker in it.'

Effie was reluctant to read it at first. She didn't want to be reminded of what had happened in the ballroom, the beastlike baying of the guests, the discordant music and the broken glass. But Pepper said, 'Go on, please. It's important.'

The passage read, 'There is incontrovertible scientific evidence that "ghosts" as they are popularly imagined to be (that is, the unquiet shades of the dead) cannot exist, except as hallucinations or figments of a disturbed imagination. The most convincing demonstration of this were the series of Herzberg Tests carried out between 1965–1968 on reputedly "haunted" properties on New York's Upper West Side, and by the Bright-Williams experiments in the East End of London, England, during the early part of the 1970s, before the slums of Hoxton and Whitechapel were demolished. These tests proved that there were no external manifestations either physical, optical, electrical, chemical or tactile. But there have been several instances in which it appears from closely-examined records that two lives from different periods of time have become coin-

210

cident. This is often mistakenly called "regression" – a condition in which a person believes that he or she can remember a "past life", as a medieval peasant, for instance, or a notable character from history. Using exactly the same proof that "ghosts" do not exist, we can show that regression is also a fallacy.

'But it can be demonstrated by comparatively straightforward means that it is not time which moves forward from minute to minute, but *only our perception of it*. The events of what we consider to be "the past" and the events of what we consider to be "the future" exist coincidentally with the events of what we consider to be "now". History is like a house with an infinite number of rooms, through which we pass on an unguided tour. Just because we have walked from one room into another, that doesn't mean that the previous room ceases to exist, even though we may not have the ability to be able to return to it.

'There are specific locations where chronological events are very thinly separated; and where "the past" and "the present" and even "the future" are being played out within sight of each other, like dramas performed behind net curtains. In such locations, dominant personalities from different "times" can occasionally often find themselves sharing the same thoughts, the same concerns, and even (in at least three well-documented instances) the same physical bodies.

'In 1983, in Antlers, in Pushmataha County, Oklahoma, an auto mechanic called Roger Freeman suffered constant hallucinations that he was a sodbusting farmer named George Poltuk. Although Freeman was earning a reasonable living and had a good family life, he woke up one night and murdered his entire family – his wife and three daughters – by stabbing them in the eyes with a screwdriver. He claimed in court that he was George Poltuk and

211

that he had killed his family rather than see them starve to death. He was asked repeatedly what his name was, and each time he answered "George Poltuk". When he was asked his date of birth, he answered "April 17, 1901", and claimed that he was three days short of his 33rd birthday. County records showed that a farmer called George Poltuk had murdered his entire family on April 14, 1935, after a dust storm had wiped out his failing farm.

'There was no evidence to suggest that Roger Freeman could have known anything about the Poltuk murders; but he gave accurate and comprehensive details about the Poltuk family, and could even tell the court what had been playing on the radio the night the Poltuk murders had taken place. *Amos 'n' Andy*, on NBC-Red.'

Effie passed the book to her mother. 'Do you think that's what happened to me?' she asked Pepper.

'Your feet were all cut up. You didn't even take your shoes off, but your feet were all cut up. Could the doctors explain it?'

Effie looked shamefaced. 'I didn't tell them. I just said that I was barefoot, and that it happened by accident. They wouldn't have believed me, would they? I didn't want to be kept in hospital for psychiatric tests, as well as stitches in my feet. The doctor looked as if he didn't believe in repetitive strain injury, let alone what-do-you-call-it, "coincident living." '

'But when you were in that ballroom, dancing, that was what you were doing. You weren't acting out your life, you were acting out someone else's, some woman who lived at Valhalla before. For those few moments, *you* were *her*, who-ever she was. You and she lived coincident lives. Whoever this woman was, or *is*, she has the kind of strong personality that can reach from one decade to the next.'

'But if she had such a very strong will, why had she

212

agreed to dance on broken glass?'

Pepper shrugged. 'I wish I knew. But see here, Effie . . . it looks like Craig's going ahead with the sale. It's a kind of an embarrassing question, but – are you going to be living there with him?'

Effie hesitated for a moment. 'I guess I don't have any choice. I don't like Valhalla, no, but I don't want to jeopardise our marriage.'

'If you ask me,' said her mother, 'Craig's acting like a selfish little boy. He *knows* you hate that place.'

'Once it's restored, maybe I'll grow to like it. It's in a beautiful setting.'

Pepper said, 'You won't grow to like it until it's been cleansed. That's why I had to ask you whether you were going to live there or not. You'll go on experiencing psychic incidents like cutting your feet and hearing that woman cry, again and again. They won't be any fun and they could be dangerous.'

'How, dangerous?'

'You've already chopped up your feet. Suppose that woman commits suicide? Stabs herself, or something like that? She may have a powerful personality but she doesn't seem very stable, does she?'

'You keep talking about her in the present tense.'

'Of course I do, because she's still with us, she's still at Valhalla. If you're seriously thinking of living there, I have to go back and do what I left unfinished last week.'

'The hazel twig, and the salt?'

'A whole lot more than that. This isn't like the milk turning sour or mirrors getting breathed-on when there's nobody there. This is much, much stronger than that. This is the strongest psychic upheaval I ever came across, ever.'

Effie's mother said, 'Will it be dangerous for you?'

'I don't know. That kind of remains to be seen. It won't

213

be *easy*, I know that.'

'You don't have to take any risks for me,' said Effie.

Pepper smiled. 'As a matter of fact, I'm doing this more for me than I am for you. A little excitement? I love Cold Spring but it isn't exactly the centre of the known universe, is it?'

Effie said, 'When do you want to do this . . . cleansing?'

'As soon as I can. There's one thing, though. I think it'll be safer if you don't come with me. It's something that I'll be better off doing alone.'

'I don't want you getting hurt.'

'Don't you worry. I'll have my tonka beans and my mugwort and my verbena. I'll have some dried moss that grew on a dead man's skull. I'll have my golden crosses and my ouanga.'

'What's an ouanga?'

Pepper reached inside her blouse and produced a small red leather pouch which had been dangling on a yellow ribbon between her breasts. 'You burn balsam and lime leaves, grind them to a powder and mix them with wine. Then you mark some balsam and castor leaves with a chalk cross. You put the ashes on a small piece of red leather, then cover them up with the leaves, and cover the leaves with a crucifix, a tuft of hair tied with a white thread, a fingernail clipping, a piece of red cloth and a copper coin – and a piece of gold or silver, if you have it. Then you tie the whole package up with a brightly-coloured ribbon, and there you have it. The good luck talisman to end all good luck talismans.'

Effie's mother made a doubtful face. 'Is this *witchcraft*?' she wanted to know.

Pepper shook her head. 'You wouldn't go out in the pouring rain without an umbrella, would you? You never go near a serious psychic disturbance without an ouanga.'

214

On the way back to Cold Spring, Pepper asked Norman, 'How about that barn-door track? Did they have what you wanted?'

'They're delivering it Thursday. This is a big job, fixing up Valhalla. You should be proud of me.'

'I am proud of you,'

Pepper took out a small tobacco tin, and started to roll herself a thin and straggly joint. She lit it up, and inhaled deeply, and the sunlight angled through the smoke.

'I was talking to Jack Register about Valhalla,' Norman remarked. 'I've been looking for some curved timber joists to fix the library floor. Like, the floor is constructed in a really odd way. The main joists radiate outward from the centre, like the spokes of a cartwheel, and then there are curved joists forming larger and larger concentric circles. It's really weird. I never saw a floor built like that before. Jack Register said the only other one he knew about was in the Benton House up at Salt Point.'

'That's famous. Or notorious, should I say?'

'Never heard of it. But I might go take a look, just to check out the floor.'

'The Benton House was where all those people disappeared, back in about 1890 or something.'

'What people?'

'They all belonged to some kind of extreme religious sect. They wore very plain black clothes and always kept their heads covered. The local people thought they were into black magic or something like that. Anyway as far as I remember some woman went missing, and everybody blamed the people who lived in the Benton House. They stormed the house but the sect people locked themselves in. When the mob broke down the door, the sect people had disappeared. There were no trapdoors, no secret passages, nothing. They just disappeared, and nobody

215

ever saw them again.'

'Hey, weird.'

'Oh, it was probably some trick, that's all.'

'All the same, I'll still go up there and see how they made that floor. Jack Register reckons it was built on the same technical principles as a spiderweb.'

'Maybe you should go ask a spider how it's done.'

'Not me. You know what I'm like about spiders. Hairy, scuttly . . . urgh.'

Pepper laughed, and leaned her head back. The ouanga around her neck nudged against her cleavage. The talisman to end all talismans, she thought. She just hoped that, when she went back to Valhalla, it was going to be strong enough to protect her against the psychic disturbance to end all psychic disturbances.

Monday, July 12, 2:47 p.m.

The two men in crumpled, unseasonable suits were waiting for them when Craig brought Effie back to Pig Hill Inn. One of them was black and very tall, and must have weighed well over 225 pounds. His hair was cropped so short that his scalp shone through it. The other was thin-faced, more grey than white, with a bony, complicated nose and eyes that were hooded and expressionless, like a basking lizard.

'Mr Craig Bellman? Lieutenant Hook, Sergeant Winstanley.'

Craig made no attempt to shake their hands. 'You made good time. I heard the traffic was heavy.'

'Judicious use of the siren, Mr Bellman. This your wife, sir?'

216

'Yes, this is my wife. I just brought her back from her mother's at Carmel. As you can see, she had an accident.'

'Sorry to hear it. Nothing too serious, I hope?'

'I cut my feet on some broken glass, that's all,' said Effie. Her feet were still bandaged and she was wearing Craig's bedroom slippers, but she didn't hobble any longer.

'Gotta be careful where you're treading,' remarked Lieutenant Hook. 'Look – is there anyplace here we can talk?'

'Effie, sweetheart, why don't you go on upstairs and take a rest?' Craig suggested. 'This won't take long, will it, Lieutenant?'

'I'd rather stay,' said Effie.

Sergeant Winstanley put in, rather mournfully, 'I'm not sure that you do, Mrs Bellman. We have to talk about the details of six pretty nasty homicides.'

'I'm not squeamish, Sergeant,' Effie told him.

'You don't want to stay,' said Craig, taking hold of her elbow.

Lieutenant Hook shrugged and said, 'There's no harm. Maybe she can think of something helpful.'

'You never know,' Effie retorted. 'Maybe she can.' She was in a stubborn mood.

It was so warm that they sat out in the garden, and the two detectives took off their coats and hung them from one of the trees. They ordered iced tea for four and club sandwiches for two (Hook and Winstanley hadn't yet eaten). Craig sat with his hand resting possessively on Effie's thigh. Even in his short-sleeved shirt he looked hot and boiled.

'We've been looking into the killing of your partner Mr Steven Fisher,' said Lieutenant Hook, opening his notebook. 'As you're probably aware his throat was cut causing almost instantaneous death. The girl who died with him,

Ms Khrystyna Bielecka, died the same way, immediately or very soon afterwards. The weapon was a carving knife from Ms Bielecka's own kitchen drawer.

'The forensic evidence doesn't add up to much. We have one or two fingerprints, notably on the bellpush of the girl's apartment, and on the drawer handle. The perpetrator was male, right-handed and reasonably strong. Judging from the angle of the wounds, he was probably six, six-two. There are no hairs, no fibres and no footprints that didn't belong to the deceased, apart from some that were traced to three of Ms Bielecka's friends, all of whom proved to have rock-solid alibis.

'We're working on the assumption, though, that the assailant was known either to Ms Bielecka or to Mr Fisher or to both of them, because there were no signs of forced entry. Mr Fisher and Ms Bielecka had had sexual intercourse shortly before they were killed, although Mr Fisher hadn't succeeded in ejaculating. You'll excuse me, Mrs Bellman.'

'Of course,' said Effie.

Lieutenant Hook paused for a while, and finished a bite of sandwich. Then he said, 'The only really interesting piece of evidence was this . . . it was found on the bed, in between the victims' bodies.'

He took down his coat from the tree, reached into the pocket, and took out a clear plastic envelope. He gave it to Craig to take a look, and watched him while he looked at it with his lizard eyes. Effie didn't need Craig to pass it to her, she could see what it was quite clearly. A playing-card, the nine of diamonds.

'There are fingerprints on this card that match the fingerprints on the bellpush. For some reason we don't yet comprehend, the perpetrator left this item at the scene of his attack. It could be a coded message: it could be a symbol of something the perpetrator wanted to say. We really don't know.'

'How do you know that the perpetrator left it there?' asked Craig. 'It might have been there already. It might have fallen to the floor, he might have picked it up.'

Lieutenant Hook politely took the card back. 'We're assuming that he left it there because there were no other playing-cards in the apartment, only this one. What's more, an identical card was found on the body of an Egyptian-born hack, Mr Zaghlul Fuad, who was found with his throat cut in his taxi only about an hour later. Different knife, but a right-handed assailant, quite tall, who had the nerve and the strength to cut through his windpipe with one quick slice. Rare that, to do it in one. Takes extreme nerve.'

'And, again, you found a playing-card at the scene of the crime?' asked Craig.

Sergeant Winstanley nodded. 'Not just any old playing-card, sir. The nine of diamonds.'

'Fingerprints?'

'Partially smudged, but identical. Mr Fuad was almost certainly killed by the same person who killed your partner Mr Fisher and his girlfriend.'

'Killer on the rampage, huh?' said Craig.

'That's right, Mr Bellman. Killer on the rampage. And he didn't stop with Mr Fuad. A little under an hour later, he killed three members of a black gang that hangs out around the theatre district, the Aktuz, they called themselves. He didn't use a knife this time, he used an eight-pound cast-steel blacksmiths' sledge, oil-finished, with a thirty-six inch hickory handle. Samuel Joseph Carter, aged twenty-four years, also known as Up or The Prince; Malcolm Oral Deedes, aged twenty-two years, also known as Tyce; and Susan Amelia Clay, aged nineteen years, also known as Scuzz or Suzi-Kue. He hit those kids so hard and so often that nobody could recognise them, except by their clothes. They were pulp.

'And, lo and behold, what should we find on the dressing-table where their bodies were discovered? The nine of diamonds, no less.'

Craig sat back. 'The nine of diamonds. Any idea what that means?'

Lieutenant Hook shook his head. 'We've tried all kinds of leads. We've talked to cardsharps; we've talked to fortune-tellers; we've even talked to a voodoo guy on 116th Street, Doctor Deadeye. So far nothing.'

Effie suddenly frowned. 'The nine of diamonds? Why does that ring a bell?'

'I don't think it does, sweetheart,' said Craig.

'But wasn't that the card that –?'

'No, no,' Craig interrupted her. 'That was the seven. You can look it up.'

Lieutenant Hook said, 'You want to tell me what was on your mind, Mrs Bellman?'

'I don't suppose it's relevant . . . but there was a gambler in the 1920s, Jack Belias. We're just about to buy his house. He played against the Greek Syndicate, did you ever hear of them? And there was one time when he was playing baccarat with Nico Zographos, who was one of the leading members of the syndicate, and he almost bankrupted him.'

'I don't get it,' said Lieutenant Hook.

Craig laughed. 'When Effie tells a story, nobody gets it.'

'Listen. It's in the book I read about Belias,' Effie retorted. 'Nico Zographos saved himself with one card, the nine of diamonds.'

'The seven,' Craig interrupted.

'The nine, I'm sure it was the nine. Anyway, Jack Belias was so impressed that he bought Nico Zographos a diamond pin, with nine diamonds in it.'

'Seven,' Craig insisted.

'*Nine*, I'm positive.'

'Well, why don't you go get the book and prove me wrong,' Craig suggested, and his voice was throaty with annoyance.

Lieutenant Hook picked cress from his lip. 'Why don't you do that, Mrs Bellman? It could be helpful. Right now we're looking for anything.'

Effie said, 'Right then, I will.' But it was only when she stood up and Craig looked up at her that she understood the implications of what she was doing. Supposing Nico Zographos *had* played the nine of diamonds? She was sure that he had, and she was sure that Craig remembered it, too. So why had Craig insisted it was seven? There was no reason for him to say that at all. Except if –

'I think I took the book back to the library,' she said, sitting down again. She felt chilled and sweaty and trembling, in spite of the heat.

'That's okay,' said Lieutenant Hook. 'If you can tell me what it was called, I'll drop by and pick it up myself. No need to bother you, not with those feet.'

Sergeant Winstanley said, 'Did you know Ms Khrystyna Bielecka, sir?'

Craig thought for a moment, and then slowly shook his head. 'If she was Steven's girlfriend, I might have met her without knowing it. But that's all.'

'Your name and office telephone number were entered into Ms Bielecka's telephone book, sir. Can you account for that?'

'I can't, no. Maybe Steven gave her my number in case of emergencies. She never called me.'

'Some of Ms Bielecka's friends say that she told them about her lover . . . a married man, a lawyer. A man who

221

was really going places, that's what she said.'

'That was Steven all over. I was the plodder, but Steven was always the star.'

Lieutenant Hook took another sip of iced tea. Then he leaned back so that his face was concealed in shadows from the tree. 'On the night of March 16 this year, you were admitted to the Emergency Room at New York Hospital suffering from a severe injury to your genital region – inflicted, you said, with a hammer. Subsequently you told one of my detectives that you had been attacked by two black youths in a disused drugstore on 48th Street. The description you gave of those two dudes leaves me in not very much doubt as to who they were. Samuel Joseph Carter and Malcolm Oral Deedes . . . Up and Tyce.'

'So what are you trying to suggest?' asked Craig, without any hint of emotion. 'You're trying to suggest that *I* killed them, in revenge for what they did to me?'

'That would be sufficient motive to make you a prime suspect, sir, yes. And since all of the homicides were distinguished by the perpetrator leaving the nine of diamonds at the crime scene, that would be sufficient circumstantial evidence to make you a prime suspect in all six homicides. Killer on the rampage.'

'*Craig!*' Effie whispered. She couldn't believe what she was hearing. Craig could be obstinate and bad tempered if he didn't get his own way, but she couldn't imagine him killing anybody. She felt suddenly chilled, as if somebody had opened an icebox door right behind her.

'Well?' said Craig. 'What are you going to do? Read me my rights?'

Lieutenant Hook leaned forward again, so that his face came back into the light. 'No, sir. I just thought you'd be interested to hear how a case like this can seem so cut-and-dried – we can have motive, opportunity, evidence – when

222

all the time the truth lies someplace else. As I said, the per-petrator left fingerprints on the bellpush of Ms Bielecka's apartment, and on the playing-card that was found on her bed. Matching prints were found on the door handle of Mr Fuad's taxi, and again on the playing-card that was left next to Mr Fuad's body. We lifted even clearer prints from the playing-card left in the dressing-room at the Lyceum theatre, and yesterday a patrolman found the blacksmith's hammer under the Henry Hudson Parkway at West 82nd Street. More prints on the head and handle. Very good prints on the head, because of its oil finish.'

Effie felt like clutching Craig's hand, but at the same time she thought *supposing it was him? Supposing he really did it?*

Sergeant Winstanley said, 'You were kind enough to let us take your fingerprints when we interviewed you on Wednesday. None of the fingerprints we lifted from the crime scenes remotely matched yours.'

'Which leads me to the surprising but unavoidable con-clusion that the perpetrator wasn't you, sir,' said Lieutenant Hook. 'Couldn't have been.'

'That doesn't mean that I couldn't have paid somebody to do it,' Craig put in. 'You know, a hired hitman or some-thing like that.'

'That possibility hasn't escaped me,' said Lieutenant Hook. 'With your permission, I'd like to access all of your bank accounts and telephone charge records. Only rou-tine, to make my superiors feel happy.' He paused. 'I could get a warrant if I have to.'

'You can look through anything you want. I don't have anything to hide. Anyway, I've spent most of my money buy-ing Valhalla. I couldn't afford a hitman even if I wanted one.'

Lieutenant Hook was unamused. 'I'd also appreciate if you didn't stray too far. I might have a few more questions for you.'

223

Sergeant Winstanley said, 'Would you have any idea, sir, who might have wanted this particular combination of people dead, apart from you?'

'You're making a false assumption, Sergeant. I didn't want them dead. How could I possibly know why anybody else would?'

'A close friend of yours, maybe, who knew what had happened to you, and wanted to take revenge on your behalf?'

'Craig doesn't have any friends who would do anything like that,' said Effie.

Lieutenant Hook turned towards her, cold-eyed. He looked as if he was capable of flicking out his tongue and catching one of the midges that were dancing in the sunlight under the tree. 'You never know what your friends are capable of doing. Some people have a very distorted sense of loyalty.'

On the way up to their room, Effie hissed, 'It *was* the nine of diamonds. I'm sure of it.'

'Seven, nine, I don't remember.'

'It *was* the nine. And it's such a coincidence. You know, one minute we're reading about Jack Belias and buying his old house, and now there's *this*. My God, if it hadn't have been for your fingerprints not matching, they probably would have arrested you.'

'They still think I had something to do with it. They're not very good at lateral thinking.'

'What does that mean?' asked Effie, unlocking the door. The bedroom was filled with sunlight and flowers.

'It means that Sherlock Holmes didn't get it quite right. He said that when you have excluded the impossible, whatever remains, however improbable, must be the truth. But supposing nothing remains, not even anything improbable?'

224

'I don't know.'

Craig nudged the door shut with his back and reached behind him to twist the key in the lock. He took hold of Effie quite roughly and looked down at her with an expression that was almost approaching a leer. 'If nothing remains, then the impossible must be the truth. It's as simple as that.'

He started to unbutton her blouse.

'Craig, not now. My feet ache.'

'Unh-hunh. Feet-ache doesn't count.'

He lifted her up and carried her over to the bed.

'Craig . . .' she said, as he leaned over her to kiss her.

'What is it? You're going to ask me if I killed those people, is that it?'

She didn't answer, didn't dare to, but looked intently into his eyes and saw nothing at all. It was like staring down two deep wells, in a vain attempt to catch the glitter of water, far below.

She touched his cheek and she was surprised how smooth it was. He seemed to have lost some of his freckles, and she was sure that his eyebrows were browner. He seemed to have acquired a new allure; a dark glamour that he had never had before.

For the first time since he had quoted to her Mallarmé's line about a distant ghost, seen in a mirror, she began to wonder who he really was.

Friday, July 16, 5:56 p.m.

A V-shaped formation of Canada geese suddenly burst over the rooftops, dolefully honking, and startled her. Valhalla had been creepy enough when she had visited

225

with Effie, but now she was here on her own she felt as if the whole house was alert to her presence, as if the walls were whispering to the stairs, as if the windows were turning their glassy eyes toward her, as if the floorboards were silently running up behind her.

She decided to start with the ballroom. It was here that the psychic vibrations had been at their strongest and their most disturbed. It was here that times past and times present overlapped each other like flickering cinematic negatives, one event dimly perceived through the shadows of another.

This time, she intended to take no risks of being overwhelmed by the psychic panic that had affected her so strongly before. She had brought a circular mirror, which she propped in the centre of the floor. If anybody from another time *did* manifest themselves, they wouldn't be able to touch her, because her soul was contained in the mirror for as long as she was reflected in it. At least, that was the theory. Catherine de Medici had used a circular mirror to foretell how long her sons would live, and the Prince of Navarre had circled around it twenty-two times before vanishing. Tribespeople in New Guinea and parts of Southern Africa still refuse to look into mirrors in case their souls can never escape.

Pepper had studied a book called *Lookynge-Glass Magyke* by Thomas De La Raiz, published in Massachusetts in 1650. She didn't believe very much of it, and some of it was nothing more than idiotic superstition; but one night she had used a mirror to tell the fortune of a young folk-guitarist and his mirror-image had been crowned with flames. Two days later he had burned to death when his tour bus overturned in heavy rain on the Garden State Parkway. She always remembered his name, Orkney Taylor. He was so burned that firefighters had thought at first that he was

226

a monkey. Pepper had prayed for weeks afterwards that it wasn't her fault.

She looked around the high, dusty ballroom, with its leaf-clogged skylights. She wasn't entirely sure why she was doing this cleansing. Maybe she had told Effie the truth, that she was lacking some good old honest excitement, here in Cold Spring, with its tourists and its bed-and-breakfasts and its prissy stores. But maybe it was more than that. Maybe she needed to test her strength. Maybe she needed to find out what she was made of. It was all very well purveying pantry-magic in little jars and pouches; but what of real magic? What of lives that were lived in parallel? What of coincidence? And by that she meant *coincidence*, two things happening at one and the same time, even though they might be separated by seven decades of calendar years.

She stood up, making sure that she could see her reflection in the mirror. She was wearing a long white dress of very thin linen, with small puffed sleeves. Underneath it she was completely naked except for the thin silver chain that she always wore around her waist and her ouanga, her talisman. Her nipples showed through the dress like the petals of fading roses seen through thin curtains. All around the mirror she had placed a circle of seven pink candles, handmade out of beeswax. Their small flames nodded in the draught from the broken windows. They made her silver eyes shine.

On a glossy tablet of white marble she had placed her other magical accoutrements: her moss, and her peony, and her verbena. These were surrounded by a pattern of small gold crosses, eight altogether, seven for the magic number and one for the soul she was trying to protect.

She didn't have the same hazel twig this time, but a twig with seven different branches which she had cut from her own yard. It was not as sensitive as the usual two-forked dowsing rod, but it would help to diffuse the potent energy of Valhalla's disturbances, and protect her from any serious harm. It was the psychic equivalent of an electrical transformer.

All the same, it was necessary for a psychic cleanser to be vulnerable. Hence her nakedness under her dress; hence her bare feet. As she had explained to Effie, ghost-busting aggression would simply make the memories of what had happened here – what was *still* happening here – flicker and melt away as soon as she approached.

She lifted her hazel twig and slowly moved it from side to side. At the same time, she opened her mind, in the same way she did when she meditated. It was almost like gradually opening a canal lock, so that the cold water of everybody else's unconscious mind could come pouring in. She didn't use chants, or mantras, or any of the spoken spells which she had learned in her Aquarius days. What was needed here at Valhalla was silence, complete openness, complete neutrality.

At first, she had no response at all, and she began to wish that she had brought her two-forked twig. She shuffled around a little more, so that she could dowse the area behind her, although she still made sure that she didn't lose sight of her reflection. She emptied her mind even more, until she was thinking of nothing but time and space and the infinite rooms of the house known as immortality.

The candles dipped and swayed. The ballroom seemed to darken a little, as if the sun had been masked by a cloud. She glanced down at the mirror and it looked strangely misted, so that her reflection was blurred.

Something –

Very faintly she felt the hazel tingling in her hands. She thought she could hear music, too – not *The Blue Danube*

228

that Effie had heard when she was dancing, but jazz music. Tinny, flat jazz music, playing on an acoustic Victrola.

She moved the hazel in a hesitant semicircle. When she pointed it towards the north-western corner of the ball-room, it faded away. When she pointed it back at the south-eastern corner, she could hear it more distinctly, although it was still very faint. It sounded like one of those really early Chicago jazz bands, Johnny Dodds and the Footwarmers, or King Oliver, or Johnny De Droit.

She heard doors opening, and footsteps. It sounded as if a man were running quickly and lightly downstairs. She heard more doors opening. A draught blew into the ball-room, and three of her pink candles were snuffed out. Broken, scented smoke drifted across the floor. Pepper felt the seven-branched hazel shiver and twist, almost as if it were frightened, almost as if it wanted to break free.

The footsteps came nearer, across the library. There was a moment's hesitation, and then the double doors were flung open, and Craig walked in.

'Well, well,' he said. 'If it isn't Ms Moriarty.' He came towards her, and looked around at her candles and her mirrors and her dishes of magic plants. 'What's this, then, raising the devil?'

'I didn't see any vehicles. I didn't think there'd be any-body here.' Pepper lowered her hazel, although it was still twitching and writhing, and the branches were bending back like spindly fingers.

Craig paced around the magic circle. He was wearing a black turtle-neck and black slacks and shiny black shoes. His eyes looked puffy, as if he hadn't been sleeping well.

'There are no vehicles here because Norman drove me up here, and he's gone over to Carmel to order some more coving. I have to say that I'm not too happy about people just wandering in here without asking me,' he said. 'We've already had one fatal accident; we don't want any more.'

'I'm sorry,' said Pepper. 'I guess I should have asked. I'm only doing this for Effie's sake.'

'Doing what? Conjuring up ghosts?'

'Mr Bellman, I don't believe in ghosts, you know that. But the psychic atmosphere here is very threatening. If I can cleanse it, I'm sure that Effie will be very much happier about coming to live here.'

'Oh, you're sure, are you? Well, may I ask what gives you the right to poke your nose into my affairs? How would you like it if I went around to that crackpot store of yours and fumigated it because I didn't like the smell of crushed spiders or dried dogshit or whatever it is you put in those potions of yours? You'd be angry, wouldn't you?'

Pepper bit her lip. 'I guess I would, Mr Bellman. But that doesn't really give you the right to be so offensive.'

'You think I'm being offensive? I'm very sorry, I apologise. Next time that you try to come in here with your mumbo-jumbo I'll throw you out without a word.'

Pepper hunkered down and began to blow out her candles and collect up her crosses and her potions. 'I've said I'm sorry. I didn't mean to poke my nose in. I was thinking of Effie, that's all; and I was thinking of you, too.' She stood up. 'Whatever you say to me now, Mr Bellman, you won't be happy here at Valhalla until you've cleansed it from top to bottom.'

He reached out and gripped her left wrist, so that she dropped the hazel. He looked directly into her eyes.

'I'm happy here already,' he said. 'This house is me. This house is what I am.'

'Please, let go of me, Mr Bellman.'

But he kept on gripping her wrist until it hurt. 'You know something, you have very special eyes. I never saw eyes like yours before. What colour would you say they were?'

'Please, you're hurting me.'

Craig paused for a moment, and then released her. 'Maybe I was wrong about you. Maybe you should cleanse the house, after all. Do you want to try?'

'I think I'll call it a day,' said Pepper. 'If there were any psychic vibrations, they'll have taken a powder by now. They don't react well to boorish behaviour.'

'You're angry with me now,' Craig grinned. On the floor, only two or three inches away from his left foot, the hazel was still twitching and rearing, as if it were a skeletal hand that was trying to take a grip on his ankle. Pepper glanced down at it, and then back at him.

'I'm not angry with you, just disappointed. You're so darned – testy.'

'Testy? And that surprises you? I was a high-flying inter-national lawyer who had his career cut short by a stupid taxi driver and a bunch of geeks. I thought I was one of the glittering few. I thought I was invulnerable. I feel cheated. I feel frustrated. I feel furious, too. *You're* dis-appointed? I have an anger inside of me you could never understand. I never expected life to be fair but I didn't expect it to be vindictive.'

'So, life didn't turn out the way you expected. You feel pissed. But why take it out on Effie?'

'What do you mean? I'm not taking it out on Effie! We haven't had such a good time in years!'

'She doesn't like the house, Mr Bellman. She hates it.'

'Unh-hunh.' He wagged his finger at her. 'At *first* she hated it, I'll grant you that, but not now. She's beginning to like it now. Last night she told me that it was really start-ing to grow on her.'

'She's only saying that because she doesn't want to wreck your marriage.'

'Wreck our marriage? Are you crazy? We're closer than

231

ever. We talk together, we go places together, our sex life's terrific. Okay, I'm very far from being perfect. But our marriage is helping me to convalesce. Just like this place. I love it. It gives me strength. It gives me actual, physical strength.'

'Effie thinks it's frightening. That's why I offered to cleanse it.'

Craig kept on circling around and around her, outside the circle of unlit candles. 'And if you do manage to cleanse it?'

'Then you may still experience some psychic vibrations, but there won't be any noises or visions or anything like that. You probably won't feel anything more than a faint disturbance in the air.'

Craig said, 'You remind me of somebody. It's your cheekbones. Maybe your mouth, too. You remind me of – no, I can't remember.' He turned around, so that he was standing with his back to her, and he didn't say any more.

'I'll be going now,' Pepper told him.

'Why don't you stay?' His tone sounded different now, much colder and much more controlled.

'I thought I was poking my nose in. I thought you didn't want me here.'

'You came to cleanse, why don't you cleanse?'

'I'm not sure that I can do it while you're here. You're very vibrant. Psychically speaking, of course. You're not sensitive, not like Effie. But you're definitely vibrant. I'm trying to pick up other emotions, but all I can pick up is you.'

'Then maybe you should start with me.' He turned back and his eyes were even blacker than before.

Pepper lifted her head and listened. She could still hear the jazz playing in another room. 'Are you having a party?' she asked him.

Craig listened too. Then he said, 'I don't hear anything.'

'Jazz, I thought it was.'

'Jazz?'

Pepper picked up her hazel twig. It was still quivering; and there wasn't any question that it was bending its branches towards Craig. She pointed it directly at him, while he watched her with a small, amused smile on his face. She slowly paced around him, and wherever she went, it kept on bending itself in his direction.

'This is very unusual,' she said. 'Most of the time, when there's a strong psychic vibration, the hazel shies away. I never saw it showing such *attraction* for anything before.'

'I guess I must be a very attractive guy.'

She stepped a little closer to him, and now the hazel began literally to *writhe*, like octopus tentacles. All the time, Craig kept his eyes on her, unwavering, with the same small smile.

'What do you think?' he asked her.

'You're right,' she said. 'It *is* you. Or at least, it's using you. The house itself is filled with psychic disturbance; but *you* are the point of focus. It's like the house is a camera full of psychically-sensitive film, and you're acting as the lens.'

'You mean Effie's been seeing things because of me? Half of the time I wasn't even there!'

'You wouldn't *have* to be there. You started something the moment you stepped into this house, you really did. You triggered it off. I don't know how, but we can try to find out, and I'm pretty sure that we can cleanse it.'

Craig looked down at her array of magical accoutrements. 'How do you normally cleanse things? Eye of newt and leg of toad, and then abracadabra?'

'As a matter of fact I was going to use mirrors. You reflect the image of the room in which the psychic disturbance is taking place from one mirror to another, through thirteen mirrors, until the image of the room is so dim that you can hardly see it. If that sounds like superstition, actually it's quite scientific. It's like Einstein – if you slow down the time it takes for you to *see* something, you slow it down in real time, too. Right here, we need to separate what's happening yesterday from what's happening today, and to do that we only need to lose the teentsiest fraction of a second. That's all.'

'What about a man? How do you go about cleansing a man?'

'It's pretty much the same. He has to be reflected in thirteen mirrors.'

'Do you think I need cleansing?' His voice was lower now, and slower. She took one step back but he took one step forward.

'I don't know. I'd have to do some more research. I never came across a situation like this before.'

She stepped back again, and again he stepped forward.

'Ms Moriarty,' he said, 'you know how I feel about this house. I want to live here and I want Effie to live here with me. Happily, and because she really wants to. If there's something about me that causes these – disturbances, whatever – don't you think you owe it to Effie to stop me doing it?'

He laid his hand on her shoulder. For some reason Pepper found it a most disturbing gesture, as intimate as if he had laid his hand on her breast. Up until now, she had only seen Craig as Effie's bossy, overbearing husband, a big man with the kind of bluff good looks that she had always found far too bluff and far too good. She preferred darker men, men with quirky faces and suggestive smiles. Gypsy-like men, who rarely shaved. But suddenly she sensed that same kind of darkness in Craig: that same kind of danger.

234

She suddenly thought: *this man's sexy, and he wants me*.

'I never did this before. It might not work. It might be dangerous.'

'You weren't afraid to cleanse the house. Why should you be afraid to cleanse me?'

She stared at him and he looked different. She said, 'We'll have to have mirrors. Full-length mirrors.'

'We have plenty of mirrors in the anteroom upstairs. Why don't you do it up there?'

She took hold of his wrist and lifted his hand from her shoulder. Again, there was an intimacy about touching him that was quite out of proportion to what she had actually done. She had only held his wrist: and she had felt his skin and his wristbones and the dark hairs on the back of his hand. She had even felt his pulse.

'I don't think I'm experienced enough for this.' She was increasingly conscious of her nakedness, and the thinness of her dress's fabric.

'You can try, can't you? Maybe you can solve all of our problems.'

'Well, I –'

'Please.'

She gathered up her candles and her jars while he stood and watched her. Occasionally she glanced up at him, and he gave her a little nod of encouragement. He made no effort to help, even when she had to carry her heavy tapestry bag across the ballroom and out to the hallway.

The windows along the corridor had all been replaced, and they were hung with dark blue velveteen curtains. The floor had been cleaned and polished, and the oak panelling had been taken back to its original honey beige.

He saw her taking it all in. 'There's still a long way to go. But not many men can build the house of their dreams, can they?'

Pepper nodded. 'You have to think of Effie, though. You have to consider your wife. She's your *wife*.'

'Oh, I think of my wife all right. And my wife thinks of me. My wife would do anything for me.'

They started to climb the stairs under the coat-of-arms that said *Non omnis moriar*, I shall never completely die.

Craig said, 'If I asked her to, she'd cut her wrists for me. She'd dance barefoot on broken glass.'

Pepper stopped, halfway up the stairs. Her bag was heavy and her hands were beginning to tremble. '*Would* you ask her to?'

'It depends. Asking a woman to prove her devotion is one of the last great masculine prerogatives. You love me? Go on, my darling, cut off all your hair! You love me? Have yourself tattooed with roses all over your breasts! You love me? Walk round the house naked in front of my friends! Show me how much you love me! Prove it! Do whatever I tell you! Crawl through mud on your hands and knees, and then get up and kiss me and thank me for making you dirty!'

Pepper's mouth was dry. 'You don't ask Effie to do things like that, though, do you?'

He continued upstairs, and then pushed open the doors to the anteroom. Inside, the room had been spectacularly refurbished. She couldn't believe how quickly it had been done – and why hadn't Norman told her about it, brought her here to see it? A huge chandelier sparkled from the ceiling, and all the gilt-framed mirrors had been immacu-lately restored. Even the thick red carpets had been relaid, and the room refurnished with three gilded ottomans with fat red cushions, occasional tables and gilt-painted chairs.

Pepper put down her bag, still looking around her in amazement. Craig closed the doors. He crossed the room with a gliding walk, and a dozen more of him crossed the

236

room, too, in their different mirrors. 'I have to applaud your mirror theory,' he smiled. 'Sometimes I walk into this room and I don't know whether the same "me" is going to walk out at the other end. Why should *this* "me" be any more valid than any of those other "mes"? He turned towards the right-hand mirrors and seven of him turned left.

Pepper looked around, unsettled. All that Norman had told her this afternoon was that Fulloni & Jahn had let them start basic roof-repair work before the final sale went through, so that Valhalla wouldn't deteriorate any further. But he hadn't said anything about mirrors and carpets and curtains and lavishly-gilded antique furniture.

'You see these carvings?' said Craig, approaching the solid oak doors that led into the master bedroom. 'They tell it all, the whole story. Women should be silent, and obedient, and keep their eyes closed except when told to open them. Men should turn their backs to them, and show them nothing at all. The first woman was made from dirt and women have been dirt ever since.'

He turned around, and stared at Pepper, and laughed out loud. She didn't know whether he was being serious or not. 'That's the story. That's what these doors have been carved to represent. Eve wasn't the first woman: Lilith was. God agreed to make her, because Adam was so lonely. He fashioned her out of dirt, the clay that men walk on, and she was never more than dirt. But soon she wanted to be equal to Adam. She didn't want to obey him, she didn't want to work as his servant; so she left him and she was turned out of the Garden of Eden.

'You can't say that God didn't give her a chance. He sent three angels after her, to try to persuade her to come back.'

Craig traced the names that were carved on the banners with the tip of his finger. *Samsi, Sangavi, Semangelaf.* 'These are the names of the three angels. They offered Lilith everything, as long as she agreed to serve Adam and all the sons of Adam; but she refused, and so God put a curse on her that made a hundred of her children die every day. Because of that, Lilith hides herself in every marriage bed, hoping to catch drops of semen so that she can have more children. Because of that, parents sing their children a song of love every night before they go to sleep, and call it a lullabye, which means nothing more nor less than "Lilla-bi!" – *"Lilith, be gone!"* '

Pepper came up to the doors and stood beside him. The carved faces looked so real that she reached out and touched them to make sure that they weren't. 'How do you know all this?' she asked.

He touched the same face that she was touching, drawing his fingertips across the lips as if he expected them to kiss him. He wouldn't stop smiling. She sensed that alluring darkness even more strongly. It slid beneath his shallow, self-satisfied exterior like a shark sliding almost invisibly beneath the faintly-ruffled surface of a shallow bay.

This man's not only sexy; he's dangerous.

What disturbed her even more was the ambiguity of her own feelings. She began to think that it was wrong, calling herself Pepper. She didn't feel like a Pepper at all. She didn't completely understand who she was, or what she was doing here. And her perceptions had subtly changed. Everything around her seemed to be magnified, and almost painfully clear. She could see every detail of the wood-carvings, every whorl and chisel mark in the oak. She could see Craig's face as if she were looking at it through a crystal-clear drop of water.

Yet his voice seemed indistinct. His words came out in a long, low grumble.

'I've made it my business to know it,' Craig told her. He turned away from the door and took hold of her arm. 'If you want anything in this life, you have to do your research. I was five months in Palestine, and three moinths in Egypt, and at the end of that time I knew what I was going to do. I built Valhalla, in my own image, and I prepared to show God that women are just what Lilith was.'

Pepper said, 'Mr Bellman . . . you didn't build Valhalla. You only bought it.'

He seemed not to hear. Instead he walked across to a cocktail cabinet and flung open the doors, almost as if he expected to find the Holy Grail inside.

'Drink?' he asked her. 'I make a mean champagne cocktail.'

'I don't think so. I think I'd better be getting back.'

He poured himself a whisky. 'Back? Back to where?'

'Back to –' Pepper began, and then suddenly realised that she couldn't remember where she was supposed to go back to. In fact, she couldn't think why she had imagined that she was supposed to go back anywhere. 'Well, anyway, I don't think so. I don't drink before midnight.'

He came across to her, circling the whisky in his glass. 'If I asked you to tattoo roses on your breasts, would you do it for me?'

'What do you want, a woman or a garden?'

His eyes were dead; but he was still smiling. 'There's no difference. Both are transient beauty, fashioned out of dirt.'

'Less of the dirt if you don't mind. I'll have a cigarette.'

He went back to the cocktail cabinet and returned with a silver art-deco cigarette box, filled with Sobranie Black Russian cigarettes. Pepper took one and he lit it for her. She hadn't smoked a Black Russian for as long as she could remember, and the pungent smell of Balkan tobacco took

239

her back to the days when she – the days when she *what*? She just couldn't seem to remember.

Craig sat on one of the sofas, and patted the cushion next to him to indicate that Pepper should sit down, too.

'No,' she said. 'I really have to go.'

'I thought you were staying over.'

'I don't know. I'm confused.'

'I heard that Gordon bought you an apartment in London. Is that true?'

'Well, you know how much Gordon likes to throw his money around.' Then she thought: *Gordon? Who in the hell is Gordon? I don't know any Gordon.* But then she thought: *Of course I do. Gordon, with his pearl stickpin and his smart maroon cravat and his grey sweptback hair . . . I met him at Deauville last year.*

'You should be careful of Gordon,' said Craig. 'He's into the store for £55,000 already.'

'Why should I be careful? It's not my money!'

'Just don't rely on him too much, that's all I'm saying.'

'And what does that mean? That I should start relying on you? Jenny Dolly thinks that you're the devil incarnate!'

Craig threw his head back and laughed. 'She wishes I were! Then she could sell me her soul, and get back her chateau at Fontainebleau and her seven-strand pearls!'

Pepper slowly sat down next to him. She couldn't keep her eyes off him. She understood everything he was talking about, and yet she knew that she couldn't have done. She knew that 'Gordon' was Gordon Selfridge, who owned one of the world's most successful department stores, on Oxford Street, London. She knew that Jenny Dolly was one of the Dolly sisters, two pretty young Hungarian singers who had taken Gordon Selfridge's fancy, particularly Jenny, to whom he had proposed dozens of times;

240

and on whom he had spent a fortune before his gambling habit sank him so deeply into debt.

She held her head in her hands, staring at Craig and trying to make sense of what was happening to her. She didn't feel ill; she didn't feel frightened. She simply felt as if she were missing something important, as if she had picked up a conversation halfway through. She knew that she had intended to come here, but she couldn't remember why. Something to do with mirrors? She couldn't be sure. There were mirrors everywhere: she could see herself sitting on the sofa a hundred times over, her face in her hands, her cigarette smoke trailing.

'Mr –?' she began, but she couldn't think of his name.

He sipped whisky, amused. 'You don't have to call me Mister.'

'Then what do I call you?'

'The same thing you called me the first time I met you. Lover-to-Be.'

'I called you that? How crass can you be? I must have been drunk!'

'Probably. But you looked as though you meant it.'

'Where was I, when I made this improbable promise?'

'You don't remember?'

Pepper took her hands away from her face and half-closed her eyes. 'The funny thing is that I do. It was outside the Hotel Metropole in Cannes. I was talking to the Duke of Westminster and you came out of the door and I said, "Look at him. That's my lover-to-be." '

Craig slowly nodded, but he wasn't Craig at all. Pepper stared at him and stared at him and then she knew who he was; and who *she* was, too.

'I'm crazy,' she said. 'I'm completely crazy. How much champagne did I drink?'

'Enough to float the Duke of Westminster's yacht.'

'Oh, God. I keep making a solemn promise to myself to stop drinking and stop dancing and stop gambling.'

'What would you do? Take up mah-jongg? Drinking and dancing and gambling is all you do.'

She leaned across the sofa and laid her hand on his knee. 'That's not *quite* all, my darling. I have been known to eat and bathe and wax my legs and occasionally sleep. But not soundly.'

He looked back at her and gave her a smile that she had never seen on any man's face before.

'I think you and I have a whole lot in common,' he said. 'What sign were you born under? Taurus?'

'Aries, couldn't you guess? Aries the Impossible. Aries the Irrepressible.'

'Aries the Erotic?'

'Oh, well, that's *it!*' she shrieked. 'Any man who talks like that, he *has* to be a Virgo!'

She threw her head back; and it was then that Craig slid towards her, and in one sinuous movement took hold of her waist and leaned his head forward and kissed her on the throat. Her first reaction was to sit up straight and twist herself free. But the sensation of his lips touching her bare neck was completely paralysing; as if his tongue were spiked with curare. She sat with her head back in a kind of trance, while he kissed her cheekbones, and all around her ear-lobes, and his tongue-tip followed the curve of her jaw until it discovered her slightly-parted lips.

She opened her eyes wide and his face was so close that it frightened her.

'You're beautiful,' he said. 'Your eyes are silver, like the moon.'

'*Hey diddle-diddle, the cat and the fiddle.*'

'I don't mind if you tease me. I can take teasing. I can take anything, from a tongue-lashing to a whip-lashing.

242

The question is, can you?'

He was so close that she found it hard to focus on him. His breath smelled of something strange, something sweet and Oriental, as if he had been eating cachous. He leaned forward, and breathed into her ear, 'Would you do anything for me?'

'What do you mean by anything.'

'I mean *anything*. Anything I asked you. Would you let me spank you for example.'

'Spank me? What for? I haven't done anything wrong, have I?'

'You must have done *something* wrong! Perhaps you've been insolent. Perhaps you've eaten too many soft-centred chocolates. Perhaps you've had impure thoughts.'

'I never have impure thoughts.'

'Do you want to see my penis?'

'Is it really so special? I thought that penises were like Chinamen, can't tell one from the other.'

'That's an impure thought, don't you think? And you've just had one.'

'You're just trying to trick me.'

'No, I'm not. No tricks, no illusions. What you see is what you get.'

She turned her head away, and shrugged. 'I haven't seen *anything* yet.'

'Well, that's insolence, don't you think? That deserves a spanking.'

She said nothing for a long while. Their faces were so close that they were almost nose-to-nose. They could feel each other's breath on their cheeks. They could feel each other's warmth.

'Do you *want* to spank me?' she said, and her voice was nothing more than breathy ventriloquism, as if somebody else had said it, somebody standing close by.

243

Without another word, he dropped back into a sitting position, then forced his hands beneath her thighs, and swung her over his lap. She tried to struggle, but he was immensely strong. She had never come across a man as strong as this. He twisted both of her wrists behind her back and held them together so tightly that she felt they were clamped in a vice. Her breasts were squashed against his leg, and she had to wriggle herself ferociously until they were free.

'Let me go!' she screamed at him.

'This is what you wanted. This is what you asked for.'

'*Let me go you son of a bitch!*'

'Now, that's another transgression! That deserves at least three extra paddles!'

'*If you don't damn well let me go I'll scratch your eyes out!*'

'Six extra paddles!'

She kicked and bucked and tried to throw herself off his knees onto the floor. But he was so powerful that he held her firmly on his lap, and there was nothing she could do to get herself free. She kept trying to think of those self-defence classes she had attended, but then she wasn't sure that she had attended them at all, or even what they were. They must have been a dream: she must have imagined them. The only classes she could remember were dance classes, in Paris, and Madame Valmeuse standing in the shafts of sunlight in her dusty black dress smacking her hands together and shouting, '*Un – et deux! – et trois! – et plie!*'

Craig took hold of the hem of her thin linen dress and dragged it up at the back. She kicked and thrashed even more wildly, but he slapped the back of her thighs so hard that she stopped, shocked, and had to wheeze for breath. He pulled her dress right up to her waist, and she could hear the seams tearing.

244

'*Bas – tud!*' she gasped.

'Bastard, am I? You've been dying for this! This is what excites you, isn't it? This is what all women like! A good hard spanking, and then a good hard ride! That's all you want; that's all you dream about. Forget all that *Ladies Home Journal* nonsense about romance.'

'You damned pervert!'

He smacked her, very hard, on her bare bottom. She shouted out, and tried to twist her head around so that she could bite his knee or his wrist or anywhere.

'That's one for calling me a pervert,' he told her. Then he smacked her again, and her bottom felt as if it had been set alight. 'That's two for calling me a bastard.'

'Let me go!' she raged at him, with tears in her eyes and her teeth clenched. 'I'll have you arrested for this! I'll have you locked up in jail!'

He smacked her again, and then again. 'That's three for wriggling; and four for threatening me. Oh – and five for calling me a son of a bitch. I nearly forgot.'

The fifth time she screamed. But the sixth time she let out nothing but a low gasp. Something was happening to her; her bottom still burned but it burned with a strange, spreading warmth. She felt humiliated, and she felt hurt, but somehow both the hurt and the humiliation were exciting. To have herself forcibly exposed like this, and to be punished simply for one man's amusement, went deep to the darkest core of her sexual feelings. She had day-dreamed about scenarios like this, but she had never imagined that she would experience it for real.

'Bastard,' she repeated, and waited for the next smack.

'Haven't you had enough?' he asked her, and even though she couldn't see his face she could tell that he was smiling.

'*Bastard-bastard-bastard!*'

Still he didn't smack her. She squeezed her thighs together, and tried to press herself against his thigh, and that gave her some sensation between her legs; but what she really craved was another smack, and then another.

'Don't tell me you've grown to like it so much already?' he taunted her. He trailed his fingertips over her reddened bottom, down between the cheeks, almost to the place where she wanted him to touch, but then he took his fingers away again.

He released her wrists, and said, 'There . . . you're free to go. If you hate me so much, if you think I'm so much of a bastard and a pervert, far be it from me to keep you here against your will.'

Without a word, she rolled off his lap and knelt on the floor in front of him. Flushed, perspiring, she frantically unfastened his belt and tore two buttons off his shirt in her hunger to get at him. She pulled open his pants and took out his penis, which was huge and hard and upcurving, so engorged that it was almost maroon. It was more like a bloodstained tusk than a human organ.

She looked at it for one long moment, stroking it slowly up and down with her fingernails. Then, with a slow diving motion of her shoulders, she buried her head in his lap, so deeply that she momentarily gagged; and that was where she stayed, her hooped earrings swinging and jingling as her head bobbed up and down; while he sat back on the sofa with an expression of benevolent disdain, and occasionally fingered her hair, or touched her shoulder.

'Don't be too long,' he told her. 'Gordon and Nico are coming around this evening, for dinner and a few hands of cards.'

He inspected his nails. He yawned. But after a while he began to tense, and to grip the seat-cushions. When he eventually ejaculated, he clutched her hair fiercely so that

246

she couldn't break free, and there was a look on his face of such malicious triumph that it was just as well that she couldn't see it.

Friday, July 16, 7:24 p.m.

Effie was walking back from the river when Norman drove past, his Charger burbling noisily and blowing out smoke. He leaned out of the window and called, 'Hi! How's it going?'

She had to shield her eyes against the sinking sun. 'I'm fine, thanks, Norman. My feet are pretty much healed up. I thought Craig was with you.'

'Craig stayed up at the house while I went to buy some supplies. Brads and stuff.'

'Are you going back there now? Hold on, I'll come with you. It's time I started to get involved.'

Norman waited outside Pig Hill Inn for her while she changed into jeans and a lumberjack shirt. He played Nirvana at top volume and ignored the frowns of passers-by who had to walk through the dense exhaust of his idling engine. As soon as Effie had climbed in, he roared off along Main Street, leaving behind him a cloud of smoke that wouldn't have disgraced an atom bomb.

'I guess the house should be liveable-in by Christmas,' said Norman. 'The pest control guys are coming a week Wednesday; the roofers shouldn't take more than like a month to weatherproof the worst sections of the roof. The glass guy is taking measurements and working out some costings. And Monday – guess what – they're going to start, like, clearing the loggias and cutting down the kitchen garden.'

'It's not the sticks and stones I'm worried about,' said Effie.

'Well, I know,' said Norman. 'Mom told me what really happened with your feet.'

'And what do *you* think about it?'

Norman drew back his hair with one hand, and looked at her in surprise. 'What do *I* think about it?'

'Well, sure. It's all so strange. Don't you have an opinion? I mean, do you believe in it, or what? What do you think's happening up there?'

'I don't know. I haven't, like, really thought about it. The only opinion that I ever get asked for is what mix of sand and concrete they should use, or maybe how to stop their sash window from sticking. I guess my generation isn't so spaced-out as yours. You know . . . we're not kind of looking for the same things.'

'I know you don't believe in ghosts . . . but you *do* believe in psychic vibrations, don't you? And what about those organic buildings you were telling us about, that rebuilt themselves?'

Norman shrugged. 'I'm totally open-minded. If something happens – if I can see one in front of my eyes – then sure. A whole lot of people have seen all kinds of weird things, haven't they, and they can't *all* be lying. Like old Henry Sneider, and his Magic Barn. It's there, I've seen it, and I believe it. I guess you just have to remember that I was brought up on all of that occult stuff that mom does; and I guess I take all it for granted. Most of it's hokum, like some of those spells she cooks up. Great for constipation but that's about all. I mean she's the Laxative Queen of Putnam County, that's what my friend Marty calls her. But as for psychic vibrations . . . I don't know. I know mom can really feel something bad in Valhalla, but to tell you the truth I've never seen anything or felt anything, and sometimes you have to wonder how much of it is down to the place, right, and how much of it is down to what's going on inside of your own head.'

'What are you trying to tell me? You think she could be *imagining* these psychic vibrations?'

'Who knows? It's a possibility.'

'But I've seen them, too. And heard them. And look what happened to my feet.'

Norman turned into the sloping, narrow road that led up to Valhalla. 'Listen, don't get me wrong. I really don't know.'

'You think I imagined these cuts on my feet? I almost lost my toes.'

'I don't know, Mrs Bellman. I've heard of spontaneous bleeding and things like that. People going blind for no reason that anybody can think of. But whether it's something to do with Valhalla, I truly can't say. I don't think you should worry too much. Once we get that house weatherproof and warm, and cut out all of that dry rot, you're going to love it. And when it's fully restored, I can tell you, it's going to be amazing.'

As they drove up the hill, under the darkening shadows of the trees, Effie fell silent. It seemed that Norman was so excited by the prospect of restoring Valhalla that he was quite prepared to dismiss his mother's fear of it as nothing more than hysteria. What had happened to his tart defence that 'she's entitled to have her opinions' – and that 'people who can't sense psychic vibrations are suffering from mental gangrene'?

Effie may not have been able to count on Norman as an ally – she had known from the moment she had met him how much he had dreamed of restoring Valhalla, and Craig had given him the opportunity to do it. But she had felt that he was sensitive and sympathetic, and that she could rely on him.

249

Now she wasn't so sure. She was beginning to feel that Valhalla was nothing more than male vanity and male aggression, transformed into bricks and slates and stained-glass windows; and that every man who came close to Valhalla would eventually succumb to the moral licence it gave them, just by its very existence. A very big house for a very big man.

'Your mom's going to cleanse the house for me,' she said; as they drove past Red Oaks Inn.

'Well . . . she's in demand for that kind of thing. She cleansed a house in Peekskill last year. They said they kept seeing these transparent faces, floating in the hall.'

'Do you think she can? I mean, do you think it's possible?'

'To cleanse it? I guess. So long as there's something to cleanse in the first place, apart from dirty floors.'

'You seem so *sceptical* all of a sudden.'

Norman changed gear to climb up the last steep slope. 'Listen, Mrs Bellman . . . I don't get regular work. Valhalla's been my passion since I was small. Now I got the chance to work on it. Like, give it back its glory.'

'The way I feel about it, it was never glorious.'

'Depends on your definition of glory, I guess.'

They drove through the gates of Valhalla and jolted down the long, curving driveway. Behind the trees, the house came into view, with the setting sun burning behind its rooftops.

'Hey, that's your mom's pick-up,' said Effie. 'Don't tell me she's started her cleansing already.'

'She never said a word to me.'

Norman parked the Charger right up behind Pepper's battered blue Chevrolet pick-up, with all its peeling moon decals along the sides. They climbed out, and Effie listened, and for the first time she heard the wind moaning softly through the rooftops, the gentlest of dirges through the chimney stacks. She shivered, although it wasn't cold.

They climbed up the steps. The front door was closed, but when Norman tried the handle they found it wasn't locked. He opened it, and it swung back in total silence, as it always did. A perfectly-joined door, on perfectly-balanced hinges. Inside, it smelled the same. That odd aroma of camphor, and menthol and aniseed. Spicy, but stale, like opening Tutankhamen's tomb and finding a crisp, bandaged mummy.

They crossed the hallway. The light in the broken windows was beginning to fade. For some reason this gave Effie a strong sense of urgency, as if they had to complete their business here before it grew totally dark. Then she thought: *Dracula*. It's a memory from *Dracula*. Everything had to be done before the sun dropped below the horizon.

She looked up at the galleried landing, and the coat of arms with all its heraldic symbols on it. Bobbin, dice, dragon and skull. The four quarters of Jack Belias' life. And its legend, *Non omnis moriar* – 'I shall never completely die'.

The windows grew darker and darker, and Effie's feeling of panic began to increase, although she kept telling herself that everything was fine, everything was under control. She was here with Norman; and Pepper was here, too. Before his accident, she would have been reassured by Craig's presence, too.

'Halloooo!' called Norman. 'Anybody, like, home?'

There was no reply, so he called again. 'Hallooo, everybody! It's us! Is there anybody home? If not, why not? Come out and explain yourselves!'

Effie couldn't help giggling. 'Come on, Norman, if they're not here, how can they explain themselves?'

Norman listened, turning around and around. At last,

he said, '*Ssh!* I can hear something!'

They both listened intently. Nothing. Only the wind, sighing through the broken window panes. Only the quick, furtive scuttling of rats.

'I can't wait to get rid of those rats,' said Norman, wrinkling up his nose. 'Mr Bellman and me went down to the cellar a couple of days ago, and the whole damned place is squirgling with them. Literally squirgling, everywhere.'

'*Squirgling?*' asked Effie.

'That's right. That's when they like squirm and wriggle and writhe, all at the same time. Jesus, you should see them.'

'I think I'd rather not. And thanks for telling me, before we spent the night here.'

'I'm sorry, Mrs Bellman. But they're cellar rats. Like, live-in-the-dark rats. They wouldn't dare to come upstairs.'

'I'll believe you.'

They walked through to the ballroom but when they opened the doors it was deserted. Even while she was standing in the doorway, uncertain about whether she should venture inside, Effie could see the daylight dying and dying in the tall, tainted-glass windows. She tried not to think about the *The Blue Danube*, or the broken champagne glasses slicing into her feet.

'Halloooo!' called Norman.

They listened; but there was no reply.

'They must be upstairs.'

They returned to the hallway, and climbed the left-hand staircase to the galleried landing. 'This place is killing me,' said Norman. 'All you have to do is forget your screwdriver on the third floor, and you have to like walk back thirty-five miles.'

Effie said, 'Where do you think they are? I hope they

haven't had an argument. Your mother asked me not to tell Craig that she was coming here.'

'They've probably met by surprise and, like, frightened each other to death.'

Effie laughed. 'That wouldn't surprise me.'

They reached the landing. The doors to the anteroom were slightly ajar, and as they approached them, Effie could hear Pepper calling out. She couldn't make out what she was saying, but she sounded as if she had hurt herself. Then she heard Craig's voice, shouting back at her. Effie turned to Norman and frowned in bewilderment.

She was just about to push open the doors when she distinctly heard Craig saying, '*Bitch!*' and she took her hand away from the door handles as if they were red hot.

'What's up, doc?' asked Norman.

Effie swallowed. The only time that Craig had ever called her 'bitch' was when he was having sex with her. He hadn't called her bitch at any other time, even when they were going through a hell-blazing row.

Pepper cried out yet again. This time – with a jerky thrust of both hands that was more like a nervous spasm than a deliberate act – Effie threw the doors wide open.

At first she couldn't understand what she was looking at. The anteroom was already filled with shadows, and the thing that writhed in the middle of it looked for one skin-prickling instant like a single distorted creature, like the plaster monster on the landing. But then it moved, and resolved itself, and she saw Pepper lying on her back, with a flimsy cotton dress dragged right up around her neck, both bare feet up in the air, her thighs impossibly wide apart, while Craig crouched between them, like a supplicant at some unholy ritual, wearing nothing but his black polo-shirt.

Effie stood in utter silence. Norman, just behind her,

turned his head away in embarrassment.

'*Bitch!*' Craig snarled at Pepper, pushing himself into her. His bare buttocks tightened like a fist.

It was then that Pepper, as she clung to him, glanced over his shoulder and saw Effie standing in the doorway. An extraordinary expression crossed Pepper's face – not of shock or surprise, as Effie would have imagined, but complete mystification, as if she couldn't remember who Effie was, or why she should be standing there looking at her. It was the expression of somebody who glimpses an old acquaintance in a busy street; knowing that friend to have died, years ago.

Norman tried to catch Effie's arm, but Effie said, 'Take me back to the Inn, please, Norman. Please, Norman – now!'

She crossed the landing and ran down the stairs. She didn't want to see, she didn't want to think. Most of all she didn't want to hear any explanations. She tugged open the front doors and hurried out onto the steps. A soft still darkness was gathering, and the sky around Valhalla was speckled with bats.

'Effie!' It was Pepper. 'Effie, wait!'

Effie ran down the steps and across the shingle to Norman's automobile. Her forehead felt as if she had been pressing it against a block of ice for ten minutes: numb and cold and physically hurting. She wished to God that she had brought her own car: then she could have sped away from here directly, and never, ever come back.

Norman came out, closely followed immediately by a flustered Pepper. She was white-faced, except for two crimson spots on her cheeks. In her diaphanous white dress she looked as if she were playing Lady Macbeth. She came hurrying barefoot down the steps, overtaking Norman, and she came right up to Effie and caught hold

254

of her sleeve. Effie twisted herself free, and turned her face away.

'Effie, I didn't realise! Effie, listen to me, it wasn't even me!'

'Please, Norman,' said Effie, ignoring her. 'Can we just get out of here, pronto?'

Norman opened the car door for her, and Effie climbed inside. Pepper clung onto the door to stop her from closing it. 'Effie, you have to believe me! It was a psychic vibration, the worst one yet!'

Effie looked up at her coldly. 'From where I was standing, it looked more like a physical vibration. Now, do you mind.'

'*Effie it wasn't me!*'

'In that case, my eyesight must have got worse than I thought.'

'*It wasn't me, just like when you were dancing in the ballroom, that wasn't you!*'

'I cut my feet in the ballroom. At least I didn't screw somebody else's husband. What's happened to you? Come on, Norman, please, I'm tired of this.'

Norman started up the Charger's engine with an ear-splitting roar. '*It wasn't me!*' screamed Pepper, over the noise. '*It wasn't Craig, either!*'

Effie pried Pepper's fingers off the edge of the door, slammed it and locked it. Norman looked across at his mother and shrugged in resignation. There was no point in them standing on the steps having a screaming contest. Craig and Pepper had been caught in the act, and no amount of emotional opera was going to change that.

They burbled up the driveway, and Norman switched on his headlights, freezing six or seven rabbits in their tracks. Effie sat repetitively rubbing her left arm; too shocked to cry. She couldn't see rabbits. All she could see

255

were Pepper's bare feet, and the whiteness of her thighs, and the blackness of Craig, kneeling in between them.

'Did you know about this?' she asked Norman, as they passed back out through the main gates.

Norman shook his head. 'I don't know what to tell you. You could have knocked me over with a goose-feather.'

'You're telling me the truth? You really didn't know?'

'Cross my heart, Mrs Bellman. I never knew nothing. Mom has plenty of men friends. She likes to call them her "beaux". She's been in trouble a couple of times with, like, married guys. But I didn't know nothing about her and Mr Bellman, no way. I would've warned her off. You can't mix business with hanky-panky, no way. This has ruined everything.'

'You bet it's ruined everything. I'm going down to see Walter Van Buren tomorrow morning to have the sale blocked.'

'Oh, shit,' said Norman, under his breath.

Effie said nothing. There was nothing else to say. She would call her lawyer in New York as soon as she got back to Pig Hill Inn; and then she would call her mother. But before she did either of those things, she would order a large vodka-tonic on the rocks and put the chain on the bedroom door.

Friday, July 16, 10:10 p.m.

She was sitting in front of the fireplace nursing the last of her second drink and staring at the slowly-collapsing logs when the door suddenly opened – only to be sharply arrested by the chain. She heard Craig say, 'Damn it to hell, Effie!'

256

He rattled the door a few times, and then stopped. 'Effie! Effie, are you listening? I have to talk to you!'

'Go away, Craig. I don't even want to look at you.'

'I have to talk to you!'

'Whatever it is, I don't want to hear.'

'But I can explain everything!'

She sipped her drink. It was so watered-down now that it scarcely tasted of vodka. 'I know. You slipped on the underfelt and accidentally fell on top of Ms Moriarty, who just happened to be lying in front of you with her legs open.'

'Those people you saw making love, they weren't us at all. Pepper will tell you.'

'You hired look-alikes, I suppose?'

'They genuinely weren't us! Not in the sense that you're actually Effie and I'm actually Craig. Pepper was right about Valhalla, it *does* have psychic vibrations. There are all kinds of lives being lived out there, at one and the same time. There's all kinds of people living there, all at the same time.'

'There's all kinds of cheating going on there, too. I don't want to hear any more. I really don't. I wasn't sure that I believed Pepper when she talked about coincident lives. It seems to me that the only coincidence she was interested in was her body coinciding with yours. I mean, come on, Craig, this must be the most bizarre excuse for adultery that anybody has ever come up with.'

'You don't believe me, then? You *won't* believe me?'

'You got it. I don't and I won't. And I'll tell you something else that I don't and I won't, and that's go along with your buying Valhalla. That place has brought us nothing but grief ever since we walked through the door.'

'You can't stop me buying Valhalla. In fact it's already bought. I gave Walter Van Buren our banker's draft before

257

I went up there this afternoon, and I'll be picking up the titles Monday morning.'

Effie stood up and stalked across to the door. 'You gave him the banker's draft? At least a quarter of that money was mine!'

'Joint account, sweetheart, with single-signature authorisation. Besides, I got the impression that you were coming around to the idea of buying it.'

'That was before I caught you and that hippie witch bitch fucking on the floor!'

'Sweetheart, how many times do I have to tell you that it wasn't us?'

'Oh, no? What do you think I've got for brains? Cream of Wheat? You're looking at a divorce, mister. Don't even dream that you're not. I'm going to take you for everything, and if we've already bought Valhalla then I'll take you for that, too. Then we'll see whether it was you or not.'

Craig hesitated, leaning against the inch-wide crack in the door. Effie could smell the alcohol on his breath.

'Effie, this is serious. This is really serious. What happened this afternoon was something extraordinary.'

'I'll bet. How did you like her? Did she have better vaginal grip than me? I notice she was noisier than me.'

'Effie, I think I was Jack Belias.'

She said nothing, but looked at him with tired contempt.

'I met Pepper in the ballroom,' he blurted. 'She was doing some kind of psychic ritual – you know, trying to get rid of all the disturbances. At first I was me but then for some reason I wasn't me. I don't know what happened after that. The house was different, Pepper was different. *I* was different. I was married. I knew I was married, but it wasn't to you.

'I had *power*, Effie. I had all of my confidence back. What those people took from me . . . that taxi driver, those

258

gangsters . . . I had it all back. I was full of energy, full of – I don't know. You know they talk about these black holes, these collapsed stars, that have such intense gravity that even light can't escape? They suck in everything around them – meteors, whole planets, even. That's what I felt like. And I sucked in Gaby, too.'

'Gaby?' asked Effie, sharply.

'I didn't say Gaby. I said Pepper.'

'You distinctly said Gaby.'

'Well, for Christ's sake, Effie. Pepper, Gaby, whatever. But it wasn't me. I didn't know anything about it till Pepper got up. She said, "Effie's here – she's seen us", and then I was back to being me.'

Effie drained her glass. 'Then you were back to being you?' she mimicked. 'You must think that I'm sceptically challenged.'

'I swear it. It's true. I really believe that I was Jack Belias.'

'You mean that your hippie mistress has invented some hotch-potch story about psychic disturbances to get you off the hook? Listen to me, Craig, I'm talking to my lawyer, and that's all I have to say to you, except that you'd better find someplace else to stay. There's probably an empty bed at the Hungry Moon.'

'*Effie!*' Craig bellowed, unexpectedly. '*Effie, it's true! I was Jack Belias! I am Jack Belias!*'

Then there was silence, punctuated only by Craig's over-exerted breathing.

Effie stood very still for a moment. She should have known that she was making a mistake by supporting his obsession for Valhalla. He hadn't been rehabilitated, after his 'accident.' He wasn't cured at all. He was still so vulnerable that he had embraced *anything* that might restore his virility. A big house for a big man; or a loose, pretty, devil-

259

may-care woman who believed in spells and mirror-magic and hocus-pocus. She thought about the night that they had stayed at Valhalla. Maybe Pepper had been hiding somewhere, in one of the upstairs bedrooms, and Craig had left the futon to go and make love to her. After all, Pepper had known where they were. And maybe, when Craig had called her, Pepper had adopted an aggressive attitude to hide the fact that they were already lovers.

Effie felt grievously wounded; but at the same time she had been expecting a crisis like this, sooner or later. It was almost a relief that Craig had given her an excuse for turning her back on him; and on Valhalla, too.

'I'll call you,' she said, pressing against the door, to close it. 'Let me talk to my lawyer, then I'll call you.'

'Effie – please, listen to me. I was Jack Belias. I *am* Jack Belias. I can prove it.'

'Go away, Craig.'

'Effie, he's inside of my head, just as much as I am! I can't help it!'

'Craig, if you don't go away, I'll have Ms O'Brien call for the police.'

'You want me to tell you how to cheat at baccarat? Did I ever know how to do it before? Do you want me to tell you about *poussettes*, or how to sandwich the shoe? Do you seriously think that I would know anything about baccarat, if I hadn't been him, if I *wasn't* him?'

'Craig, go away. I don't want to talk to you. It's over.'

'What more do you want, for Christ's sake? Do you want me to tell you about the night that I won £60,000 against Nico Zographos and the Greek Syndicate? Listen – listen – I was sitting at table two at Deauville and my table won 26 out of 29 coups against the bank. I won 12 coups myself. I went for a drink but Nico Zographos wanted me back at the table so that he could win his money back. I sat down

260

and promptly won five more coups. I won so much damn money that Zographos asked me if I wanted to join the syndicate.'

'Craig –'

'I can tell you how I ruined Bert Ambrose at the Winter Casino at Monte Carlo? That was October of 1934. I can tell you coup by coup; every card that was turned.'

'Craig, this is madness. I want to talk to my lawyer. I want to think.'

'Effie, I need you.'

'What for? Because you're short of people to laugh at?'

'I really mean it, Effie. I'll do anything.'

For one long moment Effie didn't speak. She thought of all the happy times they had spent together, from the moment he had quoted Mallarmé to their long sunlit vacations on Key West and Hilton Head Island. She thought of hamburgers at P. J. Clarke's and walks in the park. Then she thought about those interminable business meetings with Koreans and Japanese. *My name is Mrs Bellman. How are you?*

She closed the door, and double-locked it. Craig didn't call out, didn't knock. She stayed where she was until she heard him walk away.

Saturday, July 17, 10:21 a.m.

She had to walk past the Hungry Moon to get to Walter Van Buren's office. As she did so, Pepper called, 'Effie, wait!' and came running out of the store after her. She was wearing a black bandanna and a black T-shirt and there were plum-coloured circles under her eyes as if she hadn't slept.

Effie didn't break her stride; and Pepper almost had to run to keep up with her.

'Effie, will you please wait? I have to talk to you.'

'Whatever you have to say, I don't want to hear it.'

'Effie, what happened yesterday evening – it was like a nightmare.'

'I never thought that Craig was *that* bad in bed.'

She crossed the street, but Pepper continued to walk beside her. 'When Craig said it wasn't us, he was telling you the truth. It wasn't us. And it wasn't yesterday evening, either. It was another time altogether.'

Effie stopped outside the Country Goose. 'Oh, *really*,' she said. 'How naive do you think I am?'

'I don't think you're naive at all. In fact I think you're sophisticated enough to understand what I'm trying to say to you, and to believe it.'

'All I know, Ms Moriarty, is that I saw you with my own eyes lying on your back with your legs in the air and my husband on top of you.'

'Wrong. What you saw was Gaby – Gaby Deslys, a dancer. She was Jack Belias' mistress.'

'Well, well,' said Effie. 'You two have really cooked up an excuse between you, haven't you?'

'God help me, it's true. The same way that you were dancing in another time, and cut your feet.'

'Norman put that down to spontaneous bleeding.'

'Norman's a builder, not a psychic sensitive. You were in another time, the same as Craig and I were.'

Effie started walking again. 'I'm sorry, Pepper. I talked to my lawyer last night and he's already taking steps to freeze our joint assets and register my interest in the marital home.'

'Oh, come on! You're not thinking of divorce?'

'I don't know yet. I'm just protecting myself.'

262

Pepper said, 'You have to believe me, Effie, please. There is absolutely nothing between Craig and me. For God's sake, I called him Mr Bellman until yesterday evening.'

'At least the affair was polite.'

'It wasn't an affair, and it wasn't us! There's something happening at Valhalla which even I don't understand.'

'It's called two-timing. Now do you understand?'

'Effie, please. Valhalla was always a disturbed place . . . I always sensed that there was something unbalanced about it. But it's just as if Craig has triggered off a huge psychic upheaval. Yesterday evening, when we went up to that room where you found us together, that room was fully restored, fully furnished, with gilt mirrors and velvet curtains, everything. The room looked like new. In fact I think it *was* new. Effie – that's a psychic disturbance of *incredible* proportions. I've experienced sounds before; and distinctive smells; and the feeling that there's somebody there. I've even experienced emotions which were nothing to do with the way I was really feeling . . . like terrible sadness, in a room where a woman had to sit and nurse her dying child. But I *saw* this room. I experienced it. I felt it. And I talked and behaved like Gaby Deslys, not like me at all.'

Effie looked at Pepper steadily. Her expression was entirely serious; and sympathetic, too. The cool breeze from the river rustled the lime tree under which they were standing, and the shadows dappled her face.

'I don't know,' she said. 'I think you'd agree that it's pretty damn hard to believe.'

'You danced in that ballroom, Effie. You saw people who weren't there and cut your feet on glass that didn't exist. Yet it must have existed, at some time, and you have the scars on your feet to prove it.'

263

'So what proof do *you* have that you were Gaby Deslys?'

'The very fact that I know her name, and almost everything about her. I know where she was born, I know what her mother looked like. I know that she set off the riots that deposed King Manoel of Portugal, by saying that he had given her three fantastic pearl necklaces, even though he hadn't. I know something else, too; that she had roses tattooed on her breasts, just to please Jack Belias.'

With that, she unbuttoned her blouse and bared her breasts, right out there on the street. Several passers-by stopped and stared, and one elderly man nearly walked into a tree.

Effie said, 'Pepper – not here –'

But Pepper said, 'You want proof? Here's proof.'

Very, very faintly, Effie could see pinkish smudges on each of Pepper's breasts. They were so faint that they were almost invisible, and yet she could distinctly see that they were meant to be roses.

She nodded, and said, 'Yes. I see them,' and Pepper fastened up her blouse.

'Effie, this is a psychic disturbance that's powerful enough to make actual physical changes. Look at me! Not only do I have Gaby Deslys' memories but I have her tattoos, too. What's going to happen to me next? I don't *want* to be Gaby Deslys! I want to be me! Gaby Deslys lived in the 1920s and I don't want to live in the 1920s.'

'Craig kept saying he was Jack Belias.'

'I know how he feels. I'm sure, for a while, he *was* Jack Belias. And himself, too. But I swear to you, Effie, I wasn't me when Craig and I had sex yesterday evening, and he wasn't him. I did things with him that I never did with any man before – things that I never want to do again.'

'I don't want to hear about it,' Effie interrupted her.

'But you must; and you have to believe me. If Valhalla

264

isn't cleansed, then Craig is going to become more and more like Jack Belias until he *is* Jack Belias, not just mentally, but physically. Jack Belias was a very strong personality, very dominant; whereas Craig is much weaker. Gaby Deslys was obviously stronger than me, and that's why I wound up with her tattoos, instead of *her* winding up with my bust size. Like I said, this disturbance makes actual physical changes to people.'

Effie suddenly thought of the way in which Craig's skin and colouring had been gradually altering in the past two weeks. She also thought of the impression that he had given her, the last time they had made love, that he had two testicles instead of one.

And then she thought of something else. His fingerprints. If his skin could be smooth like Jack Belias, and his hair darker, why couldn't his fingerprints have subtly altered, too?

Saturday, July 17, 11:03 a.m.

Walter Van Buren was wearing his Saturday-morning clothes, a sports coat and a turtle-neck sweater, both in the same beige as his weekday clothes. Effie was sure that if they started to produce automobiles the colour of bracken he would have been first in line. He was stoking his pipe, biting the tip of his tongue in concentration, when she was shown into his office.

'Ah . . . Mrs Bellman. Good of you to visit.'

'You got my message?'

'I surely did, and I have to say that I'm very distressed about it. Effectively the sale has gone through. All the contracts have been signed and the vendors have your banker's draft. I don't know what the position is going to be when Fulloni & Jahn find out that your accounts have been frozen. They'll probably sue. In fact, I have to say that they're certain to sue.'

Effie said, 'I think I may have changed my mind. My husband and I had a – well, we had a misunderstanding yesterday. I haven't spoken to him today, but I don't see why we shouldn't be able to work something out.'

'I'm very relieved to hear that, Mrs Bellman. You know, house-buying is the single most stressful human activity after armed combat.'

'In this case, I think it beats armed combat hands down.'

'Well, yes, you're right. But you should try the Feldenkrais method . . . wonderful for getting rid of strain. You have to think of your rear end as a clock, you know.'

'Pardon?'

'You have to rotate it, you see. Your rear end. It's very relaxing.'

Effie ignored his advice. 'I'll talk things over with my husband. Then I'll talk to my lawyer again and get back to you.'

'I'm pleased. Valhalla needs somebody like your husband to get it back into shape.' He sat back in his chair, and there was a faraway, unfocused look in his eyes. 'Somebody with passion. Somebody *big*. It would be a hell of a pity to see it deteriorate any further.'

'You sound almost emotional about it,' Effie smiled. She was aware that it was the first time she had smiled since yesterday evening.

Walter Van Buren blinked his eyes back into focus and sat up straight. 'Let's just say that I have a personal interest in the old place.'

Effie waited, but it became obvious that he wasn't going to tell her what this personal interest was, and so she stood up to leave.

He showed her to the door. As she left, he gently put his hand on her elbow and said, 'I like you, Mrs Bellman. You kind of remind me of somebody I used to know, a very long time ago. So please take care. We wouldn't want anything happening to you, would we?'

'I'm not sure what you mean.'

'Old buildings can be very dangerous places sometimes. Don't forget your hard hat.'

'I won't,' said Effie, baffled.

She left the office and walked back up Main Street. As she crossed the road, however, she glimpsed him watching her from Van Buren Realty's front window, his face as pale as liverwurst. She couldn't think why, but the way he was watching her seemed deeply sinister.

Saturday, July 17, 11:57 a.m.

Norman must have been waiting for her. As she quickly walked past the open door of the Hungry Moon, he came leaping out like a jack-in-a-box. He was wearing a huge Indian shirt in purples and greens and he was wearing tiny sunglasses with amber lenses.

'Mrs Bellman!' he called. 'Mrs Bellman, I really have to talk to you!'

Effie glanced inside and she could see Pepper standing in silhouette at the crowded counter, wreathed in cigarette smoke.

'If you're worried about your contract, Norman, stop worrying. Your mom persuaded me to stay cool.'

Norman said, 'She told me about it. You know, like, she's not often sorry. But this time she's real sorry. She didn't want to hurt you, not for nothing.'

'It's all right, Norman. I think we've come to an understanding.'

'Well, I'm glad about that. And not just because of the work I was doing, or the money I was making. I mean, like, work is work, and money is money, but friends are friends.'

'That's right. Friends are friends.' She turned to walk on.

'Hey – you're not going?' said Norman, in alarm. 'I have to show you something.'

'I'm tired. I've had a bad week, okay? Can't it wait for some other time?'

'Please,' said Norman. 'This could be the answer to what's been happening up at Valhalla. It's true, I've seen it for myself. I don't know whether it's anything to do with occult disturbances or any of that stuff. You know what I think about that. Pretty sceptical, most of the time. But this is different.'

'Well, what is it?' asked Effie, impatiently.

'Do you know the Benton House, up at Salt Point?'

She shook her head.

'Well, I hadn't either. But mom had. She said that it's pretty famous, at least it is in psychic circles.'

'I think I've had enough of psychics for one day.'

'I guess so – but listen: the Benton House was built by this nutty religious sect in the 1890s, the Brotherhood of Balam. It belongs to the Historic Hudson Valley people now; but they've never got around to restoring it. Seems like they've tried about four or five times, but each time they've had to stop work because of some serious accident; and so the place is closed up. But Jim Bogard, one of the trustees, he let me borrow the keys. He wasn't supposed to; but I restored this gazebo for him last year, you know,

268

and did a real special job on it, so he like owed me.'

'Norman – what has any of this to do with me?'

'It could have a whole lot to do with you, Mr Bellman. No, I'm serious. The Brotherhood built the house in a special way . . . like the floor-joists were fitted circular, like a spider's web, which is a *very* unusual construction.'

'So?'

'So the only other place I've ever seen a floor constructed in the same way is the library floor at Valhalla.'

'Well?'

'The Brotherhood of Balam kind of upset their neighbours, so mom says, because of their rituals and stuff. But when their neighbours came looking for them, they locked themselves in their house. And then disappeared, totally disappeared, and nobody ever saw them again.'

'Oh, come on. I expect they had a secret tunnel.'

'Unh-hunh. I went all through the house, top to bottom. No secret tunnel. No secret doors. It's as solid as a rock.'

'Then what are you trying to tell me?'

Norman raised a hand to indicate that she should stay where she was. He disappeared back inside the store, and after two or three minutes he returned carrying Pepper's huge grey cat, its eyes squeezed shut in displeasure, its heavy body dangling like a gamekeeper's sack.

'You met Houdini before, didn't you?'

'I saw him in your mom's kitchen. I didn't know his name was Houdini.'

'Hairy Houdini. He used to be called Merlin, after the magician, but he got caught in the dough-mixer once, down at the bakery; and he managed to squeeze his way out between the cogs and the beaters and get himself out of there. Didn't you, Hoods? A true escapologist.'

Houdini squeezed his eyes even tighter and looked as though he would happily scratch out Norman's eyes, if

269

only he could wake up.

'Norman,' said Effie, 'I'm not in any kind of mood for games.'

'No game . . . I swear it. But if you don't see come to the Benton House to see this for yourself, you won't believe it.'

'You want me to drive up to Salt Point with you? *Now*?'

Norman dropped Houdini into the back seat of his Charger and took off his sunglasses. He pushed back his hair, and suddenly Effie found herself looking at a serious, thin, but quite good-looking young boy. 'I couldn't get the connection myself,' he said. 'But then I looked up the Brotherhood of Balam in *Nonconformist Theology* in back of mom's store. The Brotherhood were very ethical, as a matter of fact, but they worshipped fallen angels, because they thought, like, that everybody should be given a second chance. That's what upset the local populace. That, and totally nude baptism. In particular they worshipped Balam, who used to be an angel of the Order of Dominations. Balam was kicked out of heaven because he argued with God that women were equal to men. Kind of a really early version of women's liberation.'

'And?'

'And – Balam was the spirit of yesterday, today and tomorrow, all three. Balam was the spirit of time, and invisibility, and everything happening at once . . . coincidence. Balam could tell you when you were born, what you were going to do in five minutes' time, and when you were going to die. And, listen, the floor that the Brotherhood built – this weird spider-web-type floor, it wasn't so much a floor to stand on, although you could stand on it, it was like a *clock*.'

'You're losing me.'

'But don't you see? Jack Belias must have found out about the floor at the Benton House before he built

270

Valhalla. He *must* have – the design is identical, except for the scale. Because what could a gambler have wanted more than anything else in the world? To talk to Balam, right? To ask him questions, right? To know what would happen before it happened!'

Effie said, 'You're talking – *madness*! Time, spirits, floors! What the hell are you trying to say to me?'

Norman reached out and took hold of her hand. His fingers were surprisingly dry and comforting and warm. 'I'm trying to find out what's going on, that's all. I'm trying to find out what's real and what's imaginary.'

'I think we can safely say that Balam is imaginary.'

'What about the man you danced with? The man who cut your feet? Like, how imaginary was he?'

'I don't know. As far as I'm concerned, it's finished.'

'Mrs Bellman,' Norman said, with great gravity. 'It's far from being finished. Please – come with me to Salt Point? We could eat at St Andrew's Café. I have a friend who's studying at the culinary institute there . . . he can get me a table almost anytime.'

'I appreciate the offer, Norman, but I'm not particularly hungry and I don't want to go to Salt Point.'

Norman stared at her for a moment and then he let his hair fall back over his face. He looked so disconsolate that Effie reached out and took hold of his hand. 'Norman . . . I've had so much grief with Valhalla . . . I don't want any more.'

'Okay, then,' said Norman. 'I understand. But I took Houdini up to the Benton House early this morning, and it worked, and there's no reason why it shouldn't work now.'

'What worked?'

'I have to show you. You won't believe it, else.'

It was just then that Effie looked up the street and saw a

taxi stop outside Pig Hill Inn. The door opened, and Craig climbed out. She knew that she needed to have a long and soul-searching talk to him. In an odd way she had almost forgiven him for what had happened between him and Pepper Moriarty up at Valhalla. She didn't logically know why. But she could almost believe that he and Pepper were telling the truth about it. Craig, in spite of his irascibility, had always told her the truth; and she had a strong feeling that Pepper wouldn't dare to lie – that Pepper believed too strongly in the powers of light and darkness and mystical retribution.

If Pepper was convinced that she could use a few pinches of magic herbs to make a mistress's skin wither like an old apple, her eyes dull over and her breasts sag, then she obviously believed that somebody could do it back to her.

Craig disappeared into Pig Hill Inn's front door. Effie hesitated for a moment, then opened the door of Norman's car, and climbed into the passenger seat, and said, 'Sure, yes, why not?'

Norman looked pleased, and started the engine. He turned north-east, towards Nelsonville, and the Taconic State Parkway. Houdini sat up in the back with his eyes closed, his fur ruffled by the warm wind.

Saturday, July 17, 4:04 p.m.

They turned off the road and bounced along a rutted, rock-strewn track that ran down one side of a cornfield. Black clouds were building up from the north-west, but the sun still shone warmly on the varnished corn-ears and the shivering leaves of the aspens that bordered the field on two sides.

They turned into a scrubby, pentagonal field of about two-and-a-half acres. Almost in the centre stood a large, boxy-looking house, with steeply sloping roofs and four pentagonal turrets, one at each corner. The house was painted in flaky grey, and the roof was green. The windows were as empty as picture frames with no pictures in them; except for one large window on the left-hand side, which reflected a shining-perfect view of the sun, and the gathering clouds, and the shivering aspen trees.

Norman stopped and they climbed out of the car. A thin wind was blowing, and Effie wished that she had brought her coat. He said, 'You should see the way they put this baby together. This was housebuilding. I mean this was like *joinery*.'

Effie looked back towards the sun-gilded cornfield. It appeared curiously unreal, as if it were a background painting for *The Wizard of Oz*. She could imagine Judy Garland walking through it, accompanied by the Scarecrow. Then slowly the clouds began to nibble at the edge of the sun, and the field darkened, and the wind blew stronger through the stalks.

'Come on,' Norman urged her. He was carrying Houdini under his arm. 'You have to see this, you really do.'

They climbed up the front steps to the verandah, and he unlatched the screen door. 'They don't build houses like this any more. They *can't*. They may have the skill but they don't have any, like, *psyche*. This house was built on this exact spot because it was the right spot, whichever way you look at it. And it was built of the right materials and painted the right colour. That's what we call architectural psyche.'

He unlocked the front door. There was a dulled brass knocker on it, in the shape of a long, attenuated goat's face.

'Balam,' said Norman.

'Looks kind of miserable, doesn't he?' said Effie.

'Notice that he's facing east . . . same as the knocker at Valhalla.'

They stepped into the house. It was gloomy and silent and smelled of disuse. 'It's not damp, though,' said Norman. 'They built it so well that it never got damp. You look at the roof. Could've been finished yesterday.'

He led her through an empty hallway across floors that were immaculately boarded in limed oak, not a trace of discoloration or warping, and still gleaming faintly under their coating of dust.

'Look at these floors. I could cry. And do you know something? If the Hudson Valley Historical Society records are right, they were laid by a boy of nineteen called Ethan Carter. A boy of nineteen! I can't find men of twice his experience to lay a decent floor.'

He took her through to the largest room. It was high and rectangular, and almost four times the size of any other in the house, but the odd thing was that it had no windows. Any light which penetrated came from the open doors.

'Look at *this* floor,' Norman enthused. 'Now tell me, come on, like, is this a floor; or is this a floor?'

Effie walked across it, her training shoes squeaking on the once-polished oak. 'It's circular, for sure.'

'It's *amazing*!' Norman cried out, almost in anguish. 'It's the single most incredible piece of joinery I've ever seen in my entire life!'

Effie looked down, and Norman was right. It *was* amazing. It was made up entirely of curved oak boarding, laid out in perfect concentric circles, like a bullseye.

'How did they *do* that?' she said, turning around and around.

274

'Easy – well, simple in concept, rather than easy. George Carter sawed out acres of wood from mature oaks, *by hand*, right? and fitted them together like a massive jigsaw-puzzle. But think of the skill it needed! Every circle has to have a greater diameter than the circle next to it. And there must be over a thousand pieces here.'

Effie kept on turning around. 'What a dance-floor! It's incredible!'

'Hey – don't,' said Norman. 'Mrs Bellman – don't do that!'

She stopped circling. 'Don't do what?'

'All that around-and-around stuff. Like I told you, it's more than a floor, it's a clock.'

She looked down at it again. 'I still don't understand what you mean.'

'That's why I brought Houdini. You can't explain this floor. You have to show people.'

He dropped the cat into the very centre of the room. Then he hunkered down beside him, and stroked him. Houdini stretched and yawned and nuzzled up against his knee. But then Norman reached into his pocket and took out a small bow-tie shape, made out of folded white paper with an elastic band around it. While he tickled Houdini under the chin with one hand, he slipped the paper bow over his tail with his other. Houdini immediately turned around. He snatched at the bow, but missed it, and turned around again. Soon he was flying around and around, furiously trying to catch this irritating white butterfly that seemed to be following him wherever he went.

'Now, watch,' said Norman quietly, standing up. 'Watch what he does, and, like, watch his colour, too. See? It's starting to change already.'

The cat was chasing his tail so fast that he was nothing more than a furry blur. Even so, Effie could see that something was happening to him. He appeared to be bigger, and darker, and he kept on growing darker until he was almost black.

'What's happening?' asked Effie. 'He looks like a different cat altogether.'

Still Houdini went on circling and scratching and growing larger. Effie took a step closer to him, to try to see what was actually happening to him, but Norman caught her arm. 'Careful – he won't know me any more. Not for a few moments, anyhow.'

'Look at him! He's really going crazy!'

Norman checked his watch. 'I think he's done enough ... I'd better get that bow off of him.'

He knelt down on one knee, and reached out to catch Houdini as he came circling around. His hand struck the cat just once. Houdini suddenly stopped chasing his own tail and jumped at Norman's face, spitting in fury.

Norman lifted his arm to protect himself and fell over sideways. But Houdini wriggled viciously under his arm and raked his claws all the way down from his eyelid to his chin. Norman shouted out, rolled over, and tried to stand up again. Houdini leaped onto his back and started tearing at his ears.

'*Get him off!*' Norman screamed. '*For Christ's sake, get him off!*'

Effie wrenched off one of her sneakers, and hit the cat on the side of the head with it, and then on the back. Each blow made a horrible hollow thumping sound. She was just about to hit the cat again when it twisted around and hissed at her, a thick crackling hiss of pure hatred.

And she saw that it wasn't Houdini at all, but a huge black tom with glaring yellow eyes and filthy, matted fur, and a wedge-shaped head that was more like a cobra's than a cat's.

276

She screamed and threw her sneaker at it, and it dropped off Norman's back onto the floor. Norman scrambled to his feet and kicked it, twice. It lashed out at his foot, but then he kicked it even harder, and it fled into the next room.

'For God's sake, what happened to him?' said Effie. 'Are you all right, Norman? Look at your face!'

'I'm fine.' He took out a grey-looking handkerchief and dabbed at his cheek. 'Let's just get after that cat.'

'Get after it? It could have taken your eye out!'

'Come on,' Norman urged her, and took hold of her hand. He led her to the next room, where the black cat had run off to – taking just a quick cautionary peek through the crack in the door before he stepped inside.

Effie warily looked around. The doors were locked. The windows were closed. The fireplace was firmly boarded up. But there was no sign of the cat at all.

'Where did it go? It was *huge*, Norman. Where did it go?'

'Back to its owners, I guess. The Brotherhood of Balam.'

'That was *their* cat?'

'Fits the description in the records. A black cat with a vicious temper that always kept watch on the porch and attacked anyone who came close.'

Effie looked around again, because she couldn't believe it. There was no way that the cat could have found its way out of the room, and yet it had vanished. And it *must* have existed, because Norman's scratches bore witness to that.

It was then that she heard a low, doleful mewing sound. She turned around, and there, back in the centre of the main room, stood Houdini. Cowed, confused, but physically unchanged.

'He's back,' she breathed. 'He was here – then he was there – and now he's back. It's like magic.'

Norman shook his head. 'Not magic. It's science. It's

277

architecture. Mom knows more about it than I do. The Mayans were the first people to build floors like these. I mean, like, anybody could have done it, the Romans, the Greeks, whoever. They had the math, they had like all of the technical skills, but you had to believe that it was going to work, otherwise you wouldn't even try, would you? It's what I call the Deadwood Bicycle Syndrome.' He went over and picked up Houdini and stroked him. Houdini struggled a little, but he seemed unharmed by what had happened to him. 'A guy came out West in the 1880s with plans for a bicycle, and gave them to this blacksmith in Deadwood. The blacksmith refused to make it because he said he never put his name to anything that couldn't possibly work.'

Effie reached out her finger and Houdini licked it with a rasping tongue.

'The Brotherhood's cat is still here,' Norman continued. 'And so are the Brotherhood. When they disappeared, they didn't actually *disappear*, they just used this floor to take themselves through to another time. Maybe backward, maybe forward. More probably forward, I guess. They'll probably turn up again one day, right as rain.'

'They took themselves *forward*? Into the future?'

'I think so. I mean, like, who's an expert? But you turn clockwise for forward and anti-clockwise for backward. Haven't you ever thought *why* clocks go round the way they do? Like, there's no particular mechanical reason for it. It's just the way that time fits together, like this floor.'

'So what's been happening at Valhalla, you think it's the same as this?'

'Pretty much. Houdini got close to a cat with a strong personality, and he started to look like him and act like him. Mr Bellman got close to Jack Belias, and Jack Belias took him over. My mom got close to this Gaby Deslys

278

woman, and the same thing happened to her.'

'You didn't give me this little demonstration just to prove that your mom was innocent, did you?'

Norman looked embarrassed. 'Partly, if you want to know the truth. She said it wasn't her and even though it sure as hell *looked* like her, I believe her when she says that it wasn't. I want you to believe her, too; because we have to cleanse that house for good, and she's the only person I know who can do it.'

They walked back to the car. Effie was feeling very tired now, and all she wanted was a strong cup of coffee and a few hours' rest. While Norman dropped Houdini into the back seat, she turned around and took a last long look at the Benton House. The black clouds almost completely filled the sky now, and the first few drops of summer rain were falling. The windows of the house were so dark that it was impossible to see inside; but for a moment Effie was convinced that she could make out the shadow of a man, with his back turned to her.

Tuesday, July 20, 7:36 p.m.

Pepper snapped shut the last of the books, tossed it to one side, yawned and gave an extravagant stretch, so that an irritated Houdini almost slipped off her lap. Effie had finished reading over a half-hour ago, and she was leaning back against a huge Indian cushion with her eyes closed, listening to the tinkling of the wind-chimes in Pepper's living-room window.

'Didn't *anybody* ever write *anything* about Jack Belias?' Pepper demanded. 'He was a millionaire, a gambler, and he deliberately ruined more of his so-called friends than

279

you could shake a stick at. He knew the Aga Khan, the Dolly Sisters, the goddamned Duke of Westminster. Sure, they wrote about the money he won, and the hands he played. But what about *him*, and his wife, and his love-affairs? What about Gaby Deslys?'

She pried open her tin and took out an anorexic joint. It flared up when she lit it and left her with only a few shreds of grass and tobacco and an evanescent smell of Woodstock. 'How's Craig?' she asked, brushing ash off Houdini's fur. Her voice was deliberately soft and diffident. Craig was still a tender topic of conversation between them, in spite of Pepper's assurances and Houdini's apparent transformation.

'So-so,' said Effie. 'We haven't been talking too much. I wanted to discuss what happened up at Valhalla – you know, to clear the air, and to try to find out what's been happening to him. But he says he's not interested in talking about it any more, and if I don't believe him then maybe I should go back to the city.'

'You do believe him, though?'

'I don't have much choice, do I, if I want to stay with him? But he's acting so strange. He spent most of Sunday sleeping; and all of yesterday up at Valhalla. And I swear he's changing. He *feels* different, talks different. He doesn't even smell like Craig any more. To tell you the truth, I'm frightened for him. But he won't even think of giving up Valhalla. All I have to do is mention it and he flies into a rage.'

'Doesn't he have any other friends who could talk to him?'

'He won't speak to any of his friends any more. He says the house is all he needs. I made some diplomatic noises about him talking to his psychiatrist, Dr Samstag, but all he did was turn his back on me and walk out of the room.'

Pepper was silent for a while. Then she said, 'You don't think it might be a good idea if you *did* go away for a while?'

And risk the possibility that he wasn't Jack Belias when he was having sex with Pepper, and that she wasn't Gaby Deslys . . . and leave them both alone together?

'Of course I've thought of going away. But what's going to happen to Craig if I do? He's been violent and angry and very, very strange, but I still love him.'

Pepper said, 'You *have* forgiven me, haven't you?' Her eyes like silver; like polished dimes.

'I don't know. Is it you that I'm supposed to forgive; or this Gaby woman? And is it Craig that I'm supposed to forgive, or Jack Belias?'

Pepper came across and sat next to her. She was wearing a loose-woven indigo shirt and skintight jeans and a jingling gold-coin headband. Effie was very aware of her sensuality; how her breasts swayed heavily under that diaphanous cotton. By comparison, she felt over-smart. She wore a pink-and-white checkered shirt from Bergdorf Goodman and a pair of expensive white canvas slacks. Pepper smelled of herbs and spices, the larder of love. Effie smelled of Fifth Avenue cosmetic counters.

'I think this is all down to Jack Belias,' said Pepper. 'He built the house to cut himself off from the world around him, except for those gamblers he invited back for his baccarat parties. He wanted to live his life on his own terms. He wanted to rule the world, and he wanted to ruin everybody who challenged him. I'm sure that nobody could have liked him, but in none of these books does anybody actually say so. One summer he was screwing some poor guy's wife every night on top of a chemin-de-fer table, before she went home; but this same guy gave him a racehorse. Two of these books mention it; neither says why.'

Effie picked up one of the books and frowned at the spine. 'Maybe they're still alive, some of these authors. Maybe we could talk to them.' She checked the inside fly-leaf. 'Harry Rondo . . . born 1917 . . . author of six books on gambling and gamblers . . . a confirmed bachelor who now lives in Pocantico Hills.'

'Well, that's not far,' said Pepper. She stood up and tramped barefoot across the cushions to the small Indian table where she kept her telephone and her fax. She licked her thumb and noisily leafed through the local directory. 'Here we are . . . Harold A. Rondo, 7773 Bedford Road, Pocantico Hills. The directory's two years old, but if he's managed to survive, he could be worth talking to.'

Effie looked at her watch. 'I have to be back by eight-thirty. Craig's taking me to dinner at the Hudson Inn.'

'Lucky you. I love that restaurant. Here – let me give Harold A. Rondo a call before you go . . . we might be able to fix up to see him tomorrow.'

She punched out the number and waited while it rang. It was almost half a minute before anybody picked up, and then all she could hear was quavery breathing.

'Hallo?' she said. 'Is this the residence of Harold A. Rondo?'

'Who wants to know?' said a thick, soft voice.

'Well, if you're Mr Rondo, sir, my name's Pepper Moriarty and I run the Hungry Moon health food and herbal store in Cold Spring.'

'Are you trying to sell me something healthy? If you are, you're about thirty years too late.'

'Mr Rondo, I'm not calling you to sell you anything. I have some friends who have just bought Valhalla.'

'They did what?'

'They bought Valhalla . . . the house that Jack Belias built.'

282

'What are they?' asked Harry Rondo dryly. 'Some kind of outpatients?'

'Mr Bellman is a very well-respected business lawyer, Mr Rondo. His wife is an expert on modern art. The point is, they're going to restore Valhalla the way it was when Jack Belias first erected it. They're very keen to know more about him, because it seems like very little was written about his personal life.'

There was a lengthy pause. Pepper could hear Harry Rondo moistening his lips, and she could almost hear him think. After a while, he said, 'Did you read my book?'

'*Chance In A Million*, yes, I have it here. It goes into quite a lot of detail about his card-playing, sir. But it doesn't really say too much about him. I mean, not *personally*. You did know him personally, didn't you, sir?'

'I was a very young man. But, yes. My father played baccarat with him. That was how my father got himself bankrupted; and that's why I'm living here at the scruffy end of Pocantico Hills, rather than Park Avenue. My father was a very wealthy man; but he had a weakness for cards; and Jack Belias gutted him like a fish.'

'Did you ever write about Jack Belias' personal life?'

'Thought about it, but decided not to chance it.'

'Chance it? What do you mean? He's been dead since 1937.'

'I just decided not to chance it, that's all. He ruined my father in three hours flat . . . a whole lifetime of struggling and striving in the construction industry, all of it gone. And he did it in nine coups; that's all it took.'

'Would you mind talking to me and my friend about Jack Belias?'

Another pause. 'I don't know . . . talking's as risky as writing, I'd say.'

'I think I know what you mean. That's why my friend

and I want to know more. Listen, I'll come clean with you. I'm a psychic sensitive. I've visited Valhalla, and I've had some pretty unpleasant experiences up there.'

'Psychic, huh?' asked Harry Rondo, suspiciously. Effie looked away. She didn't want to think about Pepper's experiences up at Valhalla. She kept picturing her bare legs pedalling in the air, and Craig's tightly-clenched buttocks.

'Mr Rondo, if you're trying to tell me what I *think* you're trying to tell me, then Valhalla needs to be cleansed. All of its psychic disturbances put to rest. But I do need to know a whole lot more about Jack Belias' background; and what he was really like.'

This time, Harry Rondo paused so long that Pepper thought that he had hung up. Then, with his voice lowered, and trembling a little, he said, 'You want to know what he was really like? He was Satan incarnate, that's what he was like.'

'Satan?'

'Not too strong a name for him, no ma'am. I never met any man in the whole of my life who gave off an aura of evil like Jack Belias. 'Course, women loved it. He could make any woman do what he wanted, just by lifting his eyebrow. He used to take other men's wives, and he used to flaunt his conquests openly. Then, when the men played cards against him to get their revenge, he used to fleece them of their fortunes, and leave them broken. The men he ruined. Rich, confident men. Men with beautiful women on their arms, and yachts, and everything that money and breeding could offer. He brought them low. He humiliated them in front of their friends. And he took everything. He went into George Michel's chateau once and personally tore down these forty-foot high velvet curtains because Michel owed him so much money. He

284

reduced some of the richest men in the world to the gutter, one after the other. Sometimes they killed themselves; one or two of them tried to kill him. But you can't imagine the misery that man trailed in his wake. He visited Deauville, Cannes, Aix-les-Bains, la Baule, Biarritz ... smooth and charming most of the time, although they say he had an evil temper, too, if you tried to cross him. He went through all of those places and he left dead and ruined people behind him, like a plague had passed through.'

'But why did he ruin so many people?' asked Pepper. 'What was his motivation?'

Harry Rondo coughed. 'You still don't get it, do you? There was no motivation. He did it for no other reason except that he could.'

Tuesday, July 20, 9:06 p.m.

Craig ordered a vodka martini on the rocks and drank most of it straight down, like a man who has just escaped a potentially fatal accident. They were sitting on stools at the bar of the Hudson Inn, waiting for their table. They had booked for eight o'clock but Craig hadn't arrived back from Valhalla until a quarter after eight, grimy and tight-tempered and badly in need of a shower. Their table had already gone to another couple when they finally arrived; one of the best tables in the large oak-beamed dining-room, in a brick alcove surrounded by flowers.

The maitre-d', a small smooth man with well-polished hair, had tried to mollify Craig with an offer of free cocktails while they waited, but Craig had told him with deadly calm that he wanted his table and nothing else. Effie had dug her fingernails into the palm of his hand and said, 'Craig, don't. I don't want a fuss. Otherwise I'm going right back to the Inn and order myself a sandwich.'

Now he was at the bar staring at the middle-aged couple who had taken their table as if he could give both of them heart attacks by malicious intention alone.

'Craig . . . it wasn't *their* fault. Stop staring at them.'

'That's *our* table. The table I reserved.'

'But we were late. They're running a business here, they're crowded.'

He banged his glass on the bar, and snapped his fingers at the barman to bring him another vodka. The barman was a tall, shy young man with a drooping blond moustache. He said, 'You can call me Michael, sir. Or Mikey. Most people do.'

Craig stared at him. 'Do I *know* you?'

The barman flushed. 'I'm just introducing myself, sir. Just trying to be friendly, that's all. Don't take it the wrong way.'

'What is your job here?' Craig asked him. His voice was soft and menacing; so soft that the barman didn't hear him the first time.

'Keep bar, sir.'

'That's right. They don't pay you to make friends. They don't pay you to do anything except serve drinks when you're required to serve drinks. So serve me a drink. Please. And if you took offence at my popping my fingers at you, I'm sorry. Next time I'll whistle; or wave a flag, maybe; or set fire to something and send up smoke signals.'

The barman glanced at Effie, who gave him a quick, sympathetic shake of the head which meant, *don't rile him, not just now*. He took Craig's glass and brought him another vodka martini, and a glass dish of pecans and salted almonds.

286

'Your nuts, sir,' he said, with the straightest of faces.

It was a pun, in retaliation against Craig's arrogance. He couldn't have known that it had another meaning – a meaning that went right to the heart of everything that had happened to Craig since Zaghlul Fuad had picked him up that rainy night in March. When Mikey said 'nuts', he wasn't making a joke about Up and Tyce and K-Plus Drugs.

Craig stood up, as fast and smooth as some kind of predatory animal, and snatched an ice-pick from the top of the bar. Effie watched in horror as he seized the young man's shoulder with his left hand and lifted the ice-pick in his right. There was a millionth of a second in which she thought that Craig was actually going to stab him in the heart; but then Craig tossed the ice-pick aside. It clattered onto the floor and a man who was sitting at the other end of the bar quickly picked it up.

The young barman backed away, his eyes wide with shock and his face white as his apron. The man who had picked up the ice-pick moved down the bar to them, and said, 'Come on, buddy, calm down.' But Craig lifted one warning finger to him and he decided to stay where he was.

Effie caught hold of Craig's sleeve. 'Craig!' she pleaded. 'Craig, how could you!'

'Craig?' he asked, as if he didn't know his own name. He turned to stare at her and his face was so congested with anger that he was almost maroon, and his eyes were swollen and bloodshot. He could have been a demon rather than her own husband.

The maitre-d' came over, closely followed by a huge young crewcut man in a tuxedo. 'I'm going to have to ask you to leave.'

'What?' said Craig, in a thick voice. 'What are you

talking about? Effie, what's he talking about?'

'I'm sorry, madam,' the maitre-d' said to Effie. 'I can't accept any kind of attack on my staff. If you don't leave now I'll call for the cops.'

Effie tugged Craig away from the bar. He dragged his feet and he swayed against the maitre-d' as if he were drunk. As they were escorted to the door, the restaurant progressively fell silent, table by table, and the diners all turned to stare at them. Effie felt her cheeks flaming; and she was suddenly so hot that she thought she was going to faint.

The maitre-d' held Craig's arm as they reached the door. 'I'd consider it a favour if you didn't come back.'

Craig said, 'You really don't know who you're talking to, do you?'

'Please . . .' said the maitre-d'. He looked at Effie. 'Are you all right, ma'am? You're looking kind of pale.'

Craig pushed him away. 'This lady belongs to me, my friend. She is mine and mine alone.'

'Come on, Craig,' Effie urged him. 'Let's just call it a night.'

'This lady is mine,' Craig repeated. 'She belongs to me completely, body and soul. Don't you even dare think of speaking to her again, because if you do I'll tear off your head and piss down your neck.'

They went down the steps and Effie guided Craig across the parking lot.

'I'll drive,' she said, opening the driver's door. But Craig pushed her quite roughly aside and sat down behind the wheel.

'You'll do what you're told, like you always do.'

'If you're going to drive, I'm going to catch a cab.'

He sat quite still for a moment, staring directly ahead of him, as if he were thinking about something else

288

altogether. Then he climbed out of the car, stood in front of Effie, and laid both hands on her shoulders.

'When you came to live with me, the deal was that you were going to be my property. You were going to do whatever I wanted you to do, without argument, without hesitation, without flinching.'

'Listen to me, there's something wrong with you. Something's happening to you, you're changing.'

'Was that the deal or was that *not* the deal?'

'Craig –'

'Was that the deal?'

'No, it wasn't the deal! I promised to love and honour you, in sickness and in health, which is the only reason I'm staying with you right now, because something's happened to you, and you're sick! But I sure as hell didn't agree to be your property, and I never would!'

He stared down at her as if he couldn't believe that she had actually dared to argue with him. His eyes were even more swollen, his nostrils were flared, and his breath came in deep, harsh gasps.

'Get in the car,' he told her.

'I've told you, if you insist on driving, then I'll take a cab.'

'This is the last time. Get in the car.'

She shook her head emphatically from side to side. 'No.'

His response was to seize the thin straps of her short red evening-dress and yank them down. He pulled again, and again, and ripped the dress right off her. She was so shocked that she couldn't breathe, let alone scream. He took hold of her bra and yanked it up over her head, grazing her arms and scratching her face; and then he threw it into the darkness.

Finally she found her voice. *'What are you –!'*

She tried to run, but he held her tight around the waist

and while she kicked and struggled he dragged her panty-hose down to her knees and then stepped on the wide-stretched gusset to push them down to her ankles. Naked, she twisted around and started to scratch and punch him. He didn't hit her back. He didn't have to. He was far too strong for her and he didn't seem to care if she slapped his face and tore at his ears with her fingernails. He picked her up, hoisted her over his shoulder, and then walked around the car with her and threw her against the passenger door.

'I told you,' he said, his face looming large. 'The deal was, you belong completely to me. You're mine.'

'I'm going to divorce you,' she spat at him. 'This time I mean it. I'm going to divorce you and I'm going to take you for everything.'

'You can't divorce somebody you're not married to.'

'What are you talking about? What do you mean?'

'I think you've been drinking too much,' he said. 'You've been hitting the bottle. You're married, sweetheart, but not to me.'

'I don't know what the hell you're –'

'Open your legs,' he demanded.

'Craig, if this is Jack Belias affecting you, then please try and fight him back. *Please*, Craig! You're Craig Bellman, and I'm Effie Bellman, and we're married. We live at The Sutton Buildings, East 86th Street, New York City, and right now we're staying at Pig Hill Inn, in Cold Spring, and – *Craig, don't let him do this to you! Don't let him take you over!*'

'Open your legs,' he repeated.

She squeezed her thighs tight together. 'Craig . . . if you're going to drive me back to the Inn, then please get in and drive me back to the Inn. You're scaring me, Craig. You're really scaring me.'

290

He leaned forward and cupped the back of her neck in his left hand, firmly but not bruisingly. 'Open your legs or I'll break your neck. And you know I can do it.'

'Craig –' her eyes were swimming with tears. 'Craig, please don't do this!'

He clamped her neck tighter. She gasped for breath and let out a high, painful sob.

'You know I can do it,' he repeated, in the same flat voice.

Quaking with fright, Effie gradually opened her thighs. Still staring at her, still slightly smiling, Craig slid his hand between them, with his middle finger held out rigid.

She felt her tears dropping onto her bare breasts as he pushed his finger inside her. He held it there for five or ten seconds, and then took it out again.

'I told you,' he said. 'You belong to me. Completely.'

Miserably, still weeping, she pulled on her dress and climbed into the car.

Tuesday, July 20, 11:36 p.m.

She waited until she heard him drive away; then she climbed out of bed and quickly dressed in a soft white angora sweater and a pair of jeans. He had taken the room key with him, but she wedged a folded-up Pig Hill Inn leaflet in the door so that she could get back in again. She tip-toed along the corridor and down the stairs, and peered cautiously around the lobby in case she had made a mistake, and it hadn't been him driving away.

Wendy O'Brien came out with a smile and said, 'Help you, Mrs Bellman?'

Effie smiled back, and said, 'No thanks. I couldn't sleep.

291

That's all. I just thought I'd take a walk.'

'You don't want a glass of warm milk or anything?'

'No thanks, I'm fine.'

'You'll excuse me for asking . . . but everything's okay, is it?'

'Everything's great! We're really enjoying ourselves.'

'It's just that . . . well, I don't want to intrude or anything. But I have heard some raised voices, coming from your room. And your face. . . '

'I went for a walk in the woods around Valhalla, that's all, and scratched myself on some briars. It's nothing to worry about. And I'm sorry if we've been disturbing anybody. My husband's been kind of excitable since we've bought Valhalla, and he does tend to get carried away.'

She walked down the street to the Hungry Moon. It was a warm, still night, and the real moon had just appeared over the top of the Old Post Inn, so that it illuminated the greedy-mouthed moon which hung outside Pepper's store. Effie pressed the bell and waited for a while. Then she pressed the bell again. Further down the street, the Hudson glittered slow and treacly in the darkness like an oil spill.

Inside the store, a light was switched on. Then Pepper appeared, tousle-haired, wearing nothing but a man's striped shirt. She peered through the window at Effie and mouthed the words, 'What is it?'

'Let me in,' Effie mouthed back. 'Something's happened.'

Pepper unlocked the door. Effie stepped in and smelled all the dry herbal smells of the magical concoctions and potpourris.

'I was sleeping,' said Pepper. 'What the hell's happened to you? Your face is all scratched up. I thought you were having dinner at the Hudson Inn.'

Effie told her everything that had happened, trying not

292

to cry. But she couldn't help herself. She clung to Pepper and her sobs were so deep and so agonised that they hardly sounded human.

'He tore – he tore off my clothes. Everything. There was nothing I could do. He didn't talk like Craig or behave like Craig . . .'

'It's getting worse,' said Pepper. 'There's no question about it, it's getting worse.'

Effie wiped her eyes with her fingers. 'I told him I was going to divorce him, but I don't want to divorce him. Not him, not Craig. It's that *person* who's taken control of him. He talks to me like he doesn't even know who I am, and when I said I was going to divorce him, he said that I couldn't divorce somebody I wasn't even married to.'

'God Almighty,' said Pepper. 'This is much more serious than I thought it was going to be. Jack Belias has almost completely pulled him in. He's beginning to *look* like Jack Belias; and to *talk* like Jack Belias, and *behave* like Jack Belias. Before you know it, he'll *be* Jack Belias, and you'll have lost your Craig forever.'

'I don't understand this at all. How can this *be*, Pepper? How can this *be*?'

'I don't know. All I know is that sometimes we can see and talk to people from other times. But it looks to me as if nobody can stay permanently in any other time unless they make an exchange. Trade bodies, if you like.'

Effie watched silently as Pepper paced around the shop.

'I think Jack Belias wants to live in the present, but to do that, he has to send Craig back to the past. I've read about it, but I never thought it was possible, to tell you the truth. I have a terrible feeling that this is what Belias is trying to do . . . using Craig as a surrogate to send back to 1937.'

'I can't believe it. I just can't believe it.'

'Effie, you've seen it for yourself. Jack Belias disappeared in 1937, but he's trying to make a comeback and he's been using Craig to do it. Craig's body, Craig's intellect – everything.'

'What's going to happen?' Effie pleaded. 'If Jack Belias takes him over completely, where will he be?'

'I don't know the answer to that. I simply don't.'

'But if I lose Craig –'

'Effie, I simply don't know. I wish I did. Half of this is only guesswork. I could be completely wrong. I always believed that the days of your life never disappeared – that they were always there, if only you could get back to them. But I never knew that a dead person from a long time ago could take over the mind and body of somebody from here and now.'

'It's impossible,' said Effie. 'I know it's impossible. It *must* be impossible.'

'But don't you see . . . it *is* possible. This is the first rational explanation of ghosts that anybody has ever come up with. And this is the first rational explanation of people who mysteriously disappear. The truth is that they *don't* disappear – they simply walk to another room. You saw what happened to the cat, too.'

Effie sat down on a small wheelback chair beside the counter. 'Oh God, Pepper. I'm so damn tired and I'm so damn confused.'

Pepper hunkered down in front of her and rested her arms on Effie's knees. 'Come on, honey. Don't give up. We're going to do something about it. We're seeing Harry Rondo tomorrow and we're going to find out all we can about Jack Belias. We need to know why he's doing this, and how. I mean, is he consciously doing it, or is it just happening?'

Pepper squeezed her hand. She was trying to be reassuring, but she couldn't hide the troubled look on her face

– the look of a woman who dreads the past as much as the future.

Wednesday, July 21, 11:32 a.m.

Harry Rondo turned out to look just as close to death's door as he had in his book jacket photograph. He lived in a shabby green-painted house that was nearer to Route 117 than it was to the picturesque village of Pocantico Hills. The driveway was barred by a dilapidated iron gate, wound around with rusty chains, and guarded by a fierce brindled mutt with a neck that was wider than its hips.

Pepper tooted the horn of her pick-up and eventually Harry appeared. He walked around a sagging Lincoln Continental Mk IV that was parked right outside the front door, whistled sharply to the dog, and then proceeded to unravel the Gordian knot which held the gate in place.

'Had a couple of break-ins,' he explained. 'Don't know why they bothered. I never keep more than a hundred dollars in the house and my microwave's busted.'

He was lean and stooped, with a skeletal head and thinning, brushed-back hair that he had dyed to a strong shade of orange. He wore a soft charcoal grey shirt that was dusted in cigarette ash, and baggy black pants that would have looked the business in a Havana casino circa 1955. He had one of those odd, angular faces that nearly reminds you of somebody you know, but his washed-out eyes kept reminding you differently.

'I'm still not sure whether I want to talk about this,' he remarked, over his shoulder, as he led them to the house. 'Dangerous does as dangerous is. Jack Belias was dangerous; and for my money, he still could be.'

'Do you have any evidence of that?' asked Pepper.

'Depends what you mean by evidence. If a feeling in your guts is evidence, then yes.'

The house was cramped and stuffy and there were books and papers stacked everywhere. The walls were papered with a pattern of faded yellow flowers, and an odd assortment of prints and photographs were hung all over them, apparently at random. Effie saw a sepia photograph of ex-King Manuel of Portugal and his Hohenzollern wife walking on the promenade at Cannes – he very dapper with a wide-brimmed hat and walking-cane, she wearing a white cloche hat and a long blazer and looking bored. There were cartoons of famous 1920s gamblers like Berry Wall and Solly Joel; and framed menus from The Sporting Club, Rue Francois Premier in Paris, and the 43 Club in London. There was still a brown stain on the Sporting Club menu, a permanent souvenir of a sauce prepared and eaten one evening more than sixty years ago.

Harry went across to a cluttered rolltop desk, picked a cigarette out of a pack of Camels, and lit it with a book match. 'So many people suffered at the hands of Jack Belias – so many people were ruined or humiliated – that it was considered bad luck even to mention his name. And you know how superstitious gamblers are.

'When I came out of the service in 1946 I started writing articles and books about gambling and gamblers, and one name kept on cropping up: Jack Belias. I tried to talk to my father about him but he didn't want to know. I tried talking to some of the big names of gambling – men who used to play baccarat with Belias in the twenties and the thirties. What did I get? The complete loss of memory, that's what I got. All I had to say was, "Tell me about Jack Belias", and instant amnesia set in.'

296

He blew smoke, coughed, and looked around him. 'You want to sit down?' he suggested. 'How about some coffee. You may not believe it, but I make excellent coffee. With chocolate flakes.'

Effie cleared a sheaf of papers from a green upholstered armchair, and awkwardly sat down. Pepper managed to find a dining-chair with no back to it.

'Are you the lady who's bought Valhalla?' Harry asked Effie.

'It was my husband's idea, more than mine. I don't really like the place at all.'

'If I tell you what happened there, do you think you're going to be upset? I mean, I don't want to put you off living there.'

Pepper said, 'She needs to know, and I do, too. Listen, you don't know what's been happening in that house. Effie here had a kind of waking daydream that she was dancing on broken glass, and when she came out of it her feet were all cut up. Another time she heard a woman crying in one of the upstairs bedrooms, and she's seen a strange man going downstairs. I went there myself, and I saw the whole place like it used to be, with furniture and mirrors and everything.'

She paused, and then she said, 'While I was there, I truly believed that I was Gaby Deslys, the dancer; and that Jack Belias and me were lovers. But I wasn't Gaby Deslys and Jack Belias wasn't Jack Belias. He was Effie's husband Craig.'

Harry smoked and nodded, and then he found himself a wheelback chair and dragged it up close. 'It's just like I always said. Jack Belias never died. Not in the way that ordinary people die. Jack Belias left his automobile next to Bear Mountain Bridge because he wanted people to think that he had done away with himself. But did he shit. All he did was leave one time and step into another; and the only reason he left that automobile next to Bear Mountain Bridge was because he couldn't take it with him, not where he was going. He was trying to get into the future . . . be immortal. And he was looking for somebody who was weaker than him, somebody who needed what he had to offer, which was strength, you understand me? Strength, and a total lack of scruples, didn't care who he hurt, or how badly, or whether it was justified or not. Not only that, virility. Jack Belias was a very virile man, he needed sex like most people need to breathe, and he used his virility to dominate people, too.'

'So what *did* happen at Valhalla?' asked Effie. She couldn't help thinking of Craig, in the days after his 'accident'. What had he needed more desperately than strength and virility? If Harry Rondo could be believed, the influence of Jack Belias had caught him at his lowest ebb.

Harry said, 'If you want to understand what happened at Valhalla you have to understand who Jack Belias was. What shaped him, what motivated him. I spent years traipsing from one side of the Atlantic to the other, trying to find out everything I could about him. In the end, it didn't amount to very much more than a few proven facts, a hundred guesses, and a thousand assorted riddles. Like I told you, the only real evidence lies here in my gut.

'You want the proven facts? He was born John Henry Belias in the winter of 1897, in Pittsburgh, Pennsylvania. His father was Walter John Belias, also known as Jack, who worked for the First National Bank of Pittsburgh, as chief teller. His mother Annette Belias doted on him, and spoiled him so much that his father threatened to send him off to boarding school. But Annette Belias died in 1906, when Jack was nine, from complications following the birth of a daughter, Lily. From what I gather, Jack

298

never forgave his sister for killing his mother; and he never forgave his mother for betraying him by having another child. From that time on, it seems that his opinion of women in general was very low.'

'Do we have any evidence of that?' asked Pepper.

'Oh, sure we do. Reports from the Pittsburgh newspapers of 1919 and 1922, when one Jack Belias was accused of kidnapping and torturing prostitutes. In the first case he was alleged to have abducted a prostitute called Mary O'Hagan for seven days, and nailed her nipples to a kitchen table. In the second case he forced an empty gin bottle into a prostitute called Georgina French, and filled up the bottle with boiling water.'

'Oh, my God,' said Pepper. 'Oh, my God it doesn't bear thinking about.'

'He did worse than that to other women, so they say; but these are the only cases that are backed by evidence. As it turned out, he was found innocent on both charges; although there were several accusations of jury-rigging, especially from the state's attorney Nathan Tidyman. Tidyman was found dead four weeks after Jack Belias' last acquittal, in his overturned automobile, with his neck broken.

'Jack Belias' father had never liked him – and after the court cases he cut him off completely. When he died he gave over $3 million to charity, and Jack Belias got nothing. I believe that's what gave him his special taste for bringing rich men low.

'In 1923 he was appointed a junior accountant at Penn Textiles. He wasn't liked, but he was such a whiz with figures that he saved the company hundreds of thousands of dollars in his first six months; and at the end of his first year he was appointed chief accountant. He took over the running of everything, right down to buying the raw cotton on the Memphis cotton market. By the spring of 1925 he was appointed to the board, and by the winter of 1925 he virtually controlled the whole corporation. He pressed ahead with all kinds of experiments with synthetic fibres, and in 1926 he produced Fresh-Press, which wasn't a true synthetic fabric, not like nylon, but it was a chemical-treated cotton that didn't crease anything like as badly as natural cotton.

'He made a fortune out of Fresh-Press. That particular textile dominated the world market until 1938, when W.H. Carothers discovered nylon. Penn Textiles went out of business in three years; but by then, of course, Jack Belias was what you might call dead. Or moved on. Depends which definition you prefer.

'By 1927 Jack Belias was worth more than 11 million dollars. He started to travel, and to gamble; and he became a regular visitor to Deauville and Monte Carlo and Biarritz. He didn't set out to win money. He set out to ruin people. That was what turned him on. He treated women like dirt and men like potential victims. I never talked to a single person who knew Jack Belias and wasn't afraid of him. He nearly bankrupted Nick Zographos, of the Greek Syndicate; and there were dozens more gamblers who weren't so skilful and weren't so lucky. He desecrated their wives and he took their money.'

'He married, though, didn't he?' asked Effie.

'Sure. He married a French movie actress, Jeannette Duclos. She was beautiful, I can tell you. There were no two ways about it.'

'She died, didn't she?' asked Effie.

Harry crushed out his cigarette into a crowded ashtray emblazoned Hotel Ritz, Paris. 'Yes, she died. In mysterious circumstances, that's what most of the books will tell you. But I went through the medical records and there was

300

nothing mysterious about it, nothing at all. The only mystery was that Jack Belias paid a large sum of money to the coroner to testify that it was anything else but what it was.'

'And what was it?' asked Pepper.

'You really want to hear this?' asked Harry.

'If we don't hear it, we'll never know what we're up against.'

'Well, your funeral,' said Harry. 'She died by setting her head alight.'

'She did *what*?' asked Pepper.

'Belias wanted children. He wanted a son and heir, somebody to carry on his name. You've seen his coat of arms, and that motto of his, *Non omnis moriar* – "I shall never completely die". He couldn't accept the fact that he was mortal. He believed that he could live for ever, if he used all of the right rituals and prayed all the right prayers. But he still wanted a son and heir, in case the rituals and the prayers didn't work.

'What he didn't know was that Jeannette Duclos had had an illegal abortion at the age of thirteen and had never been able to have children.

'He was always ranting and raving at her. I have several eyewitness accounts of how he slapped her and screamed at her at the Golf Hotel at Le Touquet. He shouted at her again in the Palm Court of the Plaza, in New York, and called her a sterile, ugly bitch. I'll tell you who heard him say that: Harold Ross, the guy who founded *The New Yorker*. It's in one of his diaries.

'Less than a month after that, Belias held a big gambling party up at Valhalla. Just about everybody was there. They had dancing, fireworks, a whole thirty-piece orchestra. Eyewitness reports say that Belias spent the whole evening with Gaby Deslys, the dancer. Then halfway through the evening, Jeannette walked into the ballroom and it looked like her hair was wet. Nobody realised it, but she had dipped her whole head into a pailful of gasoline. She walked across the ballroom, faced up to him, and then she struck a match.'

Harry lit up another cigarette. 'The police came but everybody said they were out of the room when it happened. "I was having a smoke in the library". "I went to the powder room". "I was making a telephone call to my Great Aunt Matilda". But I talked to some of the people who were there. They don't all tell the same story, but some say she ran around the ballroom screaming, and others say she danced, she actually did a dance for him, with her head on fire.'

Pepper said, 'What about Gaby Deslys? What happened to her?'

'Oh, well, she was pretty fortunate. Belias went through a long run of bad luck on the tables, and spent so much time gambling that they kind of drifted apart. After that, he went through a whole string of mistresses. I've talked to some of them, even though they're pretty old now. They all said how cruel he was. He loved to hurt them; and of course some of them were young and stupid and drugged up, and they let him do whatever he wanted. He kept horses. Some of them even did it with horses, while Belias watched.'

Effie pressed the back of her hand against her mouth. She hadn't eaten breakfast this morning, and she was almost choking on Harry's cigarette smoke.

Harry said, 'I'm sorry. I don't mean to disturb you. But you wanted to know, and this is more or less what happened, so far as anybody can tell.'

'How did it end?' Effie asked him. 'Why did Jack Belias have to disappear?'

'There are rumours about this; and there are counter-

302

rumours; and it's very difficult to know what to believe. But one thing's certain. In the spring of 1937, Jack Belias invited eleven of his friends up to Valhalla for a non-stop weekend of baccarat. He had one every year, and it was quite an occasion, because he always held the bank and he always did what the Greek Syndicate used to do at Deauville, and allow *tout va* – that is, "anything goes", meaning there was no limit on what his guests could bet.'

'I'm surprised he had any guests, from what you've been saying about him,' said Effie.

'Don't you believe it. He had more gamblers wanting to play against him than Valhalla could accommodate. Almost every baccarat player on both sides of the Atlantic wanted the chance to break Jack Belias, and every year he gave them the opportunity, and he wined them and dined them, too, and every year he ended up richer. That man may have been Satan, but he could play baccarat like God.

'Nobody knows who all of the eleven guests were that year, but Nico Zographos and Val Castlerosse certainly were, as well as Michael Arlen and Remy Morse and Karl Marjorian and Douglas Broughton. Most of them came because they wanted to settle old scores, win back some of the money that Belias had taken from them during the past year. But Broughton needed more than that. In the summer of 1936, Belias had taken him for over a million pounds sterling, which Broughton had been forced to borrow from his own company, Broughton Steelworks. He had been forced to sell his country house in England, his chateau in France, and his apartment on Fifth Avenue. He wasn't just looking for revenge. He badly needed to win his money back, or else he was facing bankruptcy.'

Harry crossed the room and lifted a framed photograph off the wall, which he handed to Effie to look at. It showed a bluff, handsome man of about fifty-five sitting in a garden. He was wearing a wide-brimmed hat and an expensive three-piece suit, with spats. He had a white moustache and a white goatee beard; and rings on his fingers. He looked as if he had just said something which he considered to be terribly droll. Sitting on a low wall next to him, swinging her legs, was a very much younger woman, with dark hair perfectly cut in a long, shining bob, and wide dark eyes. She was nothing short of beautiful – and she had the extra allure of looking as if she were unconscious of her beauty, a dreamy erotic innocence. She wore a short white low-waisted dress, with a large bow at the hip, and white stockings. She, too, was smiling, but for some reason she didn't look to Effie as if she were smiling at what the man had just said, but at some secret amusement of her own.

'Is this Douglas Broughton?' asked Pepper.

'That's right. And the woman sitting on the wall is his wife Gina. She was twenty-three years his junior when they married. Miss Pittsburgh, 1923. He saw her picture in the newspaper when he was visiting the US Steel Corporation in Pittsburgh, and he sent his chauffeur around to her home with two dozen roses and an invitation to dinner. Hard line to resist, wouldn't you say?'

'She looks like a child, compared to him,' said Effie.

'That's right. On first meeting, most people used to think that Gina was Douglas Broughton's daughter. But she was very much in love with him. She was absolutely devoted. Even when he lost his money and they had to sell all their houses and their cars, she still stood beside him, and did everything she could to cheer him up. For his part, Douglas Broughton believed that Gina always brought him luck, and that the only time he lost money at the tables was when she wasn't there. So that was why he took her to Valhalla that spring.'

304

He squashed out his second cigarette. 'It was the worst thing he ever did in his life.'

'What happened?' asked Effie.

'They played baccarat, of course. Val Castlerosse won almost eight thousand dollars in the first few hours, and for a while it looked as if luck was running Douglas Broughton's way, too. By midnight on Friday he was up sixteen thousand dollars and according to Michael Arlen he was really hot. But he was playing by the Martingale system, which means that every time he lost a coup he doubled his stake in an attempt to get his money back. The Martingale's terrific if luck's running with you; but if it isn't, it's a very quick way to dig your own grave. It wasn't even two o'clock on Saturday morning before he was into a hole for eleven thousand, and most of the others were well down, too. It seemed like Jack Belias was unbeatable.'

He reached for another cigarette, but as he did so he paused and listened, almost as if he were expecting to hear someone entering the front door.

'Are you all right?' Pepper asked him.

'Just had one of those feelings.'

'One of what feelings?'

'It's always the same when I talk about Jack Belias. Maybe I'm just spooking myself. I always feel that he's right outside the door, listening to me.'

Pepper said, 'I don't feel anything.'

Harry listened a moment longer, and then shook his head at his own edginess. 'Stupid, I guess. But it's always the same. I started to write a magazine article about him once, and my typewriter keys kept jamming. I finished about half a page and then I gave it up as a bad job.'

He lit his cigarette very carefully and then dragged at it with as much relish as a man who hasn't smoked in a week. 'I don't really know what I've got to be afraid of. But then

I don't want to find out, either.'

Effie said, 'The baccarat. . . . did Jack Belias win all night?'

'By dawn the others had lost so much money that they were threatening to quit the table and cut short the whole weekend. So Belias came up with a suggestion. If they were real gamblers, they should each of them bet the one thing in their lives that they prized the most . . . the one thing that they couldn't bear to lose.

'None of them were interested at first, but then Belias himself said that he would stake Valhalla and everything in it, and that was more of a temptation than any of the others could resist. I don't know what Val Castlerosse staked, but Michael Arlen offered the copyright to *The Green Hat*, which was his bestselling novel, Remy Morse staked his yacht, and Karl Marjorian put up his favourite racehorse. Douglas Broughton had no yachts, no racehorses, no houses, nothing. All he had was his percentage share in the family steelworks, and his wife Gina. She wouldn't hear of him gambling away his livelihood, so she offered herself. Three nights and three days, for the winner to do with her whatever he wanted.'

'I can't believe it,' said Effie.

'I've seen gamblers stake more than their wives,' said Harry, waving smoke away with his hand. 'Maybe it seems unbelievable now, but you have to remember that Douglas Broughton was desperate, almost suicidal, and that Gina would have done anything for him. She was that kind of a woman.'

He paused. 'I don't exactly know how they arranged the game. I guess they agreed that each player would be allowed to lose a certain number of coups before he had to surrender his prized possession. As it is, it took Jack Belias less than an hour to win everything, Gina Broughton included.'

'And she really stayed with him, for three days and three nights?'

Harry coughed, and shook his head. 'She stayed with him for eighteen months. Nobody knows why. She followed him everywhere he went, and yet he treated her worse than a dog. Whenever he held a party, he used to show her off; show how obedient she was. Whatever he asked her to do, she always did it. Once he dropped a spoonful of caviar on to the end of his shoe and made her kneel down in her evening gown, in front of all of his guests, and lick it off. And another time he made her do exactly what happened to you – he made her dance barefoot on broken champagne glasses. He probably did far worse things to her, but if so he did them in private.'

Effie turned to Pepper, her eyes wide. 'Oh my God,' she whispered.

'Didn't Douglas Broughton try to get her back?' asked Pepper.

'Of course he did. He even called the cops and accused Belias of kidnap. But when the cops went to Valhalla and talked to Gina, she said that she was staying with Belias of her own free will. There was nothing they could do.'

'So what happened to him?'

'To Broughton? Nothing dramatic. He lost control of his steelworks. He went bankrupt. He contracted Parkinson's disease and he died in 1941 in a charity hospital in England. Three people went to his funeral. He was just like everybody else who tried to stand up to Jack Belias: ruined, cuckolded and humiliated.'

'And what happened to Gina?' asked Effie.

Harry went over to his desk, unlocked one of the side drawers, and took out a newspaper clipping, amber with age. He gave it to her as reverently as if it were a holy relic.

The clipping was marked *Poughkeepsie Sentinel, November*

11, 1937, and headlined *Blind Pregnant Heiress Falls To Her Death* and subheaded *Impaled on Railings, But Baby Saved.*

The story read: 'Sheriff's deputies and firemen were called yesterday to Valhalla, palatial mansion home of textile tycoon Jack Belias, to discover that the recently-blinded wife of a close friend and business associate had apparently flung herself from an upper window to be impaled on iron railings 30ft below.

'Mrs Gina May Broughton, 32, estranged wife of British steel millionaire Mr Douglas Broughton, 55, was said last night to have died shortly after her arrival at Poughkeepsie Memorial Hospital. She had been blinded in an accident last August, and since then she was said to have suffered deep depression.

'Doctors disclosed last night that Mrs Broughton was approximately seven months pregnant, and that the child had been removed on her death by Caesarean section and placed in an incubator. A boy, the child was apparently "poorly, but holding onto life".'

'Mr Belias, 40, was in residence at Valhalla at the time of Mrs Broughton's fatal fall, but declined to comment on the accident. He also declined to say how close his relationship with Mrs Broughton had been, or to answer suggestions that the child that she was carrying was his.'

Harry handed Effie a second clipping, dated the following day. *Textile Tycoon Vanishes*. It told how Jack Belias' automobile had been found abandoned by Bear Mountain bridge, its doors open and its lights still shining. There was no trace of Jack Belias himself. It was thought that he might have drowned himself, but no body was ever recovered from the Hudson, in spite of the river running exceptionally low because of the dry winter.

'That's it?' said Pepper. 'That's all you know?'

'That's all I know. And a whole lot of that is theory and

308

speculation. Only one of Jack Belias' weekend guests was prepared to talk about the game they played that night, Remy Morse, and by the time I was able to talk to him he was eighty-seven and wandering. But he said that he distinctly remembered the moment that Douglas Broughton lost Gina. He said that he let out a cry like an animal that's been mortally wounded. And I guess he was. Jack Belias killed him; just as sure as if he'd taken out a knife and stabbed him in the heart.'

'But why did she stay so long?' Effie wanted to know. 'She was only supposed to stay three days. Why did she stay for eighteen months? I mean, what did he *do* to her? And how did she get blinded?'

'I don't know about the blinding,' Harry shrugged. 'The sheriff opened an investigation but just as suddenly closed it. Maybe somebody paid him off. As for the length of time she stayed – your guess is as good as mine. Why do some women stay with men who beat them? Being beaten makes them feel wanted. Being beaten rouses up the adrenaline, puts some excitement into their lives. I don't know what Jack Belias did to Gina Broughton, and I don't suppose I ever will, but in my opinion it was worse than anything you can even think about, and in the end it got so bad that even *she* couldn't take it. Listen – if you were seven months pregnant, what would drive you to throw yourself out of an upstairs window, with a 90 per cent chance that both you and your baby were going to be killed?'

Pepper said, 'Jack Belias still frightens you, doesn't he?'

'Give me one good reason why I shouldn't be frightened.'

'He died in 1937?'

Harry looked at her narrowly. 'You don't believe that any more than I do. That's why you're here. You believe that Belias is still living in Valhalla, excepting he wants out

309

of the past and into the present day. And he's using these folks to do it . . . Mrs Bellman here, and her husband.'

Effie didn't have to ask if it were possible for Jack Belias to return from that long-ago evening in 1937. She had already seen what had happened to Craig, the way his face had changed, his voice had lowered, his skin had softened. She had seen changes in Pepper, too, and not just the tattooed roses on her breasts. It was the way in which she herself was changing that worried her the most. She felt the same, and yet she was beginning to suspect that she was growing weaker, and more acquiescent, and that soon she would be nothing more than a brainless, obedient puppet, quite willing to lick men's shoes if they asked her to, dancing on broken glass, opening up her body and her soul to anything that they wanted to do to her.

The terrible part about it was that she found the idea of being degraded vaguely exciting. To be exposed, to be opened up, to be punished in front of other people.

Harry said one thing more. 'Jack Belias built that house because he wanted to live for ever. He thought he was holy, almost, from what people say. He was going to write his own bible one day; his own book of magic and ethics and revelations. Megalomaniac bullshit, of course. But if you could ever find his diaries, you could probably find out why Gina decided to stay with him, and what happened that night she threw herself out of that window.'

Pepper said, 'Did the baby survive?'

'I surely have no idea. If it didn't, they'd have cremated it. If it did, it'd be – what – fifty-nine years old by now, going on sixty.'

Effie said, 'Do you have any pictures of Jack Belias? I've only been able to find one.'

'There was only one picture taken of him that I've ever seen.' He reached into an old brown envelope and drew

310

out a print of Jack Belias standing on the boardwalk at Deauville. 'Is this the same as the one that you found?'

Effie took it, and nodded. But then she looked at it more closely. A cold feeling of dread crawled down her back.

'Look,' she said, and passed the photograph to Pepper. There was no question about it. The man in the photograph was standing in the same place and in the same position as Jack Belias had been in Effie's book. But his face was different. He looked distinctly like Craig.

'Something wrong?' asked Harry. 'You look kind of pale all of a sudden.'

Somewhere in the house, Effie heard a door quietly closing. She was sure that she heard the lightest of footsteps, crossing the hall. A man's feet, in evening pumps. A man who listened when you least expected it. A bad, immoral, exciting man, who brought people to their knees, just because he could.

Wednesday, July 21, 3:01 p.m.

When she returned to Pig Hill Inn, Lieutenant Hook and Sergeant Winstanley were waiting for her. Both of them looked tired and hot. They were accompanied by a podgy deputy sheriff who kept blinking and clearing his throat.

'We called,' said Lieutenant Hook, 'but they said you were out.'

'I've been sightseeing, that's all,' Effie told him, guardedly.

'You didn't go with your husband?'

'I went with a friend. My husband's been busy, sorting out our new home.'

'Mrs Bellman . . . did you and your husband visit the

Hudson Inn yesterday evening?'

'Yes, we did. We were supposed to have dinner there. Why do you ask?'

'You were supposed to have dinner there, but you didn't?'

'That's right. We were late, and they gave our table away, and so we left.'

'Peacefully?'

'What?'

'Did you leave peacefully, or was there some kind of fracas? Some kind of contretemps between your husband and the management? What I'm trying to say is, was this a resigned shrug of the shoulders and a strolling out of the door, or was it an ear-on-the-sidewalk job?'

'My husband may have been less than patient. I don't want to say anything more than that.'

'Your husband was violent and abusive and they frog-marched him out. Isn't that nearer the truth?'

'He was provoked! They gave our table away to these –' she stopped herself, suddenly realising what she was saying.

'Yes?' prompted Lieutenant Hook, patiently. 'They gave your table away to these *what*?'

Effie was silent for a long time. Then she said, 'These people. They gave our table away to these people. They looked like they were wearing polyester.'

She was quite aware of the insanity of what she was saying. Yet she knew that she had to defend Craig, no matter what. Craig had acted irrationally, but that wasn't important. What was important was that they stay together, and that she helped him, and gave him whatever he wanted, no matter what it was. The very thought of it made her feel excited.

Sergeant Winstanley said, 'I was in the prosecutor's

312

office yesterday afternoon; and the last I heard, it still wasn't a crime to wear polyester.'

Lieutenant Hook said, 'Your husband threatened the barman, didn't he? We have plenty of witnesses to that.'

'He was upset, that's all. We were planning on a special evening out, and it all went wrong.'

'It couldn't have gone as wrong for you as it did for the barman. His name was Michael Shelby and he was twenty-five years old and he was engaged to be married in six weeks' time.'

'But Craig didn't hurt him. He didn't even touch him.'

'Somebody did. Michael Shelby was found in the parking-lot about a half-hour after closing time. Somebody had stabbed him in the neck with a broken beer glass, and then mutilated his face. Cut off his nose and his lips, if you want to know the grisly truth.'

Effie said nothing. She pressed her hand against her mouth. She felt as if time had slowed down; as if the whole afternoon was suspended in treacle. She could see every detail sharp and hot: the brickwork on the wall just behind Lieutenant Hook's shoulder, and the pale ivy leaves that slowly fluttered on it, like the handkerchiefs of hundreds of orphans, waving goodbye. The black unshaved prickles on Lieutenant Hook's upper lip. The fork-shaped scar on Sergeant Winstanley's cheek.

Sergeant Winstanley reached into his coat and produced a plastic forensic envelope. Effie found herself glancing at it sideways, as if she were afraid to confront it directly. She could clearly see a playing card, a nine of diamonds, stained with blood.

'They found this lying on top of the body. The county sheriff immediately remembered those homicides in Manhattan and called us late last night.'

'But those other murders . . . you checked the finger-

313

prints, didn't you, and they weren't Craig's.'

'We brought copies of those fingerprints with us today, and we've already had the chance to check them up against the fingerprints that were lifted from the broken beer glass that was found beside Michael Shelby's body. Whoever killed Michael Shelby also killed those other three.'

'But it wasn't Craig, was it? You said so yourselves.'

'Fingerprint evidence says it wasn't, Mrs Bellman. But all the other evidence strongly suggests that it was. Your husband had a possible grudge against all four victims. Even before this happened, we were prepping ourselves to come up here and talk to him again.'

'What grudge did he have against Steven Fisher? Steven was his partner, they'd known each other for years.'

'Mrs Bellman, we have eyewitness evidence that a man answering your husband's description was regularly seen at the apartment belonging to the victim Khryssa Bielecka, and a check on his phone records shows that he called Ms Bielecka's number two or three times every week.'

Effie was so stunned that she couldn't think what to say. Lieutenant Hook said, 'Listen . . . why don't we go inside and sit down. You're going to find this pretty difficult to take.'

'Craig . . . was having an affair with her?'

'It looks that way. I'm sorry that you had to find out about it like this.'

'Do you know how long it had been going on?'

'Over a year, from what our witnesses told us.'

Effie said, 'I think I do need to sit down.'

They went into the lobby of Pig Hill Inn and sat down next to the window. Sun shone through a large bowl of sweet peas; and flashed on the swinging pendulum of a long-case clock which stood against the wall.

Lieutenant Hook offered Effie some gum, but she shook

her head. He folded a stick between his teeth and started to chew. 'Your husband placed a call to Ms Bielecka on the morning before he was attacked at the K-Plus Drug Store. The last call he placed to her was a week after he returned to your apartment from hospital. Well, the last call we know about. We haven't checked the phone company records for this place yet.'

'What did she look like, this Khryssa?' asked Effie. 'I never saw her picture.'

Sergeant Winstanley searched through his pockets again and eventually produced a Polaroid of Khryssa on the deck of the Staten Island ferry, smiling and finger-waving.

'She's very pretty,' said Effie. She kept on staring at Khryssa as if the photograph could talk to her, and explain why Craig had been unfaithful. What did this face have that hers didn't? Was she funnier? Was she more passionate? Was she better in bed?

Lieutenant Hook gently took the photograph from her and handed it back to Sergeant Winstanley. 'I think I know what you're asking yourself, Mrs Bellman, and she's none of those things. She's dead.'

Effie swallowed. Her mouth had no saliva at all. 'What about those other people?' she asked. 'That taxi driver, and those gang kids?'

'The taxi driver is harder to figure out. But the day after your husband was hospitalised with his groin injury, he made a statement to the police in which he said that some "dumb, know-nothing immigrant taxi driver" had failed to get him to his destination because of gridlocked traffic . . . which is why he was walking along 48th Street in the first place. The driver who was killed was an immigrant Egyptian name of Zaghlul Fuad, and he was working the night that your husband was attacked.'

'But you don't think that Craig would have hunted him

down and killed him, just because he got stuck in traffic?'

'Sounds kind of cold-blooded, doesn't it, Mrs Bellman? But Mr Fuad had no other enemies that we know of, and no money was taken from his taxi when he was murdered.' He paused, and chewed, and then he said, 'As for the gang kids, it's extremely likely that your husband was attacked by Samuel Joseph Carter and Malcolm Oral Deedes, with the collusion of Susan Amelia Clay. It turns out that a hammer found in the dressing-room where they were killed hadn't been left around by a stage carpenter, as we originally thought, but that it was habitually carried by Samuel Joseph Carter as a weapon.'

'So he could have been the one who attacked Craig in the first place?'

'We don't have incontrovertible proof of that; but it seems like a strong possibility.'

'What about the fingerprints?'

Lieutenant Hook gave a laconic shrug. 'That's why we're here. We've had cases of criminals burning off their fingertips with acid, and I've seen two or three attempts to produce false fingerprints by using surgical gloves with latex prints moulded on to the fingertips. But none of those has been at all convincing. No – what we want is to make quite sure that some kind of clerical error wasn't made when your husband was fingerprinted at the precinct. And, of course, we'd like to talk to him, too.'

'He's up at our new house, supervising the building work.'

'We've already been there, ma'am,' said Sergeant Winstanley. He took out his notebook, licked his thumb, and leafed through it. 'Mr Bellman wasn't around, but Mr Norman Moriarty was repairing the library floor with three other carpenters. Mr Moriarty said that he had given Mr Bellman a ride to the house round about nine o'clock and that Mr Bellman had told him that he was going to continue drawing up his priority list of what restoration work needed attention first. That was the last time that Mr Moriarty saw him.'

'Then he must still be there.'

Lieutenant Hook said, 'We searched that old house from basement to attic, Mrs Bellman. Took us over an hour. If your husband *is* still there, he's been playing a pretty good game of hide-and-go-seek.'

'Do you have any idea where your husband might be, Mrs Bellman?' asked Sergeant Winstanley. 'Have you heard from him at all?'

'We had breakfast together. I thought he was going to spend the day at Valhalla, that's all. We agreed to meet back here at six o'clock, to get ready for dinner.'

'Did he seem strange in any way? Unsettled, maybe? Preoccupied?'

She shook her head. 'Just his normal self.'

Lieutenant Hook stood up. 'Mrs Bellman, Sergeant Winstanley and I are going to be around here for a little while. The minute you see your husband, can you please call the county sheriff's office and ask to speak to Deputy Shrike?'

The deputy handed Effie a card, and said, 'We really need to clear this up as quick as we can, ma'am.'

The three of them left, and Effie found herself standing alone in the lobby, overwhelmed with grief and hurt, which would forever be intermingled in her mind with the strong fragrance of sweet peas.

Wednesday, July 21, 4:06 p.m.

She rifled through his closet, searching through his socks and his shorts and every single pocket. In his leather toiletry bag, she found a bill from the Restaurant Lafayette, at the Drake Swissôtel on Park Avenue. It could have been an expense-account dinner for one of his clients. But she also found book matches from the Richmondtown Country Club on Staten Island, and he had never talked about entertaining any of his clients across there. In fact, he had never taken Effie there, either.

She felt shaken and upset, but at the same time she wasn't reacting in the way that she thought she would, if she ever found out that Craig was having an affair. She felt disturbingly *aroused*, too, at the thought that he had such virility. She tried to stop herself from feeling that way, because she knew she ought to be blazing with fury. But the more she thought about Craig the less angry she became, although she was still seethingly jealous that he hadn't devoted all of his virility to her.

The right-hand top drawer in the bureau was locked, and Craig had taken away the key. She tugged it and rattled it without success; and then she took out the drawer below and tried to reach into it from the back. In the end she took the long shoe-horn out of the bottom of her closet, wedged the end of it into the gap at the top of the drawer, and forced it downward, breaking the lock. The bureau was a fine Colonial antique, but Effie thought, damn it, Craig can pay for it.

She tugged out the drawer, accidentally spilling its

318

contents all over the carpet. Packs of playing cards, twenty or thirty packs of professional playing cards, most of them still sealed up in cellophane. But at least three packs were unwrapped, and they scattered across the floor.

Effie knelt down and quickly began to pick them up and arrange them back into suits. Clubs, hearts, diamonds and spades. It was when she reached the first suit of diamonds that she knew what was wrong. There was no nine of diamonds anywhere.

She sat up on her heels, and she felt shivery with dread. She could guess where those four nines had gone to; and the thought was more than she could bring herself to accept.

She stood up, sat on the edge of the bed, and picked up the phone.

'Can you put me through to the county sheriff's office, please?'

She waited for a while, and then a snappy voice said, 'Sheriff's department, how can I help you?'

Effie looked down at the cards lying all over the carpet. A house of cards, collapsed. A marriage, fallen apart. Four lives, savagely taken away.

'Hallo? Sheriff's department, how can I help you?'

'I'm sorry,' she said. 'It's nothing.' She replaced the receiver, and continued to stare at the cards.

In the book that she had read about Jack Belias, the author had quoted Athanase Vagliano, one of the Greek Syndicate, who had asked Belias why he gambled. 'What else is there?' Belias had replied. 'The cards are life, and the cards are death, and beyond life and death, what is there to worry about?'

She picked up the phone again and called Pepper. Pepper said she was mixing up an ouanga for one of her regular clients, and could she call back later?

'Pepper, this is *it*. We have to do the cleansing right now. The police have been here looking for Craig. They said they went to Valhalla but he wasn't there. Pepper, he went up there with Norman and he wouldn't have tried to walk back. The police think he's killed some people. The police think he killed the barman from the Hudson Inn. Please, Pepper, we have to do something *now*!'

'Hey, hey, hey, calm down,' Pepper soothed her. 'Now what's all this about killing a barman?'

'They found him dead last night and he was the same barman that Craig was arguing with. And they found a nine of diamonds on him and I've opened up Craig's drawer and there's all these packs of cards but none of them have the nine of diamonds.'

'And the nine of diamonds was the card that Jack Belias used to mock Zographos, right?'

'Pepper, I don't know what's happened to Craig but *please*, please help me.'

'Okay . . . give me twenty minutes to get my stuff together and then you can come pick me up in that fancy BMW of yours.'

Wednesday, July 21, 5:26 p.m.

They drove up past the Red Oaks Inn and down through the weather-twisted trees. It had clouded over, and a strong, unpleasant wind had risen, so that the lawns were scuttling with leaves and twigs. As they pulled up outside Valhalla's front steps, they heard a deafening *slap*-rumble noise, and looked up to see a huge tarpaulin flapping on top of the roof like a manta ray swimming through a powerful current.

320

Builder's sand whipped up from the patios, and Effie caught some of it in her eye. She was still trying to nudge it out with the tip of her handkerchief when the front doors opened and Norman appeared. He was brown with dust and his head was wrapped in a green bandana.

'Mom? What are you doing here? Hi, Mrs Bellman.'

'Hi, Norman. Is Mr Bellman anywheres around? We know the cops have been looking for him.'

Norman shook his head. 'He came up with me this morning. I saw him walk upstairs and that was it. I never saw him again. We looked for him just about like everywhere, but I guess it would be pretty easy to hide for ever in a house this size.'

Effie said, 'He's done it. I'm sure he's done it. Just like Jack Belias did when Gina Broughton was killed. He's vanished, he's gone. He's left us all behind.'

'You can't be sure about that,' said Pepper. 'He may just be hiding in the house.'

'We still have to cleanse it,' Effie insisted. 'Maybe if we cleanse it, he'll have to come back.'

'One of them will have to,' said Pepper, picking up the hem of her long maroon kaftan and hefting her tapestry bag on her shoulder. 'The only reason that Jack Belias has been able to take Craig over is because this house is so disturbed. Take away your disturbance, and they'll have to separate – body, personality and spirit. And since two people can't normally occupy the same body at the same time, you're going to have the psychic equivalent of organ-transplant rejection.'

'Sounds, like, messy,' Norman remarked.

'I've never seen it happen, but I guess it could be,' Pepper replied. 'Look what happens when two people in automobiles try to occupy the same space.' She walked into the house and Norman followed close behind her, carrying her battered brown suitcase full of mirrors. Norman snarled at the knocker on the door and Effie almost expected it to snarl back.

'We've been working on the library floor today,' said Norman, as they traipsed along the corridor towards the ballroom.

'Do you think that Craig is still here?' asked Effie.

Pepper put down her bag in the centre of the ballroom floor, knelt down, and rummaged around inside it. Eventually she produced a dried-looking root on a silver chain. 'Mandrake,' she explained. 'If he's here, it'll soon tell us.' She held it up so that it dangled in the air. 'The legend is that mandrakes grew where the sperm of hanged men dropped onto the dirt underneath the gallows. That's why they're so sensitive to the presence of any man, particularly an evil man.'

'Come on, Pepper. Craig may have got himself into trouble, but Craig isn't evil.'

'Maybe not. But Jack Belias was; or is; and right now, who's to lay money on which of them is which?'

They watched the dried mandrake root slowly winding and unwinding itself on its silver chain.

'What's it supposed to do when it senses that somebody's here?' asked Effie.

'Watch,' said Pepper.

'But the root did nothing but wind and unwind, wind and unwind.

'Nothing?' said Norman.

'Not yet,' Pepper told him. 'But I can still feel some serious disturbances. My God, it feels like a storm's brewing up. Can't you feel it, Effie? Can't you feel it in the air?'

Norman looked around the ballroom. 'I can sure feel *some* kind of atmospheric tension. You know, like, very low barometer weather. Like it's going to storm soon.'

322

'It's not the weather,' said Pepper. 'It's Jack Belias. He's found his way from one page of history into the next.'

She laid down her mandrake necklet, and then she started to set up her mirrors and her candles like she had before, when Craig had interrupted her. Effie meanwhile paced around the perimeter of the ballroom, listening for any doors opening or closing; or any footfalls. She went over to the library doors, and was about to open them when Norman said, 'Careful! Half of the floor is still, like, up. I'll show it to you later.'

Effie carried on circling around, waiting for Pepper to finish lighting her candles and angling her mirrors and setting up her herbs and talismans and her pot-pourri. The ballroom was already beginning to smell like the inside of the Hungry Moon. Effie was just about to walk around for a third time when she heard footsteps approaching along the corridor from the direction of the front door. Sharp, decisive footsteps, like those of an angry man.

'Pepper – he's here!' she hissed, as loud as she dared. 'He's coming along the corridor!'

Pepper said, 'Who's here? Craig your husband or Jack the gambler?'

'I don't know – it's just that he's –'

At that instant, the ballroom doors shuddered open. They all stepped back, Norman included. A tall, dark figure stepped inside, carrying in its arms a large metal box, almost the size of a baby's coffin. It walked slowly to the centre of the room, right up to the circle of candles, paused, and then laid down its burden with infinite care.

'I found something that might interest you,' it said; and as it turned towards Effie the candlelight swung and brightly illuminated its face, and Effie could see that it was Brewster Ridge, the black surveyor whose partner had died on their very first day of evaluating Valhalla.

'Mr Ridge, what are you doing here?' asked Effie.

Brewster jerked his head towards the battered, green-painted box. 'I took it down to Pig Hill Inn, but they told me you were gone, headed up here. I found it in Albany, in the New York State Archives, while I was searching for any old planning permits that might enhance Valhalla's value. I didn't find any, but this box has been rusting in some old storeroom since 1941. It's padlocked and nobody has the key. Nobody seems to care, either. In all of that time, nobody has claimed it or even asked to see what's inside it.'

'Well, what *is* inside it?' Effie demanded.

'Catalogue number 13444965/JB . . . a fireproof box containing the diaries and construction plans of Mr J. Belias, of Valhalla, Red Oaks Lane, Highland Falls, state of New York.'

'Have you tried opening it?' asked Pepper, excitedly.

'I wasn't sure that I had the authority.'

Norman was down on his hands and knees, peering closely at the padlock. 'Want me to give it a try, Mrs Bellman?'

'You might as well, seeing that Mr Ridge took the trouble to bring it all the way up here.'

Norman reached into a pocket and produced a screw-driver, prised the padlock off and opened up the box.

They all gathered around it. On the left side, in two neat stacks, were calfskin and crocodile-skin diaries, in red and black, neatly bound together with black ribbon. In the middle were rolls of architectural tracings of Valhalla, plans and elevations. On the right side there were five or six decks of cards, the larger professional size, unopened, a black leather-bound book with gold lettering *The Edicts of Balam* and a large manila envelope, sealed with black sealing-wax.

Norman lifted out the diaries, untied one of the ribbons, and flicked through two or three of them. They were all written in a slanting, precise hand, in black ink that had faded to a rusty colour with age.

'Anything interesting?' asked Pepper.

'If you're a card-sharp, maybe. This is like a record of every game of baccarat and chemin-de-fer and *trente-et-quarante* this guy ever played in his life. Nothing else, by the look of it. No intimate confessions. No juicy scandals.'

Brewster took out the plans and carefully unrolled them. 'These are worth having,' he said. 'Copies of the original architect's drawings. They could help you a whole lot with your restoration. Look here – the way this parapet was designed, up on the roof. That parapet's gone now, but you could restore it just the way it was meant to be.'

'Yes,' said Norman, without much enthusiasm; and it was then that Brewster looked around and saw the candles burning and the mirrors and the bowls of herbs.

'You people having some kind of a party here?'

'More of a ceremony,' said Pepper.

Brewster prowled around the candles and peered into the bowls of herbs. 'My grandma used to do something like this . . . said it chased away the evil spiritis. That's not what you're doing here?'

'Well, no, not exactly. We're just . . . housewarming.'

Brewster stood still, and looked around, and then he said, 'I've been surveying houses in the Hudson Valley since I was twenty-four, and I've been in houses like you wouldn't believe. I've been in houses where the person who built it was *dead* for twenty years, but you can still feel them there. You can feel their pride. You can feel their arrogance. Sometimes you can feel the love they had for the countryside around them; or the person they built it for.

'But this house . . .' He shook his head. 'It wasn't built to live in. Nobody builds a house like this, not just to live in. This was built for a very special purpose. The windows are out of proportion, the doors are too wide, the floors are built like no floors I ever saw before. This is like the crazy house they have at the carnival. It was deliberately designed to make a visitor feel small, and unsettled, and indecisive. Two staircases in the hall, both leading to the same landing? Which one are you supposed to take? And when you do, the risers are slightly higher than normal, to make you feel small. Stained-glass windows of nuns with their eyes closed and people with their backs turned? The Garden of Eden, gone to ruin? This house was made for something; I can tell you. I just can't figure out what.'

Norman had opened the manila envelope and pulled out some of its contents. They looked to Effie like large black-and-white photographs. He frowned at two or three of them, and then he shoved them back.

'Norman?' asked Effie.

'Maybe you should see these later.'

'Why, what are they? Let me see them now.'

'I don't think so,' said Norman, uncomfortably.

Pepper snatched the envelope, went through the photographs very quickly, her face expressionless. Then she handed them to Effie. 'You'd better see them. That was what Harry Rondo was talking about.'

The photographs were very dim and lacking in contrast. They showed a bedroom with an iron-framed bed in it, a small fireplace and a window overlooking a rooftop. Effie recognised the bedroom at once. It was the blue-carpeted bedroom where she had heard a woman sobbing. When Effie had ventured into the bedroom, it had been bare. But in these pictures, there was a nightstand and a closet and religious pictures on the walls.

326

And on the bed, a woman. A woman whom Effie recognised.

She was naked, tied hand-and-foot with ropes. Her white skin was blotched and bruised; although the photographs weren't clear enough to show her injuries in any detail. She was obviously pregnant: six or seven months, Effie would have guessed.

In another photograph, she was covered in masses of cockroaches. They were crawling all over her, and she was powerless to brush them away. A close-up showed cockroaches crawling in and out of her mouth, and up her nose. Her eyes were staring directly at the camera, unblinking, as if she were dead.

There were more photographs, and they were all worse. Although she knew that this must have happened almost sixty years ago, Effie was still appalled. She found herself biting her left thumbnail, digging her teeth into it, which was something she hadn't done since she was at high school. She glanced at Pepper and Pepper looked back at her: but Pepper's face was unreadable. Effie had the feeling that a long time ago, in her Woodstock days maybe, something like this may have happened to her.

She didn't want to go on looking but she did. Every photograph was a cold, straightforward record of unspeakable degradation – degradation without any meaning or purpose, except that the woman was helpless, and her persecutor could do with impunity whatever he chose.

She glimpsed a photograph in which a man appeared to be holding a long needle close to the woman's left eye. The expression on the woman's face was so terrible that she pushed all the photographs back into the envelope, her heart racing and her cheeks flushed. 'You know who this is, don't you?' she said. She felt so disoriented, so angry,

327

and yet so excited too.

Pepper nodded. 'Gina Broughton. The woman who agreed to stay for three days and ended up staying eighteen months. The woman who was blinded.'

'Why?' Effie demanded. She was almost screaming. 'Why did she let Jack Belias *do* that to her?'

'You remember what Harry Rondo said. She let him do it because he could. She let him do it because her husband agreed to stake her in a game of cards. What did anything matter, after that? Three days, three weeks, three months. It didn't matter any more. At least Jack Belias wanted her enough to degrade her. Her husband didn't want her at all.'

'My God,' said Effie. She was hyperventilating. 'We are dirt, after all, aren't we? We're *all* Lilith; none of us is Eve.'

Wednesday, July 21, 6:17 p.m.

While Pepper finished setting up her arrangement of candles and mirrors, Norman and Brewster went around the house one more time to see if they could find any sign of Craig.

'He could have tried walking, or hitching a ride,' Pepper suggested, but Effie knew that she didn't mean it. If Craig had wanted to leave Valhalla early, all he had to do was ask Norman to drive him. He was paying Norman's wages, after all.

'This house has been waiting for somebody like Craig for years,' Effie said. 'The very first time we drove up here, it *drew* him, almost like a magnet. You don't know how completely that mugging destroyed his self-confidence, his pride in himself. It must have been bad enough knowing that somebody else can hurt you like that, and get away with it. But to have them damage your whole manhood like that . . .'

Pepper said, 'It isn't the house that wants him. It's Jack Belias. He wants to live again, for real. He wants to live in the here-and-now, and if it means that he has to live in somebody else's body, then that's what he's prepared to do. It's just too bad for you that he found Craig.'

She lit another row of candles with a long sandalwood spill. Her eyes shone silver. 'When you first saw Jack Belias running down the stairs, he saw you, too, but only as an unreal figure, the same way that you saw him. In other words, you were haunting him in 1937 as much as he was haunting you. You were both caught in the same psychic disturbance, which is like somebody thumbing the pages of a book backwards and forwards, backwards and forwards, so that two events become superimposed on each other and you can't tell which is which. Like a flicker-book. He must have realised then that you and Craig had arrived in his life, and you were his chance of escape.'

Effie said, 'Maybe I should go look for Craig, too.'

'Unh-uh. I wouldn't if I were you. The psychic disturbance is very strong. You never know what might happen.'

'I'll just take a quick look in the kitchens.'

She left the ballroom and walked through the library. Half of the floor was still under repair, and the gaping hole through which Morton Walker had fallen was still covered with a tarpaulin, but she was able to walk around the right-hand perimeter of the room, and out into the hallway. She stood for a moment at the foot of the stairs, listening to the wind whistling through the ill-fitting window-frames, and the intermittent tapping of overgrown branches against the glass, as if some skeletal visitor were trying to attract her attention.

She climbed the stairs a little way until she could see the lumpish plaster figure on the far side of the landing. Since Norman had waterproofed the roof, it had begun to dry out, and a gaping crack had appeared beneath its nose, so that it looked as if it were just about to speak to her in some hideous, occluded voice. Its eye was less glutinous, too, and looked more focused and accusing.

'Craig?' she whispered. 'Craig? Are you there, Craig?'

There was no reply. The wind sang secretly under the bedroom doors, and sucked the air out of empty fire-places. Effie paused, still listening, but she knew that Craig wasn't there. Craig might, in fact, have been nowhere at all. Not here, not today, but in another time altogether, beyond her reach. She could search the whole world and never find him, and that was as good as his being dead. *'Gut ist der Schlaf. . . .'* the stained-glass window reminded her. *'Der Tod ist besser.'* Now she understood what it was trying to say.

Now she understood the nun amongst the lilies, and the man with his back turned. A woman of pure appearance but filth at heart, Lilith, who defied man and consequently defied the will of God. Jack Belias' primary intention hadn't been to destroy the men with whom he played cards. He had been showing that their women were nothing more than dirt – quite prepared to cuckold them, and to betray them, and then to desert them when their money ran out.

She retreated slowly downstairs. She waited in the hall-way a moment longer, and then she went through to the kitchens. They were silent and chilly, even though the evening was still warm. A tap was slowly dripping into one of the sinks, which showed that Norman must have re-connected the water supply. Through the dusty kitchen

330

window she could see the newly-cleared garden, with stacks of overgrown weeds and vegetables ready to be burned.

'Craig?' she called again, and her voice echoed in the scullery.

No reply.

She opened the door to the cellar, and immediately she heard a thick, rushing noise somewhere in the darkness below her.

'Craig?' she called, quite loudly this time. 'Craig, is that you?'

But then she heard the scrabbling of claws along water pipes, and she realised that what she had heard was rats. Hurriedly she closed the cellar door and turned the key in it. She loathed rats. In fact she loathed anything that scurried or crept or slid itself along the ground. Maybe that was proof that she wasn't descended from Eve after all, she thought, wryly: *she* would never have been tempted by a serpent.

She was walking back across the kitchen when a dark movement in the garden caught her eye. She stopped, her scalp tingling, and looked at it again. At first she couldn't see anything at all, only a scraggy line of rusty-coloured broom that bordered the vegetable beds. But then a man appeared, a man dressed in black, with a black wide-brimmed hat, and he was walking quite quickly towards the house.

She couldn't see his face clearly. He kept passing through sunshine and shade, which gave his progress an odd flickering effect, like an old movie printed on deteriorating stock. He seemed almost to appear and then disappear. *I shall never completely die.*

Effie walked swiftly out of the kitchen and back across the hallway. She reached the ballroom at the same time as

331

Norman and Brewster, back from their search of Valhalla's upper storeys, and almost collided with them.

'I've seen him,' Effie said breathlessly. 'He was out in the garden, coming this way.'

'Craig?' asked Pepper.

'Craig, Jack, I don't know. Either, or both. I couldn't see his face.'

Pepper stooped down and picked up her mandrake root. She held it up, and watched it, and for a long while it did nothing more than it had before, wound and unwound. Then suddenly Effie heard a thin, high-pitched scream. It was so piercing that it left the taste of salt in her mouth, and she felt as if her ears had been boxed.

They all looked at each other in astonishment, except for Pepper.

'Did you hear that, too?' asked Brewster. 'That was like somebody screaming inside of my head.'

'Mine, too,' said Effie.

Norman dug his finger in his left ear and twisted it around. 'Like, I'm going to be deaf for life now.'

'That was the mandrake,' said Pepper. 'It screams when you pull it up, and it's supposed to scream when murderers come near.'

'You're kidding me,' Brewster told her. 'A plant made all that noise?'

'There's a perfectly logical psychobotanical explanation for it. Their juice is sensitive to human alpha waves; and people who are capable of killing other people have distinctively different alpha waves from the rest of us. The mandrake isn't actually screaming in fear. It doesn't have any imagination. But all the same, it's screaming.'

She picked up her two-branched hazel twig. Effie glanced at her in concern, but she said, 'The seven-branched twig isn't sensitive enough. It's like trying to eat

332

cake with a dental dam in.'

Brewster said, 'Do you mind if I stay for this? Your son here was telling me all about it; all about that library floor and everything. I'd be fascinated.'

'Long as you stay at your own risk,' Pepper warned him.

'You mean this is dangerous?'

'Is an earthquake dangerous?'

Effie stood close to Pepper, among the candles and the mirrors. Pepper slowly moved the hazel twig from one side of the room to the other, her eyes still open, her lips slightly parted.

She carried on sweeping the room, very concentrated and very patient. Brewster started to say something but Norman pressed his fingers to his lips. 'Have to have silence. Sorry.'

After only two or three minutes, the hazel began to shudder and twitch. Suddenly, its stem jerked up in the air, and it stood erect, quivering so fiercely that Pepper could hardly hold it.

'Holy cow,' breathed Brewster. 'I never saw anything like that before.'

Pepper gritted her teeth. 'It's strong today, it's very strong. And it's very chaotic, there's no order to it, it's like everything's fluctuating all over the place. Music, can you hear it? And then different music. And voices!'

Effie listened, and Pepper was right. First she heard jazz music, playing very faintly in another room. Then she heard women's laughter, and *The Blue Danube*, and then jazz again, and men discussing something between themselves in deep, confident voices.

'Is there a *party* going on someplace?' asked Brewster, in awe.

'Sh,' said Norman.

Effie heard laughter, more laughter. She thought she

was standing next to Pepper, and yet in a peculiar way she wasn't, she was standing much closer to the doors that led to the library. She looked back at Pepper but Pepper didn't seem to be able to see her. Another man was walking across the room. She didn't know who he was. He was a big, balding man, with a face that had the pale lumpy texture of a root vegetable. He was wearing rimless spectacles with clip-on sunglasses, which made him look like a croupier. His shirt was stained with sweat and his beige cotton trousers were creased. He was carrying a cassette recorder and a flashlight, and he was talking to himself.

He passed right by Effie without even acknowledging her. As he passed, he said, '*Dry rot, wet rot, extensive termite infestation . . .*' He opened the library doors, stepped inside, and closed them behind him.

Effie turned to Pepper and said, 'Did you see that? Pepper, did you see that? Who was that man?'

But for some reason Pepper ignored her. She kept slowly waving the hazel twig from side to side, in smaller and smaller arcs, until at last she had located the point at which it twitched at its strongest.

'Pepper –' Effie began. But Pepper had her eyes closed now, and it was obvious that she was meditating. Whoever the balding man had been, he obviously wasn't very important. Maybe just one of Norman's carpenters, making some last-minute notes. Maybe Effie had imagined him.

She opened the library doors, and went inside. The room was lined from floor to ceiling with bookshelves, and each shelf was packed with leather-bound, gilt-embossed books. They gave off a rich aroma of Morocco and calfhide, and this mingled with the smell of cigar tobacco and men's cologne, Floris Special No 27 if she wasn't mistaken (although how she knew that, she couldn't understand). The windows were heavily draped with green-and-white striped curtains, and the floor was carpeted in bottle-green. In the middle of the room stood a baize topped table, with ornate mahogany legs, around which a dozen men in evening dress were sitting, playing cards, and over which a cadaverous-looking croupier stood guard.

She recognised most of them: Michael Arlen and Viscount Castlerosse; Karl Majorian and Remy Morse. Nico Zographos with his pout and his little moustache. And of course there was Douglas – dear, dear Douglas, with his white wavy hair and his panicky smile.

On the far side of the table, in a revolving captain's chair upholstered in black leather, a dark-eyed man with a dazzling white shirt front was dealing from the shoe. She knew him, too. Jack Belias. Momentarily, he raised his eyes to her as he dealt. His look was neither crude nor lustful. It was a look which meant nothing less than: *you will very soon belong to me*.

She was afraid of him. She had always been afraid of him. He had the coiled-up tension of a man who knows that he is stronger and crueller and far more skilful than any of those who sat around him. His face was well sculpted and refined, with deep-set eyes and sharply defined cheekbones; but his refinement was compromised by the scars which pitted his skin – evidence of poor nutrition when he was a child, and a harder upbringing than most people care to think about.

It was always his eyes which terrified her most. The last time she had seen anybody look at her the way that Jack Belias looked at her, that person had been sitting in the back seat of a crashed DeLage tourer, on the coast road just west of Nice, with a lapful of blood, dead.

All the same she walked up to the table and ostentatiously caressed Douglas' cheek. He glanced up at her, and kissed her wrist, but his jovial expression seemed to be held onto his face with two-inch nails.

'You shouldn't distract him, sweetheart,' said Jack Belias, gently tapping an inch of ash from the end of his cigar. There was no humour in his voice at all; no pretty-please; no cajolery. He said it as if he would happily stub his cigar out on her forehead. 'Now, why don't you run along and let the men get back to what they're doing.'

She walked around the table, staring at each man in turn. 'What did you stake?' she asked Remy Morse.

He slicked back his greasy black hair with his hand. 'My yacht, the *Agrippina*; and all her crew.'

'And you?' she demanded of Karl Majorian.

'My racehorse, Great Pretender.'

'My chateau,' said another player; and still another said, 'The Cope Diamond; all 47^1/$_2$ carats of it.'

She returned to Douglas, and wrapped herself around his shoulders. 'My husband, though, he doesn't stake horses or trinkets. He's far too daring for that. My husband stakes his wife; his own wife; the same woman with whom he walked up the aisle. I have every right to distract him. He's my husband. If he loses, then I lose.'

'He could still win,' said Jack Belias, lifting his sockless ankle and revealing a bony ankle, scarred with mosquito bites. 'You know what baccarat's like. Ruination one minute, salvation the next. It all depends on your nerve.'

Effie leaned close to Douglas' ear. 'I've given you every-thing,' she whispered. 'I've given you money; I've given you confidence; I've given you luck. If I have to sleep with Jack Belias because of you, then I swear to God I'm never coming back.'

Douglas looked up at her, his eyes wide. 'It's only for three days and three nights. For God's sake, Gina, what are you trying to say to me?'

'Is that what you thought? Three days and three nights? I agreed to this, yes, because I love you, and because I promised when I married you that everything I had belonged to you. But once I've done this, I've given you everything. There isn't any more of me left. Not money, not possessions, not body, not soul.'

'But you said –'

'Yes! I said! I offered! I agreed! But you didn't have to accept my offer, did you? You were my husband, Douglas! Didn't it ever occur to you to say no?'

Douglas was grey now, the colour of rainsoaked newspaper, and his hands were shaking. 'When you said yes, I didn't realise.'

Effie stood up straight. Jack Belias was watching her with huge amusement; especially since she was destroying Douglas Broughton wholesale, and ruining his concentration. She couldn't have done better for him if she had picked up Douglas' hand and showed him his cards.

'It doesn't matter who wins, and it doesn't matter who loses,' Effie declared, right into Douglas' face. 'You can't lose me playing baccarat, because you've lost me already.'

'Please! Please! May we continue to play?' asked Jack Belias. 'I hate to see a good game of cards spoiled by a little domestic unhappiness.'

'My God,' said Effie. 'Do you know what you are? He's down on his knees and you still want more! Why don't you just get it over with, and shoot him?'

'I don't want your husband, Mrs Broughton. As far as I'm concerned, he's nothing but whalemeat in a three-piece suit. I don't care if he lives or dies. I don't care if he contracts plague or wins the Nobel Peace Prize. I don't care if he's happy and I don't care if he's miserable.'

He picked up a card from the table between two fingers,

and twisted it around so that Effie could see it. The Queen of Hearts.

'I want *you*,' he told her, and grinned even wider. Some of the other players sat back in obvious embarrassment. Michael Arlen said, 'Come on, Jack, this isn't the way,' and Remy Morse wreathed his head in cigar smoke as if he were trying to hide.

'Very well, you want me,' Effie retaliated. 'But this is the only way you could ever have me. By winning me, at baccarat, like a racehorse, or a diamond, or a house. You could never win me any other way.'

Jack Belias continued to smile, but his eyes looked oddly piggy. 'First of all let me win you at baccarat. Then let's see if I can't get you to change your mind. I promise you, Gina, I'll have you crawling on your hands and knees for me. I'll have you dancing barefoot on broken glass. How about that? Would you dance barefoot on broken glass for me?'

'Come on,' Douglas protested. 'Let's get on with it.'

He didn't look at Effie again; but Jack Belias gave her one last Cheshire-cat grin, which seemed to linger on his face long after he had returned to the serious business of dealing cards.

Effie was about to return to the ballroom, to see what Pepper was doing, when a jerky, shadowy motion caught her eye. She looked back at the baccarat table. Jack Belias was slowly, almost casually spinning in his revolving chair: two, three, four times. She couldn't think what he was doing at first. Was he *playing*? But then – with a prickling feeling all the way up her neck and into her scalp – she saw a shadowy, semi-transparent figure rise out of Jack Belias' chair and move rapidly around the table, lifting up the three hands of cards he had dealt to see what they were. Then he returned to his seat, and seemed to become solid again. None of the other players appeared to have noticed – neither they, nor the croupier. It was just as if the spirit of Jack Belias had left his body and checked on his opponents' cards.

It's not a floor, it's a clock, Norman had told her. And that was why Jack Belias played baccarat in the library, where the very construction of the room would allow him to turn the page of time, just for an instant, so that he could see what was going to happen next . . . or with complete impunity look at the cards that he had dealt. Effie saw the cards flutter slightly as they reached the moment in time when Jack Belias had lifted them up to look at them; but then the room returned to normal, and the baccarat players continued to play.

'*À cheval*,' said Douglas, and placed a thousand dollars between 1 and 2.

Effie left the library. Just before she closed the double doors behind her, she saw Jack Belias raise his head and give her a cold, possessive, reptilian stare. At that moment, he looked more like Craig than Jack Belias, but she knew that Jack Belias had taken him over so completely that there was no point in trying to appeal to the man who had once said he would love her 'for all eternity, and a couple of months more'.

Once she had closed the doors, she hesitated for a split second, wondering if she ought to open them up again, just to check that Jack Belias and his fellow gamblers were still there. But then she walked quickly across to Pepper, and touched her shoulder. Pepper was engrossed in her dowsing, and she turned and blinked at Effie as if she hadn't realised that she was there.

'It's Jack Belias – he's here.'

'How do you know?'

'I've just been into the library. He's playing baccarat

with his friends.'

'What do you mean you've been into the library? When?'

'Just now. About twenty seconds ago.'

Norman came over and said, 'What?'

'Effie says she just went into the library.'

Norman looked perplexed. 'Like, how did you manage that? You've been standing here the whole time.'

'I went into the library. I swear it. Jack Belias is there, and so are his friends. They're real. They're really there. Come take a look if you don't believe me!'

Pepper looked down at her hazel twig. It was still bent back, but it wasn't twitching any longer. 'Shit,' she said, and dropped it onto the floor.

'What's the matter?' Effie asked her.

'Don't you understand? All of these spells, all of these candles, all of these goddamned mirrors. They're not having any effect at all.'

'But I saw a man walking across the library, and when I followed him, Jack Belias was there.'

'We didn't see any man. What did he look like?'

'Well, he was balding ... not very good-looking. He wore a white shirt and creased-up pants – and, yes, a pair of red and green braces.'

'My God,' put in Brewster. 'That sounds just like my partner, Morton Walker.'

'You saw Morton?' asked Norman, incredulous.

'Red and green braces, who else could it be?' Brewster replied.

'But for Christ's sake, Brewster, Morton's dead.'

'And Jack Belias is dead,' put in Pepper.

'I can't understand why you didn't see him,' said Effie.

'For the same reason that none of my spells are any use, and my hazel's a waste of time. These psychic disturbances

340

are not just happening on their own. They're all to do with *you*, and Craig, and Jack Belias, and whatever he did to Gina Broughton.'

'So, like, what's going on?' asked Norman.

'Jack Belias is back, that's what's going on. Don't you see? He must have had the idea of building Valhalla the same way as the Benton House so that he could shift himself seconds forward in perceived time, and cheat at cards. He certainly didn't build it for religious reasons: he was an atheist. He made millions out of it, and nobody ever guessed, because how *could* they guess, especially when they were angry, and they weren't thinking straight.

'Originally, he built the house this way to help him to cardsharp. But when Gina Broughton fell out of that window and died, that was when he thought of using it for something else. I think I made a mistake when I thought that Jack Belias was trying to get away from the law when he disappeared down by Bear Mountain Bridge. He didn't give a monkey's ass for the law. When Gina Broughton died, she robbed him of the chance to break her completely. No woman had ever done that to him before. So that's what he's doing here now. He's back for another try.'

'Can't we stop him?' asked Effie. 'I thought you said these mirrors would help to get rid of him.'

'There's only one way to stop him,' said Pepper. 'And that's to demolish the whole house.'

'You're kidding, aren't you?' Norman protested. 'The Bellmans have their entire savings sunk into this property, and I've done thousands of dollars' worth of work already.'

'There's no other way,' Pepper insisted. 'So long as this house goes on standing, Jack Belias will always be able to move from one decade to the next, and one person to the next.'

'But come on, mom, supposing you're wrong?

341

Supposing we pull down the house and the guy's still here, like strolling around the gardens and smelling the flowers? Then what?'

Effie said, 'If we demolish the house . . . do you think that I'll get Craig back, the way he was?'

Pepper nodded. 'Almost sure of it.'

'*Almost* sure of it?' Norman protested.

Effie said, 'I'll have to think. I'll have to talk to our lawyers. I'll have to talk to Craig.'

'It's too late. You can't talk to him any more. Craig is Jack and Jack is Craig. They're living completely co-incident lives.'

Norman checked his watch. 'Why don't we do one more search, and then call it a day? This coincident stuff is like making my head hurt.'

'Okay,' said Pepper. 'What do you think, Effie? One last look around?'

'Yes,' said Effie. 'And I think I'll start with the library.'

She went across to the library doors and opened them wide. It was empty. Not a bookshelf in sight, no baccarat table, no cigar smoke, no gamblers. She cautiously stepped inside and walked around it, trailing her fingers against the walls.

Where are you, Jack Belias? she thought. *You must be hiding close . . . in the darkness of tomorrow morning, just before dawn . . . or the shadows of yesterday morning.*

She walked to the very centre of the room, where the baize topped table had stood. She looked down; and saw a small greyish object on the floorboards. When she bent down to try to pick it up, it crumbled between her fingers. Cigar ash.

'What is it?' asked Pepper, coming across to join her.

'He's so close,' Effie whispered. 'He and Gina Broughton, both of them. I can almost *feel* them, they're so close.'

'I can feel them, too,' Pepper agreed. Her feet were bare and gold coins jingled on her headband.

Effie went to the window. 'What I don't understand is how Gina could be here, too, trying to take over *me*? She was dead, wasn't she, stuck on the railings? *He* could come back here and use the house to turn to a different time; but she couldn't.'

Pepper lit an awkwardly-shaped joint, and blew smoke out of her nostrils. 'Maybe he went back before he went forward, and got her while she was still alive. Who knows? Suddenly I feel like nothing but a quack.'

Effie held her hands over her breasts. She felt a sensation inside her that was nothing like anything she had ever felt before. It was a warm, blossoming feeling, similar to stepping out into the sunshine, but on the inside.

'Do I look different?' she asked Pepper.

'In what way?'

'I don't know, just different. I *feel* different. Do you think that Nico is coming tonight?'

'What?'

'I said I feel different.'

'No, after that. You asked me if Nico was coming tonight.'

Effie walked slowly back across the library floor. 'I really said that? Yes, I did, didn't I? And I knew who I meant, too. Zographos.'

Pepper took hold of her and gave her a quick, warm hug. 'Come on,' she said. 'Let's go on looking. We might find something that gives us a clue.'

Effie said, 'It's started, hasn't it? This is what Jack Belias came back for. Or *forward* for.'

'Don't be frightened,' said Pepper. 'He didn't break Gina and he won't have the chance to do the same to you.'

Wednesday, July 21, 7:42 p.m.

Norman and Brewster climbed the main staircase for the second time that evening, Norman taking the left-hand flight and Brewster taking the right.

'My grandma believed in magic,' Brewster remarked, as they joined up together again on the upper landing. 'If anybody bullied me at school, she used to make me take a secret snip of their hair and bring it back home to her. Then she used to mix it with chicken's blood and salt and a handful of wheat, and hang it up on the porch so that the moonlight would get to it. She used to say that it would make my enemies go crazy, but at our school most of the kids were crazy anyway so I never knew if it really worked.'

They opened the doors to the anteroom. For a millionth of a second, Norman was almost expecting to see his mother lying on the floor with Craig Bellman on top of her, her feet lifted in the air. But it was empty and shadowy and it smelled of dust.

'I can't believe that my mom could think of demolishing this place,' he said. 'I mean, it's totally unique.'

'Do you believe that this Jack Belias is *really* using it to come back?'

'What can I say? He built it on the same principles as the Benton House . . . and you can sure use *that* place for some pretty weird effects.'

'Do you think Mrs Bellman really saw Morton?'

'It sure sounded like him, didn't it? And as far as I know, she never met him.'

'Jesus, poor Morton. My grandma believed in ghosts.

344

She wouldn't have an empty vase in the room, in case a ghost was hiding in it.'

'What was your grandma's name? Winnie the Witch?'

They crossed the anteroom and approached the master bedroom doors with their silent, carved faces. 'This place might be totally unique, but I wouldn't want to live here,' said Brewster. 'I'd have to cover up these doors, for one, in case one of these faces suddenly opened its eyes.'

'Come on, man, you're spooking me.'

'Sorry. We searched the master bedroom, didn't we?'

'No harm in taking another look.'

They opened the double doors and went into the huge, churchlike bedroom. The windows were juddering in the gale, and outside the house, they could see the trees thrashing and bending like demented dancers. Brewster said, '*Urgh*,' and trailed his hand away from his face.

'What's wrong, man?'

'Spider web. I can't stand spiders.'

'This house is full of them. It's like Arachnid Apartments.'

'You're determined to spook me, aren't you?'

They crossed the bedroom and peered into the en-suite bathroom. Cold, empty, with a large black spider sitting in the white tub. Brewster promptly closed the door and locked it. 'I'd rather face a ghost than one of those suckers any day.'

They left the bedroom and walked along the south-facing corridor. 'Looks like a storm's getting up,' Brewster commented, as they looked into the sewing-room. Almost on cue, lightning flickered on the distant peak of Storm King Mountain. 'I should be getting back soon. My wife's going to be wondering where I am. She's expecting a baby.'

'You told me.'

'Did I? Sorry. I'm still so proud.'

They reached the landing where the plaster-creature stood. 'You start looking upstairs and I'll finish off this floor,' Norman suggested. 'Otherwise this is going to take us forever.'

'You got it,' Brewster agreed, and climbed the staircase past the stained-glass window. He started to walk along the corridor, opening each bedroom door in turn and taking a look inside. He didn't like this house at all. Although it was so huge, there was something about its atmosphere which made him feel edgy and trapped – as if, once he was in it, he was never going to find his way out. As he made his way along the corridor he made up a rap, singing it under his breath. The wind tugged at the window-frames as if it wanted to shake them out, and the tarpaulin which covered the collapsed section of the roof began to rumble and snap.

'I was checking out this spooky house the other day . . . the ghosts came out and they began to play . . .'

He reached the third door, and placed his hand on the handle. As he did so, he thought he heard somebody let out a suppressed sob. He froze, and listened. All he could hear was the windows rattling and the *boom*-flap-*boom* of the tarpaulin on the roof.

He thought he glimpsed a fleeting shadow, out of the corner of his eye. He looked back along the corridor, towards the landing. There was nobody there. His heart was knocking against his ribcage, and his breathing seemed to be absurdly noisy, like bellows blowing in and out. *Somebody's here*, said his instinct. *They can't be*, his logic replied.

Somebody's here! his instinct insisted. *Somebody's here!*

Brewster waited and waited. Then he heard it again, quite distinctly this time, a high muffled sob, like a child

346

crying or a woman in pain.

I don't want to do this, somebody's here.

But all the same he turned the handle and opened the door. 'Anybody here?' he asked, in a phlegmy, constricted voice. Then, 'Anybody here?'

There was a figure in white standing at the window, looking out. It had its back to him, and it didn't move, although its sheet-like covering was idly stirring in the draught. Outside, the sky was intensely grey, like moleskin rubbed with charcoal, although the rooftops were still gleaming. The empty fireplace sighed, and whistled, and sighed again.

'Pardon me,' said Brewster. 'I'm looking for Mr Bellman. Have you seen him at all?'

The figure said nothing; and didn't move. Brewster took two or three steps across the blue-carpeted room, but he wasn't sure that he had the courage to go any further. The figure hadn't acknowledged him in any way, and it surely wasn't Craig Bellman. It was far too slight, far too narrow-shouldered. It had to be a woman, rather than a man. But that didn't lessen Brewster's apprehension. He took another step forward, and then another, but he kept thinking of the red-coated dwarf in *Don't Look Now* and all of the other horror movies he had seen where people keep their backs turned, and then suddenly look around to reveal terrible faces.

He raised his left hand toward the figure's right shoulder. At the same time, clouds rolled over the last remaining brightness in the sky, and the room was plunged into gloom. Brewster thought *I just can't do this, I'm too damned scared.* But before he had time to stop himself, he grasped the figure tightly, feeling bones beneath the sheet, and twisted it around to face him.

He was so shocked by what he saw that he involuntarily

347

jumped back. It was a woman's face, as white as the sheet she was wearing. Her eyes were milk-white, too, and totally blind.

'Oh shit,' said Brewster, and crossed himself, and crossed himself again. 'Oh shit I didn't mean to –'

The woman said nothing at all but stepped forward with her left hand outstretched. Brewster tried to back away, but she found his arm, and then his shoulder, and gently curled her fingers around the back of his neck. Brewster stepped back. I mean this was a *nightmare*, man! But then he felt a punch in the stomach, not hard, but painfully, and sharply.

'What the hell are you trying to do?' he demanded. 'Are you crazy or what?' He pushed himself away, trying to untangle himself from her arms. It was then that he saw that her sheet was splattered with red, and that she was holding something that looked like a sharpened poker. He stepped back again, and felt an excruciating pain gripping his stomach, like the worst indigestion he'd ever had. The front of his shirt was glistening wet and soaked in blood.

'For Christ's sake, what did you do that for?' he shouted at her. 'I came here to help you!'

Either she couldn't hear him or she didn't care to hear him, because she suddenly groped towards him again, her left hand sweeping wildly from side to side; her poker upraised.

Brewster staggered back against the bed, then turned, tilted, and tried to make it to the door. The woman came rushing after him, her left hand still sweeping from side to side. She stabbed at the air, then she stabbed at Brewster's shoulder, and he actually *heard* the point dig into his muscle, as well as feeling it. He dropped on his hands and knees onto the carpet, coughing up blood. But then he felt the woman's hand touching his back, deftly and excitedly,

348

to locate where he was. *Gala*, he thought. *My darling Gala. How the hell am I going to explain all of this to you, baby?*

Gripping the poker two-handed, the woman stabbed Brewster in the back and the shoulders, six or seven times. Brewster felt each stab like a sharp, painful knock. He heard the woman gasping, but that was all she did. She didn't speak. His back felt as if it had been beaten with a baseball bat, but what he didn't realise was that she had already punctured both of his lungs, and pierced his liver, and that her last stab had missed his heart by less than a quarter of an inch.

He stayed on his hands and knees, unable to move, dripping blood like a slaughtered pig. He was conscious of the woman circling around him, and the sheet sliding to the carpet. He tried to raise his eyes, but all he could see was her bare feet and her ankles. He tried to say 'Why?' but all that came out was a large glutinous bubble of blood. He could taste it. It tasted like metal.

Slowly, very slowly, he bent forward until his forehead was touching the carpet. He couldn't feel any pain now, but he knew with absolute clarity that he was dying. The woman's bare feet prowled around him but he didn't bother to look. She didn't matter any more, no matter who she was. He thought: *Only the living worry about the identity of murderers. The dead are always too dead to care.*

He thought that was so stupidly profound that he almost laughed. And it was that choking attempt at laughter that was the last sound he ever made, before he dropped heavily sideways onto the carpet.

The woman stood over him, although she couldn't see him. She was completely naked, but her body was decorated with scars and burns and scratches and bruises. She was heavily pregnant, and her swollen breasts rested on her stomach like two overripe fruit.

After nearly a minute, she knelt down next to Brewster's body, touching it gently, feeling its contours. Anybody watching her would have thought that she felt regret. But after a few moments, she stood up, and picked up the sheet, and wound it around herself like a toga, and inched her way carefully out of the room.

Brewster lay where he was, his eyes still open. The blood from his wounds spread across the carpet, and formed a shape like a goat's head, with asymmetric horns.

Wednesday, July 21, 7:53 p.m.

Norman checked all of the guest bedrooms and all of the bathrooms, right the way down to the very western end of Valhalla, which overlooked the Hudson Highlands. Some of the rooms were bare-boarded, with peeling wallpaper and damp patches which looked like the maps of undiscovered continents. Others still had beds, and carpets, and yellowed curtains, and spare linen stacked neatly in the closets. The folded edges of the linen were stained with age, and some of the pillows had been ravaged by mice. But Norman still had the feeling that the people who had slept in those rooms had only stepped out for a moment, and might soon return.

Whether they were furnished or not, every bedroom shared a view of the blackening sky, and the swathes of rain that were trailing over the Hudson Valley from Kingston in the north to Tarrytown in the south; and the thin, snakes'-tongue licks of lightning. It felt to Norman that apocalypse was coming: the day of judgement. He was beginning to wish that he hadn't volunteered to have any part in his mother's attempts to cleanse Valhalla of its

350

psychic disturbances. He would have been better off at Clarke's Bar & Grill, talking joists and covings with his building buddies.

The bathrooms were the creepiest, as far as he was concerned. Every time he opened a bathroom door, he saw his own pallid face in the mirror, and every basin seemed to have a spider in it, black and impossibly long-legged. It was the rain, he guessed. Spiders always came into the house when rain was imminent.

After he had checked the rest of the second storey, he came out onto the landing where the plaster-creature was hunched. He hadn't seen it as a creature until Mrs Bellman had pointed it out to him, and now he found himself staring at it uneasily, and making sure that he didn't turn his back to it. He could just imagine it shuffling across the landing and jumping onto his back, and then biting into his jugular vein with that cracked, lopsided mouth.

He checked his watch. Brewster shouldn't be long. There were only twelve rooms and eight closets and four bathrooms on the third storey. He leaned against the banister-rail and drummed his fingers and whined Nirvana's *All Apologies* through his nose. It was the most miserable song he could think of. He checked his watch again. Come on Brewster, man. You don't have to make a meal of it.

He was still waiting when a large chunk of plaster unexpectedly dropped off the plaster-creature and broke into dust and fragments on the floor, making him start.

The creature now looked grimmer and more distorted than ever, with half of its forehead missing. Norman walked across to it and said, 'Fuck you, man,' and kicked it in its bulging, misshapen midriff.

At first he made no impression on it, but then he kicked it again, and again, and its belly collapsed in a shower of plaster and fungus and sodden, discoloured wallpaper. He

351

kicked its face, and its jaw fell off. He kicked its eye, and its eye disappeared. He kicked it and kicked it until it was nothing more than a heap of crumbled off-white fragments, spread across the landing.

He was kicking so hard that he didn't hear the light, quick footsteps on the stairs. He sensed that there was somebody there, but he assumed that it was Brewster, and so he gave the plaster-creature one last kick and said, 'What do you think, man? Bit of impromptu restoration.'

He stepped back, brushing his hands together and admiring the mess he had made. 'I should have been a kick-boxer. What do you think? Eat your heart out, Steven Seagal!'

He took another step back, and turned, but it wasn't Brewster at all. It was a tall, dark man with a blurry, indistinguishable face. He was dressed in black and carrying a walking-cane. Norman leaned forward a little, trying to focus on him; but it didn't seem to be possible.

'Are you here with –?' he began, but the man took one step towards him and he shut his mouth.

'This is my house,' the man told him. His voice was very deep; very courteous; but frightening none the less.

'Well, I don't think so,' Norman corrected him. 'This house actually belongs to Mr and Mrs Craig Bellman. I'm Norman Moriarty by the way. I've been commissioned to take care of the restoration work. Are you interested in that kind of thing? You can have my card.'

'This is my house,' the man repeated. 'I thought of it, I created it, I built it.'

'In that case,' said Norman, flippantly, 'you'd have to be Jack Belias.'

The man said nothing, but lifted his walking-cane and gripped it as if he were going to break it in half.

'Trouble is, Jack Belias went off to the house not made

352

by hands; and that was in 1937.'

'When was 1937?'

'What do you mean, *when* was 1937? Nineteen thirty-seven was, like, 1937. That's like asking when was five o'clock.'

The man took a step closer and Norman could smell his strong, floral toilet-water. 'I'll tell you when was 1937, you ignorant puppy. Nineteen thirty-seven was *now*; and 1937 was tomorrow; and 1937 was fifty years hence.'

Norman cleared his throat with a sharp barking sound. 'You're trying to say that you *are* Jack Belias?'

The man came up close and stood over Norman in the same way that the thunderclouds stood over Storm King Mountain. His voice was rich with corruption and threat.

'You don't doubt me, do you?'

Norman lifted both of his hands. It was not only a gesture of conciliation; it was a way of warding Jack Belias off.

Jack Belias took one step forward, and then another. 'You've been trespassing here, haven't you? You haven't been upstairs, have you? You haven't let my little captive free?'

'Listen, man, I don't know what you're talking about. I don't know what you mean. If you want me to leave, I'll leave.'

Jack Belias' voice suddenly rose to a roar. 'You think you can get away with it that easily? You think you can get away with it without being punished?'

'Listen, I'm out of here. I promise.'

But without warning, Jack Belias lifted his walking-cane and struck Norman a cracking crosswise blow on the right shoulder, close to his neck. Norman said, 'Shit, man!' and lifted his arms to protect himself, but Jack Belias struck him again and again and again, so hard and so savagely that there was nothing Norman could do but stagger backwards.

353

'I don't brook trespassers and I don't brook vandals and I won't brook you!' Jack Belias raged at him. He hit him on the fingers of his left hand, and Norman heard two of them crack.

'Leave me alone!' he screamed. 'Leave me alone! I haven't done anything to you!'

But Jack Belias ignored him, and continued to strike him again and again – on the arms, on the shoulders, on the side of the head. Every time Norman tried to step back, Jack Belias took a step forward. His face was still blurry and unfocused, but Norman could see that it was contorted with anger, his eyebrows locked in a frown, his mouth dragged down like a Japanese demon mask.

He turned, stumbled, and Jack Belias thrashed him across the back. It was the noise that frightened Norman just as much as the pain. It sounded as if a madman were trying to beat a sofa to death. He limped along the corridor with Jack Belias walking behind him, hitting his back and his legs.

'You thought you could get away with it?' Jack Belias kept on roaring at him. 'You thought I'd let you go free?'

Norman ducked, and twisted around, and snatched at the walking-cane. He caught hold of the end of it, and tried to wrench it out of Jack Belias' hand. They wrestled and pushed and grunted. Norman turned the walking-cane around and around like a clock-hand, trying to break Jack Belias' grip. Neither of them spoke.

There was a moment when Norman thought that Jack Belias was going to break the rest of his fingers, but then he suddenly twisted the walking-cane one way, and then the other, and Jack Belias dropped it. It fell on its tip and danced away down the corridor as if it had a life of its own.

Norman gave Jack Belias a single huge shove, and then limped towards the nearest window. His ears were ringing, his jaw was aching, and his body felt as if it had been crushed under a falling joist. He heard Jack Belias shouting with rage as he went back to pick up his cane; and he knew that he couldn't stand any more beating. Jack Belias would kill him next time.

He banged open the window catch with his bruised fist. The gale-force wind instantly blew the windows open, and one of them swung against the panelling and smashed. The rain hit Norman in the face like frozen gravel, and the net curtains blew wildly up into the air.

'Vandal! I'll teach you!' Jack Belias bellowed. He struck at the top of Norman's head, and Norman lost his balance and almost fell down onto the stone patio thirty feet below. He managed to save himself only by catching hold of the window, which swung unnervingly towards him.

For two or three terrifying seconds, he was half in and half out of the window, clinging onto the sill to stop himself from falling, while Jack Belias thrashed at his legs. Then he managed to kick back, and heave himself out onto the narrow stone ledge that ran the whole length of the second storey to the front of the house.

'I'll get you, you bastard!' Jack Belias shouted at him. Lightning crackled over the trees, and for an instant everything was lit in dazzling blueish-white. Then thunder detonated directly overhead, and Norman clung to the wet stone as rain lashed against his back and turned his jeans into grotesque, wet, overweight leggings.

Sniffling with pain, he edged away from the open window and began to creep slowly towards the next. His only fingerhold was a rough, narrow crevice between the bricks. Three of the fingers in his left hand were fractured, and he had to hold them straight, so that he was keeping a grip with only his little finger, with his thumb pressed against the brick facing for balance. Up above him, the

355

guttering was broken, and gallons of rainwater were splattering down the wall and onto his head.

He was clear of the first window when he heard a banging sound. Jack Belias had opened the next window, and was leaning out.

'You really thought that I would let you go? You really thought that I wouldn't punish you! You can't escape from me!'

Norman rested his forehead against the wall. He couldn't go forward and he couldn't go back. Whichever window he went for, Jack Belias would be waiting for him. He couldn't stay here much longer, either. He was soaked through to the skin, and his fingers were aching so much that he almost didn't care whether he held on or not. He didn't want to look behind him because he knew it was a long drop to the rain-slicked patio below.

'Come on, then, what are you waiting for?' Jack Belias taunted him.

Norman edged a little further along. His hair was hanging down over his face in wet rat-tails and he was beginning to whimper. He glanced at Jack Belias again and suddenly saw that there was a metal pipe running vertically down the wall. If he could fasten his belt to that pipe, he could stay out here until help came, or Jack Belias grew tired of waiting for him.

He shuffled further along the wall. Jack Belias reached out of the open window and rapped his cane against the bricks, trying to dislodge him, or at least to frighten him, but Norman knew that he was out of reach. He inched his way nearer and nearer to the pipe, and at last his right hand closed around it. He swayed for a moment, and had a sickening feeling that he was going to fall over backwards, but then he managed to grip the pipe tight.

The most difficult part was unbuckling his belt. He had

to do it with his right hand because the fingers of his left were so damaged. Clinging on with nothing but his left-hand pinkie, he swayed two or three times and had quickly to let go of his belt and snatch at the pipe to regain his balance. By the time he managed to thread his belt behind the pipe and buckle it up again, he was crying with pain and exhaustion.

'So you're going to stay there, are you?' Jack Belias mocked him. 'Well, in that case, stay there, and be damned. I hope the crows come and peck out your eyes!'

Norman turned to him. 'Fuck you, man!' he screamed. 'What did I ever do to you? What are you, some kind of sadist? What did I ever do to you? I wasn't vandalising your rotten house, I was trying to restore it!'

'Then you're a bigger fool than I thought!' Jack Belias shouted back at him. 'It *is* restored! It will always be restored, just as it will always be ruined!'

'Well, fuck you!' Norman retorted.

At that instant, the faint leader-stroke of a huge lightning discharge came flickering like a viper's tongue through the clouds above Valhalla, searching for a line of least resistance. It was momentarily attracted by Valhalla's tall chimneys, but then it suddenly forked sideways and touched the copper fleur-de-lys that surmounted Valhalla's lightning-conductor. Instantly it was followed by a massive return stroke, and then another, each of more than 200,000 volts – and then an ear-splitting crack of superheated, air, hotter for one-hundredth of a second than the surface of the sun.

Norman's chest glowed orange from the inside, like a hideous Hallowe'en. Then he literally exploded, and blackened arms and legs were flung across the patio. His charred head, with the stubble of his hair still smoking, rolled into the bushes.

Thunder shook Valhalla and made the window frames rattle. But the window where Jack Belias had been standing was empty, with the net curtains dragged out into the rain like shrouds.

Wednesday, July 21, 8:17 p.m.

Pepper looked up.

'What was that?' Effie asked her.

'Lightning-strike.' She paused, her silver eyes darting from side to side. 'But there's something else, too.' She turned to Effie and she looked suddenly bloodless. 'Something's wrong,' she said. 'I felt like – I don't know – I felt like I suddenly lost something.'

'Come on,' said Effie, 'it's just this creepy atmosphere.'

'No,' Pepper told her. She pressed the heel of her hand against her forehead. 'It's like – something disappeared. I can't explain it.'

'Maybe we should go look for Norman and Brewster, and call it a night.'

'What about Craig? Effie, if you lose Craig tonight, you've lost him for ever.'

Effie said, 'You've done enough already. This is my battle. Mine and Craig's. You've seen that for yourself.'

'I can't leave you here alone.'

'You said yourself that it was me that was causing all this psychic disturbance – me and Craig, anyway. What can you do?'

'I guess I could give you some moral support.'

Effie shook her head. 'There's only one thing that needs to be done, Pepper, and you know it. Jack Belias has to be shown that no matter how many times he tries to break

358

Gina Broughton down, he's never going to do it. He may take over Craig, and he may use me to re-create Gina. But no matter what he did to Gina, she wouldn't give in to him. He whipped her, Pepper, and he abused her, and he tied her up, and he blinded her. She still wouldn't give in to him. And I won't give in to him, either.'

'Well, well,' said Pepper, with a tight, puckered-up smile. 'The daughters of Lilith say thus far and no further.'

'If you like.'

Pepper reached into her kaftan, took out her ouanga, and handed it to Effie. 'I don't know whether it'll do you any good. None of my other spells seem to work around here. But maybe it'll help just a little bit to keep you safe.'

Effie took the ouanga and kissed Pepper on the cheek. 'Faith, hope and a home-made ouanga. I can't go wrong.'

'Just be extra careful,' Pepper warned her. 'Time has gone haywire here tonight. It's like all the pages of the book have got stuck together. I mean, anything could happen.'

'I know,' said Effie. 'But I'm just going to have to risk it. I think I was drawn here almost as strongly as Craig was. There's so much unfinished business to take care of.'

Pepper said, 'I'm going to go find Norman. I still have this real bad feeling about him.'

Effie watched Pepper leave the ballroom. Now that she understood exactly what she had to do, she felt stronger and more determined than she had ever felt in her life. She had fallen for Craig when he was younger, with his mystical, romantic quotes from Mallarmé. She had devoted her life to helping him at work. She had soothed him and flattered him and flattered his clients, too. She had given him too much to let Jack Belias take him now; or to let Jack Belias take her.

She heard laughter in the library. She could smell the

359

cigar smoke even though the doors were closed. She took hold of the handles in both hands, and opened them up.

The library was fully furnished and lined with books; although it was so dense with smoke that she could hardly see anything except the baccarat table, lit with a green-shaded lamp, and the men who were sitting all around it. They turned to look at Effie and their faces were universally despondent – all except for Jack Belias, who was leaning back in his chair and laughing and lighting another cigar.

'Well, well,' he said. 'It looks like the first of my winnings has turned up in person.'

Douglas Broughton turned around in his chair and his expression was desperate. 'Gina,' he said. 'Gina, I really believed that I was going to win.'

Effie walked up to the table and the men turned away in embarrassment. All except for Douglas Broughton, who kept on looking up at her, his forehead crowned in perspiration, begging for forgiveness. And all except for Jack Belias, with that strange square face of his, and those eyes like burn-holes, who smiled, and sipped at his cigar, and smiled some more.

'Forgive me,' wept Douglas Broughton. He dropped onto his knees on the carpet and took hold of her hand. 'Gina, please forgive me.'

She lightly touched his white fraying hair, the prawn-pink scalp beneath. 'Why do you want me to forgive you? For staking your wife at a game of baccarat, or for losing?'

'Oh God, Gina, forgive me for everything.'

'There's nothing to forgive. I agreed because you wanted me to. Isn't that what wives are for, to do what their husbands want them to do?'

Jack Belias made a little beckoning gesture with his finger, and a servant with white gloves came up and

360

poured him another bourbon. 'You're mine now,' he told her, in a tone of voice that was surprisingly matter-of-fact. He scooped up the last of the cards, shuffled them, squared them, and tucked them back in the shoe. 'Your husband can send over your clothes, and anything else you want for your creature comforts. Otherwise, you can go upstairs with Lettie and find yourself a bedroom. I'll be up later, when I've finished stripping my friends here of a few more assets.'

'I'm out,' said Remy Morse, looking at his watch. 'As usual, *mon cher* Jack, it has been very dangerous, very exciting, and not very much of a pleasure. I wish some day that a black cat would cross your path and trip you up, so that you break your callous neck.'

'I'm not going anywhere,' said Effie. 'The fact is that I'm not Gina and that you can't win human beings in a game of cards.'

Thunder rumbled outside the house, but already it was beginning to move away. Pepper meanwhile was crossing the patio in her wind-whipped kaftan, her bare feet crunching in ashes. She found a triangular trowel that wasn't a stone-age artefact, but a human scapula, a shoulder-bone. Then she discovered more bones, and a whole burned-out ribcage, and a spine. She found a scorched pack of orange Tic-Tacs and a half-melted pack of lime Tic-Tacs. Two small items from Norman's balanced diet.

It was then that she understood the empty sensation that she had experienced in the ballroom, and it was then that she thought of all the days of her life she had spent in bringing up Norman, from a fat white baby who never slept, to a lanky grunting teenager who could tile, and plaster, and cut immaculate dovetail joints, and who never

361

talked about anything but Nirvana, karmic diets, and bringing old houses back to their former glory.

Norman had never been old enough to realise that glory is only the golden shine of arrogance; and that the great houses of the Hudson Valley were monuments built in their own honour by men for whom nobody else would ever pay a penny to build a monument.

Pepper bent down in his rainsoaked ashes and wept and wept, while the last lightning-flickers disappeared east-ward, towards Connecticut, and the wind began to die down.

At last, however, she raised her head and wiped her eyes with the back of her hand. She turned towards Valhalla, with its spires and its chimneys and its dark, asymmetric windows, and she knew what she had to do. She stood up, and walked back to the front door. She climbed the steps and touched the wolfish door-knocker with one hand, as if she thought it would give her strength. It was there to pro-tect the house against evil spirits. Perhaps this evening it would fulfil its task.

She walked across the hallway, along the corridor, and into the ballroom. Without hesitation, she went across to the five-gallon cans of cleaning fluid stacked for the house restorers. She hefted one of them up, and carried it across to the middle of the floor. Then she went to fetch another. She unscrewed the caps, and began to empty them all across the room. The cans noisily gulped in air as the fluid poured across the shining Canadian maple. Fumes rippled up like heatwaves from a summer highway.

In the library, Jack Belias stood up and tugged down his waistcoat. 'You're wrong, Mrs Broughton,' he told her. 'You were staked by your husband; and he lost. Therefore, you're mine, and completely mine, for three long days and three long nights, to do what I will with. You agreed to it, Mrs Broughton, don't forget that. You gave your word. And in gambling, your word is your bond.'

'I think you've forgotten something,' said Effie. 'This isn't the first time you've played this game. This isn't the first time you've won this prize. You may not have changed, but times change; and society changes. You've discovered the secret of Balam, Mr Belias. You've skipped from time to time, from life to life. But you're a man of the age you were naturally born in, and you always will be.'

Jack Belias' face was rigid with anger. Without taking his eyes off Effie, he said, 'Are you welshing on a bet, Douglas? Is that it?'

'I don't know,' said Douglas Broughton, miserably. 'If she really doesn't want to do it –'

'She doesn't have a choice,' Jack Belias snapped back at him. 'You staked her. She agreed. Now she's mine. Just like the chateau is mine and the racehorse is mine and just like the goddamned yacht is mine, too.'

'No,' said Effie. 'I'm nobody's. I'm me.'

She had never believed in the whole of her life that she would be capable not only of saying those words, but believing them, too. If Douglas Broughton wanted her, he would have to stand up for her, and repudiate his stake. If Jack Belias wanted her, he would have to treat her well.

If Craig wanted her, he would have to overcome the brutal personality that had taken his soul.

She was nobody's. She was her own woman. And the full realisation suddenly made the tears pour down her cheeks, because she was free. God only knew what she had lost. Her marriage, maybe; all of her money. Twenty wasted years. But she was free.

Jack Belias tossed down the last pack of cards so that they scattered. He walked around the table and stood in front of Effie with his fists propped on his hips. He was very tall, and she could feel his magnetism like a high-powered electrical generator. He almost hummed with personal power. Slowly, she raised her head so that she was looking up into his face. She could see nothing but irritation, nothing but contempt.

'You're mine,' he said, mouthing the words with infinite softness. 'Your husband owes me ninety-seven thousand dollars, and you are the only person who can clear that debt. You have nothing at all. No money; no equity; nothing. Your husband owes me everything. And so you're mine.'

Effie looked up at Jack Belias for a very long time. She knew what she was looking for: she was looking for any trace of Craig. A look in the eye; a twitch of the mouth. She thought she detected something of Craig in the way he tilted his head slightly to one side; but anybody could have done that, Jack Belias included.

She slapped him. She didn't even know where her hand came from. Her arm just popped up of its own accord and slapped him.

'You conniving bastard!'

'Who's a bastard? Come on, bitch! Who's a bastard? Bitch!'

'You, you bastard!'

He slapped her back, hard. Her head was jerked violently to the left, wrenching her neck, and she felt her cheek flare up.

She slapped him again; and he slapped her. She was about to retaliate when he slapped her once more – so forcefully this time that she fell back against the book-shelves, and dozens of leather-bound books came tumbling out.

'Bitch! Look what you're doing to my library!'

She picked up a book and flung it at him, and then another. The pages made a satisfying flaring noise as they flew past his head, followed by a chaotic thump. The first one missed him altogether, but the second one hit him on the arm.

Now he was angry. He threw aside an occasional table with a white porcelain vase on it, kicked away all of the books that had fallen on the floor, and picked Effie up by her lapels. Flowers and water and broken pottery were spread out everywhere. Jack Belias was quaking and sweating, and his eyes unfocused like a man who can't see, or a man who doesn't want to see.

'You're mine,' he repeated. 'You're my concubine, if that's what I choose for you to be. You're my squaw.'

Effie said, 'Craig, you're overstimulated. You're over-loaded. This whole house is full of things you don't under-stand. You don't even know why it's here, or what it's for, or what it can do.'

'You're mine, sweetheart,' Jack Belias repeated, and slowly raised a warning finger to show that she should never disagree.

There was a long pause. Jack Belias took hold of her hands, both of them, and even though she knew it was Jack Belias, at least he still felt like Craig. Nobody's hands felt like Craig's hands . . . except if his prints were different.

'Craig,' she said. 'I'm begging you. Be strong. Be your-self. Don't let another man take your whole personality away. You're *you*, and that's all that matters.'

Jack Belias was silent for a moment. He lifted his head, and nodded.

Then he punched her so hard in the cheek that she flew backwards and hit her back against the doorframe.

She was half knocked-out. She tried to get up but her ears were singing and she didn't know where she was.

365

Douglas Broughton got up and said, 'Damn it, Jack, you can't do that! She's my wife!'

Jack Belias pushed him back into his chair. 'She's mine, Douglas. Fair and square. I won her and I can do what I like with her.'

'Jack . . .' begged Michael Arlen. 'Jack – this really isn't on.'

'On? On?' Jack Belias shouted at him. 'All that's "on" in this room are bets. All bets are on. *Tout va!* And I've won this woman fair and square!'

Effie sat up. Her left eye was almost closed, and she was dribbling blood and saliva from the side of her mouth. 'Fair and square?' she mocked him. She didn't care now. 'You used this library to cheat . . . you used this floor to cheat . . . I know about Balam and I know about floors that aren't floors. You cheated when you won Gina, and even then you couldn't break her.'

'What is this about cheating?' Remy Morse demanded. 'What is this about a floor?'

'Spin yourself around a few times, clockwise, and you'll see.'

'Pardon?' asked Remy Morse, completely perplexed.

But now Jack Belias was seriously enraged. He dragged Effie up from the floor and punched her on the ear, and then on the cheekbone.

'I'll kill you,' he breathed. 'So help me I'll kill you.'

'Go on then, kill me,' Effie pouted back at him, through swollen lips. 'But you will never, ever beat me.'

Jack Belias went for his walking-cane; but that was his mistake. He gave Effie time to scramble onto her feet, dodge around the baccarat table, and push her way into the hall.

'Stop her!' Jack Belias screamed, whacking his cane against the baccarat table, so that the cards jumped. But all the other men sat in their evening dress as if they were waxworks; as if they were memories, frozen in time; and perhaps they were.

Effie ran across the hallway and into the kitchen. The swing doors closed behind her: *joink* – squeak – *joink* – squeak. She went around the tables, frantically pulling out drawers, looking for knives, anything to protect herself, but there wasn't even a teaspoon. She heard the swing doors burst open again, as Jack Belias came after her, and she almost panicked. But there was the cellar door, with the key still in it. She tugged it open, and clambered in semi-darkness down the cellar steps. Two-thirds of the way down, she stumbled and almost fell, but she managed to hobble her way to the very bottom, and look around.

The cellar was illuminated by nothing more than the light from the kitchen door. She could see the floor glistening, because it was so wet. She could see vaulted arches, with nothing beyond them but blackness. She took one step forward, and then another; and behind the arches she was sure that she could hear a flurrying sound, a scratching sound. She peered into the shadows and the light reflected back at her from two red eyes, and then two more.

Oh Jesus, she blasphemed to herself. *Rats. I can't take rats.*

She was about to grope her way back up the stairs to the kitchen when she heard the sharp chipping of a man's pumps crossing the kitchen floor. Then the rap of a walking-cane, and the cellar door opened even wider.

'Gina! Are you down there? What the hell are you doing down there? I order you to come up! I *order* you to come up!'

Effie said nothing, but stood in the half-light with her hands clasped together, not knowing what to do.

'Goddamn it, Gina, I'm going to kill you for this!'

367

No, you're not, she thought to herself. *I'd rather face rats first, than give you the pleasure.*

She began to walk into the cellar – through the first row of vaulted arches, past the boilers, and into the darkest recesses where even the exterminators hadn't yet dared to venture. The rushing of rats was like the surf on the beach at Hyannis, where her parents used to take her when she was little. There must be thousands of them, nesting in this cellar. A whole subterranean kingdom, ruled by tooth and claw.

She ventured further and further, with her hands held out in front of her, in case she collided with one of the arches in the dark. She heard the scratching and scuttling very close to her now, and she started to whimper. She didn't want to, but she couldn't help herself. A rat ran over her shoe, and she felt its horrible bootlace tail whipping against her ankle, and she had to force her hand into her mouth to stop herself from screaming.

Behind her, she heard footsteps coming down the stairs. She turned, and saw that Jack Belias was following her, waving his walking-cane from side to side, like a blind man. She plunged on into the darkness, as quickly as she could, praying that she wouldn't step on anything terrible, praying that the rats wouldn't get her.

'Gina?' called Jack Belias. 'I won you, Gina, fair and square! I'm coming for you, Gina!'

Effie took one more step forward, and then another. It was then that the rats came for her. She felt one jump up on her back and dig its claws into her shirt. Then she felt two or three of them biting at her ankles, through her socks and her boots. Another flung itself onto her shoulder, but she swung herself around and it dropped off into the dark.

She was quaking with fright and disgust. But she could

see Jack Belias coming towards her, swooshing his cane from left to right, and she knew that she would rather face the rats than face up to him. To the rats, she was nothing but prey. To Jack Belias, she was a victim, a possession, the proof of man's God-given superiority.

Another rat tried to scurry up her leg. She beat it off, but she felt it nip her hand. Oh God, what kind of diseases did it carry? It was probably riddled with fleas; and the fleas had probably come from squirrels or polecats or bats or any number of wild animals that carried rabies. Another one jumped up, as heavy as a sandbag, and then another, and suddenly she was wearing thick, squirming boots made out of living rats.

She kicked her feet up in the air, one after the other, like a child kicking through heaps of leaves, and some of the rats were flung away. But then a huge rat jumped onto her right shoulder, and another followed it. She felt their claws digging right through her shirt, and their teeth tearing her skin. She tried to twist around and beat them off her, but they clung on ferociously, and she was afraid that if she pulled them away, they would take large chunks of her own muscle with them.

She dropped to her knees on a carpet of scratching, writhing rats. A rat ran up her back and into her hair, and clung to her scalp. Another tried to scurry up the front of her shirt. She knelt for a moment without moving, with her head bowed, as if she were a willing victim, and then she took a deep breath and said to herself: *I've never been a victim, ever, not of men, not of rats, not of anything!*

She climbed to her feet in a swinging coat of rats. She staggered ankle-deep in rats to the nearest wall. Then she turned her back, and deliberately collided with the brick-work, so that all the rats on her back were crushed. She heard their bones cracking; she felt their bellies burst. She threw herself backwards again and again, until they dropped off her back and onto the floor. Then she ripped the rats off the front of her shirt, and threw them as far as she could across the cellar.

Upstairs, Pepper cautiously knocked on the library doors and called, 'Effie? You there?'

She waited, but there was no reply. Very slowly, she turned the handles and opened the doors just three or four inches.

'Effie?'

The library was empty. Effie must have gone in search of Jack Belias somewhere else in the house. Unless Jack Belias had already taken her.

She glanced back worriedly at the cleaning fluid spreading across the ballroom floor. The last thing she wanted to happen was for Effie and Brewster to be trapped in Valhalla once she set it alight. But she knew that she had to do it, she had to bring it down, or Effie and Craig would never be free of it, and neither would anyone else who ever came here looking for a house to restore their status and their pride.

'Effie!' she called. 'I'm going to set a fire! Get out of the house, Effie, wherever are you!'

She listened; but there was no reply. She waited another half-minute; then she closed the library doors, crossed herself, and walked over to the centre of the ballroom floor, flicking her cigarette lighter as she did so.

Effie could see Jack Belias silhouetted in the arches, holding his walking-cane.

'Gina?' he shouted. 'Is that you, Gina?'

Around her feet the live rats were voraciusly falling on the dead rats, and tearing their skins to shreds. She kicked

370

one or two more, but they were far too greedy for their brothers' flesh to take any notice.

'*Gina!*' Jack Belias roared, into the rat-infested darkness.

Effie glanced quickly around her, wondering which way to go. Maybe she could dodge around behind him, and run up the kitchen steps before he noticed. But then she realised that light was faintly penetrating the cellar in the arch where she was standing, and she looked up to see that the ceiling wasn't a ceiling at all, but a large tarpaulin. This wasn't 1937 any more. The library floor was still broken where Morton Walker had dropped through. And if Morton Walker had dropped through, then she could climb back up.

She groped her way across the floor. She could see something shadowy in front of her, something tall and dark. Whatever it was, maybe she could climb up it, and reach the tarpaulin that covered the library floor. She made her way forward, inch by inch, feeling bruised and scratched and deeply panicky. It seemed to take her an age to reach the shape; especially with Jack Belias shouting '*Gina!*' every few seconds, and slowly advancing into the darkness of the cellar, striking with his walking-cane the few rats that scurried up to him, and breaking their backs. Every step was accompanied by a *thwack*! And another *thwack*! And a squealing of pain.

Effie blindly reached out her hands and touched the tall dark shape in front of her. It was soft and heavy and very wet and it stank of ripe blood and sour stomach-acids and something worse. She said, 'Urrh' out loud, and stepped back in disgust. But it was only when the draught momentarily lifted the tarpaulin on the library floor, and let in the briefest wash of evening light, that she realised what it was.

Morton Walker, impaled on his heating pipe, dead and eaten and ready for burial. A glistening carcass of scarlet and grey. Yet he had already been buried. He couldn't be here. His body was lying in the Cold Spring Cemetery, awaiting a headstone.

But what had Pepper said? *Time has gone haywire here tonight.*

Jack Belias whacked his cane against the vaulted arches so that it echoed. '*Gina!*' he called. 'I know you're in here. You're mine, Gina! I want you to come back and give yourself up to me, just like you promised. I won you, Gina! I want you back!'

Effie covered her face with her hands and said a prayer for Morton Walker's departed soul. Another rat jumped for her ankle, and tore her sock open, and she kicked it against the wall and broke its neck. Then, without any further hesitation, she walked up to Morton's body and started to climb it, using his knees and his pelvis as footholds, and his collar bone for a handhold.

The climb was slippery and greasy and total disgust. She kept grasping handfuls of spongy lung and body fat. His bones fell out of his arms when she tried to use them as supports, and his bloody head fell backward in utter resignation.

With one foot on Morton's collar bone and the other perched on his rubbery, collapsing face, Effie managed to reach up and grip the rope that fastened the tarpaulin. She was smothered in blood and mucus, but she didn't care. Jack Belias wasn't going to get her, no matter what. She thought of the pictures Jack Belias had taken of Gina being abused, and she was totally determined that he would never lay hands on a woman again.

On the very top of Morton Walker's impaled body, she swayed like a circus performer. His ribcage lurched under the weight. For a moment, she thought she was going to join him, impaled on that pipe. But then she reached out

372

and seized the edge of the crumbling floor. 'Oh God,' she prayed. 'Never again. Not rats. Please, not ever. Not rats.'

She heaved herself up, and lay panting on the library floor. She felt bruised and torn and shaky. Both eyes were closing up, and the left-hand side of her jaw was hugely swollen. Her hair was clogged with blood, and looked more like a rat's-nest than a real rat's-nest.

She couldn't help thinking of those photographs, and what Jack Belias had done to Gina Broughton.

Tortured her, raped her, tattooed her, scarred her and blinded her. And on top of all that, had given Douglas Broughton the greatest insult of all: he had made her pregnant.

Effie painfully climbed to her feet. As she did so, she thought she smelled burning. She sniffed, and sniffed again, and she was sure that she could definitely smell smoke. She looked toward the library doors and saw pale ribbons of smoke pouring out from underneath them.

She went to the doors and listened. From the ballroom, she could hear a brisk crackling sound. She pressed the flat of her hand against the wood panels. They weren't warm yet: maybe the fire had just started. She knew that she shouldn't open the doors, but supposing Pepper was still in the ballroom? Supposing she was hurt, or unconscious?

She hesitated for a moment, and then she risked it. Shielding her face with her hand, she opened the doors just a couple of inches.

Instantly, she shut them again. The ballroom was a dazzling, dancing inferno of fire. The whole floor looked like medieval paintings of hell, with tongues of flame licking twenty or thirty feet in the air, and a huge column of black smoke was billowing up to the oval skylight.

There was no sign of Pepper. Even if she had been there,

373

it would have been too late to save her.

Effie hurried back through the library and out to the hallway. She stopped and listened. The wind had died down now that the storm had passed, and apart from the spitting and the rumbling of the fire, still muffled by the solid oak doors, Valhalla was unnervingly quiet.

'Pepper!' called Effie, as loud as she dared. She glanced at the kitchen door, terrified that Jack Belias was going to come bursting out of it at any moment. 'Pepper! Where are you? Norman! Brewster! Is anybody there?'

She started to climb the stairs. It was then that she heard a woman sobbing. Painful, and low, and agonised; and this time she knew who it was.

She hurried up to the landing. She saw the plaster-creature lying smashed to pieces, scattered across the floor. She stopped for a moment, to listen again, and the woman was still sobbing. *I'm coming, Gina*, she thought to herself. *And this time I'm going to set you free.*

Downstairs, she heard a door slam. She knew what that was. Jack Belias, coming out of the cellar, angrier than ever. She started to climb the second flight of stairs just as she heard the swing door *joink*, and Jack Belias crossing the hallway. She heard his pumps scuffing quickly up the stairs, and the tip of his cane rattling against the banisters.

Gasping, she reached the turn in the stairs, just below the stained-glass window. But Jack Belias was too fast and too angry for her. He came running up the stairs like a dark automaton, and caught hold of her sleeve.

'Let go of me!' Effie screamed. 'Norman! Norman! Help me!'

Jack Belias swung his cane, but Effie deliberately dropped onto the floor, and rolled around, and he missed her. She felt the sharp draught of the cane, less than an inch away from her face.

'Get up and take your punishment!' he roared at her. 'Get up, you bitch, and take your punishment!'

He swung again, but Effie clambered to her feet, and he struck a blow against the banisters that jarred his hands.

'Take your punishment, you bitch!'

He swung his cane right back and accidentally struck the stained-glass window. A whole panel of lilies broke, and dropped down onto the stairs. Jack Belias turned around, and looked up at the window. It cracked, and began to slip, and he shouted out, '*No!*'

But the lead between the glass panels was crumbling and fatigued, and the frame was half-rotted, and with no warning at all the whole window collapsed on top of him, showers of splintering coloured glass. It sounded like hailstones falling, it sounded like bells chiming. Jack Belias stood with his arms shielding his head, and then – when the last pane had dropped to the floor – he lowered his arms and looked up at Effie with the most demonic expression that she had ever seen on anyone's face. He was so angry that he scarcely looked human. Pieces of broken glass surrounded his feet – a lily, a castle, and half of a nun's face, with one eye closed.

'I swear to God that I'll break you,' he told her. 'I swear to Almighty God.'

They stood in silence for a moment, confronting each other. Then Effie heard the sobbing noise again. Not loudly; not as anguished as before; but deeply sorrowful.

Without a word, she turned and hurried up the stairs.

'*No!*' shouted Jack Belias, after her. But she was determined not to be stopped. She knew what she had to do, and she knew that this was her last chance to do it.

She reached the blue-carpeted bedroom, turned the handle and opened the door. Brewster was lying on his side beside the bed, in a dark lake of blood. The discarded poker lay nearby.

Gina, thought Effie. *Oh, God. She's blind. She must have thought that Brewster was –*

She heard the sobbing again. It was coming from another bedroom, further along the corridor. Effie burst out of the bedroom just as Jack Belias reached the landing, and they almost collided. He tried to snatch her arm but she slapped the side of his head, and then suddenly stopped and tripped him up. He fell heavily sideways onto the floor, but he still managed to twist around and catch her a glancing blow on the leg with his cane.

They struggled and pushed each other. Jack Belias hit her across the shoulder and she screamed and shoved him in the chest.

As they fought, one of the bedroom doors opened and a figure staggered out of it, swathed in a white blood-spattered sheet. It bumped into one side of the corridor and then started to hobble away, groping wildly at the walls so that it could find its way. It sobbed, as it ran, a high-pitched desperate sob.

Effie tore herself free from Jack Belias and started to run.

'*Come back here, bitch!*' he shouted, and came after her in furious pursuit.

Up ahead, the white staggering figure almost tripped on the temporary flooring that covered the place where Morton Walker had fallen to his death. Effie ran after it, her whole body exploding with adrenaline.

The figure was Gina Broughton; and she, Effie, was Gina Broughton, too – just as Craig had been over-whelmed by Jack Belias and Pepper had been taken over by the body and soul of Gaby Deslys.

Effie understood now. Coincident lives, simultaneous events. *She* was Gina at the moment that Jack Belias had won her in his baccarat game; but up ahead of her was Gina after he had tortured her. Events were overlapping. Lives were overlapping. But the same nemesis was hard on both of their heels.

'*Gina!*' screamed Effie. '*Gina, keep running! He's here!*'

The figure hesitated for a moment. In the gloom at the end of the corridor, it looked like a white candleflame flickering.

'*Don't stop!*' Effie kept screaming. '*Whatever you do – don't stop!*'

Too close behind her, she heard Jack Belias' walking-cane beating at the walls, and the thick avid gasping of his breath. He was too breathless to curse at her now, but she knew that he wasn't going to stop. He wasn't going to stop until he had broken both of them; and made them admit what dirt they were.

The white figure reached the floor-length window at the end of the corridor, one of the windows that looked out over the front of the house. Effie could see that she was struggling with the catch, and then suddenly she opened it.

'*Not that way!*' Effie shouted, her voice hoarse. But it was too late. The figure had climbed out onto the parapet. Effie ran right up to the open window herself, and looked out, and the night was warm and breezy now, with a strong smell of smoke and recent thunderstorms. She could feel wind, she could see stars.

The white figure was standing on the very corner of the parapet, twenty feet away. Her head was thrown back, her arms were outstretched. Her toes were curled right over the very edge. Thirty feet below her, the railings waited, with their tall, elaborate points.

Her dark hair billowed and curled, and the breeze blew the sheet against her heavily-pregnant stomach. She looked wild and beautiful and infinitely frightening.

'*Don't!*' Effie called. '*You don't have to! You never have to!*'

But at that moment, Jack Belias reached the window, and thrashed at Effie with his cane, striking her shoulder.

'*Where is she?*' he raged. '*Where is she?*'

He leaned out of the window and saw her balanced on the parapet.

'*No!*' he screeched at her. '*No – not again – you can't do it again!*'

Effie seized his sleeve and tried to twist him around. He cuffed her with the back of his hand so that she fell heavily against the wall. Then he cuffed her again, and kicked her in the hip. She raised both arms to protect herself.

At that moment, however, he staggered and seemed to lose his balance. There was a deep *whoomph* further back along the corridor, and both of them turned. Out of the patch of temporary flooring, smoke was pouring, smoke mingled with thick orange sparks. The fire must have burned through to the library now, and the holes in floor and ceiling where Morton Walker had fallen were acting as a chimney.

Jack Belias stared at the smoke for a long, horrified moment. The sparks flew out even more thickly, like a Roman candle, and then they saw tongues of flame. The whole house began to rumble and whistle as the fire relentlessly drew in air through any aperture it could – windows, doors, keyholes, ventilators. It sounded as if a giant locomotive were bearing down on them.

Jack turned back to Effie. 'You did this! You did this, you bitch!'

But there was something strange about his face. It was very much less like Jack Belias and very much more like Craig's. He seemed confused, and kept jerking up his walking-cane as if he were going to strike her, and then

378

changing his mind and putting it down again.

Flames began to leap out of the hole in the corridor floor and lick at the ceiling. Two bedroom doorframes were already alright, and fire was beginning to run along the varnished skirting boards.

Jack Belias stepped away from Effie, his legs moving as if his knees had rusted up. 'You did this, you bitch. I should have known.'

He turned wildly back to the window. Gina was still standing on the parapet, her arms outstretched.

A heavy explosion shook the house, followed by a seemingly endless cascade of broken glass. Another explosion, and another.

'*Bitch!*' raged Jack Belias. '*Bitch, I'll kill you for this!*'

'Oh, you can kill me,' said Effie. 'You can do what you like to me. But you can never, ever break me. Look – there I am, standing outside, blinded, and tortured, and you *still* haven't broken me, and you never will.'

Jack Belias smashed his cane backward and forward against the wall. 'Break you! I'll break you! I'll break you now and I'll break you then!'

He heaved himself out of the window, catching his shoe on the sill. Effie tried to snatch at his arm but he struck her again, and almost lost his balance.

She looked into his face and he looked into hers.

'Craig,' she said. 'Don't.'

He frowned at her, and he *did* look like Craig. He looked even more like Craig than he had just a few moments before. The library floor was burning now. The clock was being destroyed: the device that had allowed Jack Belias to move from one year into another.

'Craig,' Effie begged, a second time. 'Craig – come back in. It's over.'

Jack Belias thought for a few seconds, and then gave her

an almost imperceptible shake of his head.

'Bitch,' he mouthed. Then he turned his back, and started to edge his way along the coping-stones, his feet spread like a tightrope walker.

He was only six or seven feet away when Gina turned towards him. In spite of her blinded eyes, in spite of her bruises, she was desperately beautiful. She unwound the sheet from her body, and held it high, so that it billowed in the breeze. As for herself, she was pale and pregnant and perfectly naked, and she shone in the starlight like a statue.

'*No!*' said Jack Belias, and lunged at the sheet.

His feet scrabbled on the coping-stones, trying to catch his balance. He swayed forward, and then he swayed back. For one moment Effie thought that he would fall backward against the roof, and save himself. But then he suddenly screamed, '*Effie!*' and dropped down into the night. There was a terrible pause. Then Effie heard a deep crunching noise, and the terrible resonance of iron railings when a heavy object is dropped on top of them.

Effie stared at Gina in shock. Gina, still naked, standing on the parapet, her hands cupped under her swollen stomach.

But then Gina seemed to fade. Her face began to melt like spun-sugar; her body became transparent. Within a few seconds her outline was nothing more than a pattern in the evening clouds. Effie found herself standing by the open window all alone, her eyes unexpectedly filled with tears.

In the distance, down the driveway that led between the weathered trees, she saw blue and red lights flashing. An ambulance, and two police cars, closely followed by a firetruck. Tyres slewed on the shingle, doors slammed. She saw Pepper hurrying out of the house, and heard police radio voices, and then she heard somebody say, 'Jesus. . . . have you seen this? There's a guy here, stuck on the railings. Musta jumped.'

Effie saw Pepper turn around in shock, and then look up to the window where she was standing. Something passed between them then that only two women could understand.

Valhalla burned throughout the night. At one point, there were eighteen firetrucks in attendance. Valhalla burned like the Norse palace it was named for, the palace of the dead. It burned as if it were determined to burn; as if it refused to be extinguished until it had completely consumed itself. Flames reached more than two hundred feet into the sky, and the blaze could be seen for nearly twenty miles.

At dawn, the house was nothing more than a charred shell, with only one of its walls standing. The wind blew its ashes to the east, where the demons come from.

Thursday, July 22, 7:16 a.m.

She stood in the Putnam County morgue and looked at Craig's body and didn't know what to say. She supposed she ought to have kissed him and wished him goodbye, but somehow she felt as if she had already done that, a long time ago. There was still some coarseness about his face that reminded her of Jack Belias. Maybe he had always been a little like Jack Belias, in a way.

'Okay?' asked the morgue attendant, and she nodded.

Outside, looking crumpled and unshaven, Lieutenant Hook and Sergeant Winstanley were waiting for her. 'Mrs

Bellman? Just wanted you to know how sorry we were.'

'Thank you,' she said, and kept on walking.

'By the way,' called Lieutenant Hook. 'We checked your husband's fingerprints, *post mortem*. I thought you'd like to know that we've cleared him. Whoever killed those people, it wasn't him.'

Effie said nothing. She didn't even turn around. She already knew that Craig was innocent.

Friday, July 30, 10:28 a.m.

It was a warm, overcast morning. She sat in Walter Van Buren's office, dressed in black. Walter Van Buren was a few minutes late, and he came in flustered, balancing a Styrofoam cup of black coffee.

'I'm real sorry to keep you waiting . . . I've been closing a deal over at West Point.'

'That's all right, Mr Van Buren. I've got all the time in the world.'

Walter Van Buren sat down, spilled part of his coffee, and tried to mop it up with a sheet from his tear-off notepad. 'I was very sorry to hear what happened. Your husband, I mean. Tragic.'

'You think so?'

Walter Van Buren frowned at her. 'Of course I do. Tragic.'

'You know what happened, don't you?'

'Well, yes. Your husband slipped. Fell on some railings.'

'The same railings that Gina Broughton fell on, in 1937.'

'Excuse me?'

'Come on, Mr Van Buren, you know what's been happening at Valhalla, right from the very beginning. All of those tragedies, all of those suicides. All of those so-called hauntings. You know why Valhalla was built the way it was, and you knew what was going to happen if the right couple just happened to come along to buy it.'

'I'm not sure I know what you're talking about.'

'Oh, sure you do. Because I do. My friend Pepper Moriarty and I have been doing some research into the history of Valhalla. Newspapers and county records and such; and Mr Harry Rondo's been very helpful, too. Do you know him? He's thinking of writing a book about Jack Belias. It's long overdue.'

Walter Van Buren rearranged his pens and his pencils and looked intently down at his blotter.

Effie said, 'We weren't trying to track you down or anything. We were just interested in what happened after that night at Valhalla, when Gina Broughton died. We were interested in what happened to her baby, and whether it survived.'

'Oh, yes?' said Walter Van Buren, coldly.

'We checked county records. The baby *did* survive. It was fostered to the Berrymans, who used to run Red Oaks Inn, up near Valhalla. But they had difficulties with it, according to the records. The baby wouldn't sleep, and was always distressed; so in the end they passed it on to another family, in Albany. Obviously, Albany was sufficiently far away for the baby to escape the influence that surrounded Valhalla. He grew up fit and well, and graduated from high school with honours. Maybe his career hasn't been too distinguished since. But then, we can't all be high-flyers, can we, Mr Van Buren?'

Walter Van Buren said nothing at all, but watched his coffee steaming.

'What was it, Mr Van Buren? You wanted revenge on Jack Belias, for killing your mother? Or you blamed him for abandoning you, and disappearing, even though you knew that he was always there? You could sense that Craig would fall for it, didn't you? You hooked in, didn't you, and you hauled him in.'

Walter Van Buren took a deep breath. 'I'm sorry about your husband,' he said. 'I'm just real glad that his fingerprints didn't match any of those homicides. It's sad enough to lose a loved one, without finding out that they might have done wrong.'

'Yes, Mr Van Buren,' said Effie.

He looked up at her with his colourless face. 'I suppose you'll be wanting to sell the land?' he asked her 'May I help you with that?'

Effie said, 'Of course. We were almost related, weren't we, when you come to think about it?'

Walter Van Buren nodded. 'Strange, isn't it, this business of time and memory? Do you think that, now it's burned down, Valhalla will still exist?'

Effie stood up and firmly held out her hand. 'Even if it does, Mr Van Buren, I'm not going back there.'

She walked out into the street, where Pepper was waiting for her, wearing a black kaftan.

'Everything sorted?' asked Pepper.

Effie nodded; and together they started walking up the street.

Pepper suddenly stopped. There were tears in her eyes. 'Do you know something?' she said. 'We look like widows.'

Epilogue

Seven months later, Pepper sent Effie an advertisement clipped from the *Poughkeepsie Messenger*.

THE BROTHERHOOD OF BALAM

This newly-formed brotherhood will be holding inspirational meetings Tuesday and Thursday evenings at 7.30 p.m. Come join a close circle of friends who believe in tolerance and forgiveness and the wholeness of the Universe. We have recently acquired the historic Benton House from the Hudson Valley Historical Society and all meetings will be held in these famous and hallowed surroundings.

Underneath, she had scrawled in red ballpen, *They came back!*